MW00415924

MURDER
at KING'S
CROSSING

MURDER *at* KING'S CROSSING

ANDREA PENROSE

KENSINGTON
PUBLISHING CORP.

www.kensingtonbooks.com

KENSINGTON BOOKS are published by

Kensington Publishing Corp.
900 Third Avenue
New York, NY 10022

All Kensington titles, imprints, and distributed lines are available at special quantity discounts for bulk purchases for sales promotion, premiums, fund-raising, educational, or institutional use. Special book excerpts or customized printings can also be created to fit specific needs. For details, write or phone the office of the Kensington Special Sales Manager: Attn. Special Sales Department, Kensington Publishing Corp., 900 Third Avenue, New York, NY 10022. Phone: 1-800-221-2647.

Library of Congress Control Number: 2024936522

The K with book logo Reg. US Pat & TM Off.

ISBN: 978-1-4967-3996-4
First Kensington Hardcover Edition: October 2024

ISBN: 978-1-4967-3998-8 (ebook)

10 9 8 7 6 5 4 3 2 1

Printed in the United States of America

For William Lawrence

Every historical author should be so lucky as to have such a delightfully knowledgeable and interesting Firearms Consultant!

PROLOGUE

"Damnation!" Hair spiking up in disarray, spectacles sliding down the slope of his beaky nose, the man glanced up from the work papers strewn across his desk and stared at the clock with a look of dawning horror. "What pernicious quirk of the cosmos has made six hours fly by in the space of one?"

It was, of course, an absurd question. He of all people knew that the laws of the universe were governed by a mathematical precision. *That was the beauty of the world and how it worked.* It was astounding how often one could understand so many elemental scientific truths if only one was skilled enough with numbers to figure out the complex equations that revealed the hidden secrets.

"Equations that can be put to practical use in bettering the lives of countless people," he whispered, his gaze returning for a moment to his scribblings.

But for now, the grand scheme of abstract problem-solving would have to wait. He was late—horribly late—for a very important engagement.

"I tend to lose myself in all the possibilities when I'm caught up in the excitement of discovery, but there is still time . . ."

The man gave a rueful grimace at the piece of paper pinned above his worktable. The reminder, written in giant, bold-faced letters by his good friend, stared back in stern reproach.

"But even though the hour at which I should have departed has long since passed, if I ride hard through the night and take the shortcut of North Abbey Road to King's Crossing, I can make it to the junction of the Cambridgeshire Turnpike before dawn . . ."

He was already stuffing a notebook—he called it his scribbling book—into his coat. He added the handful of papers on which he had been working to an oilskin portfolio, which he then carefully placed in the leather satchel lying beside the valise holding his clothing for the trip. "Which means that I can still arrive at close to the appointed time."

A smaller packet lay on his blotter. The man hesitated.

Choices, choices.

A recent unsettling incident had made him cautious. He knew that his fellow members of the Revolutions-Per-Minute Society—all fine fellows but limited in their imagination—were curious about his latest innovations. But they wouldn't comprehend his reasoning, even if he took the trouble to explain. Only Hypatia, his childhood comrade-in-exploration, understood that transcending the ordinary required a willingness to be bold, no matter the consequences. He couldn't wait to pay her a visit and explain all about his new calculations and what he intended to do with them.

But in the meantime . . .

The ticking of the mantel clock warned that there was no time left for dithering. He squeezed his eyes shut and forced himself to focus. And then, as often happened when he put his mind to a conundrum, the solution flashed into his head with startling clarity.

Smiling, he picked up the packet and threw it into the banked coals of his tiny hearth, then picked up the poker and stirred up flames, watching in satisfaction as the packet was quickly reduced to ashes.

The man turned back to his worktable for one last look. A good thing, for he spotted a sheet of folded stationery half hidden among his pens. "Thank God that I didn't forget this," he said, and shoved it in his pocket.

"Now, I *must* be off."

Grabbing up his bags, he hurried to the livery stable where he kept his horse and was soon galloping out of town in a cloud of dust.

At first, luck was with him. But the wind soon kicked up, fitful gusts bringing a damp chill to the late summer evening. The man looked up and muttered an oath. Iron-grey storm clouds were blowing in from the west, causing the light to fade quicker than he expected. A prick of his spurs urged his horse onward in an effort to outrace the rain. Though the North Abbey Road would shorten his journey considerably, it was a miserable excuse for a thoroughfare, unfit for man or beast when the weather turned foul.

As for the rickety wooden structure spanning the river gorge at King's Crossing . . .

"Bloody hell." Wincing in dismay as the first drops of rain spattered against his hat, he tugged his oilskin cloak from his saddlebags and put it on, hoping for the best.

But darkness soon swallowed the road, forcing him to slow his horse to a walk. Thunder rumbled, and before the echo died away, the skies shuddered and suddenly released a torrential downpour. Shrieking like banshees, the accompanying high winds forced him to shelter for a time within a copse of pine trees.

The minutes ticked by with maddening slowness.

When at last the storm abated, allowing him to continue, he found the ruts in the road were growing deeper and deeper as water sluiced through the mud, creating a helter-pelter swirling of pebbles and rocks.

His horse stumbled as the footing turned treacherous. Swinging down from the saddle, the man grasped the reins and led the way up the winding road, anger making his blood boil. He had warned the authorities on numerous occasions that neglect of the region's roadways was not only foolhardy but shortsighted. The world was changing, and forward-thinking men understood the key to progress was—

A flicker of moonlight interrupted his thoughts.

"Thank heaven," muttered the man, gazing up at the night sky, where a twinkling of stars was beginning to show through the mist. The storm looked to be scudding off to the south.

As the wind settled, the roar of the river just over the crest of the hill further buoyed his spirits. Once he traversed King's Crossing, the worst of the journey would be over.

However, his optimism proved short-lived, for when he approached the primitive bridge—it was little more than rough-hewn planking laid across two massive oak and iron support beams that spanned the ravine—he saw that the heavy downpour and high winds had caused a section of rotting planking to fall away into the ravine, leaving a gaping hole across the entire middle of the bridge.

No, no, no—I must get across!

However, there was no choice but to turn back and give up his plans.

Still, he hesitated, eyeing the exposed section of the right-hand beam where the planking had fallen away. It looked undamaged, and while his horse could not cross such a narrow walkway, it was just wide enough for him to pick his way over the gap on foot.

Daunting, perhaps, and a trifle dangerous. But he had a great deal of experience around bridge construction sites and wasn't afraid of heights . . .

Mind made up, the man unslung his bags and tied his tired horse to a nearby tree.

"I can hire a post boy at the Three Crowns to take the long way around to fetch my mount," he muttered, "and once my business is done at the inn, I can hire a new mount for my visit to Hypatia." The story of his absentmindedness and the havoc it had wreaked with his travels would likely garner a good laugh when told in the comfort of a gracious drawing room with a glass of fine spirits in hand.

Warmed by the thought, he drew in a deep breath and shouldered his bags. Without hesitation, he stepped onto the bridge and started forward.

Unsure of the planking that still remained, he kept to the outer edge of the structure, taking care to center his steps over the beam. *Focus, focus*—he needed to keep himself balanced and alert to any shifting of the rain-soaked oak. The rush of the roiling water on the rocks below warned that the slightest mistake could prove fatal.

Halfway across, the gap forced him to walk along a width of wood that was barely more than eight inches. It looked even narrower in the gloom and swirling fog, and after swallowing hard, he forced himself to lock his gaze on the silhouette of a tree on the other side.

It felt like forever, but he finally inched across the gap and onto more solid footing. Quickening his steps, he hurried across what remained of the planking and reached the other side, his boots sinking into the mud of *terra firma* with a welcome squelch.

Despite the chill of the night, the man realized that his brow was beaded with sweat—

"Halloo?"

A tentative call suddenly floated out from the darkness up ahead.

"Is someone there?" added the disembodied voice.

"Yes, yes," answered the man, feeling unaccountably comforted that he wasn't the only one traveling on such a hellish night. "But if you are looking to cross the cursed bridge, you are out of luck—unless you are willing to risk a drop to your death." He drew in a quick breath. "The planking has fallen away in the middle."

"But you were daft enough to cross the wreckage on foot?" A blade of lantern light cut through the fog. "I feared as much, Milton." The blade grew brighter. "Thank heaven you survived."

The man—his name was Jasper Milton—let out a relieved laugh on recognizing the voice. "I can't tell you how happy I am to see you, Axe!" Whatever the reason that had forced his friend—the moniker "Axe" was a private joke between them— to be on the road in this devil-damned weather, he was glad to encounter a kindred soul. "But how did you know I was traveling tonight?"

"Don't you remember me coming to your room early this morning?" interrupted Axe.

"I . . ." Milton scrubbed a hand over his face. "I sometimes get things jumbled in my head when I am concentrating on a scientific problem."

"I'm well aware of that. Which is why I decided to wait for you at the Three Crowns Inn, thinking that we could ride together for a while before parting ways for our final destinations. But when you didn't arrive at the time you should have—"

"I was late in leaving," explained Milton.

"Alas, why does that not surprise me?" replied Axe dryly. "When the inn got word earlier that the bridge at King's Crossing had been badly damaged in the maelstrom, I worried that you might have decided to take the shortcut in order to make up for a delay. And so I thought that I had better come look for you in case you had suffered some injury."

"Thankfully no," said Milton. "Though I'm soaked to the

bone, and my bags are damnably heavy." A wince. "But what are you doing here? I thought you were heading—"

"A last-minute change in plans, which appears to be a stroke of luck. My horse is tethered close by." Axe stepped free of the fog. "You're an idiot—you know that, don't you?" he added, as he set the lantern down with a long-suffering sigh. "Here, let me give you a hand."

"You're a more thoughtful friend than I deserve—always acting as the steely support to keep me from spinning out of control!" exclaimed Milton as Axe grasped the straps of the valise and leather satchel and slipped them free of his aching shoulder. "I'm very much obliged to you."

"Since we are speaking of friendship . . ." Axe paused. "Allow me to make a last plea for you to change your mind about your plans for your latest innovation. Think of—"

"Absolutely not." Milton stiffened. "If that's why you've come to find me, you've suffered an uncomfortable trip for naught. My mind is made up."

"Allow me to remind you that we made an agreement. A very lucrative one—"

"And I've explained to you why I've decided that I can no longer be part of it."

"But see here—"

"Enough!" he snapped. "You're an excellent fellow, Axe, but your vision is limited. You don't see the grand scheme or the far-reaching effects my contribution to history will have on mankind."

"You seemed to think that my vision was clear enough when I explained my idea and how we would both benefit—" began Axe, only to be cut off again.

"As I said, I've changed my mind, Axe."

"But it was *my* concept that led you to think of—"

"We both know that I am the only one who can actually make the grand scheme," said Milton.

"Because I'm not as smart as you are?"

A shrug. He shifted and made to step around his friend. "Come, I'm anxious to arrive at the Three Crowns—"

Whatever words were about to follow were swallowed in a gasp of pain as a razor-sharp length of steel cut between his ribs. An instant later, it pierced his heart, and all sensations dissolved into oblivion.

"I'm sorry." Axe pulled his knife free, allowing Milton's mortal remains to flop to the ground. "If you had only listened to reason, this wouldn't have been necessary." He put the valise and satchel down beside the lantern, careful to avoid any puddles, and then crouched down to regard his friend's lifeless face.

"But no, you were too stubborn to see beyond your world of ideals and abstraction." Axe reached out and closed the unseeing eyes. "The future will thank me for being more pragmatic."

Without further words, he searched the dead man's clothing and removed his purse and a notebook. A branch cracked close by, causing him to spin around in alarm. But the weak beam of light showed nothing but a ghostly swirl of fog, which quickly dissolved in a gust of wind.

He riffled through the valise and satchel. A grunt of satisfaction sounded as he set the satchel aside and looped the valise over his shoulder. Then he set to work dragging the body back to the bridge. It had started to rain again—which was, he decided, all for the good as it would wash away any signs of what had just taken place. However, it took some muscle and awkward maneuvering to navigate the slippery planking. He didn't dare venture too far on the damaged bridge—just enough to ensure that his act of foul play would never come to light.

An unfortunate accident would be the verdict. The violence of the body's fall onto the rocks below would make the real cause of death impossible to discern.

The wind from the new squall swirled through the nearby trees, setting off a leafy moan from the shuddering branches.

The rain stung his eyes, making it impossible to see anything more than an amorphous blur of shadows. But after another few steps, the churning of the river below told him that he had gone far enough.

Axe hoisted the dead weight of the corpse upright. And then, with one last, mighty effort, he managed to lift the body and send it plummeting down into the blackness.

A clap of thunder, a flash of lightning.

Axe flung the valise into the void and stepped back from the edge of the bridge.

"I promise you, Milton, this is all for the good," he said, and wiped his palms on the front of his coat. "You would have squandered your brilliance. While in my hands, your ideas will be developed to their fullest potential."

CHAPTER 1

"Disaster has struck!"

Charlotte, Countess of Wrexford, looked up from the half dozen checklists spread over the parlor table. "If that is a jest, it isn't remotely amusing."

"Would I jest over something as momentous as the impending nuptials of our dear friends?" replied her great-aunt Alison, dowager Countess of Peake. "Ye heavens, it has taken Kit and Cordelia long enough to admit that they are perfect together."

It was true, conceded Charlotte with a wry sigh. Her husband's best friend, Christopher Sheffield, had dithered and dithered, thinking that the brilliant Lady Cordelia Mansfield would have no interest in leg-shackling herself to a rakehell fribble. However, Cordelia had been smart enough to see Kit's true colors—

Alison thumped her cane on the parquet floor, drawing Charlotte's thoughts back to the present moment. "And so, I'm not about to let any last-minute tempest in a teapot bollox the wedding."

"Tempest in a teapot?" repeated Charlotte, her eyes widening in alarm. "Good Lord, has something gone awry with plans for tonight's welcoming supper in honor of Cordelia's family?"

"No, no, McClellan has the kitchen running like a well-oiled machine. It's the *flowers* for the ceremony!" replied the dowager.

"But the Weasels are in charge of the flowers, and Hawk is so very clever at designing the perfect combinations of colors and texture . . ."

Hawk and his older brother, Raven, had been wild orphan urchins living in London's toughest slum until Charlotte had taken them under her wing several years ago, even though she had barely been making ends meet at the time. They in turn, had deemed themselves her protectors, and had been dubbed "the Weasels" by the Earl of Wrexford for assaulting him during his first fraught encounter with Charlotte because they thought he was threatening her. The initial clash of wills had turned to a wary friendship between the four of them, and then . . .

A smile touched her lips. *Funny what strange twists Life could take.* She was now married to Wrexford, and the boys had long since been forgiven. Indeed, through some clever sleight of hand by her husband, the boys now had fancy papers giving them a respectable pedigree and had become the earl's legal wards, though their unofficial moniker had stuck, much to everyone's amusement—

Thump-thump.

"Charlotte! Do stop woolgathering!"

"My apologies." She was usually practical and pragmatic, but the upcoming nuptials had stirred all sorts of sentimental thoughts about family and friends—and how over the last few years the lines between the two had become blurred beyond recognition. "I was just musing on how Love is an even more elemental bond than ties of blood."

Alison's gimlet gaze gave way to a softer twinkle. "True.

How else to explain what binds together our exceedingly eccentric group?"

Their eyes met for a moment . . .

And then the dowager cleared her throat with a brusque cough. "Be that as it may, let us return to the subject of flowers. Because despite Hawk's best efforts, the plans for the wedding flowers have gone to Hell in a handbasket!"

"We are very good at improvising," soothed Charlotte. "But first, what is the problem? After all, we have a large hothouse here on the estate, and I know the head gardener has it filled with all manner of lovely blooms."

"Yes, but Hawk had designed a lovely bridal bouquet for Cordelia featuring *hydrangea*," explained Alison.

Charlotte was knowledgeable about a great many subjects, but botany was not one of them.

On getting naught but a blank look, the dowager rolled her eyes. "It's a blooming shrub, and a certain mophead variety produces exquisite blue flowers which are a perfect match with the silk sash of Cordelia's wedding dress."

"It sounds lovely," murmured Charlotte. "But I take it that something is amiss?"

"The wind and rain of last night's dratted storm knocked off every last petal from the hydrangea shrubs," intoned Alison. "Blue flowers aren't easy to come by." A pause. "Unless we organize a raiding party to break into the Duke of Devonshire's conservatory at Chatsworth. Word is, there is a whole section devoted to the color blue."

Charlotte didn't like the martial gleam in the dowager's eye. "The duke has no sense of humor—and larceny is not a trifling crime. Would you and the Weasels rather spend the wedding day in a cell in Newgate Prison instead of Wrexford Chapel?"

A sniff.

"I thought not," she said dryly. "And so, I suggest that we improvise." The corners of her mouth twitched in humor. "Perhaps I could use my paintbrushes to tint a selection of white roses the exact shade of blue to match Cordelia's sash."

Charlotte was a highly accomplished artist, though her skills were usually put to use poking fun at the peccadilloes of Polite Society, as well as making sure that the leading politicians and those who possessed wealth and influence did not abuse their power. Working under the *nom de plume* A. J. Quill, she was London's most infamous—and popular—satirical gadfly.

"Oiy, oiy!" Hawk rushed into the parlor, followed closely by Cordelia and McClellan, whose official title as lady's maid to Charlotte did not begin to describe the full measure of her position within the family. *Trusted confidante, occasional sleuth, firm-handed taskmaster of the Weasels, baker of ambrosial ginger biscuits*—McClellan was, in a word, the glue that helped bind their household together.

"No need for worry, Aunt Alison," added Hawk, once he had caught his breath. "As m'lady often says, we are very good at improvising!"

Charlotte felt another sweet stirring of nostalgia. The boys had taken to calling her "m'lady" during the first days of their acquaintance, and though the relationship had undergone a number of profound changes since then, they all felt comfortable with it.

"Well, don't keep us in suspense," drawled the dowager.

"Lilacs!" He looked expectantly at the maid. "It was Mac who came up with a very clever idea."

"Watered silk," explained McClellan. "I recalled seeing a length of lovely lilac-colored watered silk in the sewing room. As you know, the sheen is slightly iridescent and in sunlight its shimmer turns into a beguiling mix of lilac and steely blue."

"It was Mr. Sheffield who asked me to include blue hydrangea in the bridal bouquet," offered Hawk, "because their petals would bring out the blue of Lady Cordelia's eyes."

Alison batted her lashes, setting off flashes of sapphire. "Men find blue eyes very alluring."

"So we had Lucy, who is the best seamstress of the house maids, replace the sash on my wedding dress," interjected Cordelia, "and just tested the effect with a bouquet of lilacs and white dahlias, and—"

"And Sheffield will swoon on the spot when you walk down the aisle," finished McClellan.

"Let us hope not!" said Alison with a mock shudder. "At least, not before the vows are said."

"If he's having second thoughts," replied Cordelia lightly, "I do hope he'll choose a less dramatic way to evade the parson's mousetrap than keeling over in the chapel."

"Oh, you know me, I seem to have a knack for making a mull of the best-laid plans." Sheffield appeared in the doorway, his wind-tangled hair damp from the morning's recent rain squall.

Cordelia's eyes took on a sapphire-bright light as she looked at her fiancé. "Yes, but I rather like your mulls." A pause. "They make life infinitely more . . . interesting."

"Interesting?" repeated Sheffield as the two of them exchanged a very intimate smile.

Charlotte repressed a laugh. "Speaking of making a mull, how bad was the damage to the road leading into town?" Wrexford and Sheffield had ridden out after breakfast to survey the damage done by the fierce winds and heavy downpours of the previous evening.

"Several large trees fell, blocking all access," answered Wrexford, who finished toweling his hair dry as he joined Sheffield in the doorway. "But we set a group of the tenant farmers to clearing the way, so the wedding guests coming from Cambridge tomorrow will have no difficulty getting here."

"It was a truly hellish night," added Sheffield, his expression turning serious. "The locals have heard that there is extensive damage throughout the area."

"Perhaps that explains—" began Cordelia.

"The two of you look chilled to the bone," observed McClellan before Cordelia could go on. "I'll go fetch some tea—as well as some good Scottish whisky." She ruffled a hand through Hawk's hair. "Why don't you take the silk sample back to the sewing room and go find your brother." A wink. "There may be a platter of ginger biscuits waiting for you two Weasels when you join us."

"Whisky would be very welcome, Mac," said Wrexford as the boy scampered off. "Come, let us decamp to the comfort of the drawing room and its blazing fire."

"I would make a jesting remark about today being the calm before the storm," said the earl after pouring a wee dram of malt for himself and Sheffield. "But there is nothing humorous about the destruction that Nature can unleash when it's in a foul temper."

"Indeed," agreed Sheffield. "But we mere mortals could do a much better job about being prepared for it. The state of our roads and bridges is shameful, and that's because our thinking about transportation is, for the most part, still mired in the Dark Ages."

"Don't get Kit started," counseled Cordelia. "Our shipping company is doing quite well, but as we've recently learned, it will be a while before technical innovations in steam power replace sails. And as he's impatient to be involved in Progress, he has turned his gaze from water to land."

"Yes, well, we have so much potential for economic growth right here on this speck of an island, if only we put our minds to improving transportation through hill and dale," responded Sheffield. "Think about it! Opening up the northern reaches of England and all of Scotland to commerce would be a boon to the country."

Wrexford thought for a moment about the challenges, which were more daunting than they might seem at first. "I imagine you are thinking of steam-powered locomotives, which travel at great speed and smoothness over roads made of rails." Sheffield had been an early investor in Puffing Billy, the prototype locomotive designed by their mutual friend William Hedley.

"However," added the earl, "our island's geology—the mountain ridges running up the spine of England, the steep gorges, the many rivers and isolated valleys tucked among the rocky hills—all present a very difficult engineering challenge for creating a network of roads, rails, and bridges to link our towns and cities together."

"The fact that it's difficult should be motivating our brightest scientific minds and forward-thinking politicians to solve the challenges," countered Sheffield.

"From what I hear, that fellow from Scotland, John McAdam, is doing some good work around Bristol in his position as commissioner of paving," pointed out Charlotte. "I did a series of drawings on his innovations a while back—"

"McAdam's efforts are hamstrung by a lack of funds," interrupted Sheffield. "Now that the wars in Europe are over, we should be investing government funds in—"

A sharp rap of the dowager's cane signaled for silence.

"Enough hot air about business and technology," ordered Alison as McClellan carried in a large tray of refreshments. "We are gathered here at Wrexford Manor to eat, drink, and be merry in celebration of a joyous occasion. Solving the ills of the country can wait for a few days."

"Oiy!" called Raven from the corridor. "At least none of us have stumbled over a dead body."

Wrexford repressed a shiver as a quicksilver chill slid down his spine. Logic and empirical evidence were the backbone of his beliefs. Superstitions were based in ignorance and fear.

And yet . . .

"*Don't* spit in the Grim Reaper's eye, lad," he muttered, tempted to sprinkle a libation to Eris, the goddess of chaos, on the expensive Axminster carpet. "And *don't* let Harper eat all the ginger biscuits."

The huge, iron-grey hound, who had already loped across the room and taken up a position by the tea table, turned his shaggy head and fixed the earl with a baleful look.

"One would think you were fed naught but bread and water," growled Wrexford.

"Sweets are not good for you, Harper," explained Hawk. Seeing Sheffield turn to exchange a private word with Cordelia, he quickly filched a slice of ham from the soon-to-be-bridegroom's plate. "Here, have some gammon."

Once the laughter died down, the talk quickly turned to lighter topics. Cordelia told a number of amusing anecdotes about past gatherings of her family, which prompted more chuckles, and Sheffield recounted a number of self-deprecating stories about his clashes with his imperious father.

"I think he's still rather shocked that someone as smart as Cordelia actually agreed to marry me."

"So am I," quipped Wrexford.

As the dowager began a long and slightly naughty story about her own wedding, the earl took another sip of his whisky, savoring the mellow warmth of the spirits and flickering fire. A quiet interlude in the country was a welcome respite. The recent murder of an old family friend had forced him to confront his own fraught relationship with his late father. And though the crime had been solved and justice meted out, allowing a number of lingering wounds to heal, Wrexford was intent on making final peace with his conflicted emotions.

Better late than never, he thought with a pang of regret. Perhaps the fact that he was now the official guardian to a pair of headstrong boys had made him far more understanding of the complexities of father-and-son relationships . . .

The chiming of the case clock on the mantel brought a sudden halt to the merriment around him.

"Good heavens!" said McClellan, shooting up from her chair. "Cordelia's brother will be arriving shortly with her aunt and cousins! You must all hurry and dress for our gala pre-wedding supper."

CHAPTER 2

"What a lovely evening." Charlotte entered the study chamber off the main room of the library and settled into one of the leather armchairs by the hearth. It was late, and while the others had all retired to their quarters in the guest wing of the manor house, Wrexford had chosen to stay up a little longer in order to continue sorting through some crates of books that had recently arrived from one of his minor estates in the north.

"Cordelia seemed pleased with the evening's festivities," said the earl absently. He turned the page of the book he was perusing without looking up.

"Relieved is perhaps a better word," replied Charlotte. "Apparently her aunt can be prickly, but with both her parents gone, she wished very much to have her mother's sister attend the wedding."

He closed the book and picked up another from the worktable at which he was sitting. "Families are complicated."

An understatement if ever there was one. Charlotte reflected for a moment on her own tumultuous relationship with her parents. The terrible rift in her family had been repaired now that her kindhearted brother was the *pater familias*. But Wrexford was still struggling with recent revelations about his younger brother's death in the Peninsular War, which had forced him to question certain assumptions about his own relationship with his father.

The books her husband was perusing had come from the late earl's personal library, as he had chosen to live at the small family estate in the north rather than Wrexford Manor after his two sons had left home to pursue their own lives.

"Anything interesting?" she asked lightly.

Wrexford hesitated, his gaze on the printed page. "I hadn't realized that my father read poetry—much less made annotations in the margins about his reactions to the sentiments."

"Wrex—" she began, only to be distracted by the *click-click* of canine claws on the oak flooring.

Harper appeared a moment later in the doorway. Nose to the ground, the big hound ignored both her and the earl as he crossed the room and paused in front of the French doors leading out to the back terrace.

"If you need to piddle, you could have woken the Weasels," said Wrexford, as he rose to undo the latch.

"He did wake us," announced Raven as he and his brother padded in from the main room. "But not for a call of nature. He seems . . . unsettled."

"Perhaps he ate too much this evening," drawled Wrexford, "and his stomach is feeling bilious—"

A sudden growl cut him off.

"I don't think it's his stomach," said Hawk. "Oiy, Harper! What's wrong?"

In answer, the hound pricked up his ears. Another growl. Hackles rising, Harper turned abruptly and left the room.

Charlotte followed the others as they hurried to catch up with the hound. Wrexford, she saw, had grabbed Harper by the collar to keep him from bolting into the corridor that led from the back of the manor house to the guest wing.

"Hold your water, laddie. Let's not wake the entire house,"

murmured the earl, ruffling a calming caress to the hound's shaggy head. After a look up and down the unlit passageway, where there wasn't a flutter of movement among the slumbering shadows, he shrugged. "I daresay he's not yet reacquainted with all the creaks and noises of the manor."

A rumble rose in Harper's throat.

Hawk crouched down beside him. "Shall I fetch you a nice, meaty bone from the kitchen to gnaw—"

"Sshhh!" Raven edged halfway out the doorway and cocked an ear. "What was that?"

Charlotte had heard it, too. A faint scuffing sound coming from the first-floor landing of the West Wing staircase. Repressing a smile, she touched Wrexford's arm. "It's likely Kit paying a visit to Cordelia's room," she whispered. "Let us not embarrass—"

But in the same instant a shrill shout—it was Cordelia—shattered that surmise.

"Intruder! There's an intruder in the house!"

Wrexford reacted in a flash. "Stay in the library and shut the door!"

Charlotte nearly tripped as he thrust the agitated hound at her and pushed the boys back through the doorway.

"And *don't* let the Weasels and Harper follow me," he added.

She nodded and managed to retreat just enough for him to slam the door shut.

In protest, Harper began barking, the throaty rumbling punctuated by indignant protests from the Weasels.

"Quiet!" she commanded.

The cacophony ceased.

"You're right," said Raven. "We need to make a plan."

"We have one," replied Charlotte. "You heard Wrex. He told us to remain here and stay out of trouble." Though in all honesty, she was no happier about the order than they were.

"But he needs our help to ensure that the intruder doesn't escape!" countered Raven. "There are any number of ways for the varlet to slip out of the house."

That was true . . .

Charlotte drew in a measured breath and glanced back at the closed door, weighing her options.

A furtive scuff and *click*.

She spun around—just in time to see the tip of Harper's tail disappear into the reading area.

"Wait!"

Too late. She heard the French doors open, and by the time she stepped out to the back terrace, the Weasels and the hound had disappeared into the midnight shadows.

"Drat," muttered Charlotte, after stepping back inside and closing the doors. She hesitated for a long moment, then picked up the wrought-iron poker leaning against the hearth and hurried for the corridor.

Wrexford skidded through a sharp turn and sprinted down the darkened corridor leading to the West Wing, mentally gauging his chances of catching the intruder as he came down the main stairs.

The odds were good, decided the earl, thanks to Raven's bat-like hearing. Unless the intruder was unnaturally fleet of foot, the fellow was likely in for a rude surprise. No doubt he had expected everyone to be sound asleep, their slumber deepened by copious amounts of celebratory champagne.

However, the thud of racing steps descending the stairs urged Wrexford to quicken his pace.

Damnation, the fellow is faster than I thought.

He rounded the corner just as a dark-clad figure leapt over the two remaining treads and hit the floor running. With a well-timed swerve, the intruder narrowly avoided a potted palm and then headed for the back entrance by the mud room for riding boots and oilskins.

Intent on catching the fellow before he escaped from the

house, Wrexford accelerated—only to collide with Cordelia as she came flying down the stairs. Her flapping wrapper tangled around his foot, causing him to stumble.

"I'm so sorry," she gasped, grabbing his arm and somehow keeping both of them upright.

The earl regained his balance, just as the sound of more footsteps echoed in the corridor. He pulled free from Cordelia's hold and spun around, shielding her with his body.

"Lower that damn poker," he said to Charlotte. "The intruder has fled, and the house is safe."

"What—" began Charlotte.

"Keep our guests calm if any of them have been awoken by the ruckus." Wrexford was already moving. "I'm going after him."

Given the fellow's speed, he doubted there was any chance of catching up to him after the unfortunate delay. However, he was not yet ready to give up the chase.

The back door by the mud room was swinging in the breeze. The earl barreled through the opening and jumped from the raised terrace down to the sloping lawns. Catching sight of his quarry in the moonlight, he threaded his way through a narrow orchard of apple trees and scrambled over a low stone wall.

The intruder was halfway across the back pasture and heading for a swath of woodland.

Wrexford set off in pursuit, only to catch a glimpse of a four-footed shadow running through the meadow grass, followed by two wraithlike figures, pale as ghosts in their white nightshirts.

"Raven! Hawk! Stop at once!" he bellowed, hoping his words weren't blown away in the wind.

The Weasels showed no sign of slowing. The intruder, however, came to halt just as he reached the trees and turned around. Spotting the boys, he fumbled with something in his pocket and then raised his arm.

A wordless cry tore from Wrexford's throat as the Weasels, suddenly alert to the danger, dove for cover.

He saw a flash and a puff of silvery smoke, which was gone in the blink of an eye. An instant later, the crack of the gunshot swirled through the night, dulled to naught but a whisper by the fitful breeze.

Heart pounding hard enough to crack a rib, the earl abandoned the chase and ran as fast as he could to where he had seen the boys fall.

"Ouch." Raven was on his knees, rubbing at his wrist. "There are nettles down here."

"Oiy. And prickers." answered his brother, gingerly plucking a thorn from his thumb.

Wrexford crouched down beside them. *No sign of blood.* Which drew a sigh of relief. "Hell's bells, I ought to birch your bottoms for disobeying my orders."

"We didn't disobey, Wrex," replied Raven. "It was m'lady you told to stay in the library." A pause. "Nor did we follow you."

"And besides, you don't believe in corporal punishment," pointed out Hawk.

"In this particular case I might make an exception." He scowled . . . and then pulled them both into a fierce hug. "Don't *ever* do that again. You scared me half to death."

"Sorry." Both boys apologized at once.

Harper, who was standing guard beside the earl, let out a low whuffle and butted his head against the earl's arm.

"Harper is sorry, too," said Hawk softly.

Wrexford helped the boys up. "You could have been killed."

"Naw, he wasn't aiming at us," responded Raven. "I saw his arm rise at the last instant and heard the bullet whistle high overhead."

"You were lucky," replied the earl. "But we all know from our previous brushes with trouble that Lady Luck can be awfully fickle."

Seeing Hawk wince from a thorn in his bare foot, he lifted the boy into his arms. "Come along, the three of you need to get some sleep." A glance at the hound, whose paws were now black with mud. "You'll need to rise early in order to bath Harper and comb every last bramble out of his fur before the wedding ceremony."

The tall grasses shivered in a gust of wind.

"Or Aunt Alison will cut off your supply of ginger biscuits for the foreseeable future."

"Thank heaven," muttered Charlotte as Wrexford and the runaways emerged from the night's gloom and trooped up the terrace stairs.

"Indeed," he replied, as she and Cordelia stepped aside from the open door to let them enter the library.

"Was that a gunshot I heard?" she pressed.

"We dodged a bullet," admitted the earl. "But I'm fairly certain it was only meant as a warning."

"That's not amusing," replied Charlotte.

Raven and Hawk avoided meeting her gimlet gaze.

"It wasn't meant to be," said Wrexford.

A single chime from the mantel clock—sounding loud as gunfire in the fraught silence—announced that the midnight hour had passed and a new dawn was not far off.

"Good Lord, the wedding day is here!" Cordelia forced a smile, trying to lighten the tense mood. "Let us hope that it will bring no more surprises."

Charlotte released a pent-up breath, which ended in a reluctant laugh. "*Deo volente*," she said in Latin, glancing up in mute appeal to the Almighty before turning her gaze back to the Weasels.

"I should ring a peal over your heads." Her expression softened as she eyed their bedraggled clothing and scratched hands. "However, I would rather that you head up to your beds without further delay."

They wisely made no peep of protest and hurried away. Ears drooping, Harper was quick to follow.

Wrexford moved to the sideboard and poured himself a glass of whisky. "*Sláinte*," he said, lifting his glass in salute. "The first of many toasts to be raised on this special day." He pursed his lips. "I'm surprised Kit wasn't roused by the commotion."

"He and my family enjoyed several more bottles of your excellent champagne after the two of you excused yourselves from the postprandial celebration," said Cordelia dryly. "I am hoping that he'll be able to walk down the aisle without falling flat on his face."

"Ha! He wouldn't dare." A moment later, the dowager came into the reading area from the main room of the library. She was wearing a flame-red silk dressing gown over her night-rail, the embroidered fire-breathing dragons rippling in the lamplight as she took a seat in one of the armchairs.

"If he does," she added, "we'll just have to pick him up and carry him to the altar."

A grim smile touched Cordelia's lips. "As you said, he wouldn't dare." A pause. "I do hope my shout didn't wake any of the others."

"No, like Sheffield, they were all three sheets to the wind when they finally retired to their quarters," answered Alison. "But just to be sure nobody had any cause for alarm, I stayed upstairs. If necessary, I would have created a diversion by claiming that I had a bad dream and cried out in my sleep."

She raised a brow at the earl. "I take it you didn't catch the miscreant?"

"No." He took a swallow of his whisky. "However, we scared him off."

"*We?*" Her eyes narrowing in suspicion, the dowager raised the quizzing glass hanging around her neck and took a look around the room. "Where are the Weasels?"

"Upstairs in their beds," replied Charlotte. "That is all you need to know."

Before Alison could respond, she turned to Cordelia. "I take it nothing is missing from your rooms?"

"The fellow didn't really have a chance to make any mischief. I was only half asleep, and the click of the door latch opening brought me instantly awake. I raised the alarm just as he was beginning to search the escritoire in the sitting room." Cordelia shrugged. "In any case, all he would have found was a pile of mail that I've not yet had a chance to open. So all's well that ends well."

Charlotte wasn't so sure.

She moved to the hearth and took a moment to warm her hands over the glowing coals. Something about the incident was bothering her, though she couldn't quite put a finger on what it was.

"Does it strike any of you as strange that an intruder would break into Wrexford Manor?" she mused aloud. "Wrex is well known in the area and has a reputation for generosity with all the locals."

Cordelia and the dowager looked thoughtful, but the earl didn't hesitate in responding.

"I doubt it was a local fellow. Earlier today, when Kit and I were overseeing the clearing of the road, the workers mentioned that several raggle-taggle groups of men have been spotted in the area."

Wrexford's expression tightened. "With peace now reigning over Europe, the army is reducing its ranks, and there are many ex-soldiers who have returned to Britain only to find there are no jobs to be had. How the devil are they supposed to survive?"

Ah. Charlotte now guessed that part of the reason he had tried to capture the intruder was to offer him food and money.

"We all have good reason to know that there is much evil in this world." Alison shifted uncomfortably in her chair. "But for today, might we not allow its darkness to overshadow the light of love and friendship?"

Charlotte felt a stab of guilt for voicing her misgivings. Indeed, it was she herself who had proposed that the family remain in the country for several weeks after the wedding as a respite from their recent experiences with murder and mayhem.

"Speaking of friends, I do hope Baz will arrive in time for the ceremony," she said. Basil Henning, an irascible Scottish surgeon, had served in the Peninsular War with Wrexford and was an honorary member of their admittedly eccentric family. "Mac heard from one of the maids that the main road from London suffered considerable flooding."

"Baz will sail here on a whisky barrel, if need be," said the earl, which made everyone chuckle. The surgeon was very fond of Scotland's *uisge beatha*.

However, Cordelia's mirth did not quite reach her eyes. "I do hope the other missing guests will also arrive in time. Oliver is usually very punctual."

"Don't fret," soothed Charlotte, knowing that her cousin was traveling from the north and several other missing relatives were coming from the university town of Cambridge, which wasn't far away. "No doubt they all simply wished to give the roads another day to dry out and will arrive in the morning."

"It already *is* morning," said Alison, punctuating the observation with a gusty yawn. "Indeed, the sun will soon be up." She rose from her chair. "So come, I suggest we toddle off for a few hours of sleep before the festivities begin."

CHAPTER 3

W rexford finished inspecting the grounds of the estate's chapel and paused in the shade of a stately yew, satisfied that all was in order.

Charlotte's question of the previous night had put his nerves on edge. Although he preferred to examine a problem through the lens of logic and evidence, he had learned to trust her intuition. And so, deciding to err on the side of caution, he and his valet had ridden out at first light to search the nearby wooded areas for any signs of clandestine activity or a hidden campsite.

It wasn't that he expected any further trouble . . .

But Trouble had a way of sneaking up on him and his loved ones. And the discovery he had made on returning to the manor house—

"Tuck that scowl in your pocket before taking a seat in the chapel, laddie." The rough-cut burr of Basil Henning, who had finally arrived from London just before the breakfast hour, cut through his brooding. "We're attending a wedding, not a funeral."

"One wouldn't know it by the looks of you," drawled the earl.

"M'lady informed me that I am the very picture of sartorial splendor," retorted Henning.

"I concede that for once you don't look as if you've been dragged by the arse through a gorse bush," said the earl. "Your hair is combed, your cheeks aren't sprouting an unsightly stubble . . ."

He feigned a look of shock. "Ye gods, will wonders never cease! Your cravat is snow-white, with just the right amount of starch—"

A rusty chuckle. "Tyler gave me one of yours."

"I see that I shall have to hire a new valet."

Henning made a rude sound. "As if anyone else would put up with your sarcasm."

Ignoring the barb, Wrexford pointed to the surgeon's coat. "I doubt that the beau monde's definition of sartorial splendor includes having a foul-looking substance smeared on your sleeve." He gave a tentative sniff. "What *is* that?"

"You would have to ask the Weasels. They insisted on showing me one of their chemistry experiments once I finished the excellent breakfast that Mac made for me." His grin faded. "The laddies seem a little blue-deviled. I take it they miss Peregrine."

"We all do," replied the earl.

Earlier in the year, circumstances surrounding an investigation into the murder of a brilliant inventor had caused the Weasels to bond with the man's orphaned young relative, and the three boys—who quickly deemed themselves brothers-in-spirit—had played a vital role in solving the crime. To the satisfaction of all concerned, Peregrine's legal guardian had agreed that the boy could come live with Wrexford and his family. But the one stipulation was that Peregrine, who had inherited his late father's title, must continue his education at Eton.

The Michaelmas term had just started, which meant that the boy couldn't be with them for the wedding.

Wrexford expelled an inward sigh. Perhaps that explained why the whole family seemed unsettled.

The ringing of the chapel's bell drew him back to the moment.

"We had better take our seats before the procession begins," said Henning, shading his eyes as he glanced back at the building. The old stones were glowing with a mellow gold light in the early afternoon sun.

The earl took one last look around. The dowager would have his guts for garters if any disturbance intruded on the ceremony.

Inside the chapel, the air was perfumed with the sweet scent of fresh-cut flowers from the hothouses. He and Henning joined Charlotte and Alison in their pew. After consulting the gold pocket watch tucked in her reticule, the dowager gave a discreet signal, and a murmur of happy anticipation rippled through the guests as the string quartet struck up Haydn's "Emperor" String Quartet No. 6 in C Major, one of Cordelia's favorite compositions.

All heads turned as one to the front entrance.

Flanked by Raven and Hawk, a perfectly clean and combed Harper appeared in the open doorway festooned with an ornate flower garland. Following them were Alice the Eel Girl, Skinny, and Pudge, former urchin friends of the Weasels who now worked at the estate. The three of them were carrying wicker baskets filled with pink rose petals, which they scattered onto the walkway.

And behind them were . . .

Wrexford finally smiled, allowing his worries to float away on the breeze as he caught sight of the bridal couple.

Pop, pop, pop. The explosion of tiny champagne bubbles added a festive note to the sounds of merriment as Charlotte gazed over the rim of her crystal glass to where the wedding guests were lingering on the sun-dappled lawn below the back terrace.

"What a perfect day," she murmured. A sumptuous post-ceremony repast had been served outdoors under a tented canopy, and though the meal was over, everyone seemed loath to leave the magic of the moment. "Kit and Cordelia deserve no less."

"Perfection is an illusion. So I shall simply wish for them to be as happy as we are." Wrexford clinked his glass against hers and quaffed the last swallow of his sparkling wine.

Charlotte leaned against his shoulder. "I confess, I shall welcome some peace and quiet—"

She paused, spotting a flicker of movement by the boxwood hedge. "Oh, dear—the Weasels have just absconded with a bottle of champagne and are heading for the stables." A reluctant chuckle. "To share it, no doubt, with Alice, Skinny, and Pudge."

Wrexford smiled. "Albert won't let them get into any real mischief." The stablemaster tolerated no nonsense within his bailiwick, but his gruff manner disguised an impish sense of humor. "Given the occasion, though, he will turn his back to their bending of the rules this afternoon."

They stood in companionable silence, watching as the guests slowly began to take their leave of the newly married couple, but she sensed that his mind was elsewhere.

"A farthing for your thoughts?" she said softly, without shifting her gaze.

In answer, he stepped back from the stone railing. "Would you mind stepping inside for a moment? Now that the festivities are coming to end, there is something I would like to show you."

"I sensed that something was troubling you," said Charlotte as she followed him through the open French door into the library. "Did you discover something new this morning concerning the break-in?"

"Actually, I did," replied Wrexford. "However, that's not

what I wish to discuss . . ." The sound of hurried footsteps in the main room of the library caused him to pause.

A moment later, the earl's estate steward looked into the study chamber. "Forgive me for interrupting you, milord, but two men are outside and requesting an audience." He tugged nervously at his coat cuff. "They say it is urgent."

The words sent a chill skittering down Charlotte's spine.

"Then you had better show them in," said Wrexford.

Charlotte looked back at the terrace, where flashes of bright sunlight were capering across the flagstones. And yet she felt a shadow approaching.

The steward returned, followed by two tired-looking men in mud-spattered riding boots.

"My sincere apology for intruding on your festivities, Lord Wrexford," said the older of the two, fiddling nervously with the brim of the hat in his hands. "I am Thaddeus Whalley, magistrate of St. Ives and the eastern towns of Huntingdonshire . . ." Recalling his manners, he quickly added, "And this is Matthew Goffe, our local surgeon and newly appointed coroner."

Coroner. Charlotte closed her eyes for an instant, knowing the man's presence could mean only one thing.

"I am afraid that my colleague and I are the bearers of bad news." Whalley hesitated, looking unsure of how to go on.

"I assume it involves a death in your jurisdiction, Mr. Goffe," said Wrexford. "Though I am perplexed by how it could relate to me . . ." He glanced at Charlotte. "Or my family."

In answer, Goffe drew a folded piece of paper from his pocket and wordlessly offered it to the earl. It was crinkled with water stains and streaked with mud, but Charlotte immediately recognized its distinctive light blue color, specially made by London's most exclusive stationery shop.

"It's an invitation to the wedding," she said as Wrexford opened it.

"Yes, milady." Goffe cleared his throat with a cough. "Forgive me, but might I inquire if any guests failed to show up for the occasion?"

"Three," she answered. "An elderly couple, relatives of the groom, who sent word that the storm had made it too difficult for them to attempt traveling." After a tiny pause, she added, "And the bride's cousin."

"A gentleman, milady?" asked Goffe quickly.

"Yes."

"Forgive me asking such an indelicate question, but can you describe him?" pressed Goffe.

She shook her head. "I'm afraid not. Neither I nor His Lordship have ever met the fellow."

"How—" began Goffe, only to be silenced by a stern nudge from the magistrate.

"We shall summon Mrs. Sheffield," said Wrexford.

Whalley looked aghast. "Isn't there someone else who might know, milord? I wouldn't want the poor bride to swoon from shock on her wedding day!"

"My wife," intoned a voice from just outside the open terrace, "is not prone to swooning." Sheffield entered and raised a questioning brow at the earl. "I saw that you had visitors. Has it to do with the break-in last night?"

Eyes widening, Whalley let out a huff of confusion.

Charlotte sympathized. *Our unconventional inner circle tends to spin in unexpected ways.*

"Cordelia would, of course, be happy to describe her confrontation with the intruder," continued Sheffield. "But he was masked, so she can't give much of a description."

"It's not about the intruder, Kit," answered Wrexford. "These men are here from Huntingdonshire because they've discovered a body, and in the unfortunate fellow's pocket was an invitation to the wedding."

Sheffield swore under his breath. "Was it Oliver Carrick?"

he demanded of Whalley and Goffe. "My wife's cousin never arrived. We assumed the storms made travel impossible."

"I'm sorry, sir, but I cannot say," responded the magistrate. "There was nothing in the man's pockets save for the wedding invitation."

"Carrick is a slender fellow, about my height and several years younger, with light brown hair," offered Sheffield. "I don't recall the color of his eyes."

Whalley looked at Goffe, who hesitated before answering. "Based on that vague description, all I can say for certain is that our corpse *could* be your wife's cousin." Goffe shuffled his feet. "Is there no specific physical detail you can tell me that might help?"

Sheffield shook his head. "I only met him once, and that was during a crowded reception at the Royal Institution."

"But as the fellow had the wedding invitation in his pocket, it stands to reason that it is Carrick," mused Wrexford.

Goffe didn't demur.

"By the by, you have not yet mentioned how he died," continued the earl.

A reasonable question, thought Charlotte. And yet the two visitors exchanged nervous looks before the magistrate cleared his throat.

"The old bridge at King's Crossing was badly damaged by the severe storms that blew through the area," explained Whalley, "and could only be crossed by walking across one of the two narrow support beams. The man was found on the rocks below—"

Wrexford couldn't contain his impatience. "So you are saying it was a wretched accident and he fell to his death."

Another awkward silence.

"What the devil is going on?" growled Sheffield after it had lingered for several long moments.

Charlotte released an inward sigh, fearing that none of them were going to like the answer.

It was Goffe who ventured an answer. "We thought it was an unfortunate accident at first. But after the body was taken to my mortuary room, I did a closer examination and . . ."

He swallowed hard. "And I discovered evidence of foul play."

"Explain yourself," demanded the earl.

"The body was lying on the rocks just below the bridge, but something about the angle of the fall bothered me," explained Goffe. "And once I had the body unclothed, I saw there was little sign of bleeding from the damage done by the fall, which made no sense. So I looked more closely and discovered a small but unmistakable stab wound between his left ribs. His clothing confirmed my surmise as I found a corresponding slit in his jacket and shirt."

Goffe squared his shoulders. "So, I am quite certain that Mr. Carrick was murdered with a thin-bladed knife."

"Thank you for being so observant," said Charlotte. "Any victim of foul play, no matter their identity, deserves justice."

"I agree, milady," replied Goffe. He turned to the earl. "The wedding invitation mentioned your name, sir, and I recognized it right away. You see, during my medical training in London, I worked at a surgery run by Basil Henning, who often mentioned you. So I suggested to Squire Whalley that we come in person to inform you."

"Seeing as you are accorded to be quite an expert in solving murders," added the magistrate.

"A skill I do not look to sharpen," muttered Wrexford. "Especially now."

Whalley shifted uncomfortably. "Again, milord, we deeply regret intruding on your celebration."

"It seems to me that we have good reason to trust Mr. Goffe's judgment," responded Charlotte, after the earl turned to stare out the windows without making a reply.

Sheffield, however, didn't appear entirely convinced. "That may be so. But I should feel more at ease if we ask Baz to take a look at the body—especially if it is Carrick—and judge for himself."

"Mr. Henning is *here*?" Goffe's expression brightened.

"He is," replied Wrexford. "I shall, of course, inform him of the situation. I'm sure he will be happy to offer a second opinion."

"However, it's too late to make the return trip to Huntingdonshire. The two of you will stay here tonight, and then leave with Henning in the morning," said Charlotte to Whalley and Goffe. "I'll have our housekeeper show you to your rooms in our guest wing and then take you to the kitchen for some sustenance. You must be tired and hungry after your travels."

She waved off the magistrate's attempt to demur. "It appears that the crime touches our friends, and thus our family, Mr. Whalley. We are all now part of the investigation." *Like it or not*, she added to herself.

Wrexford's expression was impossible to decipher.

"Please come with me," continued Charlotte. "I'll return shortly," she said to the others. "And then let us discuss how to break the terrible news to Cordelia."

A whisper of wind stirred outside . . . and then a rustle of silk.

"What news?" came a voice from the terrace.

CHAPTER 4

When Sheffield didn't answer right away, Cordelia appeared from behind one of the flower-filled marble urns flanking the open French doors and stepped into the room, her eyes narrowing in a question.

Wrexford avoided meeting her gaze. The ties of friendship that bound them all together were stronger than ever. But as of today, they had rewoven themselves in a slightly altered way, and he was intent on not inadvertently tugging at one of the new threads before it had settled into place.

"Good heavens, surely it's not *that* bad," said Cordelia with a tentative attempt at humor.

"I fear it is," said Sheffield. He moved to her side and clasped her hand in his. "A body has been discovered beneath the bridge at King's Crossing." He hesitated before adding, "These men here have come to inform us that the poor fellow appears to be the victim of foul play."

"But what does that have to do—" Cordelia froze. "Dear God. Is it O-Oliver?"

"The only thing in his pockets was an invitation to the wedding," said Sheffield.

"Then it *must* be him," she responded in a tightly controlled voice.

"Forgive me, milady—" began Goffe.

"Mrs. Sheffield," corrected Cordelia. Although aristocratic protocol allowed her to retain her title of Lady Cordelia even though Sheffield was, as a younger son of nobility, a mere "Mister," she was quite adamant about not doing so.

The coroner bobbed his head in acknowledgment and swallowed hard. "Might I inquire as to whether your cousin had any distinctive mark on his body—a birthmark or a scar that might confirm his identity?"

Cordelia shook her head. "Not that I know of. His eyes are blue—a very bright shade of sapphire—if that helps at all."

A look of puzzlement flitted across Goffe's face. "Y-You are quite sure that your cousin doesn't have a distinctive burn mark on his left forearm?"

Wrexford saw her suddenly clutch Sheffield's arm, her expression wavering between shock and relief. "That's not Oliver! It's Jasper Milton, a dear friend of mine from childhood who was equally close with Oliver. The three of us were inseparable!"

She drew in a shaky breath. "I remember the day the accident occurred—Jasper was tinkering with an experimental steam engine that he and Oliver had constructed when the firebox cracked, and he was hit with an exploding chunk of red-hot coal."

Goffe gave an apologetic look at Sheffield. "I am sorry, but I must ask your wife a very indelicate question—"

"My wife is not prone to swoons or tears, Mr. Goffe. She is, in fact, tough as nails," replied Sheffield with a note of pride. "Whatever it is you wish to know, go ahead and ask her directly."

The coroner cleared his throat with an uncertain cough but

did as he was instructed. "Mrs. Sheffield, could you perchance describe the scar? I ask because such details will help make a conclusive identification."

"I appreciate your professionalism, sir." Cordelia extended her bare forearm.

The watered silk sash of her wedding dress shimmered in the sunlight as she moved, noted Wrexford, its flickering hues of blue and violet accentuating the paleness of her flesh.

"It's located here." Cordelia tapped at a spot just below her elbow. "And is shaped like a starburst, approximately two inches wide and three inches high . . ." Her forefinger traced a jagged outline.

"Thank you," said Goffe. "Given the eye color and the scar, I think there is little doubt that the victim is Mr. Milton."

Sheffield murmured a thanks, then whispered something to Cordelia which drew a grateful nod.

"If you will excuse us, my wife and are going to take a walk in the gardens."

Wrexford waited until they had disappeared from the terrace, before ringing the silver bell on the side table to summon the housekeeper. "Mrs. Meadows will show you to your rooms and arrange for a meal to be served," he said to Goffe and Whalley. "Let us plan to leave at first light with Henning to confirm that Milton was the victim of foul play."

"Drat," whispered Charlotte after closing the glass-paned doors. "I would like to believe that Mr. Goffe is mistaken about the chest wound. Death is death, but we all know how murder can stir up unexpected secrets and cause yet more pain."

"Nobody is infallible," answered Wrexford. "But he's been well trained, and I don't think that we shall be so lucky as to have Baz overrule his verdict."

Charlotte twisted the fringe of her shawl around her fingers. "What do you know of Milton?" After a moment of thought, she added, "And for that matter, Cordelia's missing cousin, Oliver Carrick?"

"Only what little Kit has mentioned to me," replied the earl. "He said that both Milton and Carrick are very gifted in advanced mathematics and engineering, but he indicated that Cordelia had told him that Milton was the real thinker—not only a practical genius but also a fellow interested in considering the philosophical implication of Progress and Change."

Charlotte furrowed her brow in thought.

"Several years ago, the two of them formed a club with three other scientific-minded men called the Revolutions-Per-Minute Society."

"An odd name," she mused.

"Apparently the members are all interested in innovations that will make travel faster and more efficient."

"You mean modes of transportation like Puffing Billy?" she asked. Sheffield had been an early investor in the prototype steam locomotive, and several enterprises were making progress on the engineering challenges of turning the new technology into a viable commercial venture.

"It's my understanding that while the society is interested in the development of new types of vehicles, its primary focus is on improving methods of building roads and bridges in order to create a reliable transportation network connecting all parts of the country," he answered. "Sheffield says that the members are all very passionate about the subject and believe that by making the movement of goods and people swift and easy they will transform society."

Wrexford paused. "I have to say, I don't disagree."

"Revolutionary, indeed," murmured Charlotte. "Given that he appears to be the driving force, I wonder whether the society will survive Milton's death?"

"I've no idea." He pressed a palm to one of the sun-warmed panes of glass, and yet it didn't quite dispel the chill tingling in his fingers.

As if in concert with his mood, a trio of crows circled low over the terrace, their dissonate screeches shattering the stillness for a moment before they flapped away.

"Oh, bloody hell," he suddenly muttered.

Charlotte hurried across the carpet to join him and right away spotted what had caught his eye.

She turned without a word and rushed to reopen the doors and meet the Weasels as they raced up the shallow terrace stairs.

"A-A varlet—" began Raven with an out-of-breath wheeze.

"Hurled a rock—" cried Hawk.

The rest of their words jumbled together as both of them began talking at once.

"*Silence!*" commanded Wrexford.

The cacophony instantly ceased.

"Let us all step into the library." Though the last of the guests had left the lawns, he didn't wish to cloud the wedding day by stirring speculation that something was amiss.

Once they were inside, he pointed to Raven. "You first."

A deep inhale. "We were out behind the stables with Alice and Skinny and Pudge when a man suddenly appeared among the trees edging the west pasture and flung a rock at us."

Another ragged breath. "Skinny wanted us to give chase," continued Raven. "But I didn't think you would like that, so we let him get away."

"Perhaps," said Charlotte gently, "you misunderstood the man's gesture. He may simply have been hoping to forage some apples from the orchard and your presence scared him away." A pause. "I did notice the two of you absconding with a bottle of champagne."

"We were *not* foxed!" responded Raven with an indignant scowl. "Between the five of us, a bottle barely wet our whistles!"

"Oiy," agreed Hawk. "Besides, it prickles the tongue. Whisky is more inter—

A sudden nudge from his brother cut him off.

"I won't ask how you came to decide that," said Wrexford.

When the boys wisely said nothing, he continued, "As for your assailant, m'lady has a point. Are you sure our recent encounter with the intruder didn't color your thinking? I can't imagine why a stranger would hurl a rock at you." A grim smile. "Unless he was thirsty."

"Perhaps he wanted to send a message," retorted Raven as he pulled a crumpled strip of paper from his pocket. "There was a missive tied around the rock."

To punctuate his brother's words, Hawk held up the fist-sized stone, which still had a length of twine tangled around it.

"Part of it isn't in English," added Raven as he offered the muddied note to the earl.

Wrexford took the paper and read it over, then handed it to Charlotte without comment.

It took her only a moment to take in the short message. She looked up, trepidation glimmering in her eyes.

"Off you go, Weasels," he said gruffly. "M'lady and I wish to discuss this in private."

"Don't forget about the house rule that says everyone in our inner circle is entitled to attend a council of war," responded Raven. "Just because we're not at home at Berkeley Square in London doesn't mean that it is any less binding."

"She and I are merely going to share some thoughts." He wasn't ready to reveal the news about the murder quite yet. "If a council of war is necessary, I daresay it can wait until morning."

It was likely wishful thinking, but he was hoping that Kit and Cordelia would decide to take an interlude of peace and quiet on their wedding night before having their world turned upside down by the Grim Reaper.

"What are they hiding from us?" asked Hawk once he and his brother had passed through the opening in the privet hedge and into the herb garden behind the kitchen.

"Dunno," muttered Raven.

"Atten-dezz vooos, mess am-ees," said Hawk, tentatively sounding out the foreign phrase written on the note. "What does that mean?"

"It means *Beware, my friends*," replied Raven. Cordelia had been tutoring him in French as well as mathematics so that he could read the works of the legendary French mathematicians Joseph Fournier and René Descartes in the original.

"*Attendez-vous, mes amis!*" he repeated with perfect pronunciation, then added the rest of the message, which had needed no translation. "*Things are not always as they seem. Look beyond the obvious.*"

Hawk scrunched his face in thought. "What do you think the rock thrower is trying to tell us?"

"A good question," said his brother. "But an even more important one is, why did he write part of the warning in French?"

CHAPTER 5

The following morning, a pale but resolute Cordelia appeared in the breakfast room of the manor house. As planned, she and Sheffield had spent the night at the Dower House, a charming brick residence tucked in a secluded corner of the estate property, in order to have some privacy on their wedding night.

But Charlotte doubted that the occasion had been the perfectly joyful interlude it should have been.

"You are quite certain that you feel up to traveling to Cambridge?" she asked, after rising from the table and giving Cordelia a hug.

They had come up with a plan the previous evening. At first, Cordelia had wished to be part of the group accompanying Whalley and Goffe to positively identify the body. But her brother Jamie—Lord Mansfield—had insisted on being the one to view the corpse, as he, too, was well acquainted with Jasper Milton. Instead it had been decided that Cordelia and Charlotte should travel into Cambridge to speak with the three fellow members of the Revolutions-Per-Minute Society who were visiting the university for several days in order to attend a series of lectures given by an engineering expert from Bavaria.

Given that Milton had been murdered, it seemed that his closest friends would be the most likely to know if anyone had wished him ill. So Mansfield had dispatched urgent notes to them requesting a meeting, and the affirmative answers had been sent back with the same messenger.

"Of course I feel up to traveling to Cambridge." Her friend poured a cup of coffee from the still steaming pot on the table. "Marriage hasn't transformed me into a weak-kneed, spineless widgeon."

"I wasn't implying any such thing," replied Charlotte. "Indeed, the union of kindred hearts and minds makes each person even stronger. But the murder of a loved one cuts to the quick. Don't underestimate the toll it will take on your emotions."

The memories of her own experiences caused her chest to clench. "You may think you are prepared for such an ordeal. But nobody truly is."

A flicker of sympathy stirred beneath Cordelia's lashes. The two of them had met during the investigation into the violent death of Charlotte's cousin. Indeed, for a time, Cordelia was suspected of having committed the crime.

"I'm under no illusion that any previous experience will lessen the pain of the coming investigation." Dropping her gaze, Cordelia swirled her coffee and took a long sip. "But doing nothing would hurt far more."

Charlotte was about to respond, but after a moment of reflection her friend continued.

"As I told you all yesterday, Jasper was my closest childhood companion," she explained. "He, too, always had his nose in a book. Rather than join the other boys of the neighboring estates in riding like little demons and creating mischief throughout the countryside, he encouraged my interest in mathematics and was a mentor in helping me learn about advanced concepts when everyone else thought it was terribly unladylike."

"He sounds very much a kindred soul," said Charlotte.

Cordelia smiled, though it was edged with sadness. "Jasper was also key in helping me masquerade as a man so I could attend the university lectures at Cambridge. I owe him . . ." She looked away. "I owe him more than I can ever repay."

"Seeking the truth and feeling that justice has prevailed will give some solace that evil has not been permitted to triumph over good." Charlotte reached out and gave her friend's hand a squeeze. "But you must also be prepared for unexpected revelations, which may prove very painful."

"I have not forgotten that some of my own less-than-savory secrets came to light when you were investigating your cousin's murder," said Cordelia softly. Her brows then suddenly drew together. "Are you trying to discourage me from pursuing the investigation? Surely you don't really think I would shy away from seeking the truth, no matter how ugly."

Charlotte surrendered a wry sigh. "It was worth a try. After all, you and Kit are supposed to be heading off on your wedding trip to Paris. Wrex and I will make sure that—"

"Paris has been in existence for several millennia," interjected Cordelia. "I daresay it will still be there after we have resolved Jasper's murder."

"Then let us discuss our strategy for today," said Charlotte, "before Alison and any of our remaining houseguests arise. As we agreed last night, it's best not to mention the word "murder" to anyone here at the house until the official verdict of the inquest is announced." A pause. "Alison has done quite enough sleuthing of late. I would prefer that she doesn't demand to come with us."

"Yes, it's best that just you and I meet with the society members," agreed Cordelia. "I know two of them quite well from their university days. They were close comrades with both Jasper and my cousin Oliver, as they all shared a passion for mathematics and engineering. And they were aware of my masquerade and kept mum about it. Indeed, they were always encouraging of my aspirations. So I think they will be forthcoming with us about who might have had reason to wish Jasper ill."

She fell silent, looking lost in the past for a moment before continuing. "The third fellow is a more recent member."

"Did Jamie mention to them that Milton is dead?" asked Charlotte.

"No, he simply said that I had a serious matter to discuss regarding him," answered Cordelia. "I am also hoping they may have some word from my cousin Oliver. It's very strange that we've not heard from him explaining why he missed the wedding."

"As we've been told, traveling is still difficult in many areas. He's likely stuck somewhere, and any letter he sent is also delayed." Charlotte made a face. "Wrex says that's another good reason why those in the Revolutions-Per-Minute Society are right to think that improving transportation is a very important issue for the future. Communication is key for so many reasons, and currently the delivery of mail is erratic."

Before they could continue, a footman appeared in the doorway to inform them that the carriage was ready, and they hurriedly gathered their wraps and were on the road to Cambridge before anyone else came down for breakfast. The weather had cleared, and though the storm had caused severe rutting in places, the worst of the mud had dried, allowing them to make good time.

The carriage stopped on Trinity Lane to let Charlotte and Cordelia out at the imposing archway that gave access to the quadrangle of Clare College's Old Court.

"The society members said they would meet us in the Great Hall," said Cordelia, who knew her way around the university as well as any male student. She gestured toward a graveled walkway that ran down the middle of the Old Court's verdant lawn. "This way."

The voices of a choir, sweet and clear as the early afternoon sunlight, echoed softly off the surrounding stone.

"How lovely," murmured Charlotte, looking up at the Gothic spires that were visible behind the stately splendor of college buildings.

"The King's College Chapel is renowned for its choristers," said Cordelia. She, too, paused for a moment, listening to a passage of Mozart's Ave Verum Corpus. "It is nice to be reminded that there is beauty in this world that cannot be diminished by the evil that lurks in the human heart."

"Amen to that," replied Charlotte.

Cordelia sighed and smoothed at the ribbons of her bonnet. "We had better move on to our meeting."

They entered the grand building at the end of the walkway and turned left, where a short corridor brought them to an open set of carved oak doors.

"Lady Cordelia!" A slender, sandy-haired gentleman broke away from his two companions standing beneath the soaring leaded windows inset with stained glass heraldic crests and hurried to greet them. "It is always a great pleasure to see you. But I must say, the three of us were rather alarmed at Jamie's note. I do hope Jasper isn't in any trouble."

"I am now Mrs. Sheffield, Kendall," corrected Cordelia. To Charlotte, she added, "Allow me to introduce Jasper's good friend and fellow engineering wizard, Kendall Garfield." A smile. "Kendall, this is Lady Wrexford."

The other two men quickly approached to go through the required ritual of formal introductions, and then Garfield cleared his throat.

"Might I suggest that we go somewhere a little more comfortable where we can have a private conversation?"

The Great Hall, noted Charlotte, was indeed imposing and not conducive to the quiet discussion of personal matters. A cavernous space with a high ornate ceiling and intricately carved dark wood paneling, it had a rigid formality that was accentu-

ated by the gilt-framed painted portraits of solemn-faced college dignitaries from the past looking down from on high.

"An excellent idea," replied Cordelia as she accepted his arm.

"Lady Wrexford?" It was Mercer Wayland, the tallest and
best-dressed of the three men, who offered to escort her into
the corridor.

"Thank you." Charlotte smiled up at him, using the opportunity to study the details of the paneling. One never knew
when circumstances might require her to draw a scene within
these hallowed halls.

Ezra Wheeler, a burly fellow who looked cut from a rougher
cloth than his two friends, was left to follow along behind
them.

Garfield led them to a smaller sitting room with a pair of
sofas and several cushioned armchairs arranged in front of a
marble hearth. "I must say, I always feel like a naughty schoolboy in the Great Hall," he said lightly, "about to be roundly
scolded by all those intimidating gentlemen peering down their
noses at me."

Charlotte chuckled politely along with the others.

"Allow me to offer my felicitations on your nuptials, Mrs. Sheffield," continued Garfield, clearly trying to put everyone at
ease before moving on to the reason for their meeting. "If I recall what Oliver told me, the happy event was . . . quite recent,
was it not?"

"It was yesterday," replied Cordelia.

Garfield's eyes widened in surprise. "I, er, I . . ." He quickly
gathered his composure. "I would have thought that you and
your husband would still be celebrating with friends and
family."

"Alas, circumstances have demanded that we put aside our
festivities."

The three men, observed Charlotte, were now no longer
smiling.

"This sounds rather serious," said Garfield. "I would have thought . . . that is . . . er, did Oliver not accompany you?"

Seeing Cordelia hesitate, Charlotte quickly added, "I'm afraid that we have some very bad news. Mr. Milton's body was found on the rocks below the bridge at King's Crossing—"

"Good God," exclaimed Wayland. "What happened?"

"The circumstances are not at all clear," replied Cordelia. "But what we do know is . . ." Her voice faltered.

Charlotte interceded, deciding there was no point in shilly-shallying. "The incident was made to look like an accident. However, the local coroner has determined that Mr. Milton was murdered."

The dowager shaded her eyes as she looked into the sunlight, watching a breeze waft a scattering of shell-pink petals from the rose garden over the graveled carriageway.

"I can't say that I'm sorry the pressures and perils of organizing a wedding are over," she mused to McClellan. "But it was a lovely ceremony."

"It was indeed," agreed the maid. "Hawk outdid himself with the flowers, and Harper didn't filch any of my special honey-glazed ham from the serving platters."

"Ha, the hound is smart enough to know on which side his bread is buttered," chortled Alison, but her amusement quickly gave way to a sigh. "My only regret is that the wedding day was shadowed by the death of Cordelia's childhood friend. She seemed quite affected by the news."

"Sheffield mentioned that the two of them were quite close," said McClellan. She paused as shouts of mirth rose from up ahead, where Raven and Hawk were racing helter-pelter along the grassy verge, tossing a ball back and forth, just out of reach of Harper's snapping jaws. "Such tragedies," she murmured, "are a fierce reminder that the joyous moments in life are precious beyond words."

Alison regripped her cane, her gaze following the antics of the boys.

"So let us talk of more cheerful things." McClellan offered her arm for extra support as they resumed walking. "His Lordship mentioned that you will be returning to London with Henning in order to attend Sir Robert's seventieth birthday celebration."

"Yes, and it promises to be a splendid occasion," replied Alison, her expression brightening. "Horatio has gotten permission from his commanding officer to take a group of us for an afternoon cruise along the River Thames in one of the Royal Navy's new steamboats before the gala dinner." The dowager's young relative, Horatio Porter, was a midshipman and had played a heroic part in their last investigation, earning the gratitude of the government. "He has promised me that I will be permitted to steer the ship . . ."

The carriageway turned steeper as it rounded a copse of beech trees. Just as they reached the leafy shadows, the boys came running back up the hill.

"A fancy carriage has passed through the entrance gates and is coming our way!" called Raven.

"We don't recognize it," added Hawk.

"Hmmph." McClellan drew the dowager to a stop. "Neither m'lady nor His Lordship mentioned anything about visitors."

Raven whistled to Harper, and after taking hold of the hound's collar he and his brother positioned themselves in front of Alison and the maid.

Their protective measures drew a smile from the dowager. "Don't worry, I happened to grab my sword cane for today's stroll."

'But m'lady said—" began Hawk, then fell silent at the carriage lumbered around the bend and came to a halt.

The door flung open, and a figure scrambled down the iron rungs and started to run toward them.

"Falcon!" cried the Weasels, their voices punctuated by Harper's thunderous barking. The three of them flew to meet their comrade-in-mischief and in the next instant were all a blur of tangled limbs and wagging fur.

A second figure dressed in the finely tailored formality of a gentleman descended to the carriageway.

"Why, that's Peregrine's guardian," muttered Alison. "Which begs the question . . ." She raised her cane in greeting. "Welcome to Wrexford Manor, Mr. Belmont." The wife of Charlotte's brother was the sister of Belmont's mother, so their family trees intertwined. "What a pleasant surprise."

Belmont blanched at the word "pleasant" but quickly assumed a smile. "Good afternoon, Lady Peake." He inclined a bow. "My apologies for appearing without advance notice, but I am hoping that His Lordship or Her Ladyship might agree to meet with me about . . ." He blotted his forehead with the silk handkerchief clutched in his fingers. "About Peregrine."

"Oh, dear, that sounds rather ominous," replied the dowager.

"It's more than ominous, milady. It's a complete and utter disaster!" Belmont's shoulders sagged. "He's been expelled from Eton!"

"For what reason?" asked Alison.

"For setting off a noxious stink bomb in the Upper School during the Sabbath Day address to the students by the headmaster!"

The dowager and McClellan took great pains not to look at each other for fear of bursting into laughter. It was, they knew, not remotely funny if one was a stickler for the rules of such bastions of aristocratic pomp and privilege.

"Oh, dear," repeated Alison, trying to sound shocked. "Alas, Lord Wrexford is away and won't be returning until tomorrow at the earliest. And Lady Wrexford is in Cambridge. However, we expect her back by the end of the day."

Belmont blew out a sigh of relief.

"Come, you must, of course, wait at the manor house. I'm sure you are tired from your journey and in need of some refreshment." Alison regarded his wan face and added, "I daresay a wee dram of brandy would be welcome."

"A wee dram would be *most* welcome," mumbled Belmont.

"Then let us leave the boys to their mayhem and get you properly settled."

CHAPTER 6

"Murdered!" exclaimed Wayland. "There must be some mistake!" He looked at his friends in mute appeal. "We all know that country coroners are notoriously uneducated and ill-trained."

"In this case, the coroner was trained by a surgeon known for his skill in the mortuary arts as well as healing. In fact, he is a family friend, and I'm quite confident that any pupil of his will not have made a mistake as to the cause of death," responded Charlotte. "And to be sure, our friend, who was a guest at the wedding, is having a look at the body as we speak."

"Ye gods." Garfield slumped back in his chair. "Why would anyone want to harm Jasper?"

"That is why we are here. We are hoping you might be able to help answer that question," explained Cordelia. "You and your fellow members of the Revolutions-Per-Minute Society likely know him best. Please think—is there anyone who had reason to wish Jasper ill?"

"It could be a very personal grudge," suggested Charlotte. "An unpaid debt, jealousy over a lady?"

The three men frowned in thought.

Wayland, however, took only a moment before answering. "I can't think of any possible motive. Jasper was a quiet fellow who did little socializing. His work was his life." He paused. "But then, your cousin knows him better than any of us. If there was some hidden trouble in Jasper's life, he would be the one to be aware of it."

"We look forward to hearing all that Oliver can tell us. But unfortunately, the bad weather and subsequent damage to the area's roads appear to have stranded him somewhere. He never made it to the wedding," explained Cordelia.

"Perhaps it would be wise to wait for him to arrive before making further inquiries," suggested Wayland.

"In our experience, we've found that it's best to move quickly in gathering evidence of a crime," replied Cordelia.

Wayland raised his brows. "*Your* experience?"

When the only reply he received from Cordelia and Charlotte was an unflinching stare, he quickly cleared his throat with a cough. "But of course, if you think it best, we are happy to be as helpful as we can." His gaze darted to Garfield. "Kendall?"

"I have to agree with Mercer. Jasper was a bit of a recluse. He really did seem to care more about numbers and abstract ideas than he did about people and parties," responded Garfield after pinching at the pleat of his trousers. "However . . ."

"However what?" pressed Charlotte.

"It was just a far-fetched thought." He gave an apologetic grimace. "Never mind."

"No thought is too far-fetched to consider," she replied. "It's only by examining every possibility, no matter how remote, that we can hope to bring the truth to light."

"Very well, then." Garfield released a sigh. "Both Jasper and Oliver attended a scientific symposium in Paris several months ago entitled *Improving the Welfare of Mankind through Innovations in the Speed and Cost of Transportation.*"

"That's quite a mouthful," observed Charlotte.

"It sounds even more lofty in French," quipped Wayland, a glint of amusement in his gaze.

Wayland seemed quick with a bon mot, she reflected. Clearly, he thought himself a clever fellow.

"Be that as it may, what, exactly, does it mean?" asked Cordelia.

"The French have led the way in building modern roads," explained Garfield. "In the middle of the last century, a fellow by the name of Pierre-Marie-Jérôme Trésaguet developed a new method of construction that is considered the first real innovation since the Roman legions created their marvelous feats of road engineering, both here in Britain and across the vast areas they occupied in Europe."

He paused. "Napoleon recognized the military importance as well as the social and economic benefits of a good network of roads, so he encouraged the French scientific community to continue thinking about ways to improve them. It's one of the reasons he was so successful in waging war. He could move his armies far faster than other nations in reaction to where his troops were needed."

"Thomas Telford, our leading expert in road building, has based his work on the same basic method, which involves various layers of different-sized stone to make a stable surface that can stand up to the vagaries of the weather and constant use," offered Wheeler.

It was the first time the fellow had ventured to speak, save for mumbling a greeting during the initial introductions.

"It may sound simple," he continued, his voice growing more confident. "But it's not. It involves a number of complex decisions, based on the terrain, the soil, the slope of the road—"

"Let us not bore the ladies with a scientific lecture," interrupted Wayland, flashing an apologetic smile at Charlotte and Cordelia. "What Wheeler means is that road building is still an art as well as a science. There are basic principles, but we still have much to learn about refining the current techniques."

Charlotte noted that Wayland called him "Wheeler," while referring to the other society members by their Christian names. Within the beau monde, the difference indicated whether one was merely an acquaintance or a good friend.

Wheeler sat back in his chair, all spark of animation disappearing and leaving his face looking once again as if it were carved out of stone.

"Getting back to the French," said Garfield. "Oliver told me that the members of the Paris Society for Practical Science—which, by the by, includes a woman mathematician who serves as one of the group's officers—were very interested in Jasper's ideas. Not the ones concerning roads but more specifically bridges, which were his specialty. He said they seemed quite determined to coax Jasper into revealing his latest innovation."

"Indeed, it sounded like they were quite lavish in entertaining our friends, plying them with fine food and wine," said Wayland. "Hoping, no doubt, that Jasper would let slip a revelation concerning his work."

"I doubt they managed to seduce any secrets out of him," said Cordelia. "Jasper tended to be shy to the point of rudeness with strangers."

"I have heard from other scientific colleagues who have met her at conferences that Mademoiselle Benoit is *extremely* charming," said Wayland. "And *extremely* attractive."

"Jasper and I have been friends since childhood," replied Cordelia. "I've never known him to have an appetite for anything other than his mathematical and scientific work."

"Good friends are sometimes too close to see every facet of a person," remarked Garfield.

"That may be true," she conceded.

"Just in case it is of any assistance," offered Wayland, "I should mention that the members of the Paris Society for Practical Science will be arriving in London next week for the international conference on transportation being held at the Royal Institution. Of course, we all will be attending as well."

Cordelia gave a grateful smile. "Thank you. That is extremely helpful to know."

As the ensuing moment of silence stretched out, a cough and a rustle of wool warned that the meeting was on the cusp of ending. Charlotte, however, had the feeling that there was more to learn.

"You said Milton's specialty was bridges," she mused. "Was he working on something specific? Some innovation in a key component that would greatly improve the way bridges are built?"

"As a matter of fact, he had been dropping hints that he had made a momentous discovery, milady," answered Garfield. "He was always madly sketching away in a pocket notebook that he called his 'scribbling book,' which he said was where he let his imagination take flight."

"His behavior did seem to indicate that he was on the cusp of something revolutionary," offered Wayland. "However, when I asked him to show us the work papers on his latest idea—we all shared our efforts to make technological and design improvements with each other at our monthly meetings—he was awfully coy about it. He kept promising to bring them, but he never did."

A shrug. "Not that it mattered. Several weeks ago, he left his scribbling book on his worktable to fetch some other research material while I was visiting him, and I confess I took a peek at the pages. It looked like gibberish to me."

"Jasper always preferred to keep his discoveries secret until he was sure that he had worked out all the flaws and come up with the right solution," mused Garfield. "I didn't press him as much as you did, Mercer, because . . . well, because his mind spun in a special way, and I respected that."

"What about you, Mr. Wheeler?" asked Charlotte. "Have you anything to add?"

Wheeler merely shook his head.

And yet Charlotte was sure that the flicker in his eyes said otherwise.

Wayland took a discreet look at his pocket watch. "Is there anything else you wish to ask us? Otherwise, there is a reception starting shortly for the visiting lecturer from Bavaria."

As they all politely rose, Charlotte contrived to whisper in Cordelia's ear while adjusting the folds of her shawl. "Find a reason to draw Wayland and Garfield out of the room for a few moments."

Cordelia was quick to improvise. "Oh, Kendall, before you go, might you and Mercer escort me for a quick peek into the study room overlooking the King's College Chapel?" A winsome smile. "I have such fond memories of you two allowing me to sneak in as part of your group."

Garfield chuckled. "You deserved to be there far more than we did, as you actually completed the assigned lessons while we—well, never mind what we did."

As the good-humored comments trailed out into the corridor, Charlotte turned to Wheeler. "I take it you also joined the Revolutions-Per-Minute Society as a student here?" she asked as a way to begin a conversation, even though she knew he had not.

"No, milady, I did not attend this university, or any other institution of higher learning," he replied. "I learned what I know about roads and bridges by being apprenticed to various architects and builders involved in such projects."

"Practical experience is often the best education," she observed.

No reply.

Undeterred by his silence—she was used to winkling information out of far more intimidating individuals—Charlotte pressed him with another question. "So how did you come to be part of the society?"

"Milton came to work for a time on a project in which I was involved."

Charlotte noted that Wheeler did not call him Jasper.

"On completing his part of the project, he said that he was impressed by my skills and arranged a position for me with Thomas Telford."

"You must be very skilled indeed," she murmured. Telford was recognized as Britain's leading civil engineering wizard. His expertise lay in building canals, roads, and bridges, including the creation of a master plan for improving transportation in the Scottish Highlands and the design for the celebrated Pontcysyllte Aqueduct over the River Dee.

Wheeler ignored the compliment. "Our paths crossed briefly on several other projects. Milton then invited me to be a member of the Revolutions-Per-Minute Society as my current position is in the area and allows me to attend the monthly meetings."

"Then seeing as you have a personal connection to Milton, you must have some thoughts on whether someone might have wished him ill."

A spasm of emotion altered his expression, but it passed so quickly that Charlotte might have missed it if she hadn't been watching him so intently.

"Mr. Wheeler, we are trying to solve a murder. Surely you would not want to hold back any information that might help."

He still said nothing.

"I assure you that Mrs. Sheffield and I are not motivated by frivolous curiosity. We have some experience in ensuring that criminals are brought to justice for their crimes."

That finally drew a reply. "I am aware of that, Lady Wrexford. I read the newspapers—perhaps a bit more carefully than most. And so I have noticed that your husband is occasionally mentioned as having aided Bow Street in quashing some malicious evil."

Wheeler hesitated, his gaze flicking to the open doorway before locking with hers. "The question is, are you interested in the truth, or merely hearing what is convenient?"

"Truth and convenience are two very different concepts. They have nothing to do with one another," replied Charlotte. "But you must decide whether I am capable of separating them."

"Even if it affects a close friend?"

"Truth is truth. It looks the same whether one sees it in sunlight or shadow."

Jaw tightening, Wheeler considered her words. "Very well." He released a pent-up breath. "A week ago, I happened to overhear a conversation between Milton and Mrs. Sheffield's cousin at our local tavern. It was late, and there were few people around. They hadn't seen me sitting in the shadowed nook near their table, and before I could reveal myself, they started arguing— quite fiercely, in fact, though they kept their voices low."

"About what?" asked Charlotte.

"I don't exactly know," responded Wheeler. "It had to do with the plans for some sort of engineering innovation. Milton had apparently decided what to do with it, and Oliver Carrick was furious with him. He tried to convince Milton to change his mind—and when he wouldn't, Carrick said there would be hell to pay, and Milton must be prepared to suffer the consequences."

"Those were his exact words?"

A grim nod. "Yes, milady. Carrick then stormed off. Milton finished his mug of ale—he sounded as if he had already imbibed several—and then he, too, left."

For an instant, Charlotte couldn't help thinking of an old adage—*Be careful what you ask for.* But of course she knew that one couldn't pick and choose the facts if one truly believed in the concept of Justice.

No matter how much they might hurt.

Wheeler's next words were an even more visceral reminder of that.

"It was not my place to spread gossip about a private altercation. But now that you have told us the news of Milton's murder, I shall have to inform the proper authorities of what I witnessed," he reflected. "Empirical evidence is the linchpin of science. If it is ignored, it can cause a false conclusion."

Put that way, it took on a rather cold detachment, but she couldn't muster any argument.

"Is there a magistrate in charge of the investigation to whom I should recount the facts of what I witnessed?"

Charlotte gave him Whalley's name and location.

The return of Cordelia and the other two men curtailed any further probing, but she had already sensed that she would get nothing more out of Wheeler.

"That was bloody clever of you to create mayhem!" chortled Raven, after passing around the platter of ginger biscuits that McClellan had sent up to welcome Peregrine back to the nest. "But how did you manage to make the stink bomb without one of the other boys noticing?"

The *crunch-crunch* of the sweets roused Harper from his slumber and drew a baleful stare.

"Cousin George is much nicer than my late Uncle Belmont," replied Peregrine. "He readily agreed to pay for a private bedchamber in my lodgings when I told him that I needed quiet in order to concentrate on my studies."

Most Eton students were housed in private lodgings in the town. Only the King's Scholars—boys who received scholarships to attend the elite school—actually lived in the school's buildings.

"Given the chemicals we selected for you, the smell must have been disgusting," said Hawk.

"Oiy, it was so noxious that a number of the students puked, which only added to the stench," said Peregrine with a note of satisfaction. "It took several hours for them to clean up the mess and air out the Great Hall."

Raven's grin disappeared. "You told us that the school-masters at Eton beat boys who break the rules."

Peregrine, who was lying on his belly, reached for another biscuit. "It was worth it." *Crunch, crunch.* "I got the boot, as well as a thrashing. Though they waited a week to summon Cousin George to fetch me in order to allow the welts and bruises on my back and bum to fade."

Harper pricked up his ears and growled.

"Bastards," muttered Raven.

"It wasn't all bad. Mister Angelo comes weekly to give fencing lessons to the Upper School. And there is a new Classics master who makes reading the *Iliad* interesting. He's not as stuffy as the others. But as for the endlessly dull hours of memorizing Latin declensions and mind-numbing dates in history . . ." Peregrine made a face. "What if m'lord and m'lady won't agree to have me here? I fear Cousin George will either send me to another horrid school or make me stay with Aunt Belmont."

"Of course they will!" assured Hawk. He looked at his brother. "Won't they?"

Raven hesitated. "Dunno," he admitted. "Your cousin is your legal guardian, which I think makes things complicated."

"It's *not* complicated! It's simple!" protested Hawk. "We all think of Falcon as part of our family. Ergo, he belongs here with us."

"That's true in principle. But dressing it up in Latin won't make all the complexities go away," said his brother. "Wrex and m'lady both know how fraught family relationships can be, and I get the feeling they believe it is morally wrong to meddle where they have no official right to do so."

"But . . ." Hawk's voice faltered.

"Let us not imagine the worst," counseled Raven. "I'm just saying that we have to wait and see."

*   *   *

"Do you trust him?" demanded Cordelia, once the two of them had settled into their carriage for the journey home and Charlotte had recounted what Wheeler had told her.

"Ah, that word "trust" again." Charlotte sat back against the squabs. "He struck me as sincere. But as I know nothing about him, I won't form an answer based on a first impression."

The town's cobblestones gave way to the ruts of the main road heading west.

Wheeler's answers had stirred several other questions. Awkward as they might be, Charlotte knew that she couldn't in good conscience avoid asking them.

"How well do you know your cousin?"

Cordelia's face fell. She was too familiar with investigations not to hear the darker questions hiding behind the seemingly harmless query. "Not as well as I knew Jasper. It was I who introduced the two of them when they both began their studies at Cambridge. I was already sneaking into Professor Sudler's mathematics lectures, and they were quick to support my quest for knowledge by helping me gain entrance to some of the other offerings."

She seemed lost in thought for a moment, and then continued. "Oliver and I had a casual friendship, formed over the years of family gatherings. It deepened during his time at university, and we've maintained a certain closeness since then. However, his interests in roads and bridges have kept him moving around to different parts of the country, so it has been some time since we've seen each other."

A sigh. "That was one of the reasons that I invited him to the wedding. I knew he was currently working within traveling distance, and I thought we might have a chance to spend several days together."

"Can you think of any reason other than an unexpected travel delay that would have caused him to miss your wedding?"

"No."

Charlotte hated asking the next question, but it had to be broached. "Were you aware of any reason for your cousin to be angry at Milton?"

"No." Cordelia turned to the window and watched the cheery hues of the fall foliage flutter by as the carriage picked up speed on a level stretch of road. "But I've seen little of Oliver during the past year, and he's a terrible correspondent. So I am as much in the dark about his possible motives as you are."

CHAPTER 7

Afternoon was fading to dusk by the time the horses slowed to a halt in the main courtyard of the manor house. Claiming exhaustion, Cordelia had chosen to be let out at the Dower House, and Charlotte made no effort to discourage the decision. Given the recent events—a wedding and a murder within the space of twenty-four hours—her friend was no doubt craving some solitude in which to come to grips with the momentous changes in her life.

Charlotte, too, was feeling unsettled by the revelations from Milton's friends and wanted nothing more than to retire to her workroom and be alone with her thoughts.

Though a pot of tea would be welcome company.

She repressed a wince as she climbed down from the carriage. It would offer comfort rather than raise any uncomfortable questions. Enough of those were already whirling around in her head.

Their country majordomo threw open the front door as she approached. "Welcome home, milady." Something in his voice immediately stirred a frisson of alarm. "You have a visitor.

Lady Peake placed him in the main drawing room to await your return."

Charlotte untied her bonnet and shrugged out of her shawl. "Who is it?" she asked, handing over the garments.

"Mister George Belmont, milady."

Peregrine's guardian.

"He's been served refreshments—"

The rest of his words were swallowed by the helter-pelter scuff of her shoes as she sprinted for the stairs.

Belmont rose as she rushed into the room.

"Y-You bring bad news about Peregrine?" she asked, her heart clenching in dread.

He blew out his breath. "Alas, the very worst news . . ."

The room suddenly began to sway. Charlotte braced her hands on the back of an armchair to keep herself upright.

"Oh, forgive me, Lady Wrexford! I did not mean—that is, the lad is quite fine in all regards." A cough. "Save for his educational future. You see, he's been expelled from Eton."

Charlotte took a moment to steady her emotions, which required suppressing the urge to laugh once his words sunk in. "I'm greatly relieved to hear that Peregrine has suffered no harm."

She gestured for him to resume his seat and moved to take the chair facing his. "Now kindly explain the terrible transgression that resulted in such an extreme punishment."

Belmont made a pained face—or perhaps he, too, was trying to mask his inner emotions. "He set off a stink bomb during the College Headmaster's Sabbath Day address to the students."

"Ah." Her lips quivered in mirth. "I'm sorry," she added. "I realize it's not amusing, but . . ."

Belmont cracked a smile. "I know. As his guardian, I should be shocked and furious. And out of a sense of duty, I did appeal to the provost of Eton for a second chance, as it was clearly a youthful prank. But Lord Fenway is very strict in his notions of right and wrong. He absolutely refused to consider it."

He shrugged. "But the poor lad was so deucedly unhappy there that a part of me is glad that the ordeal is over. However . . . I'm not quite sure what to do."

"Well, let us discuss the options," said Charlotte, trying not to let her hopes rise.

"Peregrine insists that he would be welcome to return to your household and be tutored privately along with your two wards. However, it rubs my conscience wrong to slough off my familial responsibilities on you and your husband . . . assuming that you would even consider the arrangement."

"Mr. Belmont—"

"Wait—please hear me out."

She gestured for him to continue.

"That said, I face a dilemma. My diplomatic duties demand that I travel to the Peace Conference in Vienna, and it is expected that I will be gone until next spring. My wife just had our first child, and as her health is still rather frail, it has been deemed unwise for her and our newborn to accompany me, so they will be staying with my mother."

Who detests Peregrine, thought Charlotte.

The boy's father—the elder brother of Belmont's father— had inherited the family earldom, and then had married late in life. The birth of a son had snatched away the fortune and title that Belmont's parents had taken for granted would be passed to them. Their resentment was exacerbated by the fact that Peregrine's mother was of African descent. They thought . . .

Be damned with what they thought.

"There is no dilemma," interjected Charlotte. "On no account can Peregrine be made to stay with your mother. It would be cruel—to both of them."

"I know that," he mumbled.

"Then it's settled. Peregrine will have a home here."

"Lord Wrexford will, of course, need to be consulted—" began Belmont.

"There is no need for that," she said. "Be assured that I know my husband's feelings on the matter."

He blew out a sigh of relief. "I don't know how to repay your kindness, milady."

"As to that . . ." Charlotte's expression turned grave. "There is an important issue that needs to be addressed in order to do the right thing for Peregrine, not just for now but for the future. It's unfair to treat him like a shuttlecock, batting him back and forth between families whenever the situation changes."

"What are you suggesting?"

"That you pass legal guardianship of Peregrine to Wrexford and me. It will ensure that he has a stable home, both materially and emotionally. For us to serve merely as custodians is not ideal, as it would force us to walk on eggshells when making decisions about his well-being. You must trust us to have his best interests at heart."

Belmont didn't rush to reply. She appreciated that he appeared to be giving the decision careful thought.

"There is another consideration as well, one that is awkward to raise but must be taken into consideration," continued Charlotte. "That you have been a good guardian to your cousin despite the tug of conflicting loyalties is a testament to your integrity, sir. But life is uncertain. If anything were to happen to you, your mother would likely become Peregrine's guardian. Surely that should be avoided at all costs."

"You truly are willing to accept those responsibilities for someone who is not your own flesh and blood?"

"Ours is an unconventional family, sir. What binds us together is love."

"Perhaps that's an even more reliable bond than blood," murmured Belmont. He smiled. "Then if you are truly sure, I am happy to agree to your suggestion, Lady Wrexford."

"Excellent. Given your travel plans, we will make sure to return to London in several days so that you and my husband can arrange all the legalities before you leave for Vienna."

Belmont rose and inclined a bow. "I will bid Peregrine adieu for now and then take my leave—"

"But it's growing dark, sir. You are most welcome to stay with us for the night."

"Thank you, but I am anxious to return to London as quickly as possible, so I made arrangements at the inn in Royston, which will save me several hours."

"As you wish," replied Charlotte. "Come, I'll take you to the boys and then have our cook prepare a cold collation for the road."

Once the farewells were made—a happy occasion, with the dowager adding her heartfelt thanks to the exuberant shouts of joy from the Weasels and Peregrine—and Belmont dispatched with good wishes and a hamper full of delicacies, Charlotte was quick to retreat to her workroom.

Savoring the stillness after all the emotional turmoil of the day, she moved to the bank of mullioned windows overlooking the back lawns and faraway woods. The symphony of summer sounds had turned more muted as the fast-approaching autumn brought a coolness to the evenings. Ivy rustled against the glass. Just beyond the gardens, a breeze ruffled through a stand of rowan trees, the moonlight catching flickers of its deep red foliage.

Her breath misted the glass as she reflected on this new death that had disrupted the lives of her family and dear friends. Murder was so much more than a single act of violence. Like a terrifying kraken from seafaring legends, it flung out its tentacles and dragged one into a dark maze fraught with unseen twists and turns . . .

A knock drew Charlotte back from her brooding.

Alison entered, carrying a bottle of champagne and two crystal coupes. "I thought a celebration was in order." She nudged the door closed behind her, and then came to a halt as she caught Charlotte's expression. "But perhaps I should have brought whisky instead."

Charlotte forced a smile. "You are right to remind me that darkness should never be allowed to overshadow the special moments of joy."

"I'm sorry that you had such a difficult day. It is never easy to be the messenger of death," said the dowager after setting down the wine and glassware. "I imagine that Milton's friends were devastated by news of his tragic accident."

Secrets and subterfuge. Disheartened by the thrust-and-parry meeting with the scientific society members, Charlotte suddenly couldn't stomach playing such games with her loved ones for a moment longer.

"We have not been entirely forthcoming with you," she confessed. "The magistrate and the coroner gave us reason to believe that Milton's death was no accident."

Alison's brows rose a notch. "And you feared that I would draw my blade and rush willy-nilly into the fray?"

"The thought occurred to me," she said dryly.

"Hmmph." But the snort held no real bite. "As a matter of fact, I *did* bring my sword cane—with our family, one never knows when trouble may strike. But I did promise you and Wrex that I wouldn't draw it without your permission, so I'm quite insulted."

"Hear me out before giving me a tongue lashing," said Charlotte. "Cordelia felt compelled to begin probing into who might have wished her childhood friend ill by speaking this morning with Milton's fellow scientific society members, who happen to be gathered at the University of Cambridge for a series of lectures," replied Charlotte. "It seemed to me that she was harried enough with all the sudden changes in her life without having her dear friends asking questions and demanding to help."

The sound of boyish laughter floated in from the corridor.

"If I erred on the side of caution, I apologize," she continued. "That is why Baz joined Wrex and Kit and Cordelia's brother in going to confirm the coroner's verdict of murder. But he doesn't expect there to be any error—he trained the fellow."

The dowager dropped any pretense of being offended. "What a tragedy. The unexpected death of a friend is unspeakably shocking, even more so when it's because of foul play." Her mouth pinched in sorrow. "After all the Sturm und Drang of her courtship, Cordelia deserved a modicum of peace and quiet in which to begin her married life."

"Peace and quiet." Charlotte heaved a rueful sigh. "Wouldn't that be lovely?"

Alison chuckled. "Now that you have officially added a third Weasel to your household, you had better surrender any thoughts of peace and quiet for the foreseeable future."

"It is a bargain I won't ever regret making."

"Ha, be careful what you wish for!" teased Alison. Her expression turned wistful. "At least boys are easier than girls. A surrogate daughter would be a joy . . . but raising her would be far more fraught with worries. Given all the strictures of Society, there are so many more perils for a girl to navigate."

"Indeed." Recalling her own youthful rebellions, Charlotte felt a little faint. "Lud, I made life an absolute hell for my parents."

"I have no doubt that you and Wrex would keep a steady hand on the tiller and sail through the rough waters and occasional squalls with flying colors."

Charlotte wasn't so certain. All of her natural inclinations were diametrically opposed to what was considered proper feminine behavior by the beau monde. How could she ever stoop to mouthing hypocrisies?

She shook off the question, relieved that it was merely hypothetical.

"Unfortunately, our meeting with the members of the Revolutions-Per-Minute Society offered no easy answers as to a motive for the crime," continued Charlotte. She told Alison about Wheeler's revelation.

"A quarrel, especially one only partially overheard, does not mean the angry party is a murderer," pointed out the dowager.

"True," agreed Charlotte. "I also had the distinct impression that Milton's two other fellow society members were not entirely forthcoming with us about who might have wished him dead. I can't help but wonder why."

"You suspect one of them might be the murderer?"

"For now, I wouldn't rule any of them out," she replied. "Wheeler might be lying." A pause. "But if that were so, why hasn't Carrick appeared?"

Silence.

And then a heavy sigh. "Having seen more than our fair share of the evil that man does to his fellow man over the last few months, I suppose we have all become rather cynical," mused the dowager. She handed the champagne to Charlotte. "Come, let us pop the cork and add some effervescence to the present. Heaven knows, the coming weeks will likely offer precious little sparkle."

Wrexford cocked an ear as he entered the manor house, taking a moment to savor the sweetly familiar sounds of his family.

McClellan's voice floated up from the kitchens as she passed on instructions for the next day's supper menu . . . Charlotte and Alison were in the Blue Parlor discussing the merits of Jane Porter's latest novel . . . the Weasels were upstairs and sounded in high spirits . . .

He turned as Harper padded across the marble entrance tiles and let out a *woof* of welcome.

"Wrex!" The hound's bark brought Charlotte hurrying from the room.

Her smile, a blaze of warmth in the late afternoon shadows, was all it took to lighten the heaviness of his heart. Wrexford opened his arms and drew her close.

They stood for a long moment in perfect silence, the tension in his muscles giving way to gratitude. Yes, life was capricious. And unfair. But at that moment the earl considered himself the luckiest man alive.

He tightened his hold.

A heartbeat passed. And then another.

Charlotte eased back and pressed a palm to his wind-roughened cheek. "I take it that there was no mistake."

"No," answered Wrexford. "The mortal wound was definitely made by a knife." He took her hand and brushed a kiss to her knuckles. "Shall we go sit by the fire? Kit and I rode hard to make it back here by nightfall. I would welcome a glass of whisky."

"Of course. But first let us go upstairs. The boys and I have a surprise for you."

His throat was parched, and his body ached from the hours in the saddle, but he forced a smile. "Please tell me they haven't concocted some new and nefarious chemical substance. Their last surprise of dusting the insides of my riding boots with itching powder was not at all amusing."

Another hoot of laughter sounded from upstairs.

"But I'm glad to hear them sounding more like their usual selves."

"It's not a prank, Wrex," she promised. "Come."

He let himself be led up to their quarters. The door to the schoolroom was half-open . . .

Hawk spotted him and gave an exuberant shout. "Wrex! Wrex!"

Raven scrambled into view, followed by . . .

Wrexford blinked.

And then all three boys began jabbering at once.

Charlotte waved them to silence. "Peregrine has returned to the nest—" she began.

"Yes, I can see that with my own eyes," he replied.

"And he's not leaving!" crowed Raven.

A surge of emotion—an elemental rush of joy—bubbled through his blood, but he forced himself to keep a straight face. "Dare I ask how this came to be?"

The three boys suddenly turned a little green around the gills. After exchanging guilty glances, they looked to Charlotte in mute appeal.

"You're not going to like it," she admitted. "But hear me out before reacting."

"Go on," said Wrexford. "Surely it can't be as bad as the possibilities that immediately leap to mind."

"Peregrine has been expelled from Eton," she explained, "for setting off a stink bomb during the headmaster's Sabbath Day speech to the upper-division students."

"A corking good one," offered Hawk with a hopeful grin. "It made several students puke and—"

A kick from Raven warned that such gory details weren't helping their cause.

"Mr. Belmont was required to fetch him," continued Charlotte, "and he came here to explain that he was facing a difficult conundrum . . ."

Wrexford listened intently as she explained about Belmont's travel plans and his laudable concerns over Peregrine's well-being if required to live with his aunt, whose prejudice against the boy was no secret.

"And so, when I proposed that Peregrine return to living with us, he readily agreed."

Wrexford masked his elation with a stern scowl. "I'm disappointed in you, Peregrine. Your actions put your guardian, who has been nothing but kind and fair to you, in a damnably difficult situation." Knowing that he ought not to be so delighted by the result of the mischief, he added, "Do not think for an instant that behaving badly will always get you what you want—and that goes for all three of you."

Charlotte drew in a quick breath but remained silent. He didn't dare glance at her, as he, too, felt his heart clench at seeing them look so remorseful as they struggled to hold back tears.

"That said, lad," he intoned, "I know that Eton can be a horrid place for any boy interested in intellectual engagement. And I do understand how unhappy and helpless you felt at being trapped in a complicated situation not of your own making. It's been hard for all of us. But Belmont is trying to do his best, and like it or not, he *is* your official guardian—"

"Actually he's not," interrupted Charlotte. "At least he won't be after next week, assuming you approve of the arrangement that I negotiated with him."

"C-Cousin Belmont has agreed to make you and m'lady my official guardians," explained Peregrine in a hesitant voice. "T-That is, if you'll h-have me."

Wrexford found his throat was too choked with emotion to reply. He swallowed hard . . .

Be damned with words.

In two swift steps he crossed the carpet and pulled the boy into a fierce hug. "My dear Falcon, as if that could ever be in doubt," he finally managed to say. "Welcome to being a full-fledged member of our family."

The tears now glittering on every cheek were ones of joy.

"But remember, that now brings both rights and—"

"And responsibilities!" chorused Raven and Hawk.

The earl smiled as the Weasels began cheering their new brother-in-spirit. "Aye, being part of a family means there are responsibilities, lads. And don't ever forget that."

Charlotte took a moment to dry her eyes before crouching down to plant a kiss on Peregrine's cheek. "Well, I think that's enough excitement for the evening." She rose, drawing the earl to his feet with her. "Come, Wrex, and let me pour you that whisky."

＊　＊　＊

The fire in the hearth had burned down to a mellow glow, the soft whisper of the red-gold coals adding a pleasant undertone to the tranquility of the library. Expelling a sigh, Charlotte let herself sink a little deeper into the soft leather cushions of the armchair, uncertain of how to define her present state of mind.

"Life," she observed, "can be such a wondrous but contradictory force of nature, bringing both joys and sorrows within a heartbeat of each other."

"I might not phrase it quite so poetically," replied Wrexford from his seat at one of the worktables. "But I shall not insult the Three Fates by calling them bad names."

"A wise choice," she agreed.

Paper rustled. He was perusing a book—another one of his father's, guessed Charlotte. Turning her gaze back to the hearth, she watched the subtle changing of the hues . . . *pumpkin orange . . . amber gold . . . lucifer red.*

The quicksilver flickers seemed to mirror her unsettled mood. Despite having spent the last hour telling Wrexford all about the meeting with the three members of the Revolutions-Per-Minute Society, she found that talking over the nuances of what had—and had not—been said had only made things seem more confusing.

"You seem pensive," said Wrexford, not looking up.

"At this moment, I should be feeling nothing but pure happiness," she mused. "And yet . . ."

"Emotions are rarely so black and white. As you just pointed out, life requires us to deal with a multitude of challenges all at once." The book snapped shut. "The beginning of an investigation is always hard. Possibilities flit around like unseen ghosts. One feels their presence and senses that they are close enough to touch, but when one grabs at them, there's nothing but air."

"I fear that Cordelia—"

The sound of footsteps on the back terrace had Wrexford up in a flash. He moved to a rosewood box on the bookshelves and clicked open the latch. "Extinguish the lamp flame," he said as he cocked his pistol.

"Halloo? Halloo?"

"It's Kit!" Heaving a sigh of relief, Charlotte turned away from the side table. "Dear God, what new mischief is afoot?" she muttered, hurrying to open the French doors.

"Sorry," apologized Sheffield as he and Cordelia stepped inside, bringing with them a swirl of chill air. "No one answered our knock on the front door, but we noticed the lamps were still burning here as the carriage turned into the courtyard, so we thought that we would check on whether you were still downstairs."

"Surely you have better things to occupy your time than coming by for a midnight chat," drawled the earl as he put his weapon back in its case.

A blush rose to Cordelia's cheeks, but she chose to ignore the gentle teasing. "I finally had the chance to sort through my mail from the last week. And given what Charlotte and I heard earlier today, we both thought you ought to see this without delay."

She held up a travel-smudged letter. "It's from Jasper Milton. He must have sent it just before he was murdered."

CHAPTER 8

Wrexford took the piece of paper and unfolded it.

"Please read it aloud." Charlotte remained standing by the doors. Moonlight glimmered through the glass panes, silhouetting her figure and making her face impossible to read.

"*My dearest Hypatia,*" began the earl.

"That was Jasper's private name for me when we were adolescents," explained Cordelia. "Hypatia was a famous woman mathematician from ancient times. That we had formed a close camaraderie through our shared passion for numbers seemed important to him. He didn't have any friends other than me among the children of the area."

"Why not?" queried Wrexford.

"Jasper was different," answered Cordelia. "He was considered awkward and aloof. I suppose that's because he felt more at home in the world of abstractions and intellectual challenges than in the everyday games and mischief-making that appeal to most boys and girls. I was the only one who understood and appreciated the way his mind worked."

Wrexford knew that to have any chance of solving the crime

they would have to learn a great deal more about Jasper Milton and his life. He wondered if that was why Charlotte seemed on edge.

Catching his glance, she moved to the hearth and put a fresh log atop the glowing coals. Sparks flared. A flame licked up.

Looking back to the letter, he resumed reading.

> *I fear that I'm being watched. I dare not say more here, but I shall soon visit you and explain further. In the meantime, I have taken precautions to ensure that nobody can meddle in my work.*
>
> *On a happier note, I made a connection at the scientific conference in France which helped me clarify my thinking and bring me to a final discovery. It's not something that I can discuss with my fellow society members—they are fine fellows but have limited vision and wouldn't understand. I expected better of Oliver, but he—well, never mind that now. You are the only one who sees beyond ordinary conventions and will comprehend my latest innovation and its implications. I can't wait to share it with you.*

The paper made a whispery sound as Wrexford refolded it.

"I admit that when read aloud, it sounds like Jasper took a page from one of Mrs. Radcliffe's melodramatic novels," said Cordelia. "It's completely out of character for him. He was always very precise and rational in his thinking. Something appears to have spooked him, and given the intruder who broke in here the night before the wedding, I am inclined to think that he must have had actual cause for alarm."

She frowned in thought. "After all, the intruder went straight for the escritoire. Perhaps he thought that Jasper had sent me the details concerning his work."

"Have you thought any more on what Milton's new innovation could be?" asked Charlotte. "As we heard this afternoon, his fellow society members think it revolves around an innovation for bridge building." A pause. "Is that really so revolutionary?"

"The answer to your first question is no. What with his various projects in the north and his travels to France, we haven't corresponded regularly over the last eight months," answered Cordelia. "As to whether a new scientific breakthrough could radically change the design of bridges—"

"The answer is definitely yes," interjected Sheffield. "Roads and bridges may seem unlikely candidates for innovation, but Thomas Telford and John McAdam are espousing some very interesting new ideas about grading, materials and basic construction that will revolutionize travel time."

"Kit," murmured Cordelia, "perhaps you need not explain—"

Caught up in his enthusiasm for the subject, Sheffield was already forging ahead. "Bridges offer even more possibility for innovation. Telford's recently completed cast-iron bridge, which crosses the River Spey at Craigellachie in Scotland, is a marvel of innovative engineering. Its innovative design features a single span of 151 feet and uses a slender arch that would be impossible to do in stone."

"Yes, I've heard that part of the reason for the latest improvements in bridge design are due to the new formulas for high-tensile iron that are being developed," mused Wrexford.

"Word is, Telford is also experimenting with a bridge design that uses cables made of wrought-iron links . . ." Sheffield looked to the earl. "Though I cannot begin to explain the scientific principles by which that technology would function."

The earl shrugged. "The mysteries of the physical world and its forces are not within my scope of studies."

"That is all fascinating and offers exciting possibilities for the future," observed Charlotte. "I must do some research on the subject and produce a series of drawings to alert the public to yet more momentous changes about to alter the world as they know it."

"Indeed, change is marching along at a dizzying pace," observed Wrexford. "But however intriguing the future is, let us step back to the present, and the mystery that currently faces us."

"Sorry, I get carried away when I start to think of all the ways to improve the movement of people and goods that will make the world a better place," apologized Sheffield. "Faster delivery of goods will stimulate the economy, workers will have more opportunity to find higher-paying jobs because they can afford to move to where their skills are needed. Communication is also important, and the mail will not be so erratic." Catching Cordelia's glance, he paused and blew out his breath. "But I will stop pontificating."

Silence settled over the room.

Finding the first thread to follow is always the hardest part of untangling all the motives and passions that cause a crime, reflected Wrexford. Truth rarely revealed itself easily.

A glance around at the grim faces showed that they, too, understood the coming investigation would demand sacrifice. And likely cause pain.

"So far, Milton's note seems to be the one tangible clue we have." It was Sheffield who first ventured to speak. "That he mentions a connection made in France stirs some initial questions," he pointed out. "The fact that a man appeared from the woods and hurled a warning note at Raven and Hawk which was partly written in French can't simply be coincidence."

"That would seem to make sense," replied Charlotte. "But how do the two things tie together? Was the intruder who entered Cordelia's rooms Milton's French connection? And was the man who threw the note a friend or a foe of the intruder?"

"Or was the intruder Milton's murderer?" suggested Sheffield.

"All good questions," muttered Wrexford. "However, it's a waste of time to speculate on the answers. Yes, we have two clues that point to a connection with France. But whether or not they are related remains to be seen."

"Actually, there are *three* clues," said Charlotte. "At our meeting with Milton's fellow society members, one of them mentioned that Cordelia's cousin said the members of the Parisian scientific society seemed particularly interested in coaxing Milton into giving them details about his latest work on bridges."

At the reminder of her cousin's close friendship with Milton, Cordelia suddenly let out a gasp. "Good God, another thought has just occurred to me." Her face lost all vestige of color. "We know that Jasper was murdered . . . and Oliver is still missing. Wheeler's information about the quarrel suggested one terrible reason for that. But what if the reason is worse and he, too has been—"

Sheffield drew her close and touched a comforting caress to her cheek. "Let us not jump to conclusions, sweeting."

"But if he's not injured . . . or worse, we should have heard from him by now," she countered.

"Not necessarily," said Wrexford. "Mr. Whalley told us that in some of the smaller valleys to the north, the roads were entirely washed away. It could take several more days before any communication is restored."

Cordelia didn't offer further argument, but her face remained shadowed by doubt.

"To return to Charlotte's point," he continued, "the fact that Milton and Carrick were in Paris for a symposium hosted by the French scientific society does seem to be the most solid clue of the three."

"So what are you suggesting?" asked Sheffield.

"That the logical place to start is in London, where according to Milton's colleagues, the Parisian scientific society will be arriving soon to attend an international conference on improving transportation, hosted by the Royal Institution. With Europe now at peace, there is much excitement over the possibilities of connecting all the nations together in bold new ways."

Cordelia lifted her shoulders in apology. "I'm so sorry for

upending your plans for an interlude of peace and quiet in the country."

"Don't fret—the idea of peace and quiet flew out the window earlier today with the unexpected arrival of Peregrine," responded Charlotte with a smile, and then quickly explained about the boy's expulsion from Eton and his new position as an official member of the family.

"Why, that's wonderful news!" exclaimed Cordelia.

"Yes, a welcome ray of light in the muddled darkness cast by murder," said Charlotte. "We must keep reminding ourselves that the joys of love and friendship are why we battle so fiercely against Evil."

"There are some estate matters that I must attend to over the next several days, but we shall plan on returning to Town immediately after they are done," offered Wrexford. "Baz will return from the inquest tomorrow, and he will escort Alison back to Mayfair so that she can attend Sir Robert's gala birthday celebration before joining her friend, the dowager Marchioness of Harkness, for a country house party. And then he is taking a short trip to Tunbridge Wells to advise a friend who wishes to set up a clinic for soldiers returning from Europe."

"Life must go on in the face of death," mused Cordelia.

"Indeed," agreed Charlotte, though she wished that the Grim Reaper's shadow would not darken their days so frequently.

"We, too, will be spending some days in the country before heading back to London," said Sheffield. "My father has asked for us to meet with him at the estate he gave us as a wedding gift in order to introduce us to the estate manager and tenant farmers."

He smiled. "Although I think the real reason is that he wishes to ask Cordelia more questions about her views on the growth of international commerce and what areas might offer savvy investment opportunities."

"Your father is far more progressive in his thinking than you led me to believe," she replied.

"He's more open-minded with you than he is with me. Perhaps that's because you're smarter than I am."

Cordelia's lips twitched in amusement before giving way to a more serious expression. "Kit, as usual, is being too modest. The main reason we are meeting with his father is to discuss the possibility of Kit standing for election to Parliament."

"Like many members of the landed aristocracy, my father controls a pocket borough," explained Sheffield.

There were a number of election districts in the country with a small number of voters whose livelihood depended on the local lord of the manor, and thus were deemed to be "in his pocket" and willing to vote for whichever candidate the local lord chose.

"So it occurred to me that rather than simply complain about antiquated rules and regulations that stifle progress, I should try to put myself in a position to actually do something about them."

"Bravo," responded Wrexford. "You'll bring a breath of fresh air to the stuffy confines of the House of Commons."

Sheffield made a face. "I'll likely just be whistling—or spitting—into the prevailing wind. But I might as well try to make some good trouble to atone for my past mindless revelries."

"Winds shift direction," said the earl.

Cordelia regarded her new husband, admiration glimmering in her gaze. "Change starts with tiny steps, and then can gain momentum."

"Solving a puzzling murder . . . embarking on married life . . . adjusting to new family dynamics . . . seeking political power to make the country a better place . . ." Charlotte cleared her throat with a wry cough. "It sounds like we all have our work cut out for us."

"There is one other thing to mention." Cordelia smoothed

open another sheet of paper. "As you and I expressed interest in the upcoming conference at the Royal Institution, Kendall Garfield, one of the members of the Revolutions-Per-Minute Society we met with in Cambridge, sent me a list of the delegations invited to attend."

Her fingers tightened on the document. "As we know, France is participating. In addition, Metternich is sending representatives from Austria, as are a number of the smaller German principalities." A hesitation. "And the Kingdom of Württemberg is also sending a delegation." She looked up. "You don't think . . ."

Charlotte felt a chill tease at the nape of her neck. During their most recent investigation, they had joined forces with the king of Württemberg's personal librarian to unmask a group of cunning villains who had committed treason, murder, and financial fraud over a period of years.

Or so they had thought. It turned out that man who called himself Herr von Münch was *not* the king's librarian. As to his real identity . . .

"Do I think he might be in the hunt for your cousin's papers?" she replied. "Perhaps. But I can't see him as a ruthless killer. While we don't know his true motives, he was never our enemy. He helped rather than harmed us, so I hold no grudge."

"And yet he lied to us." Cordelia made a face. "Surely you would never again trust someone who lied to you."

Charlotte pondered the question. "I'm not sure that's true." Cordelia looked surprised.

"It's not black and white," she mused.

Wrexford, she noted, was regarding her with an inscrutable look.

"What I mean is, look at me—I lived a lie for years." A pause. "In a way I still am. A. J. Quill is an integral part of who I am, and yet I hide it beneath a froth of expensive silk and satins."

"And what about you and Kit?" Her gaze lingered on Cordelia for another moment and then moved to Sheffield. "You feel compelled by the rules of Society to keep your business activities a secret."

"That's . . . different," responded Cordelia, though her voice lacked any real conviction.

"Again, I suggest we don't tie ourselves in knots speculating on hypothetical moral questions," said Wrexford. "We have no reason to think that the man we knew as von Münch is involved in the current conundrums. What we do know is that a murderer is on the loose. And we've taken on the task of catching him before he strikes again."

CHAPTER 9

Pausing by the closed door of the schoolroom, Charlotte listened to Mr. Lynsley question the boys on their assigned history lesson. The young man, who had been tutoring Raven and Hawk since shortly after she and Wrexford met, had cheerfully agreed to add a third pupil to his duties, and by the sound of the questions and answers, all was going well.

The boys, she reflected, were serious about their studies. They were eager to learn, and their tutor was an excellent teacher, so the arrangement seemed a perfect match.

Thank heaven.

Charlotte tucked an errant lock of hair behind her ear, tiptoed back to the main stairs, and made her way to her workroom.

They had returned to London nearly a week ago, but between dealing with all the details of their newly expanded family, keeping pace with her responsibilities as London's most notorious social commentator, and strategizing the first moves in a murder investigation, it felt as if there had been precious few moments in which to simply catch her breath and put her thoughts in coherent order.

A half-finished drawing—a parody on the Prince Regent's prodigious appetite for buying expensive art and expecting the country to pay for his pleasures—lay on the worktable.

"No rest for the wicked," she quipped, taking a seat and re-arranging her pens and brushes. But rather than set to work adding the final India ink shadings and details in preparation for the watercolor washes, Charlotte sat back and pressed her fingertips together.

She could see in her mind's eye the exact placement of the hues—a carmine red velvet coat collar to draw the eye to Prinny's avaricious face, an aquamarine blue waistcoat to accentuate his ocean-wide girth . . .

"If only I could picture a clever way to contrive a meeting with the members of the French scientific society," she muttered.

But fretting was a waste of time, and at the moment, she had none to squander.

Reminding herself that she had a deadline looming, Charlotte chose a fine-nibbed pen and began adding some cross-hatching beneath Prinny's goggling eyes.

The scientific visitors from France had arrived yesterday, and Wrexford had just left to meet with some of his friends at the Royal Institution to learn what official receptions were being planned to honor the conference's participants. Sparkling wine and potent spirits, served in the glittering splendor of a Mayfair mansion, often loosened tongues.

And loosened tongues tended to wag a little too freely.

Still, there was only so much one could learn in a drawing room. The real secrets preferred to lurk within smoke and shadows.

The clink of porcelain drew Charlotte back from her musing.

"I thought you might welcome some sustenance," said McClellan as she entered the room bearing a tray of tea things and a basket of fresh-baked muffins.

"Bless you." Charlotte quickly moved her artwork aside.

"Your company and conversation would be even more welcome."

The maid made a sympathetic sound.

A plume of fragrant steam rose from the silver pot. Tea, dark as mahogany, splashed into the two cups. Charlotte took a sip and felt the tension melt from her spine.

"Things may feel a little helter-pelter right now, but we shall manage," said McClellan after passing over a muffin.

"From your lips to Lucifer's ears," muttered Charlotte.

A chuckle. "The devil should know by now that challenging us gets him naught but a kick in the arse." After a glance at the drawing, the sounds of mirth grew louder. "That will be a hugely popular print with the public. You've caught the prince's gluttonous expression to perfection."

"It's good to make the public laugh on occasion. However, I would much rather make them think," replied Charlotte. "Milton's murder has made me aware of issues that may create momentous changes in the movement of goods and people around the country. That will greatly affect all our lives, and I'm anxious to learn more about the subject." A sigh. "And yet here I sit, swathed in silks and satins, just twiddling my thumbs."

"It seems to me that you are being a trifle harsh on yourself. But I understand your impatience." McClellan took a bite of her muffin and chewed thoughtfully. "Tyler mentioned that he met with some friends at a tavern in St. Giles last night and happened to learn that a meeting is taking place later tonight to discuss the problems of returning soldiers who cannot find employment."

Wrexford's valet, who also served as his laboratory assistant, had a number of other useful attributes, including a knack for making friends within the less salubrious sections of the city. The information he gained through his contacts there had proven very useful in previous murder investigations.

"Apparently a Frenchman will be one of the speakers," continued McClellan, "and from what Tyler has gathered, the fellow's main point will be that the lack of easy and inexpensive transportation serves as an invisible prison for the poor."

Charlotte considered what she had just heard. "Does Tyler know where this meeting is taking place?"

"I believe so."

"Please ask him. I think Magpie ought to attend it." Charlotte occasionally slipped into a third skin—that of a streetwise urchin who represented an employer willing to pay very well for certain information—in addition to her role as the Countess of Wrexford and the infamous scribbler, A. J. Quill.

Indeed, there were times when her many responsibilities became so blurred that she wasn't quite sure who her real self was.

"It will be good to get out of the cosseted confines of Mayfair and back into the stews," she mused. "What with planning a wedding and feathering the nest for our new fledgling, I worry that I'm in danger of losing my edge."

Before she met Wrexford, she had spent several nights a week prowling the hellholes and cesspools of the city for the secrets and scandals that made her pen so powerful.

"I had better make up a fresh batch of grease and ashes to rub on your face, said McClellan. "And retrieve your jacket from the cellars, where it's perfuming itself in a sack filled with rotting garlic."

"Lord Wrexford!" William Hedley, noted inventor of the steam locomotive Puffing Billy and other mechanical innovations, batted at the cloud of vapor enveloping his face and gestured for the earl to enter his laboratory. "It's always a pleasure to see you." A glint of anticipation flashed through the mist. "Voltaic batteries, computing engines, multi-shot pistols— what unusual and challenging questions do you have for me today?"

"Sorry to disappoint you," replied Wrexford over the *whoosh* and *clang* of the model steam engine sitting on Hedley's worktable. "I would just like to hear your general thoughts on a certain technological subject."

"Fire away, milord," said the inventor after pulling a few levers to silence his machine.

"I'm interested in bridge design. Have any new developments caught your attention?"

"Hmmph." Hedley rubbed at his chin. "As you know, that's not my bailiwick. I make things that move, and bridges are designed to do exactly the opposite. You would be better off asking Thomas Telford."

"But word is he's in St. Petersburg consulting with the tsar about a canal and bridge project in Russia," pointed out Wrexford, "and my interest is rather pressing."

"Then let me think . . ."

Not wishing to rush his friend, the earl turned to survey the work counters and the various projects in different stages of development.

Creativity is rarely tidy, he thought with an inward smile, as he regarded the chaotic-looking piles of screws, gears, rods, and various other unidentifiable implements of invention. One construction in particular drew his eye . . .

"Ah, you've picked out the most interesting of my various experiments," said Hedley as Wrexford moved in for a closer look. "I'm working on a new system for coupling the wheels of a steam locomotive, which will alleviate the wear and tear on the iron tracks."

A pause. "Or so I hope."

"I have no doubt you'll figure out a solution," he replied. "I look forward to the day when your locomotive design is a common sight chugging over hill and dale."

For a moment, Hedley stood very still, a faraway look in his eyes. "We shall see, milord. We shall see," he said softly, but then with a small shake returned to the earl's original question. "You might want to have a chat with Marc Isambard Brunel. He's a very clever fellow with a wide range of practical technological interests. He fled from France to America in the early days of their revolution and was chief engineer for the city of New York before settling here in Britain—so he may be of more help to you than I."

"That's an excellent suggestion. I don't know him, but I've heard he was just made a Fellow of the Royal Society, so I look forward to making his acquaintance." After another look around, he gave a nod of thanks. "And now, I'll not keep you any longer from your work."

Wrexford was halfway down the corridor to the stairwell when the sound of footsteps caused him to look around.

"I just recalled something, milord, though it may be of no consequence," huffed Hedley as he skidded to a stop. "At the last meeting of the London Society for Progress, one of my colleagues mentioned hearing a very interesting presentation by a young man who is working on technical innovations that would make it possible to construct bridges with a longer span."

"Did he perchance mention the fellow's name?" asked Wrexford.

"Aye, he did!" Hedley paused to draw in a breath.

"It was Oliver Carrick."

Charlotte swore softly after reading the note that had just been delivered by an errand boy from the Royal Institution. "Wrex won't be home until late. He met up with a scientific colleague, and they are hoping to find Marc Isambard Brunel attending the evening lecture at the Royal Society, as he may be able to shed some light on the latest developments in bridge design."

"Brunel," mused Tyler. "He's the fellow who's been working on digging a tunnel under the Thames."

"I'm not sure that speaks highly of his bridge knowledge," quipped McClellan.

Tyler chuckled. "If you can't go *over* something, might as well try going *under* it."

"Kindly stubble the levity," muttered Charlotte. "The hunt for a murderer is no laughing matter."

Tyler's expression immediately sobered. "I did not mean to make light of it, m'lady."

"I know, I know." She sighed. "It's simply frustrating to have no real leads—"

"Save for Lady Cordelia's missing cousin," interjected McClellan. "The fact that she's had no word from him strikes me as suspicious, especially given what his fellow member of the Revolutions-Per-Minute Society told you."

"Unless Carrick has also been murdered," she countered.

"No corpse that might be his has been found," pointed out the valet. "Sheffield had Mr. Goffe, the coroner who discovered Milton's remains, alert all of his colleagues in Cambridgeshire and the surrounding counties to report any unidentified bodies. So far, there's been no word."

"It's likely that Milton's killer meant for the corpse to fall into the river below." Charlotte repressed a shiver. "If it had, then God only knows if it ever would have been found. So if Carrick has met the same fate . . ."

Silence.

"But let us not be disheartened by what we don't know." Her words were as much for herself as for the others. "And concentrate on finding a thread that will lead us to the truth."

She gave a grimace. "As to that, it may only turn into a useless knot, but since you discovered that a visiting Frenchman will be spouting his views on how the poor are kept in their place by the lack of affordable transportation, I thought it might be worth it for me to attend tonight's meeting of radical thinkers. Where is it taking place?"

Tyler hesitated. "I'm coming with you."

"That's quite unnecessary." She heard the sharpness in her voice and didn't care. It rankled that he thought she had gone too soft to fend for herself. "Just because I've assumed a fancy title and live in the gilded splendor of Mayfair doesn't mean I've become a helpless widgeon."

"I meant no insult, m'lady. I'm not questioning your skills. But this is a group whose outspoken ideas can land them in prison—or worse. They know me. If a stranger shows up alone, they may very well suspect the fellow is an informer. And in a fight of twenty-five to one, I don't wish to contemplate what might happen."

"You know that Tyler isn't one for exaggeration," said McClellan. "If he says it's too dangerous to go on your own, then it is."

Charlotte knew they were being sensible. But for one mad moment, she wanted to tell them to go to the devil. The truth was, her life was feeling entirely *too* sensible. A part of her craved that fizz in the blood which came from dancing along a razor's edge.

That was the trouble with danger. It was seductive. All reason went to hell.

McClellan must have read her thoughts. Eyes narrowing, she looked about to add a more forceful warning.

"You need not ring a peal over my head," assured Charlotte. "You'll get no further objection from me."

Tyler shuffled his feet. "You'll need to do exactly as I say."

"Yes."

He looked in question to McClellan, who gave a gruff nod. "Aye, m'lady's word is her bond."

"Then you had better go dress in your rags. We need to leave shortly."

"Fawwgh," muttered the maid. "I suggest waiting until the last moment before donning your stinking coat."

A short while later, Charlotte and Tyler were headed east, winding their way through the back alleys and byways that few of the beau monde even knew existed. The surroundings grew shabbier, the stench of rotting garbage and human waste thickening the sooty air.

No words were exchanged until they passed into the slums of Seven Dials. Slowing his steps as the narrow footpath between two sagging buildings opened onto a cart path, Tyler edged closer, shoulder to shoulder.

"Once we're inside the tavern, keep your head down and let me do all the talking," he whispered. "These men are damnably good at smelling a rat." His breathing shallowed. "Though whatever godawful substances Mac used to scent your coat should obliterate all other olfactory messages."

Charlotte tugged the brim of her hat a little lower. "Oiy."

"I'll try to get myself invited to share an ale with the Frenchman after the meeting—I'm known to the group as a Scottish radical who has no love for the British. But I don't dare have you linger with us. They have sharp eyes."

"I understand," she said. "I'll leave and make my way home on my own." She knew this part of the stews well. Her old residence was close by.

Though it might well have been on the moon, considering how far removed she was from her former life. Here the ambient smells were of sweat, piss, and despair rather than of money and all the luxuries it could buy.

Tyler plucked at her sleeve. "This way."

A winding turn brought them to a lane unlit save for the greasy flicker of lamplight oozing through the shuttered windows of a low building. A fugue of sounds—rumbled voices, the thump of pewter, the hiss of cheap candles—greeted them as Tyler wrenched open the tavern door and entered, Charlotte shadowing his steps. Threading his way around the perimeter of the taproom, he headed for a door located on the far wall and led the way into a windowless meeting area.

It was half full—Charlotte gauged that there were between twenty-five and thirty men present, a mix of laborers and better-dressed men with soft hands. She guessed they were the intellectuals, hoping to use their minds rather than their fists to effect change.

A ferret-featured man with lank brown hair framing his narrow face came over to greet Tyler. No introductions were made. This was not the sort of place where the niceties of Polite Society were observed. A terse exchange followed, which Charlotte studiously ignored, while straining to hear what was being said.

Frenchie . . . delegation . . . transport—the few words she caught were promising.

The man drifted away to confer with several cronies. One of them then moved away and mounted an overturned wooden crate set close to one of the walls. The crowd shuffled around to face him, and the room grew quiet.

"It's the Frenchman," whispered Tyler as he shifted his stance. "He's come over with the scientific society from Paris, though he's not a member."

Charlotte gave no outward reaction.

The man started to talk. He spoke English quite well, with only a trace of an accent. It was a well-tailored presentation, distilling abstract concepts into practical ideas that the working men could grasp.

"The fact that travel is both expensive and difficult works as an invisible prison. You can't afford to leave a place, and so employers can pay you a pittance for your labor. If you had the freedom of choice, you would also have an opportunity to make a better life for yourselves and your families. That's why we are agitating for better roads and bridges to connect the country."

Murmurs rippled through the crowd as the men began to understand the message.

"I've seen for myself what improved roads mean for the working man in France," continued the speaker. "You deserve no less here in Britain."

The rumblings grew louder. A few shouts of support echoed through the room.

"You should also be demanding that the government establish a fund for public works—like roads and bridges—that will employ the soldiers returning home from war and unable to find jobs because steam-powered looms and lathes have taken their place!"

More applause.

Ferret Face approached the makeshift podium, and the Frenchman ceded his place. "We already have plans to start circulating printed broadsides pressing for Parliament to pass an Act to fund road and bridge improvements. Our local radical newspapers will also add their voice. If we stir enough public sentiment, the government will be forced to listen."

An overly optimistic assessment, mused Charlotte. But then, reformers needed unflinching passion to keep butting their heads against the bastions of privilege and power.

Still, the man's core point—that free movement of labor was a key element in offering workers an opportunity to improve their lives—had made her realize that it was, perhaps, an important issue, and that A. J. Quill ought to look into it more carefully.

Glancing around, Charlotte made a mental sketch of the people and venue. Perhaps in using her pen to help unmask Milton's killer, she could also help those who were still living.

Ferret Face finished his exhortation and stepped down from the crate, signaling the end of the meeting. Tyler moved away to have a word with him and the Frenchman while the crowd began to file back to the tap room. He returned after a few moments, pausing just long enough for a quick exchange.

"I've been invited to stay. We're meeting a friend of the Frenchman in a private side room."

"*Bonne chance*," she whispered. "I'll head straight back, as we planned."

"Be careful."

Charlotte acknowledged the warning with a tug to her hat and then slipped away.

CHAPTER 10

The soot-dark night air felt refreshing after the fetid heat of unwashed bodies and rancid oil lanterns. She turned down an alleyway that branched out into a maze of footpaths after squeezing between two ancient wooden buildings. A scudding of starlight fluttered over the rutted ground for just a moment before the clouds overwhelmed the feeble glow.

It didn't matter. Charlotte knew the route by heart.

Mud squelched underfoot, and for a moment she was transported back to the days when her nocturnal prowlings for information to use in her satirical drawings were the key to her survival.

From up ahead came the scrabbling of a feral cat and the faint squeak of its victim.

"Eat or be eaten," she murmured. Though these days, that stark choice no longer had real teeth.

Life certainly did take unexpected twists and turns.

As her words were swallowed by the gloom, old instincts kicked in, and she was suddenly aware that she wasn't alone. The sounds behind her didn't quite match the echo of her own footsteps.

She took an instant to gauge her options. Cutting back was out of the question, and bolting ahead was too risky—she couldn't be sure of outrunning her pursuer. And with the buildings jammed together cheek by jowl, there were no openings allowing escape to another alleyway.

However . . .

Charlotte slowly lengthened her stride. She recalled that just after the next turn was a brick warehouse where the half-collapsed overhang of the neighboring building provided a way to scramble up to a narrow ledge and reach the roof. From there, one could drop down to the other side and disappear into another web of alleys.

Assuming, of course, that the overhang was still there.

Her pursuer was keeping pace but didn't sound any closer. *Biding his time, no doubt* . . . but with luck, she could gain an extra few yards head start by seizing the element of surprise.

Just as she rounded the bend, Charlotte broke into a run. The splintered section of overhanging roof was there, and taking care to time her leap, she managed to snag hold of it.

Splinters gouged her palms as she tried to pull herself up onto the broken shingles.

Damnation—my sedentary life has left me weak as a kitten.

A shout rumbled against the surrounding brick and wood as her pursuer caught sight of her ploy.

Damn! The thud of steps warned that he was closing in. Swinging her legs side to side for momentum, Charlotte tried again to heave herself up. Pain lanced through her palms, but her grip held, and her hips came up over the edge, allowing her to claw her way higher.

A hand caught her boot, but she shook it off.

Her pursuer cursed and grabbed again, his fingers once again seizing her heel.

Swallowing a spurt of fear, Charlotte tried to lash out again, but his grip was like a vise, pulling her down. She felt herself slipping . . .

A sudden *crack* sounded as something hard—a rock?—ricocheted off the back of her assailant's head, knocking him off-balance and sending him tumbling to the ground.

Dear God, surely the Weasels hadn't—

But there was no time for such distractions. She needed to stay focused on the moment at hand.

With a grunt of effort, Charlotte scrambled free of danger and up to the peak of the overhang, then crawled over to the brick ledge. From there, the gaps in the crumbling mortar allowed her to climb the short distance to the roof. Without a backward look, she raced across to the other side, dropped down to a low-slung shed, then to the ground, and took off running.

A stitch in her side finally made her slow to a walk as she reached the streets of Mayfair. Keeping to the shadowed passageways, she made her way to the back garden gate of their Berkeley Square mansion and let herself in.

The earl looked up from his reading as Charlotte tiptoed into his workroom.

"Drat," she said. "I was hoping that you would be asleep."

He eyed her torn jacket and filthy breeches. "I can see why." He cocked an ear but heard no sound in the corridor. "Where's Tyler? I was told the two of you went out together to attend a meeting in Seven Dials."

"He was invited to stay and have a round of drinks with the radicals," she answered. "We had agreed beforehand that I would head straight home if that happened."

Wrexford held back a sarcastic retort. Her face looked unnaturally pale, and as she shifted her stance . . .

"Is that blood on your hands?" he asked calmly.

"Yes." She drew in a shaky breath. "But might I explain everything after I go to the kitchen and wash the filth from the scrapes?"

"Sit," he commanded. "I'll be back shortly." A hesitation.

"Though I might suggest that you remove your stinking jacket and hat while I'm gone."

He returned with a basin of steaming water, several soft cloths, and a jar of medicinal salve. After putting them on a small side table and moving it close to her chair, Wrexford went to the sideboard and took a bottle of amber-dark spirits from one of its lower cabinets. "As you know, Baz is a great believer in splashing a bit of whisky on a wound."

"Heaven forfend that you squander your special Highland malt on a few trifling scratches," replied Charlotte. It was said lightly, but he heard an undertone in her voice that made him uneasy.

For the moment, however, he took care to respond with an equal measure of humor. "Don't worry. Tyler keeps a bottle of cheap swill tucked away for his own medicinal purposes. I daresay his scrapes are far worse than yours."

She forced a brittle laugh.

Which made him even more concerned.

After uncorking the bottle, Wrexford crouched beside Charlotte and took one of her hands in his. She winced as he splashed a bit of the spirits on her palm and gently massaged it into the torn flesh.

"I know it burns," he murmured, "but in this case, Baz asserts that pain is good."

"Easy for him to say," she replied.

He put aside the whisky and picked out several splinters before rubbing some of the herb-scented salve over the cuts. "Do you want to tell me what's upset you? Or would you rather that I guess?" A pause. "My imagination will likely conjure up something far worse than what actually happened."

That made her smile, though her gaze remained troubled. "You keep insisting that you're ruled by facts and logic—empirical observation, not imagination."

"For the most part I am," he declared. "But not when it comes to my wife."

A sigh signaled her tacit surrender. "My pride is more bruised than my body." She made a face. "I'm upset at myself for failing to stay alert. My skills are getting rusty."

Ah. In her youth, Charlotte had eloped to Italy with her drawing teacher in order to avoid being imprisoned in the gilded cage of aristocratic life, which offered her sumptuous pleasures and gorgeous plumage . . . but no freedom.

"Go on," he encouraged, though he was fairly certain he wasn't going to like what was coming next.

"After the meeting, I did exactly as planned and set out to make a discreet return home through the spiderweb of footpaths that crisscross through the stews," she explained. "I know the way by heart, but that made me careless. I stopped paying attention to my surroundings. By the time I noticed that someone was following me, I had turned onto a narrow footpath, and it had me trapped on either side by buildings that offered no gaps between them through which to escape."

His chest clenched as Wrexford fixed her with a searching stare, trying to spot some unseen injury that he had somehow missed.

Nothing. And yet, that didn't assuage his fears. "What—"

"I had to go up," she said, anticipating his question. "I knew where there was a broken overhang that I could jump and reach, allowing me to scramble over to a slanted roof from which I could climb to the top of the adjoining brick storage building. From there, I was able to descend to a cart path and lose myself in the maze of alleyways near the Foundling Hospital."

"Your pursuer didn't try to follow?"

"He caught my boot, but by some miracle—don't ask me how it happened—a rock sailed out of nowhere, knocking him to the ground."

"The Weasels were tucked up in their beds when I arrived home just an hour ago," he mused. "I don't see how it could have been them."

"Thank heaven," she muttered. "Be that as it may, whoever decided to play guardian angel saved me. By the time my assailant recovered, I was halfway up the brick wall, using the gaps in the mortar as handholds to reach the roof." A pause. "With his size and weight, he never would have made it."

"Is that supposed to reassure me?"

"No," admitted Charlotte. "I should never have been in such a precarious position in the first place." Her shoulders sagged to a very un-Charlotte-like slump. "My arms have no more heft than those of a rag doll. I could barely pull myself up over the edge of the overhang, a feat I've accomplished countless times in the past."

"You're out of practice," he observed.

"Precisely!"

He might have smiled, but the look of distress in her eyes warned that it was no laughing matter.

"Wrex, my ability to transform into Magpie is important to me. It's integral to my ability to unearth the secrets and hidden clues that allow me to keep the public informed on the issues that matter to their lives." She looked away for a moment, throwing her face in shadow. "No one else cares about the great unwashed masses and whether they have the right to a modicum of fairness."

"Magpie may fly less frequently, but that doesn't mean—"

"I've grown too weak." Though a mere whisper, Charlotte's voice resonated with an aching vulnerability.

Wrexford rose in a flash and gathered her in his arms. "My love, you are the strongest person I know."

"My body nearly failed me. If it again in falters in a mission, I may put you or the boys in danger."

"It's the heart that matters," he said. "Physical deficiencies can be easily remedied."

"B-But how?"

"As to that, I have an idea." Touching a fingertip to her face, he lightly traced the ridge of her cheekbone. "Come to bed, and I shall explain."

"Be serious, Wrex," she murmured, though a smile quivered at the corners of her lips. "I—"

His kiss silenced whatever protest was coming. "Trust me, I take the matter of your beautiful body quite seriously," he said, reluctantly ending the embrace sooner than he would have liked.

"And I thoroughly appreciate your concern, my love." She kissed him back—a long and lingering embrace. "But I do hope you have an additional suggestion for how to regain my former prowess at scrambling out of sticky situations."

"As to that, there is an old adage about killing two birds with one stone," replied Wrexford. "You have been wanting to take fencing lessons with Harry Angelo ever since I mentioned that he is open-minded enough to teach female students. Be assured that he gives no quarter to the weaker sex—a session with him is physically grueling, and every muscle will soon be strong as steel."

The lamplight caught the luminous flash in her eyes. "And I can practice with the Weasels and Peregrine! . . . Though we must make it clear to the boys that the term of endearment now officially refers to all three of them."

He loved the fierceness of her passions, even though they sometimes scared him half to death.

"Thank you, Wrex," added Charlotte, pulling him close. "When can I start?"

"I will send a note to him in the morning." On seeing that it was still dark as Hades outside, he quickly amended, "That is, at a more civilized hour in the morning."

"Excellent." The tension in her had softened, allowing then to fit together like matching pieces of a puzzle.

Which in a sense they were. He owed the inscrutable forces

of the cosmos a great debt of thanks for bringing them together.

"Now may we go to bed?" he murmured.

A feathery laugh tickled against his ear. "With pleasure."

Charlotte sat back in her chair and blew off the plume of
steam rising from her just-poured cup of coffee. "You didn't
think it important to mention that discovery to me last night?"

Wrexford had waited for Tyler and McClellan to join them
in the breakfast room before revealing what Hedley had told
him about Oliver Carrick.

"We had other more pressing matters to discuss," he replied,
a wicked gleam flashing for an instant in his eyes as he met her
gaze.

She looked down at her plate of toast to hide her smile. He
was right to remind her that murder must not be allowed to
eclipse all that was good and joyful in life.

McClellan filled the earl's cup and moved on to Tyler, who
had just returned from his night forays.

"I hope you have made this morning's coffee as black as sin,"
said the valet as he scrubbed a hand over his unshaven jaw.

"But of course. You look like Hell, so naturally it's as dark
as the devil."

Tyler winced at the word *devil*. "I feel as if a legion of
demons is jabbing red-hot pitchforks into my skull. The piss-
poor ale served at the tavern was bad enough, but from there
our little group moved on to the quarters of the French radical
and his friends, who served a cheap red swill that doesn't deserve to be called wine."

"*Debemus pro bono superiori pati*," quipped Charlotte. *We
must suffer for the higher good.*

"They made a point of adding that it was from Corsica,"
added the valet, after a swallow of coffee.

"Corsica," repeated Charlotte, feeling a chill tickle between her shoulder blades. "Oh, surely they're not suggesting that they would support the return of Napoleon to France?" The former emperor, who was Corsican by birth, had recently been exiled to the tiny isle of Elba, off the coast of Italy. "Europe is finally at peace after over ten years of constant wars, which have wrought unimaginable death and destruction throughout Europe."

"Yes, but the Allied Coalition—led by Britain—simply returned the hated Bourbon king and his corrupt, venal court to power," pointed out Tyler. "The Frenchmen spoke eloquently about all the excellent reforms and improvements Napoleon made—from the judicial and legal systems to agricultural techniques and transportation. They claim that he has promised to abide by international law if allowed to return to France and will never again seek power outside the country's borders."

"Clearly those idealists are unaware of the former emperor's famous statement that he can never see a throne without wanting to sit on it," remarked Wrexford dryly.

Charlotte put down her knife, leaving her bread unbuttered. "But what does all this have to do with Milton's death?" she mused.

"I haven't the faintest idea," answered the earl. "But let us look again at what we do know. We received a cryptic note half in French, and Milton's fellow members of the Revolutions-Per-Minute Society told you and Cordelia that the French scientific society had seemed very interested in Milton's technical innovations. And Oliver Carrick, the only person who can corroborate what went on at the symposium in Paris, is missing."

"And you said that Milton's fellow members had heard that the Frenchwoman was particularly attentive to making friends with Milton," reminded Tyler. "Given all of that, it would seem that we should concentrate our efforts on learning as much as we can about both the radical Frenchman who is here agitating for the working class to demand better and cheaper travel and the members of the Parisian scientific society who are in Town for the international conference."

Wrexford nodded. "We'll leave the radicals to you. Charlotte and I will contrive to receive invitations to the receptions and soirees welcoming the international scientific delegations to London—including the group from Paris."

"Alison will know all the social plans," mused Charlotte.

"I've already learned from one of my colleagues at the Royal Institution that the French ambassador is holding a party tonight in honor of the Parisian delegation—who, as you know, decided to arrive early in London."

"One can't help but wonder why," observed McClellan.

"Indeed." The earl reached for the coffeepot and poured himself a fresh cup. "So let us plan to start ferreting out answers."

CHAPTER 11

The glittering light from a myriad of candles blazed through the diamond-paned windows of the town house on Curzon Street, bathing the cobblestones in a golden glow as Wrexford and Charlotte descended from their carriage. Hedley had arranged for them to receive a last-minute invitation to the French ambassador's soiree.

"I never cease to be appalled at the egregious waste of money frittered away on sumptuous pleasures for the rich that would be far better spent on feeding and clothing the poor," muttered Charlotte. "The beau monde simply doesn't care."

"That's not entirely true, my love." The earl tucked her gloved hand in the crook of his arm. "You and your pen make a number of them care."

"Not nearly enough."

"Not yet."

On that note, they passed through the portico into the grand entrance hall and made their way up the curved marble staircase. After greeting their host and his wife, Wrexford moved to the archway leading from the main drawing room to the side salons and paused to survey the crowd. "Let us part ways here. I wish to find Hedley."

Charlotte spotted the dowager near the refreshment table and raised a hand in greeting. "And I will join Alison and her friend Sir Robert. If the female member of the French scientific society is in attendance, they will see to it that I meet her."

He watched her walk away—the sight of rippling silk accentuating her lithe grace always took his breath away—and then turned his thoughts to the task at hand. There was one guest in particular whom he wished to meet . . .

"Ah, Wrexford, there you are!" William Hedley approached in the company of another gentleman. "As you requested at our meeting the other evening, I am bringing over Mr. Marc Isambard Brunel to make the formal introductions. Though I must say, I'm surprised that the two of you have never met before."

""Our paths have often crossed, but only from afar," replied the earl after exchanging polite bows with the well-known engineer. Having missed finding Brunel the previous night, he was glad to finally meet him face-to-face.

"Your reputation precedes you, milord." Brunel had lived in Britain for nearly twenty years, but his accent still spoke clearly of his French origins. He was a powerfully built fellow with broad shoulders and a long face accentuated by strong features and dark eyes that flashed with intelligence.

Brunel shifted, and although dressed in well-tailored evening clothes, he didn't look entirely comfortable in such finery. His thick, callused hand held his crystal champagne flute a little awkwardly, as though he feared an errant twitch might snap the delicate stem in two.

"As does yours, sir," said Wrexford. "Your engineering design for mass-producing pulley blocks for the Royal Navy was a stroke of genius."

Brunel gave a Gallic shrug at the mention of his innovative

factory in Portsmouth, which was capable of producing 130,000 blocks per year—a key factor in ensuring that the British Navy ruled the oceans. "It was Henry Maudslay who brought my scribbles to life by building the actual machines. He's the true genius."

"Progress in so many industries owes a great debt to him," agreed the earl, who had encountered Maudslay and his engineering work during several previous murder investigations. "His lathes and milling machinery, which allow for making better and more accurate parts for other machines, have indeed revolutionized our ability to create new technologies."

"Quite right." Brunel raised his glass in silent salute. "But I have a feeling that you did not seek me out simply to discuss the general advancement of science in Britain." He took a sip of champagne. "Through several of my friends, I'm aware that your talents occasionally go beyond solving chemistry and other scientific problems."

"As it so happens, I do have a few specific questions unrelated to laboratory results," replied Wrexford.

"I am happy to be of assistance if I can, milord."

"I'm interested in the members of the Society for Practical Science who have come from Paris to attend the conference on transportation at the Royal Institution."

"It has been years since I left France," said Brunel. "I nearly lost my head during the Reign of Terror—as did the lady who is now my wife—so I have no official ties to the country." Another sip. "However, the new generation of scientific-minded individuals in France do often seek my counsel, and so I happen to be well acquainted with the members of the Society for Practical Science. What is it that you wish to ask me?"

"I understand that the primary interest of the society is roads and bridges," explained the earl. "To your knowledge, are any of the members doing innovative work in bridge design? Or are they simply engaged in working with current technology and building principles?"

"An interesting question." Pursing his mouth in thought, Brunel considered it.

A string quartet seated in a nook by the windows overlooking the back gardens began playing a Mozart sonata, the pianissimo tones softening the trills of laughter and clink of crystal.

The engineer quaffed the last of his wine and set his glass on a marble plinth. "Most of the members—I believe that they number twenty-five—are engaged in the practical demands of rebuilding a network of transportation ravaged by over a decade of marching armies and warfare. Their efforts are devoted to practical work, not theoretical thinking."

His gaze circled the ornate drawing room before coming back to Wrexford. "There are, however, two individuals who I would say are the intellectual leaders of the group."

"Tell me a little about them," pressed the earl.

"Jean-Paul Montaigne is the society's president. I believe he has some family connection to England—an aunt, perhaps— and spent a year of university study here."

Wrexford made a mental note of the fact. "Do you perchance know where?"

"I don't."

"It doesn't matter," he said. "Does Monsieur Montaigne have a special interest."

"Bridges," answered Brunel without hesitation. "His background is engineering, but he's also apparently very talented in mathematics and is interested in creating bridges with longer spans, which would give greater flexibility in routing roads through rugged terrain."

"A possibility that is far more momentous than it might sound," observed Wrexford.

"Indeed." Brunel took a moment for reflection before going on. "Important transportation projects, like Telford's ambitious Ellesmere Canal, often run into monetary problems because the terrain demands lengthy detours which may make the cost prohibitive. New technological innovations can help us conquer those obstacles."

"Is Monsieur Montaigne here tonight?" asked the earl.

"I have not yet spotted him or any of his delegation," answered Brunel. "However, if it is bridges which interest you, I would recommend you focus your main attention on Isabelle Benoit, who is secretary of the Society for Practical Science."

"A woman as an officer?" he mused.

Brunel quirked a faint smile. "You have no great regard for the intellectual powers of the fairer sex?"

"On the contrary, I happen to think that women are every bit as smart as men, but we give them precious few chances to prove it."

"That's exceedingly enlightened thinking, milord."

"Some might call it exceedingly radical," replied Wrexford. "Be that as it may, I'm aware that France is more liberal than our country, where most intellectual societies don't permit women to be members, much less to serve as officers."

"Allowing women to have both rights and responsibilities was one of the few good legacies that Revolutionary France left to the country. It allows the best minds to flourish regardless of sex."

A pause. "So if it is bridges that interest you, speak with Mademoiselle Benoit. Her expertise in mathematics is even more impressive than that of Montaigne."

Brunel once again surveyed the crowded drawing room with his sharp-as-steel gaze. "Ah, I still don't see Montaigne. But that is Mademoiselle Benoit over by the bust of Julius Caesar, conversing with the lady wearing the smoke-blue gown."

The engineer's eyes remained riveted on the Frenchwoman's companion. "Would you like me to introduce you to mademoiselle? The lady in blue is unknown to me—"

"Thank you, but that's not necessary," said Wrexford. "The lady in blue happens to be my wife."

* * *

"Here I go away to school for a month and already the family is involved in another murder investigation," observed Peregrine. "Do you think that His Lordship has concocted some sort of special magnetic solution that draws him to dead bodies in need of someone to find justice for their souls?"

"Ha, ha." Hawk gave a weak laugh. "Don't ask me to explain the chemistry. I think it just naturally happens."

Raven looked up from the mathematical puzzle he was trying to solve. "I heard Tyler say to Mac that Wrex was very much looking forward to an interlude of peace and quiet in the country."

"Wrex does seem unsettled about something," said Hawk. "I wonder what it is?"

Harper, who was stretched out in sleep by the front of the hearth, opened one eye and gave a gusty sigh.

"Nooo, I don't think Wrex is hungry, Harper. Though perhaps he's worried because you are eating him out of house and home," quipped Raven, which drew a chortling from the others.

But it quickly died away as he set down his notebook and frowned in thought. "M'lady did mention to Aunt Alison that Wrex has been thinking about fathers and sons . . . and said something about him feeling that he hadn't been very good in either role."

"I wonder what makes a good father?" mused Hawk. Abandoned in the slums of the city as children, he and his brother had only had each other.

Raven raised his brows at Peregrine. "What do you think, Falcon? You're the only one of us who has had a real father."

"That's not entirely accurate," drawled Peregrine. "But I understand what you mean." A sigh. "I don't remember much about my real father. Just fleeting moments."

Looking thoughtful, he tilted his head to gaze out the darkened schoolroom window, where a sliver of star-dotted sky was just visible above the rooftop silhouettes.

"He had a wonderful laugh. It sort of wrapped around you like sun-warmed honey." A smile. "And very broad shoulders. I felt as if I could have touched the sky as we walked with me perched on his shoulders, and he regaled me with stories of all the places in the world he had visited."

Peregrine then lapsed into a meditative silence for several long moments. "But I guess what I remember best is that no matter what we were doing, he made me feel . . ." A watery sniff. "I suppose what fathers do is they make you feel very loved."

Hawk looked at his brother and blinked. "That's how Wrex makes me feel," he said in a small voice. "I know we're not related by blood, but it feels like he's my real father in every way that matters."

"Oiy," agreed Raven. "M'lady is always saying that love is an even stronger bond than blood." He grinned at Peregrine. "Which means we're all family now."

"Oiy," echoed Peregrine with a solemn nod. "And we don't need any fancy bits of paper to tell us that."

"That goes for you, too, Harper," added Raven.

The hound thumped his shaggy tail and gave a *woof* of approval.

"So if Wrex is feeling blue-deviled," said Hawk once their giggles ceased. "What can we do to cheer him up and make sure he knows that *he* is loved?"

"As to that . . ." Raven thought for a moment. "I have an idea."

"Do introduce me to your companion, my dear."

Charlotte looked around at the earl's approach. "With pleasure, Wrex. Mademoiselle Benoit, this is my husband, Lord Wrexford."

"Mr. Brunel has been singing your praises, mademoiselle," said the earl, "and he strikes me as a man who is not easily impressed."

"Dear heaven, you now have me completely intimidated, milord," murmured the Frenchwoman as Wrexford bowed over her hand.

Charlotte had a feeling that very little cowed Mademoiselle Benoit. But as she knew well from her own experience, it was often a useful ploy for a lady to pretend to be less intelligent that she really was while assessing an unexpected situation.

"I doubt that I shall be able to manage a coherent word, given your august reputation in the scientific world," added the Frenchwoman with a tremulous quiver of her mouth that didn't quite come across as sincere.

"Be assured that I don't bite," he murmured.

Not without cause, thought Charlotte.

The remark drew a genuine laugh. "In that case, I shall endeavor not to disgrace myself."

"You need not worry, mademoiselle," Charlotte quickly added. "Nothing pleases my husband more than conversing about scientific subjects with a fellow expert."

"Even if that fellow is a woman?" challenged Mademoiselle Benoit.

"I'm considered highly eccentric by Polite Society for having unorthodox views on a great many subjects," responded Wrexford. "One of which is that a lady's intellect is inherently equal to that of a gentleman."

"Eccentric, indeed," said Mademoiselle Benoit. "In that, it seems we are kindred souls, sir."

"I was just asking Mademoiselle Benoit about her particular field of interest—" began Charlotte.

"And I was boring your lovely wife about bridges."

"On the contrary," she protested. "I assure you that I found your explanations very interesting."

Mademoiselle Benoit's brows shot up, and then her surprise gave way to a knowing laugh. "Ah, you are just being polite. There is no need—I am used to being considered odd."

Charlotte merely smiled. *And I am used to the assumption*

that all aristocratic ladies are featherheads. She and Wrexford had decided beforehand that she would ask deliberately shallow questions in hope of piquing the Frenchwoman into revealing more than she might wish about her work and her relationship to Milton.

"Mr. Brunel was just telling me about bridges," said Wrexford, "and how the key challenge for engineers these days is figuring out how to build longer ones."

"Precisely, milord!" Her obvious passion for the subject softened the Frenchwoman's prickly demeanor. "Few people understand the significance of that. It will effect fundamental changes in how people and goods are able to move from place to place."

"That certainly sounds convenient," observed Charlotte. "But how is that revolutionary?" She knew the answer, of course, but was interested in how the Frenchwoman would answer.

A flare of exasperation lit in Mademoiselle Benoit's eyes. "It is revolutionary because it will allow roads to be built in places that previously could not be reached, as well as shortening existing routes, making it easier—and cheaper—to travel." She drew in a sharp breath. "For the rich, cost is not an impediment. But for the working class, having no option to travel at a cost they can afford makes them virtual slaves to local employers."

"You make a very compelling point," said Wrexford. "I take it your scientific work is in making improvements in building materials—iron with a greater tensile strength, cements that are more impervious to weather."

"That is the path that your leading British engineer Thomas Telford and his followers are taking," came the reply.

"And you see a different way?" asked the earl.

"There are those of us who believe that mathematics, not simply new materials, is the key to providing answers for how to effect a more fundamental change in bridge building."

"Mathematics?" Charlotte gave a dismissive laugh. "Adding

and subtracting may help keep one's household's finances from collapsing in a heap—though I must say, all those numbers make my head hurt." She flashed a smile. "But surely you are jesting about mathematics being able to build a new type of bridge."

Mademoiselle Benoit speared her with a withering look but ignored the question as her gaze returned to the earl. "One has only to look at the medieval Gothic cathedrals, and the grand curves and domes of Renaissance architects to see that mathematics can teach us lessons about dealing with the weight, strength, and stresses of large structures."

"Interesting," said Wrexford. "I have heard that Jasper Milton, one of Britain's up-and-coming engineers, has been engaged in the same sort of thinking."

The Frenchwoman's expression turned wooden. "Has he?"

"But surely you are aware of that." The earl paused. "Our friend Mrs. Sheffield, who grew up with Milton, recently mentioned that he and her cousin Oliver Carrick attended a symposium in Paris several months ago given by your scientific society."

"Yes, yes," chimed in Charlotte, following his lead. Milton's death was not yet public knowledge. The earl planned to reveal the information when he felt it would rattle the Frenchwoman's sangfroid. "Why, come to think of it, Cordelia was under the impression that Milton and you had spent a goodly amount of time together."

"She is mistaken, milady, " replied the Frenchwoman. "I barely spoke with the man—and I am sure Monsieur Milton will confirm that when your friend next encounters him."

"I'm afraid that won't be possible," said Wrexford. "Milton suffered a fatal accident during the recent storms up north."

Mademoiselle Benoit turned pale as death. "*Mon Dieu.*"

"We are also a bit concerned about Oliver Carrick, as Mrs. Sheffield expected to see him at her wedding last week. Have you, perchance, any idea of his whereabouts?"

"*Moi?*" For an instant, the Frenchwoman looked about to swoon. However she steeled her spine and drew in a steadying breath. "*Sacré bleu, je ne sais . . .* zat is, *je n'avais pas* a clue!"

All of a sudden, Mademoiselle Benoit appeared to have lost her fluency in English.

Lowering her lashes, the Frenchwoman added, "W-Why would you ask me zat?"

"Because," said Charlotte, "we were under the impression that Carrick had also formed a friendship with you during his sojourn to Paris."

"*Non, pas de tout!*" A fierce shake of her head emphasized the denial. "I fear zat you have a *very* unreliable source of information."

"A misunderstanding, no doubt," said Wrexford politely.

"*Oui!* Now, if you will excuse me, I really must rejoin my colleagues."

Charlotte watched the froth of skirts—the sea-green silk and ivory lace trim looked like storm-tossed waves—as Mademoiselle Benoit hurried away.

"What is your impression?" murmured the earl.

"I think," she replied, "that the young lady is lying through her teeth."

CHAPTER 12

Wrexford descended from the carriage and took a moment to appreciate the tranquil beauty of Berkeley Square's center garden. The night air was still—not a leaf fluttered—and the silvery moonlight cast an aura of enchantment over the foliage.

"A ha'penny for your thoughts," murmured Charlotte as she joined him on the pavement. They had not lingered at the French ambassador's reception after the encounter with Mademoiselle Benoit, and the darkness had not yet deepened to its midnight hue.

"They're not worth a farthing," he replied lightly.

She took his arm. "Nonetheless, I should like to hear them."

He hesitated, his evening shoes scraping softly over the paving stones as he shifted. "In quiet moments like these, one can almost imagine that there are places in the world where Evil dares not tread."

Charlotte drew him closer and pressed her cheek to his shoulder. "I'm so sorry about all this. I know you were looking forward to a peaceful interlude in the country in which to contemplate personal matters."

"In the grand scheme of things, sorting through the books from my father's library is not a pressing concern, given that our dear friends need our help in solving the murder of a loved one."

And yet Wrexford couldn't help but regret having to put off the chance to make peace with his own inner demons.

"I know that's true," she replied. "But it doesn't diminish your desire to . . . put to rest the ghosts of the past."

Wrexford felt the warmth of her closeness ease the knot in his chest.

"Come," said Charlotte after a long moment of companionable silence. "There is nothing more that we can do tonight concerning the murder. Let us spend an hour or two unpacking the crates of your father's books that you brought with us from Wrexford Manor." She smiled. "Who knows—perhaps we will discover some hidden papers which show that your father was a romantic at heart and secretly penned poetry."

"Heaven forfend," he said, marveling at how she always seemed to know exactly how to draw him back from his dark broodings. "Some revelations are too shocking to contemplate."

"You really think it impossible?"

"My father was a great many things. A romantic was not one of them."

Hand in hand, they turned away from the moon-dappled garden and entered their town house, taking care to tread lightly as they headed for the earl's workroom so as not to rouse the rest of the household.

"Shall I pour you a whisky to sip as you work?" asked Charlotte after pausing by the sideboard.

"A wee dram would be welcome." Wrexford rummaged through his top desk drawer and withdrew a magnifying glass, a small notebook, and several freshly sharpened pencils. "I want to catalogue the contents of the crates so that Tyler can cross-check the titles against the books in my own collection.

The extra copies I will save to gift to the boys when they are older."

"That's a lovely idea." Cupping the glass of amber spirits in her hands, she turned to the door connecting the workroom to the library—

Only to have it thrown open from the other side.

"What are you three Weasels doing up at this hour?" inquired the earl as he approached the archway.

"We know how much you were looking forward to sorting through your father's books," answered Raven. "So we decided to help."

He stepped back to join Hawk and Peregrine by the side of the door, revealing four long worktables at the center of the room, each of them holding a double row of neatly stacked books.

Wrexford paused in the opening to regard their handiwork.

"We arranged them by subject," offered Hawk. "Save for the ones in French and German, which we grouped separately."

"What a lovely surprise," said the earl after inspecting the first table. "It's an excellent job." He turned to face them. "Thank you, lads."

To his surprise, the boys didn't crack a smile.

Charlotte noted their solemn demeanor as well. "Is something amiss?" she asked gently. "If perchance an accident happened while working with the books, and one of them was damaged, I would hope that you wouldn't hesitate to tell us."

"No, m'lady, no harm has come to any of the books," assured Raven, though he didn't quite meet her gaze.

It was only then that Wrexford noticed that the boy had his hands clasped behind his back.

Which didn't bode well.

"So then, what's the trouble?" he pressed.

Hawk sidled over and whispered something in his brother's

ear. Raven nodded, prompting Hawk to gesture for Peregrine to join the huddle.

Wrexford would have been amused if he hadn't suddenly felt a prickling of foreboding at the nape of his neck.

"We found something in one of the books—" began Raven.

"The pages fell open as I was lifting it out of its crate—" explained Peregrine.

"We weren't snooping," interjected Hawk.

Wrexford tried to imagine what could possibly be making them so worried about his reaction.

Charlotte, however, was quicker to make a guess. "Books make excellent hiding places for things one wishes to keep private."

He was about to dismiss the suggestion that his father—a gentleman of exemplary character and spotless reputation—had anything to hide with a rude snort, but then thought better of it.

We all have secrets that we wish to keep to ourselves, he told himself.

"Whatever it is," she continued, "Wrex appreciates that you have found it for him."

Looking reassured, Raven revealed the piece of folded paper he was holding and offered it to the earl.

Wrexford hesitated for an instant, torn between curiosity and dread. So much had been left unsaid between him and his father . . .

However, forcing a smile, he took it and flicked it open. The sight of the familiar looping script—written in the distinctive shade of blue ink that his father had always favored over black—made his throat constrict.

Memories, memories.

But aware that all eyes were on him, Wrexford made himself concentrate on the words. It was a letter—an unfinished one—put aside, said the last line, until later that day.

Only later had never come. The date scrawled at the top was the day the late earl had suffered a fatal heart spasm while out riding with his closest friend.

He looked up. "It appears to be the last letter my father ever wrote." To his surprise, his voice sounded perfectly normal.

Charlotte, however, wasn't fooled. A look of sympathy pooled in her eyes. "To you?" she asked.

Wrexford shook his head. "To someone whose name apparently begins with *A*." He handed her the paper.

It was a short missive and took only a moment or two to read.

"Hmmm."

"Is that all you have to say?" he asked, keeping his voice light despite the emotions churning in his gut.

"For the moment, yes." Charlotte turned her attention to the Weasels. "You boys have done a splendid job in organizing the books for Wrex. But the hour is late, and it's time for you to head up to your eyrie. You have lessons with Mr. Lynsley first thing in the morning."

A shadow of disappointment flitted over Raven's face. "But who is 'A'?" he blurted out.

"Sweet dreams," she said with smile that didn't belie the note of steel in her voice.

"Oiy," Hawk tugged at his brother's sleeve. "G'night, m'lady. G'night, Wrex."

As Peregrine was already heading for the corridor, Raven reluctantly allowed himself to be led away.

"I couldn't tell the lads even if I wished to do so," said Wrexford, once they were alone. "Damn me for being such a stubborn fool." Guilt tangled with regret, making him feel achingly vulnerable.

"Ye heavens, you must stop taking on the sole blame for the misunderstandings between you and your father, Wrex," counseled Charlotte. "He admits it right here"—she waved the letter—"that he should have made the effort to reach out to you—"

"Reach out about what?" he demanded.

"About 'A' and whatever relationship the two of them had." She took a moment to reread the words. "You've told me that your mother died when you and Tommy were very young. Your father must have felt lonely over the years, especially when you both left home." She allowed a brief pause before adding, "Did he never have . . . a romantic liaison?"

"A good question." Wrexford watched the flame of the desk lamp flicker within its glass globe. "As a child, one certainly doesn't think of those things. I do remember that he would take occasional trips to his estate in West Yorkshire where he kept a small stud for breeding hunting horses."

He made a face. "I always thought that horses were his passion in life—they seemed to bring him great pleasure. However, when Tommy and I were at university, we began to suspect that he might have a mistress. Several of our friends mentioned seeing him at the Newmarket races accompanied by a very attractive lady."

A sigh. "But when Tommy ventured to mention it, my father said it was merely an old acquaintance he had encountered. We both accepted that, for there seemed no reason not to."

"Of course not," agreed Charlotte. She fell silent, but only for a moment. "Could 'A' have been a neighbor?"

"It seems unlikely. Like my father's estate, the neighboring ones were used mainly as hunting retreats. There was little in the way of social entertainments in the area. I can't imagine a widow or any unattached lady taking up residence in such isolation," replied Wrexford.

"And yet it's hard to interpret this as anything other than an exchange between two intimately acquainted people." Charlotte cleared her throat and began reading it aloud.

My Dear A,
Much as I long for your presence, I understand
your continued absence—God knows, you are right
to chastise me. I should have reached out to Alexan-
der long ago. It is a sad state of affairs when a father
is too cowardly to contact his son . . .

Wrexford looked away, throwing his face in shadow, as
Charlotte continued.

I shall do so later this afternoon, as I have prom-
ised Needham to ride out with him and give my opin-
ion on his newly purchased stallion.
As for our other concern, I promise that I—
Blast it all, Needham is here early! I will finish this
later as well.

The ensuing silence seemed to thunder in his ears, a painful
reminder of all the precious moments he had let slip by.

"I wish I could make sense of what you have just read," he
finally said. "I wish . . . Damnation, I wish a great many
things . . ."

"Sweeting, you don't think that I regret not making peace
with my father?" asked Charlotte softly. "These tug-of-heart
conflicts that occur in all families are impossibly hard. The
hubris of youth allows for little nuance—things are either black
or white. While we're now wise enough to realize the most of
Life is actually colored in a subtle range of greys."

He let out a pent-up breath that ended in a rueful smile.
"How would I live without you and your wisdom?"

"Quite peacefully," she quipped, "and free from chaos and
crime."

Wrexford laughed, and all at once the shadows seemed to
lighten.

"I can't make things right with my father," he mused. "However, I can make an attempt to find 'A' and perhaps understand a part of his life that he felt compelled to hide from me."

"The unknown 'A' is a mystery for now," said Charlotte. "But we're very good at unraveling mysteries. Once we've solved this current murder, we can turn our attention to the task. Griffin has an excellent nose for sniffing out old clues and following them wherever they lead."

Their good friend Griffin was Bow Street's best Runner and had helped them in a number of previous investigations.

After folding the late earl's letter and placing it on the side table, she took his hand. "Come, let us retire for the night and leave any further thinking until the morning."

"Yet another wise suggestion, my love. Lead the way."

"Why is Wrex upset?" asked Hawk.

"Because his father had a secret mistress—" began Raven.

"We don't know that," interjected Peregrine.

"Oiy. But it certainly sounded like something niffy-naffy was going on."

"Wrex looked more sad than angry," mused Hawk. "What can we do to help?"

"Nuffink!" said his brother with a wry smile. Hawk tended to mispronounce certain words when he was agitated. *Nothing* was one of them.

"If this was a question of ferreting out information in the slums or pilfering papers from some Mayfair mansion, we would have a good argument for being included in any plans," said Raven. "But m'lady has explained to us that the heart is a devilishly complex organ and that until we are older, we can't comprehend all the variations of Love."

"Variations?" Hawk scrunched his face in a frown. "That makes no sense. Love is love."

"Actually it's more complicated than that," offered Peregrine. "Shakespeare's plays are a good example. My uncle Willis used to tell me about how the playwright understood human nature better than most and captured both the light and the dark side of love. He said like most powerful forces, it can be used for good or for evil."

"What did your uncle mean?" asked Hawk.

"Ummm . . ." Peregrine lifted his shoulders in a baffled shrug. "I don't exactly know. But one of his favorites sayings from Shakespeare was *Lord, what fools these mortals be!*"

CHAPTER 13

Despite the ungodly hour, their early morning breakfast was interrupted by the arrival of Cordelia and Sheffield.

"Ye heavens, Kit, I would have thought that you could now afford your own sustenance," said Wrexford as he buttered a fresh-baked sultana muffin. During his rakehell bachelor days, Sheffield had been wont to frequently avail himself of the earl's well-stocked larders and wine cellar.

"Yes, but our cook can't come close to matching Mac's ambrosial coffee and pastries."

"Flattery will get you nowhere!" called the maid. She bustled into the breakfast room a moment later with a fresh pot of coffee and tray of fragrant French croissants.

Sheffield inhaled deeply and then released a blissful sigh. "Tell me, how much would it cost to lure you away from Wrex and his irascible moods and sarcastic tongue?"

"Far more that you are willing to pay," growled the earl.

Cordelia helped herself to a croissant and took a seat. "Enough banter." She pinched at the bridge of her nose. "Forgive our unannounced appearance so early in the day. We arrived back in London late last night, and I simply couldn't wait to hear whether you've discovered any helpful news regarding Jasper Milton—or my cousin."

"Help yourself to coffee," said Charlotte. She waited for their friends to get comfortable before she and the earl launched into a summary of all that had happened.

"A band of suspicious radicals, a midnight attack on Charlotte by some unknown assailant," mused Sheffield once the explanations were done. "A secretive mademoiselle..." He reached for a pot of apricot jam. "How is it that we never seem to stumble over a crime that has a simple solution?"

Cordelia rapped him on the knuckles with her butter knife. "That's *not* humorous."

Sheffield made a face and hung his head in contrition. "Forgive me. I didn't mean—"

"We know what you meant," said Charlotte. "But in all honesty, I think there is rarely a crime that can be deemed simple. The actual act is merely the stone that drops in the water. There are always ripples that spread out from the moment of reckoning which stir complicated questions about the causes and effects."

"That's all true," agreed Wrexford. "But be that as it may, let us turn from the abstract to the pragmatic. We've uncovered a few clues that call for further exploration." He paused to let his words sink in. "Mademoiselle Benoit merits more scrutiny, as does Hedley's remark that Oliver Carrick gave a talk at the London Society for Progress on the technical innovations involved in building longer bridges."

"The Royal Society is holding a gala soiree tomorrow evening in honor of all the international scientific delegations who have come to London for the Royal Institution's symposium," said Charlotte. "Alison's good friend Sir Robert is on the society's Board of Governors, so I can ask her to ensure that the board makes it clear to the French delegation that it would be a grave insult to the British scientific community if all their members, especially their officers, do not show up."

"I'll join with Charlotte in arranging that," volunteered Cordelia. "I'm very curious to meet the Frenchwoman."

"Mademoiselle Benoit turned very skittish when Wrex mentioned Milton and your cousin. We are quite sure that she is hiding something," said Charlotte. "The question is what."

The earl nodded. "The head of the London Society for Progress is a friend of mine. I will have a word with him about Carrick and with whom he might be working on bridge innovations."

Sheffield sat back in his chair. "It may not prove overly useful, but through a friend of my father I have an introduction to Lord Hugo Fenway, who is director of the government's newly formed commission in charge of the Bristol Road Project. It is a major undertaking, tasked with modernizing the route between London and the port of Bristol so that goods may be moved quickly and efficiently. We are scheduled to meet this afternoon."

"Kit is being modest," interjected Cordelia. "The reason for the connection is that his father has agreed to let him stand as candidate for Parliament in the pocket borough that he controls, and as Kit's election is certain, he's been invited to meet with Fenway because of his interest in roads and the transportation of goods."

"My father's friend said that Fenway is still in the process of putting together the commission and thinks he may have a place for me," explained Sheffield. "Not only would I find the position interesting, but in the course of learning about it, I might contrive to discover more about the activities of Milton and Carrick, who were consulting on the renovation of the stretch of road and obsolete bridges near Windsor."

"It seems we all have our marching orders," said the earl.

"Yes, but it's too early to visit anyone at this hour," pointed out Sheffield. He eyed the silver chafing dishes on the sideboard. "Besides, I haven't yet had my full breakfast."

Cordelia rolled her eyes.

"Alison won't mind the intrusion," said Charlotte. "Do you mind if we leave now?" she said to Cordelia. "I am escorting the boys to their fencing lesson at Angelo's Academy later this morning—where I, too, shall begin learning the art of swordplay from the great Harry Angelo."

"Don't tell Alison that," quipped Cordelia. "She'll be green with envy and demand to sharpen her skills as well."

"I'm actually not doing it to learn how to wield a blade, though that might come in handy. It's because living the life of a cosseted countess has left me woefully weak." Charlotte recounted the details of how she had barely managed to escape her assailant in the stews.

Wrexford made no sarcastic comment, for which she gave silent thanks. She knew he didn't like the risks that she was taking, so the fact that he supported her wish to continue as Magpie meant the world to her.

"Hmmm? Angelo teaches fencing to women?" mused Cordelia. "Perhaps I should also sign up for instruction."

Sheffield choked on a bite of eggs.

Cordelia batted her lashes at him. "Did you say something?" He shook his head.

"Wise fellow," drawled Wrexford. He poured himself another cup of coffee. "As soon as it is proper to pay a call, I shall visit my scientific friend and see what I can learn about Carrick."

Charlotte rose, eager to begin the day. "While you two lollygag over breakfast, Cordelia and I will get to work."

"Ah, breakfast is still being served?" said a voice from just outside the door. "I was hoping that I hadn't missed the chance to share a meal with you, milord." For a big man, their friend Griffin, Bow Street's most respected Runner, moved with surprising stealth. "Riche said that if I hurried there might be a crust of bread left."

Wrexford made a rude sound. "The word "share" is an interesting way of describing our dining habits—I pay for prodigious meals, and you eat them."

Charlotte waved for Griffin to enter and take a seat. "Ignore His Lordship. He's always grouchy at this hour in the morning."

"Thank you, milady," responded the Runner as she poured him a cup of coffee. To Sheffield and Cordelia he added, "Allow me to offer my felicitations on your recent nuptials."

Despite the happy words, Charlotte noted that his voice was shaded by a hint of tension.

"I take it this is not just a social call," she murmured.

"Correct," said Griffin, not looking overly happy about the fact. "Word has reached Bow Street about the murder of Jasper Milton." A pause. "And the evidence given by one of his colleagues indicates that Oliver Carrick must be considered a suspect for the crime."

His gaze had remained on Sheffield and Cordelia. "My understanding is that Carrick is your cousin, Lady Cor—"

"I prefer to be addressed as Mrs. Sheffield," interjected Cordelia. "As for Oliver, yes, you are right about the relationship."

Griffin put down his cup. "Have you any idea of his whereabouts?"

"No," she answered.

"None of us do," added Wrexford.

"And to be honest, I don't think that I would tell you even if I did know." Cordelia's chin rose a notch. "Because I simply refuse to believe that Oliver could have murdered his friend. They've been kindred spirits for years."

The Runner's eyes pooled with sympathy. "If I were you, I wouldn't want to believe it either. But alas, my experience has taught me that if provoked by certain circumstances, most every one of us mortal beings can be pushed into the abyss of evil."

"Ye gods," exclaimed Sheffield. "The evidence against him is hearsay! You know as well as I do that we all have arguments with those who are close to us and say things we don't really mean in the heat of the moment." A scowl. "An outsider might very well misinterpret the words, as well as the tone in which they are said."

"I don't disagree with that, sir," responded Griffin. "But the government has asked Bow Street to take over the investigation, and I have been put in charge."

Wrexford frowned. "Why is the government taking an interest in the murder?"

"They don't convey their reasoning to the likes of me." Griffin gave a grateful nod as McClellan bustled from the kitchen with a platter heaped with her breakfast specialties and set it in front of him. "Still, I have been tasked to solve the crime."

He made no move to pick up his fork. "And I sincerely hope that we may pursue the investigations as friends, not enemies."

"That would be preferable," responded Cordelia.

Which was, noted Charlotte, a very ambiguous reply.

The earl waited until noon before setting out for the Royal Institution, where his friend, like many of the leading scientific-minded gentlemen in London, had his laboratory.

Handing his overcoat to one of the porters, Wrexford headed up the grand staircase to the top floor of the building where sounds of whirring and clacking in the north corridor announced that he had reached one of the areas devoted to engineering.

A knock on the far door elicited a hearty, "Come in, come in!"

"Ah, Wrexford!" Parnell Hamden looked up from his worktable, revealing a long, craggy face that was currently streaked with mud-colored grease. "I thought you were rusticating in the country for the month."

"Alas, so did I," answered the earl. "However, a matter of grave importance has required my presence in London."

At the word *grave*, Hamden's welcoming smile faded. "Dear heaven, are you investigating another murder?"

Wrexford chose not to answer. "Might I ask you a few questions about a recent lecture given at the London Society for Progress by Oliver Carrick?"

"Carrick! A brilliant fellow," responded Hamden. "He isn't in any trouble, is he?"

"That is what I am trying to discern," Wrexford answered. "Have you perchance seen him lately?"

"I have not, milord. However, it is my understanding that he doesn't live in London. I believe he's currently employed by Thomas Telford as a project manager for one of the Holyhead road and bridge sections."

"Do you know exactly where?"

Hamden shook his head. "I don't, milord."

Wrexford considered what he had just heard. "You just called Carrick a brilliant fellow, and yet I've heard that it is his friend Jasper Milton who is considered the real genius when it comes to bridges."

Hamden rubbed at his chin, leaving another streak of grease on his sallow skin. "An interesting observation. I suppose it depends what materials and technology you believe are the most likely to allow the most impressive innovations."

"I've been told that Milton was using advanced mathematics to shape his structures and determine optimal weight-bearing designs. What did Carrick talk about in his lecture?" asked Wrexford.

"He seemed to believe that Telford's work with suspension cables was the right direction, but my sense was that he and his fellow collaborator were developing a new and innovative idea."

"In what way?"

Hamden chuffed a laugh. "That he didn't say. But then, inventors never give away their actual designs. Patents are potentially worth a fortune, so they merely tantalize their audience with hints of their cleverness."

Wrexford had good reason to know all about patents and their worth. But something else that Hamden had just said suddenly stirred a question.

"You mentioned that Carrick had a collaborator. Any idea of who he is?"

"Again, Carrick was rather coy about revealing any specifics." A smile. "But my guess is that it's a *she*, not a *he*."

Charlotte buttoned up the padded fencing jacket and flexed her knees, enjoying—as always—the feeling of freedom that came with wearing breeches rather than layer upon layer of stifling skirts. The carriage had dropped her and the boys off at a discreet back entrance to Angelo's Fencing Academy, allowing her to enter the building unobserved.

The boys peltered off to one of the practice rooms while an attendant led her to a dressing area attached to the room where Harry Angelo gave his private lessons.

The ring of steel against steel echoed through the outer corridor, stirring a flutter of butterflies inside her rib cage.

"What if I'm about to fall flat on my arse?" she whispered as she tugged on the heavy leather glove that she had been given. Her brush with disaster in the stews had left her confidence shaken. In the past she had never doubted her physical abilities. But now . . .

A *tap-tap* on the door roused her from such worries.

Squaring her shoulders, she clicked open the latch and stepped onto the canvas mat.

"Good day, milady." Harry Angelo cut a flourish through the air with his fencing foil and dropped into a graceful bow.

"Thank you, sir. But I am here merely as a student," said Charlotte. "Let us please dispense with social formalities."

A twinkle lit in his grey-green eyes. "As you wish." He

moved to the side wall and took down a face mask made of wire mesh. "Please put this on as a safety precaution—it goes on by tying the two leather ribbons together at the back of your head."

Once she had done so, he handed her a weapon. "As you know, there is a button on the tip, so there is little chance of drawing blood. But I do caution you, this is not an activity for the faint of heart."

"I have three boys at home who have made that abundantly clear. So far there are no missing fingers or limbs."

He laughed. "Lord Wrexford tells me that I am supposed to make you, er, exert yourself. Is that true?"

"Yes," replied Charlotte firmly. "Treat me exactly as you would a male pupil."

His lips twitched. "As you wish."

Charlotte was soon ruing her hubris. After showing her how to hold her foil and demonstrating the basic fencing stances, Angelo then proceeded to put her through a grueling series of drills that left her soaked with sweat and gasping for breath.

"You have great balance and athleticism, milady," he announced with an approving nod, once he took pity on her and ended the lesson. "We shall make an excellent swordswoman of you . . . that is, once we put a little steel in your muscles."

Fearing that she couldn't manage more than an exhausted squeak, Charlotte merely nodded.

"You are lucky—you have excellent practice partners in your Weasels and Peregrine. " He offered her a towel. "They are good lads."

She accepted it with a grateful look and nodded in answer, still not trusting her voice.

Angelo chuckled. "You know, many of my male pupils would have puked after the workout I just put you through." He gave her a jaunty salute. "Don't be too hard on yourself, Lady Wrexford. Your husband was right—you're tougher than nails."

"S-So why do I feel that someone has hammered a handful of them through my biceps?"

Another chuckle. "You may be a trifle sore tonight, but it will soon pass." He stepped back and inclined a bow. "Until next time, milady."

"A *she*," repeated Wrexford. "Are you referring to Mademoiselle Benoit, the secretary of the Paris Society for Practical Science who is part of the French scientific delegation?"

Hamden dismissed the question with a brusque wave. "The French build aesthetically lovely bridges, but as far as I know, they are not making any notable innovations in the actual engineering of such structures." He tapped his fingertips together. "Mind you, I could be wrong, but I think that the lady in question resides right here in England."

"A lady? Trained in engineering?" queried the earl.

Hamden smiled. "Obviously, she didn't attend Oxford or Cambridge. However, she comes from a very wealthy merchant family who believed in the importance of education for both their sons *and* their daughter. So she's as well-schooled as most men in science and mathematics. But more than that, she has a special flair for creating successful commercial ventures, as well as practical experience in running her husband's various businesses, one of which fabricates machinery."

He paused. "I believe that Carrick met her a little over a year ago while working on a construction project that she was funding, and my sense is that she took him under her wing, so to speak."

"Interesting." Wrexford was now on full alert. A clearly ambitious woman with business acumen and an interest in bridges . . . "Do you perchance know this woman's name?"

"But of course," answered Hamden. "She's actually very well known in the engineering world, especially after she and her husband won a very handsome contract of £40,000 from

the Royal Navy. They created an innovative design of copper
nails and sheathing to protect the bottoms of naval warships
from barnacles and hole-boring marine worms."

A very handsome contract, reflected Wrexford. Given the
woman's obvious talent for making money, partnering with
someone who was on the cusp of creating an innovative technology that would revolutionize bridge building could very
well be worth a bloody fortune.

"And then, of course, in 1811 she received a patent in her
own name for an innovation in bridge design."

"A woman with a patent in her own name?" The earl was
both surprised and impressed. As far as he knew, that had never
happened before.

"Indeed. In fact, one so important that Thomas Telford
asked permission to use her idea in the bridge design he is currently working on to span the Menai Straits." A pause. "It will
connect the island of Anglesey with the mainland of Wales, and
thus be the longest bridge ever built."

"The lady's name," urged Wrexford. "If you please, just give
me her name."

"Sarah Guppy," said Hamden. "She and her husband live in
Queen Square, Bristol's most fashionable neighborhood, and
are leading lights of the city's high society. But my guess is that
she'll be coming to London for the Royal Institution's conference on improving transportation."

"Thank you," said Wrexford. "You've been a great help." It
seemed possible that he had picked up a clue that would lead
them to Oliver Carrick . . .

But he feared that Cordelia wouldn't thank him for it.

CHAPTER 14

"Is m'lady ill?" asked Hawk as Raven tiptoed back into the schoolroom. "Though she tried to hide them, she was making some very distressing little moans during the carriage ride home."

"Hard to tell," answered his brother. "She's lying on the chaise longue in the Blue Parlor, which she *never* does."

"Maybe she ate a bad kipper for breakfast," suggested Peregrine.

"We could bring her a plate of ginger biscuits," said Hawk. "Mac says ginger is very good for belly aches."

Harper's ears pricked up at the mention of biscuits.

"I don't think it's her belly." Raven crinkled his nose. "A pot of salve smelling of camphor was sitting on the table beside her."

The three of them exchanged quizzical looks.

"But whatever the ailment, let us trust that Mac knows what to do," continued Raven. He lowered his voice to a conspiratorial whisper. "Because we have other fish to fry."

Hawk and Peregrine edged closer.

"Tyler has a surveillance task for us tonight," explained Raven.

"He wants for us to come along with him to a tavern in Seven Dials and wait in the alleyway while he attends a meeting. Then he wants us to follow the man who leaves with him and discover where he is lodging."

Hawk looked a little disappointed. "That's child's play. Doesn't he have anything more challenging? Like sneaking into the man's quarters and stealing some incriminating document?"

"For now, we just do as we're told," said Raven. But the gleam in his eye hinted that further orders might be open to interpretation.

Peregrine cleared his throat. "Just so we all understand the rules . . . as I'm now a full-fledged Weasel"—Wexford and Charlotte had used those exact words—"doesn't it stand to reason that the old restriction forbidding me to accompany you on clandestine forays into the stews is now rescinded?"

When Belmont was the boy's legal guardian, Wexford and Charlotte had refused to let Peregrine take part in any potentially dangerous activities. A fact that had not sat well with him.

"Oiy," agreed Raven after giving it some thought. "I don't see any reason why you can't now fly with us."

"Hooray!" crowed Hawk as he thumped his brother-in-spirit on the back.

"Let's gather up our urchin rags and head down to the mews," said Raven. "I think they may need a fresh layer of muck."

"Ouch!" Wincing, Charlotte shifted on the chaise longue, feeling as if a regiment of the King's Household Cavalry had just ridden roughshod over her body.

"I heard that." Wrexford came into the parlor and assessed her appearance—she was still wearing her fencing breeches and chemise, with a soft wool blanket draped over her supine body.

"How was your lesson?" he inquired, after pouring two measures of Scottish malt from the decanter on the sideboard.

"Harry Angelo is a malicious demon," she muttered through

clenched teeth, "sent by Lucifer himself to torture unsuspecting mortals."

The earl handed her a glass of the spirits. "That bad, eh?"

"I ache in parts of my body that I never knew existed," replied Charlotte, wincing as she gingerly arranged herself into a sitting position against the pillows. She took a swallow of whisky, and as its fire warmed her innards, she managed a rueful smile. "I loved it."

"I thought you might."

"But heaven only knows if I will be able to drag myself to the next session."

"You'll feel much better after a hot bath and a good night's sleep," he assured her.

"Impossible." A dubious sigh. "I feel as if I won't be able to move for a month."

He laughed.

"But enough on my travails." Another wince as she shifted her position. "How did your meeting with Hamden go?"

Wrexford pulled a chair over to the chaise longue and took a seat. "Oliver Carrick has a great deal of explaining to do." He told her what he had learned. "Granted, the fellow may be lying dead in a ditch somewhere and so is innocent of any subterfuge or crime." A pause. "But if he isn't, why the devil hasn't he shown his face?"

Charlotte couldn't think of any plausible answer.

"We need to have a talk with Mrs. Guppy," announced the earl.

"Yes. But let us pray that Hamden is right, and we don't have to travel to Bristol to do so," she said dryly. "The prospect of bouncing over rutted roads for two days is definitely *not* a tonic for my body or spirit."

"Sarcasm doesn't become you, my dear. I'm the one with the caustic tongue and cynical disposition."

"Pour me another whisky, and I promise that my disposition will greatly improve."

Wrexford did as he was asked. "Alas, I'm not sure that you should make that pledge." A sigh. "Given what I've learned so far, I fear that Cordelia is going to experience some very painful revelations."

"If what you suspect is true . . ." Charlotte knew that he thought all the evidence uncovered so far indicated that Oliver Carrick had to be considered the prime suspect for the murder.

"Then that means Cordelia will suffer a double blow, losing *two* dear friends under unimaginably painful circumstances," she finished. "I—I wish there was some way I could believe that there is some innocent explanation for Carrick's continued absence. Word of Milton's murder has been published in the newspapers. Surely, he must know that people will think the worst if he remains in hiding."

"Perhaps he has no choice," said Wrexford. "So far, it's only circumstantial evidence against him, but the investigation hasn't really begun in earnest. Now that Griffin has been assigned the case, Carrick may fear it's only a matter of time before someone will recall seeing him at a time or place that will tie him to the crime." A pause. "Indeed, he may have already fled the country—or is doing his damnedest to arrange his flight."

Charlotte put down her glass of whisky, her throat suddenly too tight to swallow.

"However, I shall try to keep an open mind as to whether he is guilty or not."

"That's only fair," she responded, even though she, too, was beginning to fear the worst.

"Speaking of fair, we ought to send word to Cordelia and Kit. They won't thank us for delaying in telling them—"

However, the sounds of voices in the corridor announced that their friends had already arrived.

"Any news—" began Sheffield, but on catching sight of the earl's expression, he swore under his breath.

Cordelia came to an abrupt halt, the color draining from her face. "Is Oliver . . . dead?"

"No," Charlotte assured her. "But what Wrex has discovered isn't overly encouraging."

Sheffield put his arm around Cordelia. "Tell us."

They listened in taut silence as Wrexford recounted his conversation with Hamden.

"I simply can't—I simply won't—believe that Oliver murdered Jasper," exclaimed Cordelia. "They've been close friends and collaborators since their university days!"

Charlotte refrained from repeating Griffin's warning that a lethal falling-out between close friends was an age-old story.

"I've heard of Sarah Guppy, and Hamden is right. She is very astute when it comes to business," observed Sheffield. "Everyone associated with the family's enterprises acknowledges that she's in charge of overseeing both the finances and the actual manufacturing of their products."

He paused. "However, she's a very wealthy woman, so why would she risk everything to be involved in murdering Milton and stealing his idea—assuming that's why he's dead."

"Because greed begets greed?" suggested the earl. "Think about it. If someone has come up with an innovation that allows bridges to span wider distances, it opens up a whole new realm of opportunities in the world of transportation. Suddenly, all sorts of new routes are possible, changing the time it takes to travel—which in turn would have great economic implications."

He looked around. "I, for one, can't begin to put a price on what that patent would be worth."

"And we know that Mrs. Guppy has good reason to understand the value of a patent," said Charlotte.

"Yes," said the earl. "In addition to the other information Hamden passed on, he told me that Mrs. Guppy actually received a patent for an innovation she created for bridge design."

Squeezing her eyes shut, Cordelia clutched at Sheffield's coat.

"Speculation does none of us any good," muttered Sheffield. "I take it you'll seek to have a meeting with the lady."

At Wrexford's confirming nod, he added, "Cordelia and I wish to go with you."

"Very well. But we ought not forget about the other possible suspects. Let's us wait and see what Tyler and the Weasels discover tonight." He explained about the plan that he and his valet had made for learning more about the French radicals. "And then we shall consider how to confront Mrs. Guppy."

A fraught silence settled over the room.

"How did your meeting go with Lord Fenway, Kit?" asked Charlotte, hoping to lighten the mood by moving on to a more positive topic.

"Quite well," answered Cordelia, beaming with pride. "Lord Fenway was clearly impressed with his knowledge on transportation and invited Kit to join the commission right away, saying there was no need to wait for the parliamentary elections."

"By Jove, that's great news. Congratulations," said the earl. "He made a wise choice."

Sheffield smiled. "Cordelia is exaggerating Fenway's reaction. However, it's true that he did offer me the position. I look forward to getting involved in the planning." His expression turned more serious. "And as I said before, perhaps in the process I can learn some facts about Milton and his fellow society members that may aid us in solving the present investigation."

"*Deo volente*," whispered Charlotte. *God willing*.

Wrexford looked to the mullioned windows, where the late afternoon light was deepening to dusk. "Let us also hope that tonight's foray will bring us a step closer to solving the crime."

CHAPTER 15

"So, what's the plan?" whispered Raven, once Tyler had squeezed into the filthy alleyway near their destination in Seven Dials and crouched down beside the three boys.

Tyler held his nose. "Hell's teeth, what does Mac use to perfume your clothes with such a stench?"

"It's disgusting, isn't it?" grinned Peregrine.

"Truly awful, but enough of that for now," responded the valet. To Raven he said, "The meeting will last a half hour, or maybe three quarters. After that, I shall exit the building accompanied by another man. Stay alert and shadow us. We will part ways where the seven roads converge at the sundial. You are to follow the man—and whatever you do, don't lose him!"

Raven made a rude sound.

"Yes, I know you imps of Satan are devilishly good at this, but it's vitally important that we learn where he is lodging, and whether he's connected with any members of the French scientific society."

"You want for us to worm our way into the building and eavesdrop?" asked Hawk.

Tyler hesitated.

From somewhere close by came the scrabbling of a feral cat.

"If we're spotted," pointed out Raven, "he and anyone else in the place will simply think we're thieving guttersnipes."

"Use your judgment," replied the valet. "But whatever you do, *don't* get caught."

Another rude sound. "Trust me," replied Raven. "We won't get caught."

The valet edged to the alleyway opening and looked around. A moment later, he slipped away.

Hawk crawled forward to a position by the corner of the wall. "I'll take first watch."

The three of them settled in for the wait without further words. Surveillance required silence as well as patience. The minutes passed, punctuated by the creaks and groans of the surrounding dilapidated buildings and the furtive sounds of creatures small and large going about their private business under the cloak of darkness.

"Pssst, Mr. Tyler has come out." Peregrine, who was serving as sentry, alerted the others.

Raven took a quick peek, watching as the valet and his companion turned down one of the crooked walkways. "I'll lead the way. Keep alert."

The three of them slithered out into the darkness, moving with wraithlike stealth over the uneven ground.

Tyler kept up a patter of conversation with the Frenchman until, as he had warned, the two them parted ways at the landmark sundial.

The valet headed west while the Frenchman chose a route winding to the east. Head down, the fellow quickened his steps, oblivious to the three flitting shadows trailing in his wake. The wretched slums soon gave way to a slightly more respectable neighborhood.

The Frenchman skirted around the south side of Lincoln's Inn Fields, then turned down a lane of modest row houses. He slowed just before reaching the next corner, then climbed a set of low stone steps and fumbled in his pocket for a key to the front door.

Raven waited for the portal to click shut and then assessed the surroundings. "Now we know the location," he said. "But I noticed there's a narrow alley running behind the houses. If we climb the back wall, we'll likely find a place where we can get a peek through one of the rear windows. Perhaps we can catch a glimpse of who else is there."

Hawk and Peregrine nodded in understanding.

It took little time for them to scramble over the alley wall and drop down into the hardscrabble cart area used by the coal monger and night-soil men. A light was visible in one of the lower windows.

Dropping to a crouch, Raven led the way around a stack of empty crates and made his way to the back wall. The iron-framed window was closed, but a tiny sliver of light between the outer edge and the wooden sash revealed that it wasn't latched shut.

The faint murmur of voices drifted out through the crack.

A flurry of hand signals indicated to the others what he wanted. Noiselessly they retreated to the crates, then carried two of them back and placed them just below the window.

Raven smudged a handful of dirt over his already blackened face and mounted the makeshift perch. Drawing a metal probe from his boot, he used the thin length of steel to ease the window a touch wider, allowing the words to become more distinct.

"What do you mean you have nothing for us, Mr. Garfield?" The voice was edged with a thick French accent.

Finding a handhold in the crumbling mortar of the bricks,

Raven angled himself just enough to look into the room without being seen. He saw that the speaker was a tall, gangly fellow with a beaky nose, and standing next to him was the French radical who had been walking with Tyler.

The radical whispered something to Beaky Nose, who nodded and then fixed Garfield with a threatening scowl. "Don't play games with us. "We're offering you a very handsome sum of money—and you've already received a down payment."

"I'm not playing games," retorted Garfield.

"But you said that you've been spying on Milton for weeks!" A woman's voice, sharp as a knife. "You assured us that you knew where he kept his work papers."

"I do! And I visited his lodging right after Lady Cordelia let me know about his death." Garfield's voice had turned shrill. "I tell you, there was nothing in the safe he has hidden in the false bottom of his armoire. I also checked every nook and cranny in his workroom. Milton must have been carrying them on his person."

He paused for a ragged intake of breath. "My guess is they were stolen by his murderer."

A French oath—a very foul one, recognized Raven—rumbled through the air.

"Then you had better hope that you can discover who killed him and retrieve the papers," said the unknown woman. "Otherwise . . ." Her voice trailed off, leaving the threat hanging in the air.

"Don't worry. I have an idea where to look," assured Garfield, though he sounded a little panicked.

The sudden fierce yowls of two alley cats in combat pierced the stillness of the night.

"If I'm right, I'll have the papers for you." A pause. "But I'll need another deposit on the sum you promised."

Another Gallic oath.

"I don't like it any more that you do," said the woman to Beaky Nose. "But it's critical that we get those papers." She took a menacing step toward Garfield. "You had better not be deceiving us. We expect delivery of what you have promised . . . or else."

The momentary silence was broken by the sudden scuff of footsteps. Raven ducked and flattened himself against the wall just as the Frenchman yanked the window shut and clicked the latch. He waited for several moments before climbing down and sidling close to Hawk.

"I think we've heard enough. But before we go, climb up and take a quick peek to see if you can get a glimpse of the woman inside—you're good at remembering faces and being able to sketch a likeness."

Hawk was up on the perch in a flash. His small size and agility allowed him to maneuver along the tiny ledge running below the sill and gain a good angle to see into the room. He was about to retreat when he suddenly stiffened and went very still.

Raven waited for a bit, but when his brother remained unmoving, he flicked a warning wave that they ought not linger any longer. Hawk nodded but waited another few moments before descending and signaling that he had all that he needed.

They picked up the crates and replaced them on the pile, taking care to brush away any sign of footsteps that might give away their surveillance. A short time later, they joined the hustle and bustle around Covent Garden, just another trio among the many roving urchins looking to wrest some meager sliver of good fortune out of the night, and then angled north toward Mayfair and home.

The earl paused to look at the mantel clock before he resumed pacing back and forth in front of the hearth in his workroom. He had given his permission for the Weasels to follow the Frenchman. But as the hour grew late, he was questioning his decision.

"Sit down, Wrex. You look like a cat crossing a hot griddle," murmured Charlotte. "Surveillance is second nature to the boys. Unlike me, they haven't lost their edge."

"Peregrine doesn't have their experience," he pointed out.

"Which is why Raven and Hawk won't allow him to do anything dangerous."

Wrexford knew she was right, and yet it didn't quiet the niggling feeling that the pieces of the investigation weren't fitting together in any logical way. And that bothered him. After another turn, he came to a halt.

"I can't make sense of how French political radicals tie into Milton's murder. Why would social activists care enough about an engineering innovation to commit murder? What do they intend to do with it?"

"Perhaps Tyler learned more about their motives at this evening's meeting," said Charlotte.

He resumed his pacing, unable to keep from thinking aloud. "The radicals are focused on the workers and their struggles, not scientific developments. They clearly understand the significance of better roads and bridges, which would allow workers more choice in employment. But I just don't see them risking all their primary goals by committing a single act of violence."

"Hmmph," grunted McClellan from her chair by the hearth. "Put that way, I have to agree," she added, after finishing the last stitch on the sock she was darning and snipping the thread.

But before they could continue discussing the possible motivations of the radicals, the sound of footsteps in the adjoining library signaled that Tyler had returned.

The three of them turned in expectation, waiting for him to throw open the door.

A smile of grim satisfaction flashed through the shadows as the valet stepped into the room and spotted them.

"Well?" demanded the earl.

Tyler allowed a prolonged moment of silence before finally responding. "Eureka."

"Bloody hell, Kit's penchant for melodrama appears to have rubbed off on you," retorted Wrexford. "Stubble the theatrics and just tell us what you've learned."

A martyred sigh. "You might show a little more appreciation for my cleverness." But sensing that the earl was in no mood for their usual verbal fencing, Tyler turned serious. "I've discovered a key connection and think it may lead us to Milton's killer. My efforts to befriend one of the French radicals paid off tonight as I plied him with the piss-poor red wine served at their gathering place. Convinced that I am a comrade-in-arms in the fight against the ruling class, he confided in me that he and his friends soon expect to possess a momentous technological innovation that will allow them to make a great deal of money."

He paused. "And that the proceeds would be used for the Higher Good."

"What the devil did he mean by that?" asked Wrexford.

Tyler shook his head. "He realized that he had perhaps let slip more than he meant to, so I didn't dare press him on that. I did, however, express admiration and ask how he had managed to make such a deal. And he said it was because a good friend from his school days—a fellow who is a staunch believer in the ideals of the radicals—happens to be one of the leaders of the French scientific society that is currently in London to attend the international conference on transportation."

"Finally a connection," murmured Charlotte.

"Perhaps," muttered Wrexford, who wasn't quite ready to accept the drunken ramblings of his valet's newfound comrade.

"I understand your skepticism, milord. But apparently the radical group has given the member of the French scientific society money for a bribe to obtain the plans for the innovation—"

"That has to mean Milton's secret," interjected Charlotte.

"It's hard to imagine otherwise," agreed Wrexford.

"It's also hard to imagine that the society member isn't Mademoiselle Benoit," said Charlotte.

"I don't see how she could have committed the murder herself," pointed out the earl. "If she's involved—which I think is likely—then she has to have a co-conspirator."

"I seem to recall you mentioning that Brunel said both the president of the French scientific society and Mademoiselle Benoit were experts on bridge design."

"True," mused Wrexford. "I suppose it makes sense that the two leaders of the group might be working together."

"The Weasels are following the French radical to learn where he is lodging. That may reveal his co-conspirators," began Tyler.

But before he could go on, the sudden flurry of steps in the corridor announced that the boys had returned.

"Wrex! M'lady!" Raven burst into the workroom first, with Hawk and Peregrine right on his heels. "We followed the Frenchman to a house near Lincoln's Inn Fields, and he is definitely up to something havey-cavey—"

"Blackmail!" announced Peregrine.

"Theft!" added Hawk.

"Possibly murder!" cried Raven, raising his voice to be heard above the others.

Wrexford placed a fisted hand on his hip and waited for the excited shouting to cease.

The boys exchanged glances and immediately fell silent.

"That's better," remarked the earl. "Now, tell us exactly what happened—calmly and with as much detail as possible."

Raven took a moment to steady his breathing. "We did what Mr. Tyler asked and followed the Frenchman from the tavern in Seven Dials to a house on a side street close to Lincoln's Inn Fields." He quickly explained about seeing a light in one of the back windows and spotting a way to sneak close to it.

"Once we climbed down into the walled yard, we found a stack of crates and carried them over to the window, which allowed me to climb up and ease the casement open."

"Repeat what you heard," said the earl, "and please do so as exactly as you can."

"Oiy, I knew you would think that important," replied Raven. "There was a group—three men and one woman—and they were negotiating a deal . . ."

"Garfield!" whispered Charlotte, once Raven had finished recounting the conversation.

"I also had Hawk climb up for a look to see if he could get a good glimpse of the woman and Beaky Nose," explained Raven. "The light was awfully dim where they was standing—"

"Beaky Nose had shifted into the shadows. But I was able to see the woman's features clearly," interjected Hawk. "If you give me a pencil and paper, m'lady, I can draw her likeness."

Charlotte quickly rustled through the items on the earl's desk and brought over what he needed.

Hawk, who had a discerning eye for detail, needed only several minutes to complete his sketch and hand it over to her.

"Well, well." The earl allowed a grim smile as he caught a glimpse of the portrait. "It appears that Mademoiselle Benoit is indeed up to her neck in intrigue."

Charlotte squeezed her eyes shut. Sometimes her reasoning worked better when she tried to picture how the pieces of the puzzle fit together.

"I don't disagree," she said after considering all the variables.

"And clearly so is Garfield. I sensed that he was hiding something when Cordelia and I interviewed him in Cambridge."

"All this could very well mean that Carrick is innocent," pointed out McClellan.

Charlotte feared that it wasn't going to prove so simple. "Perhaps. But the fact that Garfield said that he knows where Milton's papers are is unsettling."

Wrexford seemed to understand her concern. "You think he believes that Carrick murdered Milton."

She nodded. "I can't help but recall Wheeler's account of the heated quarrel he overheard between them."

"Wheeler could have been lying," pointed out Tyler.

"True. However, he was brought into the society only recently by Milton and has little in common with them socially. My sense was he didn't much like or respect Garfield, Wayland, or Carrick personally, but the chance to work with a genius like Milton overcame his distaste," replied Charlotte. "I find him a rather colorless fellow, but his devotion to facts and the scientific method of reaching a conclusion—which he said gave him no choice but to tell the authorities what he had overheard—struck me as sincere."

"And yet, as you often point out, greed is a powerful emotional force," said Wrexford. "Wheeler may also have realized what Milton's invention would be worth if it actually allows for longer bridges."

"Given that all the members of the Revolutions-Per-Minute Society possess an expertise in bridges, I'm sure that Wayland realized it as well," replied Charlotte. "So you're right. In theory, they all could be guilty of the murder." She blew out her breath. "But let us not run round and round in circles. We now have actual evidence to suspect Garfield—who is conspiring with Mademoiselle Benoit and Beaky Nose—in addition to Carrick."

"I say Mrs. Guppy and her connection with Carrick merit further scrutiny as well," said the earl.

Charlotte fetched a notebook from Wrexford's desk and wrote down the names.

A sigh. "Now, we need to come up with plans for how to uncover more information about the activities of the various people . . ."

"And hope," muttered Wrexford, "that it will lead us to Milton's killer."

CHAPTER 16

The sun was setting the next evening as Charlotte paused in the courtyard of Somerset House's North Wing, home to the Royal Society, one of Britain's most respected scientific institutions. The gala reception for the delegations attending the international conference on transportation had already begun, but she took a moment to look up at the oversized grandeur of the architectural detailing. *Soaring pilasters, elongated windows crowned with pediments . . .*

"Impressive, isn't it?" said Cordelia with a half-mocking smile.

"It's meant to be," she answered after dropping her gaze to the arched entrance. "A reminder that the gentlemen who congregate within these walls are doing important work." The sonorous notes of a cello concerto drifted out of the open doors, accompanied by the mellifluous sounds of people enjoying fine food and wine. "And for the most part, they are."

"But even the most exemplary organizations have their share of scoundrels," remarked Cordelia. Her expression turned pensive. "As we both have good reason to know."

Genius and madness. Sometimes the two went hand in hand.
"Money can corrupt the soul," observed Charlotte. "As can the lust for fame."

On that note, they passed through the entrance portal.

Given that Mademoiselle Benoit was already wary from their previous encounter, Charlotte had decided that she and Cordelia, aided by the dowager, would have better luck in trying to elicit information from her without the presence of the earl.

Instead, Wrexford and Sheffield intended to confront Garfield, for thanks to Tyler's sleuthing earlier in the day, they had discovered what secret passion could have driven the man to betray his fellow society members for money.

It had also been decided that the Weasels would follow Mademoiselle Benoit back to her residence after tonight's reception and arrange with a cadre of their urchin friends to keep the Frenchwoman under surveillance round the clock in order to report on any visitors and where she went during her daily activities.

"This way," said Charlotte, indicating an elegant reception hall decorated in muted shades of cream and taupe.

Once she and Cordelia had greeted the Royal Society dignitaries who were hosting the reception, Charlotte needed only a moment to spot their quarry. However, Mademoiselle Benoit was just as sharp-eyed and quickly sought refuge among a circle of men near one of the soaring windows overlooking the river.

"Drat," she muttered under her breath.

"Flighty little thing, isn't she?" intoned Alison, as she appeared from behind a display of potted palm trees. "Never mind—I have an idea." The dowager gestured for Charlotte and Cordelia to follow her into one of the side alcoves before continuing.

"Mademoiselle Benoit doesn't know of our family connection. So Sir Robert and I shall contrive to draw her away from her present companions for a private conversation. I daresay she won't dare risk giving offense by refusing," explained Alison. "Then, when you two come over to join us, we shall make an excuse and withdraw."

The strategy proved successful, and although the Frenchwoman fixed Charlotte and Cordelia with a mutinous scowl, she made no move to quit their company.

"*Alors*, I have told you all zat I know," said Mademoiselle Benoit in a low, tight voice. "*Je ne comprends pas* what you want from *moi*."

"The truth would be an excellent start," responded Charlotte. "And by the by, you may cease the charade of mangled English. Lady Peake happens to know that your grandmother was the younger daughter of a British diplomat posted to Paris before the Revolution."

A look of anger—or was it fear—flickered for an instant in her eyes, but then the Frenchwoman quickly regained her sangfroid. "Just because I speak excellent English doesn't mean that I'm a criminal."

"Nobody is accusing you of a crime," assured Cordelia. "We simply want your help in finding Oliver Carrick." She drew in a breath and let it out in a shaky sigh. "He is my cousin, and I wish to help him. I fear that he may be in grave danger."

"I—I wish I could help you, madame." The quiver in Mademoiselle Benoit's voice betrayed a hint of raw emotion . . .

Which was, decided Charlotte, the first glimmer of honesty from the Frenchwoman, and she reacted quickly to take advantage of it.

"You can trust us—" she began.

"Isabelle!"

A tall man with a beaky nose and a shock of unruly auburn hair curling over his forehead hurried over to join them. Charlotte guessed that he must be Jean-Paul Montaigne.

"*Excusez-moi, madame,* my apologies, but I must ask my colleague to come with me *tout de suite,*" he added brusquely to Charlotte, though he didn't look the least repentant. "A governor of the Royal Institution wishes to speak with the officers of our scientific society in one of the side salons."

"Mais, Jean-Paul . . ." Mademoiselle Benoit bit her lip, but after a flicker of hesitation, she accepted the man's arm and allowed him to hustle her away.

"Hell's bells," muttered Cordelia. "I think she was about to tell us something." A sigh. "And so did her colleague. But I doubt that he will allow us anywhere near her after this tête-à-tête."

"Yes, I'm quite sure he won't," agreed Charlotte. "Based on Raven's description of who he saw last night negotiating with Garfield, and the fact that mademoiselle just called him 'Jean-Paul,' we can now be sure that Jean-Paul Montaigne, the president of the French scientific society, is mademoiselle's co-conspirator."

She considered the situation for a moment. "But few people suspect that an elderly dowager can be a wolf in sheep's clothing. Let us find Alison. She will be able to get close to Mademoiselle Benoit and under the guise of making polite conversation can tell her that for the next three days at noon we will be waiting by the Piccadilly entrance to Green Park for a rendezvous. Perhaps she's getting cold feet about her involvement in such sordid skullduggery and will come and confide in us."

As they turned and surveyed the reception room, Charlotte suddenly spotted a gentleman wearing a distinctive striped sash over his formal diplomatic dress coat. "You go on and arrange things with Alison. I will join you shortly." Another glance. "I need to have a quick word with someone."

Wrexford and Sheffield turned the corner of Duke Street and entered Mason's Yard, a discreet enclave tucked in between Jermyn Street and St. James's Square that housed one of London's most exclusive purveyors of rare books. An auction was taking place the following day, and the shop had remained open for the evening, allowing collectors to make a private appointment to examine the items up for sale.

They took up a position near the gated entrance of the adjoining building. Tyler had paid an earlier visit to the store and confirmed the time of Garfield's scheduled visit.

"We shouldn't have long to wait," said the earl after clicking his pocket watch shut.

Sheffield cracked his knuckles. "I'm not a violent sort of fellow, but anyone who would murder a friend to possess a few bibliographic treasures, no matter how special, deserves to be beaten to a pulp."

"I don't disagree." Though Cordelia was doing her best to put on a brave face, Wrexford knew that the murder of her childhood friend—perhaps by the hand of someone she knew and trusted—had left her badly shaken. "But let us leave it to the proper authorities to mete out punishment."

"Hanging is too good for the varlet," muttered Sheffield. "What sort of monster kills a close friend for personal gain?"

Alas, human nature is such that it happens far more often than one would like to think, reflected Wrexford.

The well-oiled whisper of a door opening and shutting alerted them that their wait was over. A shadow skittered over the cobblestones as a lone figure moved through the lamplight and into deepening twilight.

"Mr. Garfield, might we have a word?" Wrexford stepped out to block the man's way, while Sheffield took up a position behind him, making it clear that the question was not really a request.

Garfield stopped short, his eyes widening in surprise. "I'm sorry, but I am in a bit of a hurry."

"Whatever it is, it can wait," said the earl.

A nervous laugh. "Come, come, auctions are meant to be

civilized competitions between gentlemen. It's rather unsporting to stoop to intimidating another player in the game."

"We don't give a rat's arse about books," snarled Sheffield.

Garfield flinched and turned to face him. "Then w-who are you?"

"Lady Cordelia's husband."

The fluttery lamplight caught the sheen of sweat beginning to bead on the man's forehead.

"And my companion is Lord Wrexford."

"I—I don't understand," stammered Garfield. "W-What could you possibly want from me?"

"The truth—and without having to ask for it again," retorted Sheffield. He flexed a fist. "I dislike the idea of having to bruise my knuckles in beating it out of the likes of you."

Garfield edged away in panic, as if seeking to flee back to the book emporium, but Sheffield shoved him back a step.

"I don't know what you mean!" bleated Garfield.

"Then allow me to explain." Wrexford gave a flash of teeth that only a lackwit would mistake for a smile. "To begin with, you have been conspiring to sell the innovation of your good friend Jasper Milton before his corpse has grown cold in the grave."

"I—"

"Which begs the question—did you murder Milton?" continued the earl. "Or did you keep your lily-white hands clean and hire someone else to wield the blade?"

Eyes widening, Garfield began to sputter in shock. "M-M-Me? Good Lord, no! I—I didn't kill Jasper!"

"And yet he is dead, and you were overheard making a deal to sell his calculations to members of the French scientific delegation, who are here in London to attend the transportation conference," said Wrexford.

"It's *not* what you think! I—I can explain."

"Then do so, you sniveling little muckworm," growled Sheffield. "Before I shove your teeth down your gullet."

Wrexford waggled a brow in warning, not wanting Garfield to become too terrified to speak. "We're listening."

"The French scientific society paid a visit to the University of Cambridge three weeks ago, before coming to London, and as Jasper and Oliver Carrick had recently been hosted by them in Paris, our Revolutions-Per-Minute Society reciprocated," explained Garfield. "In the course of entertaining them, one of their members—Monsieur Montaigne, who is the president of the group—took me aside and offered me a good deal of money for obtaining the technical papers outlining Milton's new innovation for building bridges."

He drew a steadying breath. "I refused."

Sheffield expressed his skepticism with an obscenity.

"I did!" insisted Garfield. "It was only after I learned the terrible news from Lady Cordelia about Jasper's murder that—" He gave a convulsive swallow. "That I decided to reconsider."

The breeze freshened, rustling the leaves of the lime tree planted in the center of the small square.

"It's—it's devilishly complicated to explain." Garfield blotted his brow with his sleeve. "Jasper cared more about abstractions and idealism than he did about money. He saw things differently than most people. That was the source of his genius. But it also caused him to form some rather radical ideas."

"Explain yourself," demanded Wrexford.

"Jasper had a knife-sharp mind, and he loved the intellectual challenge of coming up with a solution for a scientific problem—like bridge design—that baffled the rest of us. But he also cared about using the new innovation to make life better for everyone, not just the higher circles of society."

Garfield paused, as if choosing his next words with care. "He seemed to feel comfortable talking to me about certain ethical concerns. You see, the rest of the members of the Revolutions-Per-Minute are . . . I suppose the best word is competitive. They wish to be recognized for their own innovations—"

"And you don't?" interjected Sheffield.

"Not really," mumbled Garfield. "I am skilled at what I do, and I feel I'm contributing to the welfare of our country by helping to make travel easier and faster. But I am content with simply being a good engineer, not a great one. My personal passion—my love of old and rare books—rather than my professional accomplishments is what makes me happy."

Wrexford considered himself a hard-bitten cynic, but strangely enough, he was inclined to believe what he had just heard. "Getting back to Milton's ethical concerns, what do you mean by that?"

"Jasper was in much demand to oversee important road and bridge projects. On one of them—don't ask me which one, because he didn't say—he was very upset by the way contractors were chosen for goods and materials. He described it as rich men making extra profits through a system of bribes and favors paid for by the public. Within a grand plan to connect faraway cities and towns with each other, there are many individual projects—"

"Like Thomas Telford's master plan to open up the Scottish Highlands and connect them to the main ports," mused Sheffield.

"Yes, precisely," said Garfield. "And each of those projects within the master plan has a board of commissioners to oversee the construction, some of whom receive personal remuneration for bestowing lucrative contracts on certain suppliers."

Wrexford looked to Sheffield for his reaction. He and Cordelia ran a successful international shipping company, and so they were intimately aware of all the complex inner business workings of moving goods from place to place.

"Unfortunately, greasing the wheels of commerce is simply an accepted cost of doing business," said Sheffield. "Mind you, not everyone does it," he added meaningfully, "but those who don't often pay a price in their profits for being scrupulously honest."

A pause. "Though if that is happening on the Bristol Road

Project, I'm sure Lord Fenway would want to know about it. He has a reputation for being someone who never bends the rules."

Frowning in thought, the earl pondered what he had just heard and then once again pressed Garfield. "Where are you going with all this?"

"Please allow me to finish, milord." Garfield cleared his throat. "When Jasper returned from attending the transportation symposium in Paris, he seemed . . . different. He talked to me about how France had made great inroads in improving life for all its citizens under Napoleon, despite the former emperor's penchant for war. And at several meetings of the Revolutions-Per-Minute Society, he waxed poetic about how making a fortune on a patent seemed unethical when allowing innovations to be used by all would make life better for the common man as well for the rich and powerful."

A pause. "So, on hearing of Jasper's death from Lady Cordelia, I thought of a plan that I felt would both honor Jasper's wishes and satisfy my own desires without hurting anyone. I immediately contacted the French and offered to sell them Jasper's innovation. Given their political beliefs, it seemed likely that they were more likely than anyone to use it for the common good."

"You want us to believe you were acting out of altruism?" Sheffield's skepticism was back.

Garfield looked away to the book emporium's window, where soft flickers of light caressed the gilt-stamped calfskin bindings of the antiquarian volumes on display.

"I *do* care about improving the lives of others. As I said, I am not as brilliant or innovative as Milton or Carrick, but I am good at what I do and create improvements that benefit all travelers," he said softly. "But you are right. At heart, my motives were selfish."

He took a moment to compose his thoughts. "When I heard

that a very fine first edition of Chaucer's *Canterbury Tales* was coming up for auction, I succumbed to my lust to own it. My actions may have been less than honorable in regard to my own desires, but I swear to you that I did not harm Jasper."

Much as Wrexford found Garfield's reasoning a trifle self-serving, the long-winded explanation did strike him as truthful. And just as important, he simply didn't think that the fellow possessed the nerve or the will to be a killer.

"However . . ." Garfield blew out his breath. "I couldn't bring myself to face the possibility until just now, but I fear that I may know who did."

CHAPTER 17

Charlotte waited for the gentleman in question to drift away from the group of diplomats gathered by the punch bowl, then discreetly followed as he wandered over to admire a display of rare botanical engravings hung in one of the side salons.

"I couldn't help but notice your sash, sir," she said, joining him in front of a colorful floral specimen by a renowned botanical artist from the seventeenth century. "You are a representative of the Kingdom of Württemberg, are you not?"

"You have a very discerning eye, madam," responded the gentleman with a smile. He was younger than most of the other foreign representatives in the room, and while only of average height, he held himself with an athletic grace that made him stand out from the crowd. "Not many people here would recognize the coat of arms of my tiny country."

"You are likely right," replied Charlotte. "Even though they should, given that your ruler is married to the eldest daughter of our king."

He acknowledged her statement with an admiring nod. "You seem very well versed on international politics." An apologetic cough. "I know it is considered unmannerly by London's Polite Society for a gentleman to introduce himself to a lady, but might I have the honor of formally making your acquaintance?"

Charlotte responded with a light laugh. "Rules are vastly overrated, don't you think?"

A spark of interest lit in his ice-blue eyes. "Indeed. Those who are unwilling to improvise rarely transcend the ordinary." With that, he took her proffered hand and inclined a graceful bow over it. "I am Maximilian Conrad von Hauser."

"It is a pleasure to meet you, sir," replied Charlotte. "And I am Lady Wrexford."

"*Enchanté*," murmured von Hauser. He plucked two glasses of champagne from the tray of a liveried servant and passed one to her.

They exchanged a number of observations concerning the importance of the upcoming conference before she broached her real objective in seeking von Hauser's company. "As it happens, sir, the reason why I know a bit about the Kingdom of Württemberg is because I am acquainted with someone from your country."

A twinkle glimmered in his eyes. "I do hope that he didn't disappoint you, milady."

"Not at all. I found him quite interesting and engaging."

"I am delighted to hear it," answered von Hauser. "Might I inquire who it was?"

"Of course. His name is Ernst Joseph von Münch, librarian to King Frederick," replied Charlotte.

A look of puzzlement flitted over von Hauser's features. "I didn't realize that you had actually visited my country—"

"Oh, but I haven't," she said. "I met him here in London several months ago."

"But . . ." He shifted uncomfortably. "But Herr von Münch

is quite elderly, and these days he never leaves the Ludwigsburg Palace."

"Yes, strangely enough, that is what I was told later," responded Charlotte. "So I can't help but be curious." She looked around before adding, "Can you think of anyone from your country who might have had reason to impersonate Herr von Münch?"

If she hadn't been watching carefully for any reaction, Charlotte might have missed the tiny ripple of alarm in his eyes before von Hauser quickly covered it with a baffled shrug. "Good heavens, no. I can't for the life of me think of anyone, Lady Wrexford."

"Ah, well, I suppose it was just a silly jest," she said lightly. "No harm done."

"On the contrary, I take this impersonation very seriously, indeed. You may be assured that I shall look into the matter," he said, his voice bristling with indignation. "Such puerile pranks are undignified and reflect badly on the Kingdom of Württemberg."

Seeing Alison appear in the doorway and waggle her cane, Charlotte quickly patted his arm. "Please don't give it another thought. I'm sure you have more important things weighing on your mind."

Leaving him muttering under his breath, she hurried away to join the dowager.

"Ah, how edifying that you have suddenly found a conscience, Mr. Garfield," remarked Sheffield.

"You have every right to mock me, sir. I don't claim that what I did was admirable. But Jasper was my friend, and I care just as much as you do about seeing his killer brought to justice."

"Let us hear him out before we pass judgment on his actions," murmured the earl.

Sheffield acknowledged the suggestion with a reluctant nod.

Garfield gave Wrexford a grateful glance before commencing his explanation. "Two of my fellow members of the Revolutions-Per-Minute Society are also in Town to attend the symposium given by the Royal Institution." He hesitated. "One of them is Mercer Wayland."

"Wayland was also one of Cordelia's good friends during his university days," explained Sheffield to the earl, "and along with Milton and Carrick, he helped her sneak into university lectures disguised as a male student."

Garfield confirmed the statement with a nod. "We all respected her intelligence and determination."

A smile touched his lips for an instant, and then his expression turned deathly serious again. "About Wayland . . ." He slowly shuffled his feet. "Even back then, he was quite a dandy and enjoyed hobnobbing with his aristocratic friends. But such revelries take money, especially here in Town, and he recently admitted to me over supper that his gaming debts have become overwhelming from trying to keep his pockets plump enough to carouse with his rich friends."

Wrexford knew of more than a few reckless young men who had gambled themselves into ruin.

"And after we had a few more pints of ale," continued Garfield, "Wayland muttered that the answer to his prayers would be coming up with a momentous engineering idea that could be patented."

A pause. "The trouble is, he is quite smart, but he's not brilliant enough to come up with such a discovery on his own."

"So you're saying that he might have killed Milton to steal his idea?" said Sheffield.

"Since you apparently overheard my conversation with Monsieur Montaigne and Mademoiselle Benoit—though Lord knows how—you are aware of the fact that I made a thorough search of Jasper's lodging and found nothing. So I assume that he had his work papers on his person when he was murdered."

"What about Carrick?" asked Wrexford. "Do you think he could be the murderer?"

Garfield gave an involuntary shudder. "I can't imagine that is true. They were such close friends." A grimace. "But neither do I wish to think that Wayland—or Wheeler, for that matter—would be capable of such a heinous crime."

"Then why do you think Carrick hasn't been seen since Milton's murder?" pressed the earl.

"I—I haven't a clue." He hesitated and swallowed hard. "Perhaps you should ask Sarah Guppy."

That Guppy was again linked with Carrick put Wrexford on full alert.

"What makes you suggest that?" he asked.

"She and Oliver formed a friendship during the past spring when he was working on a bridge repair project near Bristol," replied Garfield. "She's an unofficial leader within the world of mechanical engineering, and my sense is she took him under her wing."

"Thank you." The earl stepped aside. "I think we've heard enough, Kit."

"A-Am I free to go?" asked Garfield in a small voice.

"Where are you staying?" inquired Wrexford.

Garfield replied with the address of a modest but respectable lodging house on Gerrard Street near Leicester Square.

"Yes, you may be on your way," said the earl. "But don't think of leaving London." As the fellow started to hurry away, the earl added, "And I suggest that you abandon your plan to buy the Chaucer book. The advance payment you received from the French radicals is blood money, and unless you wish to repay it in the same currency, I would give it back without delay."

The fleeing figure was soon swallowed in the shadows, leaving behind just as many unanswered questions as revelations.

"I take it we may now head back to Berkeley Square," said Sheffield, "where you are going to offer me a very fine glass of Scottish malt to wash the bad taste from my mouth." He grimaced. "Perhaps the ladies have learned something useful from the elusive Mademoiselle Benoit."

"Not quite yet," answered the earl. "Tyler's sleuthing also included gathering information on Wayland and Wheeler, the other two members of the Revolutions-Per-Minute Society, as well as Garfield. Apparently, Wayland favors a certain gambling hell in St. Giles, and since Garfield has just thrown him to the wolves, I suggest we go there now and see whether it's worth sinking our teeth into him."

"And here I was looking forward to a decent drink." Sheffield blew out a mournful sigh as they started walking east. "Please tell me we're not also planning to confront Wheeler with whatever guilty secret he's been hiding."

"Actually Tyler couldn't find one."

"Ye gods, is he a saint?"

"I have no idea," answered Wrexford. "But according to Tyler, aside from working in the library of the Royal Institution on mathematical calculations and technical drawings for his current project, Wheeler's only other forays are to the Survey Office, where he pores over pieces of land for sale near the River Thames in Berkshire."

"He sounds like a bore rather than a saint," quipped Sheffield.

"According to those who work with him—I wouldn't call them friends, for he doesn't appear to have any—Wheeler is a very serious, aloof fellow," continued Wrexford. "He's much in demand as a project manager and bridge designer and is well-paid for his services. That he wishes to acquire land where he can put down roots rather than fritter his money away on sybaritic pleasures shows a pragmatic approach to life. Most unmarried men his age are out sowing their wild oats, without a thought for the future."

"Hmmm." Sheffield thought for a moment. "Well, we know he told Charlotte that he's from a humbler background than the others. So perhaps he's experienced enough hard times to know that life can be cruelly fickle and so he is careful with the money he earns."

"We also know that he told Charlotte about Carrick having a heated argument with Milton just before the murder," pointed out Wrexford. "She seems to think he is telling the truth."

"And you don't?" queried Sheffield.

"Regardless of appearances, nobody should be considered above suspicion right now. And so we need to arrange a talk with him," countered the earl. "But first things first." He flagged down a passing hackney. "Let us find Wayland and see what he has to say for himself."

The streets soon turned to squalid lanes as they delved deeper into the slums of St. Giles, and they were forced to make the last part of the trip to the gambling den on foot.

A big, beefy porter led them through the ramshackle building's dimly lit entrance hall and wrenched open the door to the warren of gaming rooms. The fug of smoke and sweat, mingled with the sweeter scents of port and brandy, immediately enveloped them as they stepped into the haze.

Flashes of white skittered through the lamplight as dice bounced over the felt-covered tables, the muted sounds punctuated by a chorus of groans.

"I had forgotten what god-benighted places these gambling hells are," muttered Sheffield, surveying the scene with a twisted smile. "How was I so blind?"

"You were angry," said Wrexford. "And bored." Sheffield

had passed through a bad spell in his life, flinging himself into reckless behavior in retaliation for his father's attempt to control his life by keeping a tight hold on the family purse strings.

"I was stupid," replied Sheffield. "And wallowing in self-pity."

"A fact that I pointed out to you on many occasions."

"I wasn't ready to hear your lectures—"

A bloodcurdling cry rose from a nearby table as a man stood and flung his empty glass against the wall.

Sheffield looked away, a shadow passing over his face. "As the heir of an earldom, you had far more control over your life than I did. I—I resented your advice."

"I don't blame you," replied Wrexford. "Thank God you met Cordelia, who somehow managed to hammer some good sense through your thick skull."

"Amen to that," said Sheffield.

"But enough about your youthful follies." Wrexford squinted into the gloom. "We need to confront Wayland."

As a harried serving wench made to pass them with a tray of drinks, the earl stopped her for questioning, taking care to flash a bit of gold as he made his request.

But the coin only elicited a disappointing answer.

"Damnation, she says Wayland isn't here tonight," he muttered on turning back to Sheffield.

"Perhaps we should ask someone else, just to make sure."

However, passing over another guinea to the barman elicited the same information. And given that both bribes had been a very generous ones, Wrexford conceded that the interrogation would have to wait.

"At last, we can finally wash away the sour taste of unsavory friends and smarmy lies with a glass of decent whisky," announced Sheffield as he followed Wrexford into the earl's workroom and shrugged out of his overcoat.

Charlotte looked up from perusing the pile of notes she had spread out on Wrexford's desk. "Did you not find Garfield?"

"Yes, we found him." Wrexford made a face as he moved to the sideboard. "Perhaps the most interesting thing we learned tonight was how quickly a member of the Revolutions-Per-Minute Society will turn on a fellow member—and supposed friend."

Cordelia, who had returned to Berkeley Square with Charlotte to await word about the confrontation with Garfield, closed her eyes for an instant. "What do you mean?"

After passing out drinks, the earl settled into one of the armchairs by the hearth and recounted what Garfield had told them.

"We need to meet with Sarah Guppy," said Cordelia once he had finished. "And the sooner, the better. It seems like she may be the one person who can help us cut through this Gordian knot of intrigue."

Charlotte lifted her glass, but rather than drink, she watched the refractions from the cut crystal cast a pattern of whisky-colored flickers on the far wall. "Perhaps. And yet it feels as if we're missing a piece of the puzzle."

"If you ask me, I say we have too many damn pieces," groused Sheffield. "I still don't understand why the French radicals care so much about getting their hands on Milton's innovation."

"Perhaps they intend to sell it to someone else in order to fund their own objectives," said Wrexford. "From what I have heard, Russia is desperate to improve its primitive transportation system. I wager that the tsar would be willing to pay a fortune to possess such a revolutionary technology."

"That's one plausible scenario," said Charlotte. "But it doesn't feel quite right." A chill seemed to shiver through the cut glass in her hand. "If only Carrick would make an appearance."

Cordelia shifted, her shoulders sagging as the weight of the silence grew heavier. She looked down, hiding her face, and the sag turned into a quiver.

Sheffield put down his drink and moved without a word to draw her up from her chair and into his arms.

All the fear and worry that was pent up inside her broke free in a muffled sob. Sheffield held her close and stroked her hair, allowing her sorrow to run its course.

"Ye heavens, I never cry!" Cordelia finally looked up in consternation, tears pearled on her lashes. "It's just that I can think of only two possible explanations as to why Oliver hasn't shown his face." She swallowed hard, trying to steady her emotions. "He must be dead . . . Or he must be guilty."

Anguish rippled through her watery eyes. "A-And I'm not sure which one I want to be true."

Charlotte felt a clench in her chest, knowing full well that murder destroyed far more than a single life. *Trust, loyalty, love*—all the truths that one took for granted could crumble into dust in the space of a heartbeat.

"Let us not lose faith," she counseled. "We ought not jump to any conclusions until we have gathered all the facts."

"Speaking of which, did you two learn anything from Mademoiselle Benoit?" asked Wrexford.

"Alison contrived to get us alone with her," replied Charlotte. "She seemed agitated, and after assuring her that we only wished to help her if she was in trouble, she seemed on the verge of confiding in us—"

"But Montaigne rushed over and demanded that she come with him," interjected Cordelia.

"However, Alison managed to get a private word with Mademoiselle Benoit later in the evening," added Charlotte, and explained about arranging a possible rendezvous with the Frenchwoman.

"Perhaps she will come," said Sheffield, "but in all honesty, I don't think it likely. She's involved too deeply in a very sordid scheme involving theft and murder—and she knows it."

"Still, I'm willing to give her a chance," said Charlotte. "I say we go to Green Park tomorrow."

Cordelia gave a wordless nod.

"Fair enough," said Sheffield. He then gave Cordelia another quick hug and drew her to her feet. "Come, my love. I think we've done all we can for tonight. Let us take our leave and return home."

Charlotte waited until the sound of their steps died away before rising and moving to the earl's desk to retrieve her notebook. Wrexford was standing at the windows, his back turned to her as he stared out at the dark-on-dark gardens. She recognized the set of his shoulders all too well—he was deep in thought, and she didn't wish to break his concentration.

Instead, she returned to her seat and, after flicking to a fresh page in the notebook, began to draw random doodles. Sometimes the visual images that appeared when she gave her mind free rein sparked unexpected insights, though she couldn't begin to explain why.

Whoosh, whoosh . . . on instinct, her hand moved over the page, rapidly filling it with lines and squiggles. Turning the page, she began anew. Perhaps the whisper of the soft graphite point dancing over the paper was a calming sound . . .

She looked up to find Wrexford had moved closer and was peering over her shoulder at the image.

"An apt metaphor," he remarked after studying her drawing of a bridge crossing a dark and impossibly long chasm.

"I suppose it is." She sighed. "Alas, it's unclear whether the design or construction materials are strong enough to bear our weight as we attempt to cross it."

"We are moving slowly and carefully," he replied.

She was usually more optimistic than Wrexford, but the

sight of the black chasm she had sketched suddenly shook her own self-confidence. "Yes, but it could crumble at any moment."

"*Fortes fortuna juvat,*" he murmured.

Fortune favors the brave. His use of a Latin aphorism to lift her spirits made her smile in spite of her fears.

"There are risks in any endeavor, my love." He added after leaning down to brush a kiss against the nape of her neck. "And you have to admit, whatever the dangers we stumble over, we always seem to land on our feet."

CHAPTER 18

The following day proved disappointing. As Sheffield predicted, Mademoiselle Benoit failed to appear at the appointed rendezvous spot. As Wrexford watched a dispirited Charlotte and Cordelia trudge into the drawing room after lingering for more than an hour near the gate of Green Park, he offered encouragement.

"Don't look so blue-deviled. There are a great many reasons as to why mademoiselle couldn't join you," counseled the earl. "She may be afraid of her co-conspirators, she may be committed to attend one of the conference panels, she may—"

"She may be guilty as sin," intoned Sheffield. He gave the coals in the hearth another jab with the poker and turned to face them. "Let us be painfully honest. She is one of the villains, and I think we need to treat her as such."

Cordelia bit her lip but didn't argue.

"The Weasels and their urchin friends have her under surveillance," said Charlotte. "If she does anything suspicious, we will immediately know about it."

Wrexford couldn't decipher Cordelia's expression, save to

comprehend that it was a mix of conflicting emotions. She wanted very much for her cousin to be innocent, but such a hope was fading with every passing day.

"Patience," he counseled. "We all know that investigations lead us through shadows and darkness before we see a glimmer of light."

Before anyone could respond, a discreet knock sounded on the closed door.

After a moment, it opened a crack. "Milord, Mr. Griffin is here," said their butler, "and is requesting an audience on a matter of great urgency."

"Show him in, Riche."

The Runner entered the room and stopped short on seeing that the earl wasn't alone.

"Bad timing, Griffin," drawled Wrexford. "No meal is being served at this hour."

Griffin didn't crack a smile, which didn't bode well for the coming conversation. "Forgive me, milord. Riche didn't mention that you had company."

"You may speak freely." He gave a wry shrug. "You know damn well that I will immediately pass on any information you tell me in private to those who are present."

"I would hope that we are all friends, not enemies," replied the Runner after a meaningful look around the room.

"So would I."

Griffin thought over the earl's carefully chosen words before responding. "Then with that assumption in mind, I shall proceed." However, his gaze fixed on Cordelia for a moment before he continued.

"I just had a second visit from Mr. Ezra Wheeler, who as you know, is a member of the Revolutions-Per-Minute Society founded by Mr. Milton and Mr. Carrick. He seems an observant fellow." A pause. "With a sense of public duty to report any suspicious activity to the proper authorities."

"Sarcasm is my bailiwick, Griffin, not yours," murmured Wrexford. "Do go on."

"Wheeler said he saw Mr. Mercer Wayland, who is—"

"Yes, yes, who is another member of the Revolutions-Per-Minute Society," interjected Cordelia.

The Runner nodded. "Apparently Mr. Wheeler spotted Mr. Wayland working in a study room in the library of the British Museum. He said that Mr. Wayland had half a dozen rare mathematical books—including several by Sir Isaac Newton—open on the table, and there were a number of papers with calculations and drawings spread out around him—"

"That's hardly suspicious. Mr. Wayland is a talented engineer who, like his fellow society members, is presently engaged in overseeing the building of roads and bridges," pointed out Wrexford.

"Yes, but Mr. Wheeler said that Mr. Wayland appeared alarmed at being seen, and quickly shuffled all his papers together to hide their contents."

Griffin looked at Cordelia. "However, Mr. Wheeler had caught a glimpse of them. And according to him, the incident seemed very odd, seeing as Mr. Wayland's expertise is not in any area of mathematics that would require the type of book he was consulting. Would you agree, Lady—that is, Mrs. Sheffield?"

"I'm sorry, but I'm not familiar with Mr. Wayland's current work, so I wouldn't know," she answered.

"And you, milord?"

Wrexford experienced a twinge of conscience at being less than forthcoming with the Runner, who had always been forthright with him. But for now, he felt his loyalties lay with Cordelia . . . at least until they knew more about Oliver Carrick and why he was missing.

"I'm afraid that I'm as much in the dark as you are."

"Hmmph." Griffin huffed a reproachful sniff and regarded the earl with a hard stare. "And you know nothing that might shed some light on the situation?"

He shook his head.

"Well, then . . ." Griffin twisted the hat he was holding in his meaty hands and inclined a stiff bow. "I won't take up any more of your time, milord." Without further words, he turned and left the room, closing the door with a touch more force than was necessary.

"Damnation," said Charlotte softly.

"I don't like withholding information from him either," said Wrexford. "But until we know more about what is going on, we can't risk revealing what we have learned. Griffin's superiors care more about quickly apprehending a likely suspect than they do about scrabbling in the muck until they unearth the truth. And that would put our friend between a rock and a stone. We all know he's scrupulously honest, but he must answer to them."

"I agree," said Sheffield. "I suggest that tonight we make another visit to Wayland's gambling haunt. And if he's not there, then let us pay a call on him at his lodgings and see what he has to say for himself. Cordelia mentioned to me that during the first meeting she and Charlotte had with the Revolutions-Per-Minute society members, Wayland mentioned having had a peek at Milton's scribbling book. That now takes on a more ominous ring."

The earl nodded. "Indeed. It's time we cut through the smoke and lies and start eliciting the truth from Milton's so-called friends."

Charlotte flexed her shoulders, feeling pleasantly exhausted by her latest fencing lesson with Harry Angelo.

"Which is, of course, an oxymoron, if ever there was one,"

she said with a rueful sigh as she reached for a paintbrush to add the watercolor highlights to her finished drawing.

But life was all about contradictions . . . and how one dealt with them.

She sat back and regarded her drawing of a road twisting through rugged terrain and ending in an unfinished bridge that disappeared into a gathering of storm clouds. It was an eye-catching image, but composing the captions was a challenge.

Transportation—the movement of people and goods from one place to another—seemed like such a simple subject. And yet it was fraught with so many important ramifications. The French radicals had made her think about how the cost of transportation affected the common workers and their ability to look for work. From Cordelia and Sheffield she had learned about the economic ramifications . . . and then there was the question of communication and military movements, both crucial to any government.

"Transportation is fundamental to how society works, and I must make the public aware of how this matters to their own lives," she said softly. "I must make them keep their eyes on how our government deals with the issue as all the new technologies open up a whole world of possibilities."

After massaging the back of her neck, Charlotte set to work, and after an interlude of laying in the subtle washes of color, she put aside her palette, satisfied with the finished drawing, the first in a series that she hoped would raise uncomfortable questions.

Especially for whoever had murdered Jasper Milton and stolen the papers containing the secrets of his innovation.

Her work done, she cleaned her brushes and headed downstairs to the Blue Parlor. Early evening had given way to the deeper darkness of night. Wrexford and Sheffield had just left to search for Wayland, while the Weasels . . .

"Have you finished your work? inquired McClellan, looking up from the sock she was darning.

"Yes," said Charlotte.

"Then I'll fetch some tea," said the maid, rising and putting aside her sewing basket.

"Tea would be most welcome," she said, repressing a wince as she took a seat in one of the armchairs.

Cordelia, who had decided to wait at Berkeley Square for Wrexford and Sheffield to return with their report, was reclining on the sofa, reading a novel.

"I thought you had already read *Pride and Prejudice*," commented Charlotte as she caught sight of the title. "Several times, in fact."

"Yes," admitted Cordelia. "But in times of stress, a favorite book is a comfort." She smiled. "The foibles, the fears, the absurdities of the Bennet family and their friends are a reminder that we are all far from perfect."

The observation drew a sympathetic sigh from Charlotte. "All too true. But speaking of stresses, I'm so sorry that you have had no peace and quiet in which to adjust to married life." She made a face. "I doubt many brides are gifted with the task of solving a murder on the day of their wedding."

Cordelia allowed a chuckle. "Ah, well, neither of us has chosen to lead a conventional life."

"Indeed," she replied. But marriage was complicated under the best of circumstances. "How are you dealing with all the changes? And I mean it as a serious question. Please don't fob me off with platitudes."

The book closed with a whispery rustle of pages. "It would have been interesting if Miss Austen had chosen to write about the newly wed Lizzie and Darcy."

"Yes, but as insightful and observant as she is, I wonder if she would handle it quite as well," mused Charlotte. "So much of the complex dynamics of marriage is uniquely personal."

"I suppose that is why a true friendship is the best foundation for marriage," replied Cordelia. "So in answer to your question, of course there are adjustments to be made. It is frightening to realize that you are no longer an entity unto yourself, but bound together with another, body and soul." A pause. "But it is also exhilarating. Finding the right balance will take time—"

"And the balance will keep changing," said Charlotte.

"I suppose that is what will keep the journey full of surprises," replied Cordelia.

"It appears that I've missed an interesting conversation," announced McClellan as she appeared with the tea tray.

"Have you ever considered marriage, Mac?" asked Cordelia.

The cups rattled as the maid set down the tray. "I do not consider myself a good candidate for matrimony."

"Oh?" Charlotte raised her brows. "Because you are intelligent, independent-minded, and would refuse to be ruled by the whim of a husband?"

The three of them exchanged looks and burst out laughing.

"Yes, those are rather elemental reasons," said McClellan, once the chortling ceased and she began to pour the tea. "But I suppose the most important one is that I've never met anyone who has tempted me to change the status quo."

"You never know," murmured Cordelia.

"Hmmph." McClellan held out a plate of ginger biscuits. "Help yourselves. The rest I shall wrap up and give to the Weasels. They are taking the late-night shift of keeping mademoiselle's residence under surveillance."

"I'll bring the biscuits to the boys." Charlotte glanced at the clock and put down her cup. "I had better go wake them." She had insisted that they take a nap after returning from the fencing academy so they wouldn't doze off during their assignment.

"And be sure that they wear their coats, as the night is turning chilly."

*   *   *

"Wayland isn't here," muttered Wrexford after rejoining Sheffield in the shadows of the gaming hell's foyer. "The barmaid said he hasn't been seen for the last four nights, which is unusual."

"Perhaps the fellow is gambling on making his fortune on something other than the turn of a card."

"Perhaps." The earl brushed a hand over the pistol in his coat pocket. "Why don't we go and ask him?"

Earlier in the day, he had learned of Wayland's current address from the organizers of the transportation conference. "He has extravagant tastes in his lodging as well as his clothing and entertainments. He has rented a set of rooms at the Albany from one of his rich friends for the duration of the conference."

The Albany was a prestigious residence for the wealthy and well-connected located just off Piccadilly near St. James's Palace.

"At least the environs will smell a good deal more salubrious than our present location," said Sheffield. "And it's only a short stroll from there back to Berkeley Square."

Such optimism, however, proved short-lived. The porter at the Albany informed them that Wayland was out and had left no word as to when he might return. Wrexford considered asking for access to search the rooms—greasing a few palms would likely smooth over any hesitation—but decided not to reveal his interest in Milton's murder to their suspect quite yet.

They walked to Piccadilly, but instead of turning right, the earl turned left and waved down a passing hackney.

Sheffield's face fell. "Now where?"

"To Garfield's residence," replied Wrexford. "He's the man who sent us haring after Wayland. Let's press him for a more a detailed explanation as to why. Somehow, I have a feeling he hasn't told us everything he knows."

* * *

Hawk hunched deeper into the collar of his coat and blew on his bare fingers. "I had forgotten how cold an autumn night can be."

"Sleeping in a fancy mansion has made you soft," sniggered Raven. "I remember when finding a broken crate in which to shelter was cause for jubilation." He glanced out from their hidey-hole at the building across the street before adding, "Who has the ginger biscuits?"

Peregrine dutifully passed him the oilskin sack. "I'll take the first watch while you two get some rest."

Raven yawned. "Oiy, there's no sign of life in mademoiselle's residence." Indeed, every house on the street appeared to be slumbering soundly, draperies drawn, lights extinguished, a peaceful stillness blanketing the shadowed brick and stone.

Peregrine kept himself alert by silently practicing a poem by Coleridge that their tutor had asked them to memorize.

> *In Xanadu did Kubla Khan*
> *A stately pleasure-dome decree:*
> *Where Alph, the sacred river, ran*
> *Through caverns measureless to man*
> *Down to a sunless sea . . .*

A movement, barely more than a ripple within the darkness, suddenly snapped the boy's attention to full alert. He caught the pale flicker of a face as a man mounted the entrance steps of Mademoiselle Benoit's residence and thumped his gloved fist against the door.

"Oiy, someone's seeking entrance," whispered Peregrine.

Raven and Hawk came instantly awake. They wriggled over to join him.

"He's tall," said Peregrine, "and looks to be slender despite his overcoat."

A weak flutter of light—a single candle?—momentarily lit one of the upper windows, and after a minute or two had passed, the door opened, and the man slipped inside.

Hawk looked to his brother. "What should we do?"

They knew from an earlier reconnaissance that there was no easy access to the back of the house.

"We wait for now," said Raven. "Let's see if we can creep closer and try to get a look at his face when he leaves."

But before they moved, the door opened again, and the man hurried out. Without pausing on reaching the street, he turned left and quickened his pace. Within moments, he was swallowed in the gloom.

"She's gone back upstairs," observed Peregrine. Even though the draperies were drawn, they could see a faint line of light.

And then all at once it was gone.

"I guess she has blown out the candle," said Hawk.

But an instant later it appeared in one of the lower windows.

The three of them held very still, watching and waiting.

Once again, the door opened and a cloaked figure—they saw just enough of her shadowed face in the moonlight to recognize Mademoiselle Benoit—emerged. On reaching the street, she hesitated and then headed for the west corner of Eaton Square.

"Pssst, follow me," said Raven, scrambling to his feet and setting off in pursuit.

Several hackney carriages and their drivers were loitering beneath the single street lamp illuminating their small patch of King's Road. Hoping, no doubt, for one last fare before night turned to the wee hours of morning.

Mademoiselle approached one of them, and after a quick exchange of words and money, she climbed into his hackney.

Raven waited until the whip cracked and the wheels lurched forward before darting across the cobbles.

One driver pushed him away, but on seeing the flash of a guinea, the third fellow was eager to make a deal. The coin passed hands, and Raven signaled for Hawk and Peregrine to join him inside the shabby carriage.

Seeing Hawk was about to speak, Raven held up his hand for silence. "We must seize the chance to learn what she is up to. Wrex and m'lady are struggling to solve the murder, and this may provide a vital clue."

CHAPTER 19

The street where Garfield had his rooms was deserted and the buildings dark. The residents of the area were shopkeepers and clerks, sober citizens who couldn't afford the luxury of midnight revelries.

Wrexford made short work of opening the lock of the lodging house's front door, Once inside, he and Sheffield moved noiselessly to the stairs.

"Garfield is on the top floor," whispered the earl. "His rooms are the door on the right."

Sheffield heaved a martyred sigh. "Do try to frighten the truth out of him quickly. I've already worked up a terrible thirst."

They felt their way up the stairs and crept across the landing to Garfield's door. Wrexford crouched down and felt for the keyhole . . . only to have the door yield to his touch.

Not a good omen.

He eased it all the way open and signaled for Sheffield to follow him inside. He turned and locked the door before striking a light to the taper on the candlestand.

A small flame sparked to life.

Nothing looked amiss in the sitting room. The bedchamber door was closed, and the only sound disturbing the late-night silence was the muted rhythmic ticking of the mantel clock.

Wrexford moved quietly across the room, but as he touched the door latch a sharp metallic scent warned him of what he was going to find inside.

Sheffield smelled it too, for he let out a wordless hiss.

The taper's light showed Garfield lying in a twisted position, one arm extended on the dark wood floor. His sightless eyes were widened in shock, the left breast of his white nightshirt stained garnet-red by the spreading circle of blood.

The earl knelt beside the body and felt for a pulse. "He's dead. The flesh is slightly cool, so I would guess it happened around an hour ago."

Sheffield looked around. "He doesn't appear to have put up a struggle."

"Hard to say," replied Wrexford, taking his time to observe every detail of the corpse. "I—"

He stopped short and held the flame closer to Garfield's right hand, which was lying palm down, the bloodied forefinger extended.

"Have a look at this," he said.

Sheffield crouched down beside him. "Holy Hell, he's drawn some sort of marks on the floorboard. It looks like two letters, with a line between them. . ." He squinted at the reddish tracing. "Is the first letter . . . an 'O'?" He looked up in dismay. "A-And . . . second one a 'C'?"

"Yes, it looks so to me." Wrexford drew in a troubled breath. "Which doesn't bode well for Oliver Carrick."

Mist rippled over the dark water. Ghosting through the tall reeds and marsh grasses growing along its bank, Raven and

Peregrine approached the tall perimeter wall surrounding a private estate—a grand Tudor manor house and grounds set on the River Thames adjacent to Fulham Palace and its magnificent botanical gardens.

Mademoiselle Benoit's hackney carriage had just passed through its main gates. The Weasels had quickly climbed down from their carriage and paid the driver to wait in a cul-de-sac for their return. But rather than risk having the three of them spotted sneaking into the main courtyard, it was decided that Hawk—as the smallest and most agile—would slip in and observe what was happening before they decided on their next move.

To their left, Raven noted a boathouse and a dock jutting out into the water. To their right, a majestic oak loomed up from behind the weathered stone, its leaves chittering softly in the night breeze.

"We'll wait in the tree's shadow for Hawk's signal," he whispered, indicating the landmark they had picked out for the rendezvous,

"What is this place?" asked Peregrine, once they had crouched down by the wall.

"Dunno," answered Raven. He glanced around, assessing the best way to get up and over the wall. "But my guess is that despite its fancy trappings, nothing but dark mischief is happening inside it."

"Oiy. Why else would mademoiselle—"

"Sshhh!" The sharp crunch of gravel rose above the other night rustlings. "It sounds like the hackney is leaving."

A few moments later, a hiss from above caused them to look up.

"Mademoiselle entered the house," said Hawk. "It looks to be a private residence. There are no guards or dogs patrolling the grounds."

"Then let's take a closer look at what's going on." Raven was already on his feet, his hands fisted in the thick vines of ivy that were growing up the wall. He joined his brother atop the decorative limestone coping and waved for Peregrine to join them.

The stately house was dark, save for the glow of lamplight flickering in the windows of a room overlooking the back terrace.

"It took some fierce knocking on the door for someone to let mademoiselle in," explained Hawk. "I don't think she was expected."

"It looks like m'lady and Wrex were right to—" began Peregrine.

Raven hissed for silence as the terrace door opened. A short, stout woman—she was wearing a hooded cloak which hid her face—stepped out. "Fetch the box of tools from the mud room, and bring it down to the dock," she called to someone inside as she lit a marine lantern.

Raven slithered down through the ivy on the inside of the wall and gestured for the others to follow.

"Move quickly to the dock—and quietly," he said. "We need to see what they are up to."

The newly mown grass muffled their steps as they darted to the far side of the privet hedge bordering the walkway, using it as cover to make their way down the sloping lawn to the river. A cluster of barrels and crates on the dock provided a hiding place . . .

"Hell's bells—it's a steam launch!" intoned Peregrine, stopping short as he caught a glimpse of the dark-on-dark engine and chimney rising up from the middle of the boat tied to the mooring cleats.

"Stop gawking and hide yourself," ordered Raven, though he, too, was mesmerized for a moment by the sight.

Wrenching his gaze away, he ducked under a coil of rope

hanging from an iron stanchion and inched the crates apart just enough to create a peephole.

"Hold still," he warned as footsteps thudded onto the dock's wooden planking.

The eddying currents swirled against the pilings with a deep-throated gurgling.

"Remember to stoke the boiler slowly, Jed." It was the woman's voice, steely with the note of command. "This particular grade of cast iron can crack if heated too quickly."

"Aye, Mrs. Guppy."

"Better check the coal bin as well. We should have enough fuel for tonight's journey, but best to be prepared." A pause. "I'll leave you to get everything ready while I return to the house and fetch our passenger. The sooner we get this over with, the better."

Her retreating footsteps were soon swallowed by the crackle and *whoosh* of the steam engine coming to life. Metal clanked against metal as the boatman checked the level of the coal and muttered an oath. Raven saw him take up a large canvas sack and head for the boathouse.

"Mrs. Guppy—" began Hawk.

"Is a friend of the missing Mr. Carrick," finished Raven. "And so is Mademoiselle Benoit."

"Are you thinking that—"

"Yes," said Raven. "There's a chance they are going to rendezvous with him." There was no time to dither—he made a decision. "You two hurry back to Town and tell Wrex and m'lady what we've discovered." He passed over the purse, which was still well filled with coins. "I'm going to stow away in the boat and see what they are up to. I'll return as quickly as I can."

"But—"

Raven had already slipped over the rail of the launch. In a

flash, he wriggled his way inside the storage locker built into the prow of the boat and pulled the door shut just as Mrs. Guppy's helper emerged from the boathouse, dragging a bulging coal sack in his wake.

"*Dead*?" Charlotte needed a moment to collect her wits. Both she and Cordelia had dozed off while reading in the parlor as they waited for Wrexford and Sheffield to return, and her mind was a bit muzzy. "But I don't understand. I thought you went to confront Wayland—and yet you found Garfield dead?"

"Wayland wasn't at his usual haunt," explained the earl. "Nor was he at the Albany, so I wished to press Garfield further on why he thought Wayland was the most likely suspect for Milton's murder."

"W-Wouldn't the fact that Garfield is now dead seem to indicate that Wayland is indeed the villain?" ventured Cordelia.

"I fear that may not be true, my love," said Sheffield gently. "We found some evidence at the scene of the crime that . . ." He paused to choose his words with care. "That doesn't look good for your cousin."

The blood drained from Cordelia's face.

Charlotte rushed to pour a measure of brandy from the decanter on the sideboard. "Drink," she urged, bringing the glass to Cordelia and holding it to her lips as Sheffield kept a steadying arm around his wife's waist.

"W-What evidence?" demanded Cordelia after choking down a swallow of the spirits.

"Garfield wrote something on the floor with his own blood," answered Wrexford. "Both Kit and I agree that it appears to be the letters *O* and *C*."

"I *can't* believe . . ." The lamplight caught the pearling of tears on Cordelia's lashes. "I *won't* believe . . ."

"I know how difficult it is," said Sheffield, pressing a palm to her cheek, "but I fear you must."

Charlotte moved away to join Wrexford by the hearth, allowing the couple some privacy. "Do you think Henning could tell whether the murder weapon was the same used on Milton?" she said softly as he stirred the coals to life.

"Perhaps," he answered. "That would mean . . ." He hesitated. "I did send word alerting Griffin to the murder. Otherwise I feared it would cause an irreparable breach in our friendship if it came to light that I had discovered the crime and said nothing."

"But you are worried that asking him to send the corpse to Henning may reveal that the same knife was used in both murders. And that Oliver Carrick will become even more of a suspect, especially given the *O* and *C* written in Garfield's blood." Charlotte squeezed her eyes shut for a moment. "Do you think Oliver Carrick is the murderer?"

Wrexford didn't reply. Which was an eloquent enough response.

She, too, was having trouble thinking of an alternative, but before she parsed through the problem, a sudden shout caused her to spin around.

"Wrex! M'lady!" The pelter of racing footsteps in the corridor punctuated Hawk's out-of-breath shouts.

The earl rushed to the door and flung it open just as the boy skidded to a stop, with Peregrine right on his heels.

Two of them. And there should be three.

Impelled by dread, Charlotte hurried across the carpet, her heart hammering against her rib cage. "Where is Raven?"

"On a steam launch chugging down the Thames!" replied Peregrine with undisguised envy.

"Ye heavens, why—" she began, but one look at Wrexford reminded her that flinging out helter-pelter questions did none of them any good.

"Quiet, everyone!" commanded the earl with a note of measured calm. "Let us begin at the beginning. Tell us what happened, lads—but do so without any unnecessary embellishments."

They both drew in a deep breath, and Peregrine signaled for Hawk to go first.

"Mademoiselle Benoit left her residence about an hour after returning from the soiree and flagged down a hackney. It seemed awfully suspicious, and as we were tasked with keeping an eye on her movements, we decided that we ought to follow her . . ."

Taking turns, the boys recounted where the journey had taken them, and what had transpired on the estate's dock.

"And so, we rushed back here as quickly as we could to tell you," finished Hawk.

"This means—" began Wrexford.

"This means that Mrs. Guppy is in league with the Frenchwoman," said Charlotte, trying to keep fear from bubbling through her blood. "I can't think of any way to view that in a good light." She pressed her fingertips to her brow, surprised at how cold her flesh felt. "But perhaps my mind is not functioning clearly."

"Never fear, Raven is far too clever and experienced to be caught," pointed out Sheffield.

Wrexford, she noted, remained silent. No doubt he was thinking about the same grim fact that she was.

"The River Thames is notorious for its treacherous currents. Even men who are at home on the water fear going overboard." Her voice wavered, and she moved to the window, pressing a palm against the chill glass to steady her nerves. "And Raven doesn't know how to swim."

"Actually, he does," said Wrexford. "After the incident at the Serpentine Bridge, I took all three of our Weasels out to a calm spot near Isle of Dogs and made sure they learned how to stay afloat as well as deal with the dangerous eddies of the river."

"Peregrine swims like a fish," piped up Hawk. "He, too, taught us some tricks for navigating the perils."

Charlotte felt her spurt of panic ebb. But not by much.

"What's this about rivers?" McClellan appeared in the doorway, hair hastily pinned up and a heavy wrapper thrown over her night-rail. She fixed the ladies with a gimlet gaze. "Hmmph! I thought you said it was going to be a quiet evening and any council of war would wait until morning."

"So we assumed," replied Charlotte. "But the best-laid plans of mice and men—"

"And rats," muttered Sheffield.

"Evil, slithering rats," amended Cordelia.

"Name calling may help vent your spleen, but it does us no practical good," observed Wrexford. He moved back to the hearth and braced his hands on the marble mantel.

"Why a steamboat?" he wondered aloud.

"There are countless wharves and docklands just in the stretch of river between Fulham and Isle of Dogs," said Sheffield. "They could be going anywhere, so all speculation on our part is useless. We have no choice but to wait for Raven to return."

The earl grudgingly nodded his agreement.

"I'll go fetch tea and coffee," said McClellan. "And a platter of ginger biscuits."

At the mention of their favorite treat, Hawk and Peregrine quickly offered to help her.

"The resilience of youth is a godsend. It allows cheerful optimism in the face of unspeakable danger," mused Charlotte. "While we are older and wiser to the vagaries of the world."

The earl came to join her, his hand finding hers and clasping it tightly. "Kit was right to remind us that Raven is both clever and resourceful. He's no stranger to trouble, and eluding danger is second nature to him."

But it only takes one mistake. And nobody is perfect.

However, rather than cast a pall of gloom over the room, she forced an answering smile.

"Of course." She drew in a breath. "And Kit is also right to remind us that for the moment, all we can do is wait."

CHAPTER 20

Puffs of steam misted the air, and the whooshing grew louder as the boatman fed chunks of coal into the engine's firebox.

Mrs. Guppy returned with an agitated Mademoiselle Benoit in tow. A young man in an oilskin cloak trailed behind them. "Calm yourself, Isabelle," she counseled. "There is no need to panic."

"I tell you, time is growing short! Oliver—" A sob slurred the next few words. "—Jasper's papers!"

"Have courage, my dear. Just give me a moment to prepare for our journey, and then we shall discuss the current situation."

The exhortation seemed to settle mademoiselle's nerves. As she stepped into the boat, her gaze locking on the belching engine, worry seemed to give way to curiosity. "Oh, I have always wanted to experience traveling in a steam-powered conveyance!"

"You will find it exhilarating." Mrs. Guppy waved the young man to the rear of the launch. "Andrew is my top nautical engineering expert, and he's well versed in all the subtle hazards of the river. He will take the ship's wheel and navigate us to our destination faster than any traditional carriage or sailing vessel."

Mademoiselle Benoit reached out a hand and swirled her fingers through the silvery skeins of vapor rising up from the chimney. "Now that we are no longer in thrall to the vagaries of tides and currents, rivers—and soon oceans—offer quicker, safer, and more reliable mode of travel because of steam power." A beatific sigh. "And just imagine when locomotives are a common sight huffing and puffing through the countryside on a set schedule."

Mrs. Guppy smiled. "That day is coming, Isabelle. But for tonight we must concentrate on the challenges of the present."

"The steam pressure is ready, ma'am," called the boatman.

"Then cast off the lines and let us be on our way."

Moonlight flickered over the water as the steamboat chugged against the current. The dark silhouette of the slumbering city slipped by. Few lights were visible along the river's edge. At this hour of the night, any business being done was best conducted under the shroud of secrecy.

Lifting her face to the breeze, Mademoiselle Benoit moved slowly past the thumping engine to a spot by the larboard rail near the bow of the boat. Mrs. Guppy finished conversing with her engineer, then went to join her.

"I'm frightened," said mademoiselle in a low, tight voice. "As I told you, it appears that Garfield has been lying to us—I don't know why—and it is Wayland who has Jasper's papers. I just learned that he has negotiated a price to sell them to Jean-Paul Montaigne and his radical friend, and a rendezvous to make the exchange has been arranged."

A sound of distress rumbled in her throat. "It's scheduled for tomorrow night! We can't let that happen! We *must* get our hands on those papers!"

Inside the storage locker, Raven shifted and pressed an ear to the tiny gap between the door and its frame, straining to catch the words through the engine sounds.

"Let us hope that Oliver will have some idea of how to stop them!" Mademoiselle choked back a sob. "That intimidating-looking Bow Street Runner came to ask me and the other officers of our society about Oliver. I am sure that the authorities think he is guilty of Jasper's murder!"

"My dear, they can have no real evidence of his guilt, because there is none," said Mrs. Guppy.

"But what if someone witnessed the quarrel in the tavern? Oliver said he was so distraught by Jasper's refusal to listen to reason that he wasn't as discreet as he should have been."

"Sharp words are naught but hot air," countered Mrs. Guppy.

"And yet those words may convince a jury that there is no cause for reasonable doubt."

Raven jiggled the door, moving the latch just enough to open it a hair wider.

"Mrs. Sheffield and her friend Lady Wrexford assured me that they want to help Oliver." A gust of wind tugged at Mademoiselle Benoit's cloak. "Perhaps we should trust them and tell them everything."

"Let us see what Oliver has to say when we reach our destination. But I would counsel that we don't trust anyone," answered Mrs. Guppy. "Keep in mind that Jasper Milton was likely murdered by a so-called friend. If we want to get our hands on his papers—"

The boat rocked as it cut into a swirling current, and the slap of the water against the hull made it impossible for Raven to hear any more of the conversation. By the time the river turned calmer, Mrs. Guppy had moved back to the stern to exchange words with her engineer, leaving mademoiselle standing by the larboard rail, staring out into the darkness.

Shifting uncomfortably within the cramped space—the air was thick with the cloying odors of pine tar and bilge water— Raven parsed over what he had just heard . . .

"Ahoy, Jed!"

A shout from the engineer to the boatman roused him from his thoughts.

"Kindly fetch me a pair of hemp mooring lines from the storage locker."

"Aye, sir," The boatman placed a last chunk of coal in the firebox and shuffled to the bow of the boat.

Raven whispered a curse that Charlotte had strictly forbidden him to say. He slithered back as far as he could and pulled the coils of rope over his head and shoulders, hoping that the darkness would hide his presence.

The locker door opened, allowing a spill of light from the lantern by the engine to flutter over the nautical supplies. A meaty hand reached in and groped around . . .

And then seized Raven's collar and gave a mighty yank.

Struggling was hopeless. He let himself go limp and allowed the boatman to drag him out of his hiding place.

"Oiy, look what we have here—a thieving little wharf rat!" cried the boatman, lifting Raven to his feet.

Reacting in a flash, the boy drove an elbow into the man's stomach and slashed a vicious kick to his knee, allowing him to twist free. He danced out of reach, and pressing his back to the rail, whipped out the knife in his boot and turned to face the others.

"Bloody hell." The boatman edged back and took a wary sidestep to put himself between the knife and mademoiselle.

The engineer rose from his seat, keeping a grip on the ship's wheel. "If you take over steering for a moment, Mrs. Guppy, Jed and I will make short work of throwing the filthy little rat into the river."

"Sit down, Andrew," ordered Mrs. Guppy. "There will be no such violence. For God's sake, he's a child!"

"And will grow into an even more dangerous, depraved man. We would be doing the world a favor," growled the engineer. "Besides, he may have overheard your conversation."

"There is enough evil in the world," replied Mrs. Guppy firmly. "We shall not add to it by resorting to murder ourselves."

"*Oui*," said mademoiselle, repressing a shudder. "There has been too much death shadowing our efforts. The boy is innocent—"

"Innocent—ha!" said the boatman, rubbing at his bruised stomach. "The imp of Satan was planning on stealing anything that wasn't nailed down."

"Nails wuddna be a problem," retorted Raven.

Mrs. Guppy repressed a twitch of her lips at the show of spunk. "Even if the lad did overhear anything, what possible harm can he do with the information?"

The engineer grumbled but couldn't muster an argument.

To Raven, she added, "Put the knife away, young man. You are in no danger from us. When we tie up at our destination, you'll be free to go." A pause. "But in return, you must promise that you won't return to my dock and rob me blind."

"Oiy, fair enough," grunted Raven. He slid the knife back into his boot but kept a wary eye on the two men.

"Ah, the word of a gentleman," sneered the engineer. "So of course you can believe it."

"In my experience," observed Mrs. Guppy, "thieves often have a code of honor."

A snort. "Don't say I didn't warn you when you come out one morning to find this lovely craft stripped bare."

With things at a standoff, an awkward silence descended over the boat, save for the hiss and clang of the engine and *whoosh* of the water.

It was Mademoiselle Benoit who broke the tension by turning to Mrs. Guppy. "I've never been on a steamboat," she said, "and I would love to get a closer look at its engine. Might you explain to me how it works?"

"It's always a pleasure to reveal the wonders of our new

technological innovations, which are changing our world for the better." Mrs. Guppy fetched a folded tarp from the storage locker, placed it down aft of the boiler, and gingerly lowered herself to a kneeling position.

"My legs aren't quite as limber as they were in my youth," she said with a wince. Then grasping a brass ring set in a section of the floorboards, she pulled up a section of the planks, revealing the rotating crankshaft.

Raven craned his neck to see the mechanics, curious to observe the workings of the engine.

Mrs. Guppy caught his movement and regarded him thoughtfully. "Would you like to have a closer look?"

Another shrug, but she must have seen the flare of interest in his eyes, for she beckoned him to crouch down beside mademoiselle. "Come, have a look. You have my word that my men won't lay a hand on you."

He hesitated, and then decided that if she had intended to toss him overboard, she would have tried to do so already. He slid closer and dropped to a crouch — but kept himself poised to spring up at the first sign of trouble. Already he had a plan for scrambling out on the narrow deck of the prow, where the two men could not both come at him at once.

"It's really a rather simple contraption," began Mrs. Guppy. "The boiler heats water, which creates steam. The steam creates pressure, which opens and closes the pistons as they move up and down. There are gears and levers, which then move in different ways to convert that force to turn the propeller. And that is what pushes the boat through the water."

Raven watched the rhythmic up-and-down motion of the pistons with great interest. Beneath his boots he could feel the vibration of the crankshaft thrumming though the floorboards.

"So, the pistons go up and down," he mused.

"Correct," said Mrs. Guppy.

Raven moved his forefinger in a circling motion. "And a propeller has to spin round and round."

"That's right. In engineering, we call it converting reciprocating motion into rotational motion."

"So, how does that happen?"

He knew the answer in principle, but as he had yet to see a working marine engine in action, he was curious to observe exactly how all the individual parts moved.

The boatman made a rude sound. "Next you'll be lecturing the little muckworm on Newton's Laws of Motion."

"Actually, I have a feeling that the lad would catch on very quickly." Mrs. Guppy turned back to Raven. "By the by, do you have any formal education? Can you read?"

Raven let out a snicker. "Do I look like I know m'letters?"

"Appearances can be deceiving," she murmured.

Raven froze on hearing one of Charlotte's favorite warnings, suddenly aware that he must not underestimate the plain and dowdy Mrs. Guppy. Dressed in an unflattering shade of mud-brown wool, she looked like a rather dull greengrocer's wife. But clearly she was not.

He gave a rude grunt, determined to be more careful and keep his mouth shut.

"The lad asked a good question." Tucking her skirts more tightly around her legs, mademoiselle shifted her position. "Please continue with your explanation."

"If you take a closer look at the engine, you see there is a system of connecting rods and levers . . ."

Raven and Mademoiselle Benoit listened with rapt attention as Mrs. Guppy began to explain the mechanics of all the moving parts, both of them interrupting to ask questions.

"You're *very* clever." Mademoiselle smiled after Raven inquired about the arrangement of gears turning the crankshaft.

He ducked his head, once again aware that he ought not appear too clever.

Mrs. Guppy eyed him for a long moment and then resumed explaining how the technology worked.

The tide was turning, the crosscurrents churning up rippling eddies as the boat passed under Blackfriars Bridge.

"Avast, Jed, cut the steam," called Andrew over the thump of the pistons. "White Lion Wharf is just ahead."

Mademoiselle Benoit sat back, her look of enthusiasm giving way to naked fear.

"You must be brave," counseled Mrs. Guppy. "We will soon be with Oliver, and the three of us will come up with an idea of how to deal with the latest development."

"But what if . . ." Mademoiselle turned away, leaving the rest of her words unsaid.

The boat bumped up against barnacled pilings. The engineer jumped out and fastened the mooring lines around the iron cleats.

"You're free to go, lad," said Mrs. Guppy as she slowly rose.

Raven darted over the railing and crossed to the cobbled courtyard just beyond the wharf. But then he stopped and took cover in the shadows of the stone warehouses, intent on following them to where Oliver Carrick was hiding and then reporting back to Wrexford and Charlotte.

"This way, my dear." Mrs. Guppy guided mademoiselle past the storage sheds. "We haven't far to walk."

"What if Oliver isn't there?" said Mademoiselle in a shaky voice. "What if he's been arrested? How will we ever manage to help him—"

Raven had to make a rapid-fire decision.

"Oiy," he called. "If you are looking for someone to trust, you need to come with me."

All we can do is wait.

Charlotte had sat down at the earl's desk and taken up a sketchbook—Wrexford had suggested that they move from the parlor to his workroom, which offered distractions to keep their minds off brooding—and was now intent on working out a preliminary idea for her next satirical print. But as the minutes slid by with agonizing slowness, she couldn't keep her imagination from conjuring up all sorts of hideous possibilities for why Raven hadn't yet returned.

Unable to sit still a moment longer, she slipped off her shoes and moved as quietly as she could to the far end of the room in order to pace without rousing the others.

Despite their sleepy protests, Hawk and Peregrine had been sent up to bed, but Cordelia was dozing on the sofa, her head pillowed against Sheffield's shoulder. He was passing the time by reading a weighty report from Lloyd's of London on revised insurance offerings for commercial shipping ventures.

Charlotte noted that he hadn't turned a page in quite a while.

McClellan had put aside her mending and was now knitting. As for Wrexford . . .

He appeared in the doorway of the adjoining library with several books in hand.

A reminder that yet another mystery—a very personal one—hung over their family.

Charlotte felt a stab of guilt at having put aside the recently discovered letter written by Wrexford's late father and all the questions it had raised. Murder had a way of shoving every other concern into the shadows. However, she knew how much Wrexford longed to turn his attention to unraveling the conundrum of the person known as "A"—which might help him to understand the complexities of his relationship with his father.

"Have you found anything helpful?" she asked.

"Not particularly," he answered. "Though I confess that I'm surprised by what excellent taste my father had in poetry."

"I haven't forgotten about your personal quest, my love. We will find the answers to the questions about your father's mysterious correspondent as soon as we solve this present conundrum," promised Charlotte. Her heart ached for him. Putting the needs of his friends before his own was simply part of who he was. But she knew it was taking an emotional toll.

"I hope . . ." Though they had kept their voices low, she saw that the sounds had roused both Cordelia and Sheffield. Leaving the rest of her thought unsaid, she quickly turned her attention to the present moment.

"You two really should return to your residence." Charlotte moved back to the desk. "You need not wait here all night. We will send word as soon as Raven returns."

Assuming he . . . No, she wouldn't even consider the alternative.

"We've no intention of leaving," announced Sheffield. He patted back a yawn. "Mac serves a far better breakfast than our cook."

McClellan stuffed her knitting into the sack by her feet. "Speaking of which, I had better go and put a batch of muffins into the oven."

But before she could move, the clatter of fast-approaching footsteps exploded in the corridor.

Wrexford spun around and reached for the pistol case on the bookshelf behind him, while Sheffield rushed to lock the door against attack.

The latch rattled, and then a fist thumped against the paneled oak.

"Oiy, oiy! Let us in!"

CHAPTER 21

Stepping back, Sheffield quickly turned the key and allowed Raven to barrel into the room, followed by two women and a man. Charlotte recognized Mademoiselle Benoit despite the hooded cloak that concealed half of her face. As for the other two . . .

Cordelia let out a strangled shriek and darted forward to seize the man in a fierce hug.

Oh, surely not . . .

Charlotte shot a questioning look at Raven, who gave her an inscrutable smile. But before she could ask any questions, Cordelia released her embrace, and her tears of joy gave way to righteous fury. Grabbing the man's lapels, she shook him hard enough to rattle his teeth.

"You bloody idiot! Of all the cork-brained, ass-witted behavior! How *dare* you frighten me half to death?"

Oliver Carrick—at least Charlotte assumed the dazed-looking fellow was Cordelia's missing cousin—opened his mouth to speak, but Cordelia cut him off with another verbal salvo.

"What were you thinking!" she demanded. "Didn't it occur

to you that hiding made you look guilty as sin?" She thumped a fist to his chest. "Speaking of guilty, we just discovered—"

"First things first, Cordelia," interrupted Wrexford. "Let us hear what Carrick and his friends have to say before we speak of anything else."

Cordelia hitched in a breath but gave a grim nod of understanding.

"I—" began Carrick.

"As for you two, what the devil is going on?" Cordelia couldn't keep from directing her ire at Mademoiselle Benoit and the other woman. "The three of you have a great deal of explaining to do!"

"Perhaps," counseled Sheffield, "if you stop ringing a peal over your cousin's head, we can begin to make some sense of what is going on."

"An excellent suggestion. I'll fetch some tea." McClellan rose and, on catching Charlotte's gaze, gave a subtle signal to Raven.

"A very interesting young man." The older woman with Mademoiselle Benoit—based on Hawk and Peregrine's report, Charlotte knew exactly who she was—raised her brows at Charlotte as Raven followed the maid into the corridor. "I take it he works for you?"

"In a manner of speaking," she replied coolly, wary of revealing any information about her family to a woman as sharp as Sarah Guppy. "But we have more important things to discuss—and you've saved us the trouble of traveling out to Fulham to interrogate you."

Charlotte took a moment to study the woman's unremarkable face, but her expression was a cipher. "To begin with, why have you and Mademoiselle Benoit been conspiring to keep Oliver Carrick in hiding?"

A flicker of amusement lit in the woman's eyes as she moved to join Charlotte by the earl's desk.

"You must be Lady Wrexford." On receiving a nod of acknowledgment, Mrs. Guppy added, "I have heard a great deal about you from a friend who attends Lady Thirkell's salon for intellectually minded ladies." She didn't elaborate. "Are you interested in science, milady?"

"I occasionally attend Lady Thirkell's Bluestocking soirees because I enjoy intelligent conversation on a great many subjects," replied Charlotte, carefully parrying the woman's probing.

"Your husband has the reputation of being a brilliant chemist."

"Among other things," she said softly.

"Ah, yes . . . his hair-trigger temper." Mrs. Guppy tapped a finger to her chin. "Should I be worried?"

"That depends."

"On what?" asked Mrs. Guppy.

"On whether he believes that you're a cold-blooded killer."

A smile. "I'll take my chances, for I have heard that along with a fearsome temper, he also possesses an analytical mind, razor-sharp logic, and a conscience that values the truth."

Charlotte gave the woman credit for her show of unflappable calm. Indeed, her nerves appeared forged out of steel.

Whether that was good or bad remained to be seen.

"My husband and I both value the truth. So why don't you begin explaining why we should believe that you and your two companions are not guilty of a heinous crime?"

"That promises to be a rather long conversation. Might we wait for our tea?" Mrs. Guppy glanced at the sideboard. "Or perhaps pour ourselves a stronger libation before we get down to business."

Charlotte heard a whisper of wool as Wrexford came to stand behind her.

"What may I offer you?" he asked politely.

"I do enjoy a good Scottish malt," replied Mrs. Guppy.

"Ummm, make that two," called Carrick.

Mademoiselle Benoit hesitated and then requested brandy.

"Please sit and allow me to serve your drinks," said Charlotte, quickly assuming the role of a perfectly polished hostess—a lady of no substance beneath the froth of expensive silk and good manners.

If Mrs. Guppy wished to engage in a cat-and-mouse game of feminine wiles, reflected Charlotte, she would find herself matched with someone who had a great deal of experience in how to play it.

Wrexford stood in the shadows, waiting for everyone to settle themselves in the room. Patience was not usually his strong suit, but he used the delay to study Mrs. Guppy, who had not yet chosen a spot. *An imaginative inventor, a highly successful entrepreneur*—her intellect was clearly saber-sharp.

Mrs. Guppy seemed to sense his scrutiny, and while most people found his stare unsettling, she reacted by raising her glass in a subtle salute.

Or was it a challenge?

No doubt he would learn the answer to that in a moment, for after taking a small sip of her whisky, she edged away from the others, who had seated themselves near the hearth, and came to join him.

"You have a very intriguing circle of family and friends, Lord Wrexford."

The earl said nothing.

"But then, that shouldn't surprise me. You have the reputation for being a gentleman of many interesting talents," she continued. "Raven is a very clever and perceptive lad. Wherever did you find him?"

He ignored the question. "One of the first things you've probably heard about me is that social niceties bore me to perdition. So let us not engage in thrust-and-parry verbal fencing under the guise of making polite conversation."

"Excellent. I, too, prefer plain speaking," answered Mrs. Guppy.

"I imagine you have a great many questions for me. So perhaps I can help narrow them down by giving you a summary of Jasper Milton's murder, along with what we do—and do not—know."

She took a sip of her whisky. "Because, to be frank, time is of the essence. That you had Raven watching Mademoiselle Benoit was a fortuitous stroke of luck, as you shall soon understand. But to take advantage of it, we will have to move fast."

"That's a well-crafted emotional appeal, madam," replied Wrexford. "But it's wasted on me. If you wish to convince me to take a course of action, you'll have to use facts and logic."

"I expected no less." She turned slightly, the candlelight kindling a flash of sparks beneath her lashes. "So, let me begin without further ado."

Charlotte accepted a cup of tea from McClellan, listening with only half an ear as Cordelia and Sheffield peppered Carrick and Mademoiselle Benoit with questions. After the maid took a seat near the others, she drifted away from the group and shifted her attention to the interchange between Mrs. Guppy and Wrexford.

This, she knew, was where the real game would play out, with truth and lies moving around the checkered board like black-and-white chess pieces, looking to seize the advantage . . .

Charlotte caught the last few words of Mrs. Guppy's challenge and the earl's response. But before the woman could begin her summary, the earl spoke up, addressing his words to everyone in the room.

"I'm aware of Garfield's offer to sell Milton's papers to Mademoiselle Benoit and her French colleague and have heard a self-serving explanation from him all but accusing Mercer Wayland of being the real culprit."

She noted that he kept Garfield's murder to himself for now.

"So my patience, never in great abundance to begin with, is just about exhausted." The earl straightened from his slouch against the wall. "I've had enough of lies and innuendoes. The only thing I wish to hear from our three guests is the truth."

"Fair enough," said Mrs. Guppy. "So let's start with the key truth to this conundrum. Oliver Carrick did not kill Jasper Milton. But he saw who did."

Charlotte bit back a gasp.

"Why—" began the earl.

"We'll return to that in a moment once I finish with the preliminaries," interjected Mrs. Guppy. "As a man of science, I assume you prefer to have as many facts as possible before you begin trying to solve a problem."

"Correct," answered Wrexford.

In response to Mrs. Guppy's gesture, Carrick rose and moved to join her.

Sheffield found Cordelia's hand and gave it a squeeze.

"Secondly," continued Mrs. Guppy, "Mademoiselle Benoit is not the enemy, nor are the other members of the French scientific society—except for Jean-Paul Montaigne, the society's president, who is allied with a group of radical French social reformers who are currently visiting London in order to spread their message to Britain."

"Are you saying there are *two* French factions?" demanded Wrexford.

"Precisely, milord. Again, we'll come back in a moment to their motives. But now to the crux of Jasper Milton's murder." Mrs. Guppy allowed herself a deliberate pause. "The most important thing for you to know is that he is not quite the victim he seems to be."

"A bold assertion," said Wrexford. "Naturally you will have strong evidence to back it up."

"I shall let you judge for yourself, sir."

Mrs. Guppy nodded at Carrick. "Now that Lord Wrexford has heard my preamble, Oliver, perhaps you can flesh out my words with what you know."

"I shall do my best, Sarah." Carrick cleared his throat. "It's frightfully complicated, sir, and I confess I am still in the dark about a number of things. But as Mrs. Guppy has said, we must act quickly to avoid a grave threat to the present peace in Europe. We have reason to believe that Jasper's papers are about to be sold to the French radicals—"

"Wait! First things first," interrupted Wrexford. "Mrs. Guppy says you witnessed the murder. What I don't understand is, why didn't you immediately report it to the authorities and have the culprit arrested?"

"Because . . ." Carrick closed his eyes for an instant. "Because it was dark, and what with the swirling rain and fog of the storm, I didn't actually *see* the murderer. I could only make out a vague silhouette. But I heard Jasper address him as Axe and call him a good friend . . ." A hesitation. "And then Jasper added something about Axe acting as the steely force which kept him from spinning out of control."

"What about Axe's voice?" demanded Sheffield. "Given that Milton called him a good friend, and given that you and Milton were very close, surely you should have recognized it."

"It was blowing like the devil, and the river was rushing against the rocks of the gorge." Carrick gave a helpless shrug. "I just couldn't identify it. And then, they dropped their voices. I heard nothing for a bit, and suddenly the lantern shifted, and I saw the silhouette of the murderer as he cleaned a knife on his sleeve and slid it back into his boot."

The memory made him lose his composure for the moment.

Mrs. Guppy picked up the narrative. "Axe then bent over Jasper's body and searched through his clothing. He found a packet inside Milton's overcoat and slid it into his pocket."

"What happened next was horrible," stammered Carrick. "He lifted Jasper's body and maneuvered it out onto what remained of the bridge and then . . . p-pushed the corpse into the ravine as if it were naught but a sack of stones."

Cordelia covered her face with her hands.

"A branch cracked close to me, and Axe swung the lantern beam around to the bushes where I was hiding. I panicked and fled, uncertain as to whether he had seen me."

"Think!" pressed Wrexford. "Have you truly no idea of who Axe could be?"

Carrick have a helpless shrug. "He was cloaked, and as I said, the wind was blowing like the devil, so I couldn't even make out his shape. All I can say is that he was of average height."

"We all have monikers for familiar friends, often based on a diminutive of their formal name—" began the earl.

"Or a personal humorous reason, known only to the two friends," pointed out Sheffield. "So it's hard to speculate on what 'Axe' might mean."

The ensuing silence indicated that nobody disagreed.

"Given the weather and the hour, I can't help but wonder— why were you there?" demanded Charlotte. She was finding it hard to make sense of Carrick's story, and judging by Wrexford's expression, so was he.

"Because I wanted to make a last effort to convince Jasper not to do what he was planning to do with his innovation."

The earl muttered an oath. "Ye gods, if I were looking for endless melodrama, I would read one of Ann Radcliffe's horrid novels."

"Explain yourself, Oliver," counseled Mrs. Guppy.

"Jasper was always an idealist." Carrick looked to Cordelia, who gave a confirming nod. "One of the reasons he loved mathematics was because he saw it as pure and unambiguous. It could create what he referred to as 'noble truths,' which turned chaos into order."

"Mathematics simplified the universe for Jasper," added Cordelia. "He liked its world better than our unruly everyday existence."

"Jasper believed that his new innovation—"

"Which was what?" demanded Wrexford.

"I can't answer that exactly," replied Carrick, "for he never explained it in any detail. However, he did say that he had discovered the key to creating longer and wider bridges, and that such innovations would revolutionize travel, making it faster and cheaper for people and goods to move from place to place—especially as he believed that locomotives will soon replace horses and carriages."

"I understand the economics of what you've described, and it's clear that such a transformational discovery would be worth a fortune," mused Sheffield.

"But that's just it," exclaimed Carrick. "Jasper didn't care about the money! He wanted his innovation to better the lives of ordinary people. He became very upset on discovering that many of the contracts for work on the Bristol Road Project were given out based on bribes rather than expertise. And that made him even more morally opposed to licensing the rights of a patent to rich investors, who would then make a fortune building the new structures for municipalities and countries—"

"Only to have the municipalities and countries have to charge tolls or other fees to recoup their investments, and then continue to reap the profits," interjected Mademoiselle Benoit. "Thus ensuring that travel remained too expensive for the common man."

Which begged the question . . .

"So what," responded Charlotte, "was Milton's solution to the dilemma?"

CHAPTER 22

There was a long moment of silence as Carrick fiddled with the folds of his cravat. "To gift his innovation to the French radicals. During our visit to France to attend the Parisian scientific society's symposium on travel, he met a group of social agitators and admired their idealism."

"Our society's president was the go-between," explained Mademoiselle Benoit. "Jean-Paul Montaigne and one of the leaders of the radicals have been friends since childhood, and Montaigne shares the group's egalitarian beliefs. In fact..."

She looked to Carrick for an instant and then blew out her breath. "In fact, he is a staunch supporter of Napoleon and the reforms the former emperor made in France to break the stranglehold the idle rich had on the country."

Wrexford felt a chill slither down his spine at the mention of Napoleon. "But the emperor is no longer in any position to change the world—for better or for worse. Now that he has been exiled to Elba, his only empire is a tiny speck of an island off the coast of Italy."

"Which lies only 170 miles from France," murmured Mrs. Guppy.

The earl frowned. He wanted to dismiss the idea as absurd. But he had talked to enough of his military friends to know that the situation in Europe was more fraught than the British government wished to admit. Despite all the eloquent talk of camaraderie and cooperation at the Peace Conference taking place in Vienna, the European rulers were at each other's throats. The Continent needed to be rebuilt from the rubble of war, and they were all vying for any advantage that would make them more powerful and prosperous than their neighbors . . .

It was Charlotte who gave voice to the question that was forming in his head.

"Are you saying that the radicals plan to use Milton's innovation in some way to help Napoleon return to the throne?"

"Yes!" Carrick, Mrs. Guppy, and Mademoiselle Benoit all answered in unison.

Cordelia broke the stunned silence with an uncertain laugh. "Surely you're jesting."

"I wish that were so," replied Carrick. "The radicals have been secretly negotiating with Russia to sell them Milton's innovation for an ungodly sum of money. Tsar Alexander is desperate to modernize his country, and the fact that Russia has very little sea access limits its opportunities for international commerce. The ability to build a sophisticated network of roads and bridges within his vast empire and then connect it with the rest of Europe would make Russia an economic power."

"And then," intoned Mademoiselle Benoit, "the radicals plan to give that money to Napoleon to finance his return to France."

"The people of France—" began Sheffield.

"The people of France will welcome him back with open arms," said Mademoiselle Benoit.

Wrexford didn't disagree. The Bourbon king been restored to the throne by the Allied Coalition, but he was much despised by his subjects.

"You value facts, milord, so allow me to explain how we know all this," offered Mrs. Guppy.

A nod.

"During the time when Milton and Oliver were visiting Paris for the scientific symposium, Isabelle—that is, Mademoiselle Benoit—overhead Montaigne explaining to his radical friend that Milton possessed a momentous secret, one that would be worth a fortune. The two of them then came up with a plan to convince Milton to put his idealism into action. Montaigne knew Milton admired many of the reforms made by Napoleon, and he was clever enough to craft a speech describing a utopian vision of Europe rising from the ashes of war into a confederation of prosperous, peaceful nations all tied together by Milton's wondrous bridges and improved roads."

"It was seductive. Jasper imagined himself as a hero for the ages," said Carrick. "I tried to point out the realities of Napoleonic France and the fact that it was not all sweetness and light. But he chose to believe only what he wanted to believe."

A sigh, as he turned with an apologetic shrug to Cordelia. "Jasper had changed over the last year. An arrogance had crept into his once self-deprecating demeanor. It was as if his undeniable scientific genius had made him think that his view on any subject was the correct one. There was no arguing with him once his mind was made up."

"Heaven knows I tried everything to get him to see the situation more clearly," announced Mademoiselle Benoit. "Oliver and I were worried that Milton would hand over his secret without further consideration. So we decided . . ."

A flush rose to her cheeks. "We decided that I should try to charm him and win his friendship so that I might offer subtle advice." She gave a wry grimace. "Alas, I was not very successful."

"It was I who asked her to try such wiles, and she selflessly agreed," interjected Carrick. "We became friends at a conference two years ago and have corresponded—"

"Lord Wrexford doesn't need a full account of your romantic entanglement," chided Mrs. Guppy with a fond smile. "Suffice it to say, Oliver and Isabelle are engaged, and in the spirit of complete candor, I'll add that the three of us have formed a business venture and are currently working together on a way to build better bridges using more conventional ideas than those of Jasper Milton."

"You did mention that time was of the essence," said the earl. "And yet I still am not quite sure where all this is going."

"It's complicated, milord. Bear with me a little longer. I'm nearly finished with the explanation."

He nodded for Mrs. Guppy to continue.

"So, we've now come to Oliver's initial assertion that he intended to make one last attempt to sway Milton on the night of his murder, for he knew that Milton was planning to meet the French radicals at the Three Crowns Inn on the Cambridgeshire Turnpike to give them his innovation."

"I was going to appeal to his conscience, pointing out that war would likely explode again if Napoleon returned to the throne of France, bringing death and destruction to countless innocent souls. But as I've said, I never had the chance."

Carrick blew out his breath. "However, we have just learned that Mercer Wayland has arranged a rendezvous with the radicals in order to sell them Milton's papers, though God only knows how he obtained them. Perhaps he's in league with Garfield—"

"Garfield was murdered earlier this evening," interrupted Wrexford, deciding to reveal the news now and see if it would work to his advantage. "He drew an *O* and a *C* on the floor-board with his own blood just before he died. And as we've just heard, you've been hiding out in the city by yourself."

He allowed a deliberate pause. "So forgive me if I wonder whether everything I've just heard is a lie and it was *you* who stabbed him in the heart—just as you did Milton?"

Carrick looked uttered shocked and bewildered by the revelation. "I—I," he stuttered, finally managing to find his voice. "I can only assure you that I did *not* kill poor Kendall." A helpless shrug. "But I can't prove it to you."

"I swear, Oliver is innocent," exclaimed Mademoiselle Benoit. "Murder goes against everything we believe in." Tears glistened in her eyes. "We are trying to prevent more bloodshed."

"Then why would Garfield have drawn an *O* and a *C*?" demanded Sheffield.

Carrick hesitated and then expelled a resigned sigh. "I—I haven't a clue."

"Perhaps if we finish our explanation, it will help convince you of Oliver's innocence," said Mademoiselle Benoit. "Oliver and I have been planning to steal Milton's papers from the radicals if they managed to acquire them." She swallowed hard. "So that they can't be used for evil."

"Isabelle has convinced Montaigne that she is an ardent supporter of the radicals and the return of Napoleon to the throne of France," explained Carrick.

"And that now brings us to the present," said Mrs. Guppy. "And why we decided to accept Raven's offer to take us to meet you."

"We are hoping you can help—" began Carrick.

"Have you any evidence to prove that there is a single grain of truth in what you have told us?" asked Wrexford.

"Actually, we do," replied Mrs. Guppy. "In a manner of speaking."

"At this point, I'm in no mood for word games, madam. Speak plainly — and I suggest that you do your damnedest to be convincing."

Mrs. Guppy met his ire with an air of unruffled calm. "We've just learned that Mercer Wayland has arranged a meeting for tomorrow night — or rather, this evening — with Montaigne and his radical friend in order to pass over Milton's papers." A pause. "We also know the location."

"Raven implied that you have some experience in dealing with skullduggery," added mademoiselle.

"What, precisely, are you looking for me to do?" countered Wrexford.

"We are hoping that you will stop the Frenchmen from taking Milton's innovation and funding the return of death and destruction to the Continent," piped up Carrick.

"And are you also hoping that I will give the papers to your newly formed business venture?"

Mrs. Guppy looked surprised by the question . . . and then her expression turned thoughtful. "Given your reputation for unflinching honor and integrity, sir, I shall happily leave that decision to you."

Outside the mullioned windows, the moonlight was swallowed by darkness as clouds scudded over the night sky. Rain began to patter against the glass.

"So . . ." Mrs. Guppy fisted her hands together, "will you agree to take charge of ensuring that Milton's papers don't get passed to the French?"

Wrexford looked to Charlotte. Their eyes met for a heartbeat, and he knew his answer.

"Yes."

"How are you going to stop the exchange?" asked Carrick.

"Never mind, Oliver," counseled Cordelia. "Raven was right — Lord Wrexford is no stranger to skullduggery."

The less said about their methods, the better, thought Wrexford, and then turned his attention to the logistics of retrieving Milton's papers.

"Now that we've come to a meeting of minds, exactly where and when is Wayland meeting the French radicals?"

Mrs. Guppy quickly passed on the information—the rendezvous was to take place at Vauxhall Pleasure Gardens, a favorite haunt of both the high and the low society of London, where ornate pavilions provided food, drink, and music, while the unlit pathways that meandered through the shrubberies encouraged more risqué activities.

"The appointed hour is midnight, when the nightly display of fireworks begins," she added, and named the exact location—a carpentry workshop set in the wooded area on the east edge of the gardens.

"I'm familiar with the spot." Wrexford was already formulating a plan, though he had no intention of sharing it with her and her companions.

As if reading his mind, Mrs. Guppy set aside her glass. "Well, then, it seems that our business is done here, unless you have any further questions for us, sir?"

"I believe we know all we need to know," agreed the earl. *Assuming that what we have heard is true.*

Mrs. Guppy gestured to Carrick and Mademoiselle Benoit. "Then let us take our leave." To Wrexford, she added, "I imagine that you wish to know our whereabouts. I have rented a townhouse on Conduit Street, just a short walk from here, for the duration of the transportation conference, and we shall be staying there."

"A moment," said Wrexford as she started for the door. "I am willing to take some of what you have told us on faith. But for now, I'll be sending four of my footmen—all of whom are former soldiers—with you to make sure that the three of you—especially Mr. Carrick—don't decide to disappear."

"Wrex!" exclaimed Cordelia.

Mrs. Guppy held up a hand to silence the protest. "I understand, milord."

An uneasy silence settled over the room as Wrexford left to make the arrangements.

Cordelia rose and sat down next to Carrick. Pulling him close, she whispered something in his ear.

The earl returned shortly and informed Mrs. Guppy and her companions that the footmen were awaiting them outside the workroom door.

McClellan, who had been sitting quietly in the shadows throughout the long discussion, waited until the sound of steps had faded to silence in the corridor before raising her voice. "Do you trust them, milord?"

"I think," he said slowly, "that we should all be extremely careful not to let any personal emotions cloud our judgment."

"But . . ." Cordelia bit her lip. "But Oliver is not only a dear friend, he is *family*."

"Yes, but as we've seen in previous investigations, families can be a viper's nest of deceit and death," said Sheffield. "Wrex is right to remind us of that."

"For now we need to focus our attention on the task of retrieving Milton's papers," counseled Wrexford. After a glance at Charlotte, he added, "I have an idea, but it's late and we will all think more clearly after some sleep. So I suggest we reconvene here in the morning to draw up a plan."

Charlotte waited until she and Wreford were alone before moving across the carpet and wordlessly wrapping him in a hug. Strange how such a simple act—pulling him close, feeling his warmth and his strong, steady heartbeat through the layers of their clothing—could force her fears to slither back into the shadows.

"Thank you," she whispered.

"For agreeing to put all of us in danger?" he said wryly. "Yet again."

"For being you," she answered. "And choosing to do the right thing, even when it's not easy."

"I'm not entirely certain that I have made the right decision," he admitted. "I dislike withholding evidence from Griffin." A tiny muscle twitched as his jaw clenched. "What if I am aiding and abetting a murderer and his accomplices?"

Charlotte thought for a long moment. "But clearly you have your doubts about Carrick's guilt, despite the evidence. As do I," she said. "So for now, let us trust our instincts and hope they will lead us to the truth."

"Choices, choices," murmured Wrexford, and chuffed a reluctant laugh. "In truth, it was Raven who at a key moment had to make the most important choice of the night."

"While she was serving me tea, McClellan told me about what happened after he stowed away on the steamboat," mused Charlotte. "He showed great steadiness and maturity in handling a very dangerous situation and ended up making an excellent decision."

Her words sparked a sudden realization. "Good heavens, our little Weasel is growing up in every sense of the word, isn't he?" She blinked away a nascent tear. "I—I don't know whether to feel happy or terrified."

"I imagine that we shall be experiencing an equal measure of both in the days that lie ahead." Wrexford pressed a kiss to her brow. "It is the natural cycle of life." A smile. "The young make their elders go prematurely grey. No doubt we will be butting heads with him—as well as with Hawk and Peregrine—more frequently than we would like."

Charlotte shuddered, recalling her clashes with her parents.

"But we have done our best to set a good example of how to

react to the vagaries of Life with both compassion and honor."
He watched the flicker of red and gold flames rise up in the
hearth, bright against the blackness of coals. "We have lit a
spark. It will be up to them to carry the torch."

He extinguished the lamp on his desk. "Come, we need a few
hours of sleep. Tomorrow is already here, and we will have
much to organize over the coming day."

CHAPTER 23

Darkness had swallowed the last glimmer of twilight, bringing with it a chill wind. A wave slapped against the hull of the wherry, drawing a grunt from the waterman as his oars caught in one of the river's swirling eddies.

The first part of the plan to ensure that Jasper Milton's plans did not pass into the hands of the French radicals was now in motion.

Charlotte tightened her grip on the gunwale and ducked away from the spray, keeping her gaze on the opposite shore. She and the Weasels had hired a boat to take them to Vauxhall Stairs, and from there they would make their way up to the riverside gate of the pleasure gardens while Wrexford and Sheffield arrived by carriage, as befitted gentlemen on the prowl for revelry.

The waterman had looked askance at their motley appearance, but the flash of silver in Charlotte's hand had silenced any thought of refusing them passage. Money spoke louder than the cut of one's clothes or the color of one's skin.

The boys, she noted, were enjoying the trip over the choppy

water, with Raven explaining in a low voice to Hawk and Peregrine how a steamboat overpowered such currents with the
ease of a hot knife cutting through butter.

Charlotte feared that their upcoming mission wouldn't
prove quite so easy. But she pushed aside such brooding as the
wherry bumped up against the landing stairs and they scrambled out onto the wet stones.

"This way," she whispered, starting up the footpath to
Vauxhall Walk. She and the Weasels were tasked with arriving
early at the rendezvous place deep within the wooded area of
the gardens and keeping a lookout for the conspirators. But
first she had to contrive a way to get the boys inside the
grounds . . .

"I've an idea." Charlotte paused as they reached the top of
the path and explained what she had in mind. "Stay close and
be ready to move fast."

A few moments later, she sauntered up to the attendant man-
ning the side entrance to Vauxhall Gardens—an unadorned
iron gate which catered to the working classes. After fumbling
in her pocket, she purchased a ticket and waited for her change.

"Oiy, Ox Brain—I gave ye a bloody shilling!" she cried,
after looking down at the coins he had dropped into her out-
stretched palm.

"Count 'em again, Piss Breath!" came the snarled reply. "I
gave ye the right amount."

She staggered, deliberately knocking into one of the cullies
guarding the gate. He grunted and shoved her back a step, curs-
ing at the foul smell emanating from her jacket.

"What is that stink?" he growled, only to spit out another
curse as the Weasels and Peregrine seized the moment to dart
through the tiny gap in the gate and race past him.

"Stop the little gutter rats!" he cried to his comrade, who
was busy flirting with one of the doxies trying to get in for free.

Too late. The boys had already disappeared in the tangle of starlight and shadows.

Steadying her footing, Charlotte made a show of re-counting the coins in her palm. "Hmmph. Next time, keep a civil tongue in your head or ye'll be sorry," she said after a loud belch.

"Be off wid ye," warned the ticket attendant with a disgusted snort, "or I'll toss yer sorry arse into the river."

She waggled a very rude sign with her fingers and scampered away as he roared in fury. Nobody paid her any attention. Vauxhall Gardens was a world unto itself, a notorious pleasure garden spread over several acres that offered dining, concerts, and all manner of frivolous entertainments. Within its walls, high and low society mingled without constraint, and under the cover of night the rules of Polite Society gave way to secret desires—an evening visit allowed both men and women to seize an interlude of naughty pleasures.

After cutting through a cluster of shrubs to reach the adjoining walkway, Charlotte stopped for a moment to get her bearings. The infamous Dark Walk, a lanternless path leading through a maze of trees and thick shrubbery where no respectable lady would dare risk being spotted, was on her left. Its stillness seemed to thrum with the crisscrossing currents of hidden passions.

She had once done a series of drawings on the stiff-rumped government ministers who were known to take illicit pleasures within the swath of overgrown foliage. The gossip it stirred in the drawing rooms of Mayfair had resulted in several changes within the Privy Council.

A sultry laugh drew Charlotte back to the moment as a demoiselle with rouged cheeks and dressed in a provocative gown approached a tipsy gentleman and whispered something in his ear. They moved into the shadows . . . And then another figure, a man lounging against a lamp post, a pocket sketchbook in hand, caught her eye. Charlotte recognized him as

Thomas Rowlandson, one of London's most famous gadfly satirical artists, whose work she much admired. He was also one of her chief rivals for the public's attention, though thank heaven he did not have a clue as to what A. J. Quill looked like.

Still, she ducked her head and kept moving. The glare felt as bright as the sun—it was said that over one thousand glass lanterns glimmered like points of fire in the night. After another bend, Charlotte turned away from the glittering lights and cacophony of the main pavilions on her right, where an orchestra of wind instruments was playing "La Réjouissance" from Handel's *Music for the Royal Fireworks* while the aristocratic revelers who could afford the luxury dined in the fancy food pavilion on arrack punch and thinly shaved ham.

The path she chose narrowed, and the sounds around her softened to furtive rustling. Here and there, a moan of ecstasy stirred the leaves. Quickening her steps, she made her way deeper into the velvety darkness.

At the hoot of an owl, Charlotte slipped into the bushes and crouched down beside Hawk.

"We circled around the workshop," he reported. "There is a front and a rear entrance, both locked, and it was completely dark inside."

The plan they had made earlier in the day called for her and the Weasels to arrive early so that the boys could keep watch for Wayland and the Frenchmen. Wrexford and Sheffield would travel on their own and meet up with her to await word on when they could move in to confront the conspirators.

"We did see a flutter of movement in the trees behind the place," added Hawk. "But when we went to investigate, there was nothing there."

"People come here on the prowl for adventure," mused Charlotte. "A frisson of excitement, whether good or bad, relieves the tedium of their everyday life."

As A. J. Quill, she had good reason to know that the vast

majority of London's working class lived an existence of quiet desperation. It was why she wielded her pen. To make the world a better place for those who could not fight for themselves—

She made herself shake off the distracting thought. Tonight was about catching a cold-blooded killer and ensuring that the former emperor of France did not profit from the crime. Heaven only knew what misery he would inflict on rich and poor alike if he were able to return to his throne.

"Go back and keep watch with the others. Wrex and Sheffield will arrive shortly, and we'll wait here." She paused for a moment. "And remember, as soon as you alert us that both the Frenchmen and Wayland have arrived, the three of you are to head straight home."

Wrexford and Sheffield paused after purchasing their entrance tickets and passing through the ornate main entrance of Vauxhall Gardens.

"Drunkenness, debauchery, and deceptions," observed Sheffield as he regarded the revelries taking place beneath the flickering lanterns of the main walkway. "Highborn or lowborn, men—and women—find it hard to resist their primal lusts."

"People like to be shocked by things they wouldn't dare think about at home," said the earl. "Danger is like a drug. It stimulates the senses, consigning reason to perdition."

Laughter erupted nearby as a well-dressed gentleman fell into a fountain while trying to dance a jig along its stone edge.

"But the ecstasy is short-lived."

"Abandon all hope, ye who enter here," quipped Sheffield, repeating the famous line from Dante's *Divine Comedy*.

"The poet was right—life often plays out as a farce." After another look around, Wrexford turned for one of the side paths. "We need to go this way."

They were both dressed in dark clothing, with soft felt hats pulled low. Heads down, they cut around the crowd, keeping their pace slow so as not to draw attention. *Drunken laughter, ribald teasing, shrieks of delight*—the air was thick with merriment. But the weight of his pocket pistol brushing against his thigh as he moved reminded Wrexford that their reason for being here was not for pleasure.

"Is all arranged with Griffin and his men?" asked Sheffield, once the way led into a secluded glade of trees.

"It took some convincing," replied the earl. "Along with the promise of several prodigious dinners."

Sheffield chuckled. "He's far worse than I ever was about taking advantage of your largesse."

"It's a small price to pay for working with a fellow who is both trustworthy and extremely skilled at what he does," replied the earl. "He wasn't happy with the fact that we have naught but circumstantial evidence to support our claim of having found Jasper Milton's killer." A shrug. "Which is why he agreed to my proposal of us apprehending Wayland and the French radicals and then handing them over to him. That allows him to take custody of the men in order to investigate my claim that I overheard what sounded like suspicious conspiring. He and his men are waiting at the side gate by Tyre Street."

"You haven't yet failed to make him smell like roses to his superiors," commented Sheffield. "You didn't mention Milton's stolen papers?"

"No," he said. "The papers seem irrelevant to the authorities. It seems to me that their value—if any—is purely scientific. I would rather have experts who understand their significance assess them before deciding what to do with them."

"That seems a logical—"

"Sshhh," warned Wrexford, coming to a halt as voices rose from nearby. But it was merely a drunken couple who giggled again and stumbled off toward the Dark Walk to make their mischief.

They resumed walking and soon heard Charlotte's signal.

"All is well?" asked Wrexford, after slipping through the foliage and meeting her between the trunks of two tall oaks.

"The boys are in place, and the workshop is presently deserted. Hawk will alert us when both parties have gone inside."

"They know—"

"Yes, yes," she said. "Be assured that they understand that they are to head straight back home." A smile. "Or risk having their ginger biscuits cut off for the foreseeable future."

"I would dearly miss Mac's ginger biscuits," mused Sheffield.

Charlotte was about to reply when a tiny flicker of lantern light sparked through the foliage from the pathway leading to the workshop.

They ducked down and waited in silence.

After ten minutes, another flutter of light appeared for an instant before disappearing.

Wrexford drew his weapon and signaled for Sheffield to do the same. Charlotte, he knew, had come unarmed, for he had insisted that she not accompany them inside to confront the conspirators.

A breeze stirred through the branches as Hawk materialized out of the gloom.

"They're all inside, Wrex," he confirmed.

"Excellent." The earl turned to Charlotte. "Remember, you have strict orders. You are to take cover in the bushes once we get closer to the workshop and wait there until we return."

She nodded.

Satisfied, Wrexford led the way back to the path, and they continued on to where Raven and Peregrine were waiting.

"There are two Frenchmen. They arrived first and unlocked the door," reported Raven. "We didn't see any weapons, but they were carrying a valise."

The money, perhaps?

"The fancy fellow you described arrived alone," added Peregrine. "He had nothing in his hands."

"Well done, lads," he whispered. "Now off you go—straight home to Berkeley Square."

Raven hesitated—but only for an instant. His expression, however, indicated how little he liked being dismissed from the action.

However, butting heads over what risks were permitted was a problem for the future, thought Wrexford with an inward sigh. He forced himself to focus on the present moment.

The three boys disappeared with wraithlike stealth, and Charlotte retreated into the foliage to keep watch for any trouble coming down the path.

With a nod at Sheffield, he signaled for them to approach the workshop.

All at once, a momentous *BOOM* shuddered through the gardens, and an instant later the sky filled with a starburst of multicolored sparks.

"The fireworks have started," muttered the earl, pausing to look up. "Right on schedule."

Sheffield winced as another explosion rent the air. And then another.

Wrexford started forward. "Come, let us put an end to this sordid affair."

The iron-banded oak door to the workshop was shut. Slowly easing the latch up, the earl released it without a sound and gave a tentative push to test the hinges. Hearing no hint of a groan, he opened it just enough for him and Sheffield to slip into the windowless anteroom.

The air was musty and redolent with linseed oil and wood shavings. It was dark as Hades, but a crack of light was visible straight ahead, where the door leading into the main room had been left slightly ajar.

Wrexford cocked an ear but heard nothing. He waited a moment longer, then tapped Sheffield's arm and indicated for them to move ahead.

Slowly, slowly.

Still no sound of voices.

Wrexford paused to draw his pistol's hammer to half-cock, then inched forward another step and placed his palm on the rough-grained door.

His flesh began to prickle.

He exerted a touch of pressure, opening the crack just enough to peer into the room.

Charlotte changed her position. And then changed it again. The bright blaze of the fireworks continued to light the sky, the booms softening to a regular rhythm. Close by, all the little noises—the twitter of a nightingale, the ruffling of the leaves, the faint music from the main pavilions—indicated that nothing was amiss. And yet she felt twitchy.

Perhaps, she thought ruefully, her muscles were still in knots from the latest fencing session with Angelo.

A leaf tickled against her cheek, nearly making her jump. She drew in a calming breath . . .

And froze at the snap of a twig.

The sound had come from up ahead. A feral cat foraging for food? Or a more sinister predator?

Squinting into the gloom, Charlotte tried to make out any sign of movement.

Nothing.

Raising a false alarm could put Wrexford and Sheffield at risk. She waited, but all she heard between the booms of the fireworks was the thumping of her heart against her rib cage.

After another minute passed, she cursed herself for a fool and sat back on her haunches, then turned her gaze to the path and resumed her surveillance.

*   *   *

A lantern, half hidden by the legs of a worktable, was set on the floor, its wick turned low so that only a faint aureole of light illuminated the floor. It showed . . .

Holy hell.

Wrexford's breath caught in his throat as he took in the scene. Three bodies lay sprawled on the stone flaggings, their limbs unnaturally still.

A man wearing a black silk mask and holding a smoking pistol in one hand was crouched down beside the corpse nearest the door. "Damnation!" he hissed to his henchman, a muscled brute who had moved to the window to check the surroundings. "Why did the cursed fellows fire at us?"

"Only the devil knows," came the terse reply. The henchman turned back to the room, a last rippling of smoke drifting up from the two pistols clutched in his hands. "But there will be hell to pay with our superiors. There wasn't supposed to be any bloodshed."

The earl pulled back and leaned close to Sheffield's ear. "Wayland and the Frenchmen are dead," he whispered. "There are two assailants. Their weapons appear spent, but Black Mask may still have one loaded." He thought for an instant. "I'll handle the situation. You stay here out of sight—and I bloody well mean that."

"Search the bodies, and be quick about it," urged the henchman. "The fireworks likely covered the sound of the shots, but we can't afford to be caught. We must find those papers."

Before Sheffield could respond, Wrexford slipped back to the doorway and took dead aim at Black Mask as he started to reach for the pocket of Mercer Wayland's once-elegant coat.

"Don't move," warned the earl. "You and your friend have precisely three seconds to toss your weapons over here, else I will put a bullet through your brainbox."

* * *

The breeze freshened, and Charlotte felt another tickling against her flesh. She reached up to brush away the leaf, only to have a gloved hand clamp down over her mouth.

"Mmph!" She struggled to break free, but her captor had seized her from behind, pinning her arms to her sides. In desperation, Charlotte threw back her head, hoping to smash her assailant's nose. But he deftly dodged the attack and tightened his hold.

"*Achtung!* Lady Wrexford, please hold your fire!" whispered a familiar voice. "We've no time to waste."

Charlotte went slack from shock. "*You!*"

"*Ja,* me."

A myriad of questions were whirling in her head as she twisted to face the man who had grabbed her. "You have a great deal of explaining to do, Herr von Münch—or whatever your damn name is."

"Yes, yes, but not now. I fear that your husband and Mr. Sheffield are in grave danger." He drew his pistol and checked the priming. "You must hurry and fetch your Bow Street Runner friend and his men, while I take up a position to reinforce them."

She hesitated. "H-How do I know you're not lying?"

"Because I've never been your enemy." A pause. "There's no time to argue. Please trust me—I, too, wish to scupper the French plans."

Trust. Charlotte had to make a split-second decision. And Wrexford's life might well be teetering in the balance . . .

"Milady?"

She scrambled to her feet and broke into a run.

Black Mask raised his gaze, the lantern catching the malicious gleam flashing from within the silk's eyeholes. He hesitated, then a thump sounded as his pistol hit the floor and skidded across the stones to within inches of Wrexford's boots.

"Now you," said Wrexford, turning his gaze to Black Mask's henchman.

The man tossed his weapons aside.

"Who are you?" demanded the earl.

An amused laugh from Black Mask, who answered with an obscenity.

"Kit," called Wrexford. "Go alert Griffin and his men that we have a pair of murderers to hand over."

"Not a chance that I'm leaving you alone with these bloodthirsty criminals," replied Sheffield, coming to stand beside the earl. "Give the signal for Magpie. He can run and fetch them."

Wrexford hesitated, loath to draw Charlotte into the fray even though it made logical sense.

"Who are you?" he repeated, giving himself a moment to consider the suggestion.

Black Mask let out a grunt and winced. "Might I stand?" he asked, raising his hands in surrender.

"Slowly," said Wrexford after glancing at the henchman. On catching sight of a satchel lying beside one of the other bodies, he added, "Fetch that bag, Kit."

Sheffield moved just as Black Mask straightened from his crouch—and lashed out a kick that shattered the lantern's glass globe and sent it skittering into a pile of wood shavings.

Whoosh! A giant flame shot up, fueled by the spilled oil.

Wrexford shied back, blinded for an instant by the sudden blast of light.

Black Mask kicked over the table, sending an open can of pine spirits into the fire. Smoke billowed up from the burning wood.

Another heavy thud reverberated off the walls.

The earl spotted Sheffield through the wildly flickering light and shadows. The spinning table had knocked him down.

"Kit!" he cried in warning, seeing the henchman draw a knife from his boot.

Sheffield had fumbled his pistol as he fell and was just pushing up to his knees.

The blade flashed as the henchman started forward.

Wrexford pivoted to take aim, but in the same instant, another shot rang out.

A scream ripped free from the henchman's throat as the knife in his hand flew up in the air and spun away to the far corner of the room.

Bloody hell, had Charlotte . . .

As the earl whipped around to spot the unknown shooter, Black Mask and the henchman both bolted for the rear window, where they smashed through the mullions and started to scramble out into the night.

Wrexford turned back in a flash but couldn't bring himself to shoot a fleeing man in the back.

As for going after them . . .

He took a step in pursuit, but a hand caught his sleeve.

"Let them go, milord."

The earl uttered a curse on recognizing the voice.

"They are dangerous men—perhaps more dangerous than you imagine."

Wrexford couldn't help but wonder how Ernst Josef von Münch—who on their first encounter several months ago had claimed to be the personal librarian to the king of Württemberg—appeared to know far more than he did about what was going on.

"They made short work of these three men," continued von Münch. He gestured at the corpses. "One has to assume they are experienced assassins."

The word *assassin* sent a sudden rush of ice through his veins. He knew that von Münch was a crack shot . . .

He grabbed the so-called scholar by the lapels. "Where is my wife?"

"I sent her to alert Mr. Griffin and his men. They should be here shortly." answered von Münch. "But given the circumstances of my previous visit to London and the awkward questions that might arise, it would be best if I'm not here when they arrive."

"What the devil are you doing back here?" demanded Wrexford, grudgingly releasing his hold.

"I, for one, am exceedingly grateful for Herr von Münch's presence," interjected Sheffield, cradling the satchel he had just retrieved. "And for the fact that he's a damnably good shot." He took a peek inside the bag and let out a low whistle. "It looks like the French truly were willing to pay a king's ransom—"

A small sound—a rasp of breath—caused all three of them to turn and then crouch down around Wayland's body. Wrexford leaned in, close enough to feel the faint flutter of breath against his cheek.

"What happened here?"

Wayland was lying face up, a pulse of blood leaking from the bullet hole in his left breast with every fading heartbeat. His eyes were wet with tears as he struggled to form a word.

"A-Axe."

"Do you know who he is?" coaxed the earl.

"He . . . he . . ." Wayland managed to move his hand and tried to lift it to his chest. "He . . ."

A gurgle. And the pulsing went still.

"Bloody hell," intoned Sheffield as von Münch scrambled to his feet and cocked an ear.

Wrexford heard it, too. A shout from Griffin and the thud of boots as he and his men turned from the main walkway onto the side path.

"I must go."

As von Münch turned, the earl responded. "I expect you to show your face at Berkeley Square within the hour."

"With pleasure, milord. After all, nobody else in Town has such a fine selection of German wines."

Wrexford didn't smile as he began searching through Wayland's coat and found a packet of papers. "Be assured that if you don't show up, I will come find you. And the only cork I will be pulling is yours."

CHAPTER 24

"Thank heaven you are all safe!" Cordelia shot up from the sofa as Sheffield followed Wrexford and Charlotte into the earl's workroom. "Baz arrived a short while ago—" Her eyes suddenly narrowed on spotting the burn marks on their coats, prompting a suspicious sniff. "Why do I smell smoke?"

"Because where there's smoke, there's fire," observed Henning after swallowing the last of the whisky in his glass. "And these three always manage to spark Trouble."

McClellan rose from her chair by the sofa to refill his glass.

"We're in no mood for sarcasm, Baz," counseled Charlotte. She pulled off her urchin's hat and tucked a bedraggled lock of hair behind her ear. "It's been a bloody night—in every sense of the word."

"D-Did you not apprehend Wayland and the two Frenchmen and turn them over to Griffin?" asked Cordelia.

"The three of them were dead when we entered the workshop," answered Wrexford. He handed a glass of whisky to both Charlotte and Sheffield before pouring one for himself.

"Speaking of corpses, the reason I am here now is because I

arrived home late last night from Tunbridge Wells to find that Griffin had delivered a body to my mortuary, with orders from Wrex to determine whether the knife used was the same one that killed Milton," said the surgeon. "Why is it that we can't stop stumbling over dead bodies?"

"Ask the Grim Reaper," drawled Wrexford. "The deceased fellow is Kendall Garfield, one of Milton's fellow members of the Revolutions-Per-Minute Society. Were you able to find the answer?"

"As a matter of fact, I was," answered Henning. "Yes, it was the same knife. It has a tiny but distinctive nick in the blade." He swirled the spirits in in his glass. "Why is he dead?"

"Let us leave the gory details for later," said Charlotte. The unexpected twist in the investigation—all their carefully constructed assumptions had been blown to flinders—left her feeling confused and weary to the very marrow of her bones. "What matters most is the fact that all our efforts have simply spun us round and round in a circle."

She let her words sink in. "Leaving us back where we first started, with nary a clue as to who murdered Milton—and now Garfield and Wayland."

"Save for the recent evidence against Oliver," whispered Cordelia. "But surely you can't believe he is guilty. Everything he and the others have told us rings true."

Charlotte sighed. "At this point, I'm not certain of *anything*."

"Save that five men involved in this investigation now lie dead," muttered the earl. "Charlotte is right. It's hard to see what the devil is going on."

"But Oliver can't be guilty of the deaths that happened tonight. Your footmen haven't let him and the others out of their sight," said Cordelia.

Wrexford conceded the point with a nod. "I'm trying my damnedest to find an alternative. I've told Tyler to ask around among his contacts in the criminal world to see if he can uncover any information that might give us another lead to follow."

Sheffield put down the satchel of money beside one of the storage cabinets. "It's a pity that we never got a chance to interrogate Wayland, especially after hearing Wheeler's account of seeing him in the British Museum's study room working on what looked to be technical drawings."

"I was thinking about much the same thing." Wrexford shut the draperies and gave a terse account of what had happened at the rendezvous at Vauxhall Gardens before unwrapping the papers he had found in Wayland's coat and spreading them out on the escritoire.

"Please come have a look at these," he said to Cordelia, "and tell me whether you believe that they are Milton's work papers."

"Y-You think that Wayland created fake documents to pass off as Jasper's calculations?" asked Cordelia.

"Given what Wheeler told Griffin, it seems possible, but I'm not conversant enough in mathematics or engineering to make a judgment," answered the earl. "All I can say for sure is that the two mysterious men sent to retrieve the documents were desperate to get their hands on them."

Charlotte stiffened as a question suddenly reared its head. "Sent by whom?" she said softly.

Wrexford's silence was a tacit admission that he hadn't the foggiest notion of what intrigue-within-intrigue was going on.

Cordelia approached the escritoire. Paper crackled as she smoothed out the creases and subjected the pages to a careful study.

Despite the red-gold flames dancing up from the coals in the hearth, the room seemed to turn darker and colder. Charlotte chafed her hands together, trying to keep her fears at bay.

"This makes no sense." After examining the first few pages,

Cordelia looked up. "There is an error in one of the calculations. Granted, it's an advanced computation, but Jasper would never have made such a blunder."

"Perhaps he was rushing," suggested Sheffield.

"It's not the only mistake." Cordelia frowned in consternation. "But even more important, I simply don't see what the calculations are creating. They seem like meaningless bits and bobs floating over the page, having no relation to the sketches." She shook her head. "But then, I have no expertise in engineering, so I may be totally wrong."

"We need to send word to your cousin and his companions, and ask them to come here right away," said Charlotte. "The three of them are familiar with Milton's work, so let us hope they will have some notion of whether the papers are genuine."

McClellan put aside her sewing box. "I will go wake Raven—"

"I would rather send one of our footmen," she interjected. "Mrs. Guppy is both highly intelligent and highly observant. The less she sees of him, the better. I don't want to encourage further speculation as to how he fits into our household."

Wrexford nodded his agreement.

"I need to change myself into Lady Wrexford for their visit," added Charlotte. "Mac, might you come along and give me a helping hand?"

"I have been thinking," announced Wrexford once the two of them returned to his workroom. "I don't believe Wayland had the ruthlessness to kill Milton and Garfield. My guess is he somehow learned that Garfield was trying to find Milton's papers in order to sell them to the French and decided to create a false set of sketches in order to preempt his fellow society member. He must have thought that he knew enough about Milton's work to fool Montaigne and his radical friend."

"That's plausible," agreed Cordelia.

"Perhaps von Münch will be able to shed some light on what

is going on." Wrexford's brows drew together in a scowl. "Assuming he wasn't lying about meeting us here."

A noise from nearby—a light-footed shuffle—stirred a sudden foreboding.

"Oh, ye of little faith," called a voice from the adjoining library, and in another instant von Münch appeared in the doorway.

Wrexford decided not to inquire as to how the fellow had gained access to the townhouse.

"I may have misled you on several occasions," continued von Münch, as he entered the workroom. "But I was always your ally, not your enemy. Granted, circumstances demanded some sleight of tongue, but there was never any intent of malice or deceit."

"No intent of deceit?" Henning let out a snort. "Read any good books lately, Herr Librarian?" he asked with undisguised sarcasm. "Perhaps you could recommend a Germanic horror novel, complete with dark secrets, duplicitous scholars, and skulking villains."

"Oh, but you English are far more imaginative than we are when it comes to composing such dramatic and entertaining stories," replied von Münch.

"Ha!" muttered the earl.

"Enough needling, everyone." Charlotte sat down rather heavily in one of the armchairs by the hearth.

A look of contrition clouded von Münch's gaze. "My apologies, milady. Humor often helps to defuse a confrontation, but I do not mean to make light of the fraught situation." He glanced at Cordelia. "I am aware that Mr. Milton's murder has touched you and your friends personally."

"Since you claim to be our ally, why don't you start being truthful with us?" said Wrexford. "Beginning with your real identity and why you are back in London."

"Actually, my name really is Ernst Josef von Münch." A smile. "My father also happens to bear the same name. It is *he*, not I, who is a renowned scholar and holds the position of personal librarian to King Frederick of Württemberg."

"Why the masquerade?" asked Charlotte.

"There are times when a research trip would prove too grueling for my father," replied von Münch. "So I occasionally serve as his representative."

A rather amorphous answer, reflected Wrexford. But then, he imagined that the words had been chosen with deliberate care.

"Exactly what sort of research do you do for him?" asked Charlotte.

"That depends."

"Might you be more specific?" she pressed.

Clasping his hands together behind his back, von Münch turned to regard the crackling coals. Sparks flared as a chunk crumbled to ash, setting off a hiss of smoke.

"Let us just say that my father and I head up an informal council to advise Crown Prince William on the international issues that may affect our tiny country."

"One would expect King Frederick to handle such affairs of state, not his son," observed Wrexford.

"Prince William considers it his responsibility to understand the complexities of such things. His father has . . . other interests."

"Like eating, drinking, and indulging in any debauchery that tickles his fancy?" suggested the earl.

"The king wholeheartedly embraces the pursuit of pleasure. And according to his physician, that is cause for concern."

Wrexford considered what he had just heard. "Is the prince attending the Peace Conference in Vienna?"

"He is, milord," answered von Münch. "Our delegation has little actual clout, but a number of the senior diplomats respect Prince William's opinions—as well as the fact that he often knows more than they do about the intrigues going on between the major powers."

"I take it that very few people in Vienna, including your own delegation, would be happy to hear that Napoleon might be contemplating a return to the fray?" Wrexford continued.

"Correct," said von Münch. "That is why Prince William asked me to return to London, as we've heard rumors about such a possibility."

"Then it would seem," interjected Charlotte, "that we are once again aligned on the same side."

"I would hope so, milady."

Trust. Aware of what a slippery concept it was, Wrexford took several moments to parse through all the nuances of what had—and had not—been said. "Then I shall lay our cards on the table," he announced abruptly. "And expect you to do the same."

A solemn bow. "You have my word on it, milord."

"We have reason to believe that Milton meant to give his innovation for bridge building to the French radicals," explained the earl, "who in turn intended to sell it to the tsar of Russia for a king's ransom. The radicals then planned to use the money to help fund Napoleon's escape from Elba so that he might rally France around him and return to the throne."

"I feared as much," muttered von Münch. "How did you uncover all this information?"

Wrexford quickly launched into the full explanation. *The confrontations with Garfield and Wayland . . . the suspicions about Mademoiselle Benoit . . . the surveillance which led them to Mrs. Guppy . . . Carrick's eyewitness account of the murder . . .*

"Ye gods, it is truly a plot worthy of a horror novel," murmured von Münch.

"Alas, the threat is all too real," responded Charlotte. "There are still some missing pieces to the puzzle. And several clues that just don't seem to fit in, no matter how we try to find a place for them."

"Perhaps I can be of help in solving some of those conundrums," said von Münch after hitching an apologetic shrug. "To begin with, I was the intruder in your manor house on the night before the wedding—"

Cordelia uttered a very unladylike oath.

"You have every right to be angry, Mrs. Sheffield. But I had reason to think that Milton had sent you his papers for safekeeping. I had searched his quarters earlier that week—very carefully, I might add. But apparently so did someone else who was far less skilled. And so Milton was suspicious and became even more secretive about his work. When I bribed the local postmistress, I learned that he had sent you a package."

"It was merely a letter telling me he was worried that someone was trying to steal his new discovery," replied Cordelia. "And you need not bother asking me what it was. I have no idea, other than it's some sort of revolutionary innovation for building bridges."

"I still cannot fathom how a single innovation can revolutionize a structure that has been around since time immemorial," mused Sheffield.

"An excellent observation," conceded von Münch. "I have no answer for you."

"Perhaps Oliver can give us an explanation," suggested Cordelia. "The whole reason he and Jasper founded the Revolutions-Per-Minute Society was because they had a vision for changing the age-old ways of moving people and goods from place to place."

"Innovation in transportation is moving with frightening speed," observed Charlotte. "Only look at all the momentous changes we have seen in the space of a few short years. Hedley's Puffing Billy, which runs on roads made of steel rails, boats powered by steam-driven propellers . . . why, people are even beginning to talk of how to control the flight of balloons and travel through the air!"

The import of what she had just said made her stop and think. "Our world is changing right before our eyes in ways that would seem inconceivable to our forebearers." A sigh. "It frightens many people."

Wrexford picked up a pencil and rolled it between his palms. "As was said in one of the tales from *The Arabian Nights' Entertainment*, once a djinn is let out of a bottle, it is impossible to put it back and replace the cork. But disagreement over whether something new is good or evil is often the catalyst for Progress."

A thoughtful silence settled over the room. Cordelia closed her eyes and nestled closer to Sheffield. Henning rose and poured himself another glass of whisky.

"Speaking of corks, milord," murmured von Münch. "Might my appearance here, just as I promised, merit uncorking one of your fine German wines?"

"I suppose you have earned it," replied Wrexford, though he wasn't convinced that von Münch had been entirely truthful with them. He paid a quick visit to his wine cellar and returned with a superb bottle from the Rheingau.

After imbibing a glass, von Münch cleared up the confusion as to several of the other incidents that had puzzled Wrex and Charlotte.

"I confess, I was also the man who threw the rock at Raven and Hawk with the note written half in French. As I mentioned earlier, I suspected the French were up to no good, and knowing your skills in solving complicated mysteries, I wished to point your attention to the French scientific delegation in hopes that you would ferret out any suspicious activity among its members."

Wrexford acknowledged the admission with a gruff nod. He also surmised that von Münch had been Charlotte's guardian angel on the night she had been attacked in the alleyway, but he refrained from asking. He suspected that their friend was observant enough to have guessed that she was one of the urchins who had participated in their previous investigation. Whether von Münch had also figured out her other persona—

His brooding was suddenly interrupted as Riche, their normally unflappable butler, threw open the door without knocking.

"Forgive me, milord, but Mr. Griffin is at the front entrance and has a carriage waiting. He says that he needs for you to come with him. It is a matter of great urgency."

CHAPTER 25

Wrexford swore under his breath but felt compelled to oblige. Griffin was not one for histrionics. "Given the lateness of the hour and all that has happened, I suggest that you send word to Carrick and his friends and delay our meeting," he said to Charlotte. "I have no idea when I might return."

"Kit, you and Cordelia should go home and get some sleep," she responded. "I shall summon you as soon as Wrex returns."

"Is there anything I can do for you?" offered von Münch.

"*Nein*," answered Wrexford. "You, too, should seek some rest. *Schlafen Sie wohl.*"

"I didn't know you spoke German, milord."

"There is a great deal that you don't know about me," replied the earl.

"Some men might interpret that as a threat," murmured von Münch.

Wrexford opened his pistol case. "But only if they were up to no good."

"Ah." A smile. "Then I shall sleep with a clear conscience."

He stepped back, losing himself in the shadows of the work-room.

"I assume you'll soon be serving breakfast . . ." Still slouched in his chair, Henning patted back a prodigious yawn. "So if you don't mind, I shall trespass on your hospitality and spend the night here."

"Suit yourself." The earl was already reloading his weapon while Charlotte brushed the worst of the dust from his over-coat.

He caught her hand and brushed a quick kiss to her knuckles.

"Be careful," she whispered.

Their eyes met. "Always."

Wrexford broke away and hurried down to the entrance hall, where Griffin was pacing like a caged lion.

"What the devil is going on?" demanded the earl.

"You'll see soon enough." The Runner led the way out to the carriage and climbed in without further explanation.

The earl found Griffin's silence unsettling. Their first en-counter had been adversarial, but mutual suspicion had softened to a grudging partnership, and now, after working together on a number of investigations involving murder, he considered the Runner a friend.

"Given our cooperation in the past, I would have thought that I merited some sort of response to my question," he said quietly.

"I could say the same to you, milord." In the flicker of the carriage lamp, Wrexford saw an injured look flit over Griffin's features. "Please don't insult my intelligence by claiming you didn't see the letters written in blood by Kendall Garfield's corpse. And yet you said nothing to me about them when you arranged for me and my men to apprehend the supposed mur-derer of Jasper Milton earlier this evening at Vauxhall Gar-dens."

"You have good reason to be upset with me, but rest assured

that my reticence was not due to lack of trust." Wrexford decided to leave further explanations until later. "I don't believe that Oliver Carrick is the culprit."

"That is not for you to decide, milord. You are an earl, not the Almighty."

Wrexford felt a stab of guilt, knowing that Griffin's rebuke was absolutely correct. And yet . . . Carrick deserved a fair trial if arrested for the crime. And he had grave doubts as to whether the authorities would follow the letter of the law.

So yes, he thought, *perhaps I am playing God. But my conscience can live with that, at least for the moment.*

The clatter of the wheels took on a different sound as they turned off the cobbled street and made their way down a side road to a stone pier at the river's edge.

A wherry was waiting for them.

"Are we returning to Vauxhall Gardens?" he asked.

Griffin shook his head in reply.

Wrexford lapsed back into a stoic silence as two grim-faced boatmen rowed them across to the south bank.

The tide was low, and the cloying smell of decay hung heavy in the air. A fitful breeze stirred through the dark trees lining the bank, setting off a brittle rustling of the autumn leaves, which would soon be falling to join the elemental cycle of birth and death.

The essence of Life was actually frightfully simple, mused the earl, *despite all the myriad complexities that we mortals create for ourselves.*

The wherry picked its way through the narrow channel in the oozing mud flats and bumped up against a crude stone landing.

"This way," said Griffin, leading the way to a footpath that led into a glade of trees.

"Christ Almighty," growled Wrexford when a man stepped out of the gloom and raised his lantern to illuminate his face.

"Don't blaspheme, milord."

"Forgive me if I prefer not to take any chiding on morality from you," retorted the earl.

A humorless laugh. "Neither of us is as pure as the driven snow."

"Perhaps not. But at least my intentions are always honorable." Wrexford had encountered George Pierson, the top operative for the minister of state security, on several previous occasions and was of the opinion that the fellow had oil of vitriol running through his veins rather than blood.

"So you say." Pierson gestured for Griffin to retreat and wait back at the wherry, then angled the light to a spot in the small clearing where a dark tarp was carelessly draped over three corpses. "We've brought the victims of tonight's shooting here to keep the public from getting wind of what happened." He moved to it and lifted up a corner of the covering to reveal a blood-smeared face.

"Do you recognize this man?"

Wrex considered lying but decided it would only be to spite Pierson—and that was not a worthy reason. "Yes. He's a French radical."

Pierson scowled. "Do you know why he's here in London?"

"Ostensibly to foment unrest among our workers and make trouble for our government while the Peace Conference in Vienna is taking place," answered the earl. "But I believe his main reason was to convince Jasper Milton to give his bridge innovation to him and his cohorts, so that they could sell it to Russia and use the money to fund Napoleon's escape from Elba."

A gleam of surprise—which quickly turned to ire—sparked in the operative's eyes. "How in the name of Satan did you learn that?"

"Because, as you well know, my network of informants is a good deal more capable than yours."

Pierson took a step closer to the earl. "Have a care, Wrexford. You are treading dangerously close to the line separating cleverness and treason."

"Are you accusing me of treason?"

The air seemed to spark with unseen electricity. The earl was aware of a fire-sharp prickling against his cheeks.

Pierson stepped closer, then surrendered his pent-up breath in a brusque sigh. "I would rather not," he admitted. "The government is dealing with a grave threat to the security of our nation. So I would hope to have your voluntary cooperation without resorting to schoolboy threats and name-calling."

"What threat demands indiscriminate slaughter?" asked the earl, pointing to the two other victims lying under the tarp. "Why kill Wayland and Monsieur Montaigne of the French scientific society—I'm assuming it was your men who committed the murders—along with the French radical? They merited arrest, but not execution without a trial."

"My men were there simply to apprehend the three conspirators. But one of them fired first, and my men had to defend themselves. Unfortunately, they are excellent shots."

"And yet I saw no pistols around the bodies when I searched the three dead men for the papers," said Wrexford.

"My men told me they were fired upon," insisted Pierson. "And they understand that there are serious repercussions for lying to me."

Which, noted Wrexford, was not at all an answer to his observation.

When he didn't reply, Pierson added, "Regardless of your low opinion of my morals, I don't kill for no reason." He looked down at the dead bodies, throwing his face into shadow. "My men didn't recognize you or Mr. Sheffield, so the fact that you were threatened with a knife was a mistake. In their defense, they were told that retrieving the papers was of utmost importance."

"I would rather have a full explanation of the government's interest in Jasper Milton's papers than an apology."

"You are welcome to ask Lord Grentham for one. Perhaps he will humor you," replied Pierson.

"Ha!" The earl made a rude sound. "And perhaps pigs will sprout wings and fly."

Pierson allowed himself a faint smile. "I'm not sure which is more likely." He bent down to flick the tarp back over the dead man's face. "Let us return to more pragmatic questions. Since you said that you searched the bodies for the papers, I assume it was you who took them away."

"It was," answered Wrexford.

"I must insist that you give them to me."

"They are useless," said the earl. "Wayland was desperate. His gaming debts were threatening to ruin him, and when he learned that the French radicals would pay a large sum for Milton's work, he seized the opportunity to create a false set of work papers."

Pierson contemplated the earl's statement for several moments. "You are absolutely sure of this?"

"The papers are false," repeated Wrexford.

"Damnation." Pierson kicked at a clot of mud. "I need to get my hands on Oliver Carrick, who clearly lies at the heart of all this." He looked up. "Given the skills of your spies, can you tell his present whereabouts?"

"I don't possess that information." It wasn't precisely a lie. He didn't know which house on Conduit Street had been rented by Mrs. Guppy.

"If you learn anything—*anything*—about this affair, send word to me through Griffin." He clasped his gloved hands together with a muffled slap. "This is a highly sensitive government matter, milord, not a parlor game to keep you amused."

Wrexford hesitated. A part of him longed to hand over the investigation to the official authorities and be done with murder and intrigue. But he couldn't bring himself to do so. The minister of state security and his minions would not hesitate to do whatever was necessary in order to protect the government—whether it be from actual threats or mere embarrassment.

He glanced at the corpses lying beneath the tarp. Including quietly disposing of those they deemed guilty—and that likely would include Oliver Carrick—without a public trial.

However, he believed that the rule of law applied to everyone, even the most heinous criminals.

"I assure you, Pierson, murder and betrayal are not a game to me." He glanced up at the sky, where the first pale flickers of dawn had given way to morning sunlight.

"Now, if we are done here. I would like to return home for my breakfast."

"You need to take some nourishment." McClellan joined Charlotte by the arched windows of the breakfast room as dawn gave way to early morning. "One never thinks well on an empty stomach."

"Hear, hear." Henning swallowed a mouthful of broiled kidney and washed it down with a slurp of coffee. "Lud, if Mac ran my kitchen, I would soon be a genius."

The Weasels chortled over the comment as they helped themselves to fresh-baked muffins.

Charlotte forced a smile in spite of the dark thoughts that were tumbling and tangling inside her head. But the flash of humor couldn't keep her brooding at bay. It seemed as if the more they learned, the less the facts made any sense. None of the pieces of the puzzle seemed to fit together.

"Toast would be welcome, Mac, along with a dish of apricot jam," she conceded. "And coffee—a pot of it, if you please."

"And you may bring tea for me." The *tap-tap* of her cane in the corridor announced the imminent arrival of the dowager.

"Here I go away for a visit to my friend in Kent for a short while, only to discover on my return last night that you are up to your neck in skullduggery."

"Guilty as charged." Given Alison's awareness of Milton's murder, Charlotte had felt obliged to send a note to the dowager's residence updating her on the progress of the investigation.

Alison took a seat at the table. "Now that I am back, how can I help?"

"I'm not sure." Charlotte gave a nod of thanks to McClellan for bringing the coffee and poured herself a cup. "We now have a key clue, which could help us solve the murder. We know that the killer was a friend called 'Axe' by Milton, but we can't seem to make any progress in discovering his real identity."

Alison frowned. "Axe?"

Charlotte dutifully explained—with much help from the Weasels—about finding Oliver Carrick and learning what he had seen and heard at the scene of the murder.

"Hmmph." Looking thoughtful, the dowager buttered half a muffin.

"It's imperative to locate Axe, because we have found another piece of circumstantial evidence that points to Oliver Carrick as the murderer." She told the dowager about the marks found beside Garfield's dead body.

"There is much else to tell," she added. But before she could begin, Cordelia hurried into the room, accompanied by her cousin.

"I've just shown Oliver the papers that Wrex retrieved last night!" she announced.

"They were definitely created by Mercer Wayland. I know his handwriting, so I'm sure of it," said Carrick. "Furthermore, Cordelia was correct in saying that Jasper would never have made the mistakes that appear in some of the equations."

He paused. "But as for the actual mathematics, that's a more complicated situation."

"I told Oliver that Wayland mentioned having had a peek at Jasper's scribbling book," said Cordelia.

"Yes." Carrick brushed back an unruly lock of hair from his brow. "And I think that Wayland may have actually provided us with a clue pointing to Jasper's ultimate discovery. I recognized certain elements . . ."

His voice betrayed a note of rising excitement. "It's an area of mathematics called the 'calculus of variations,' first developed in the last century by the great Swiss mathematician Leonhard Euler and the Italian-born Frenchman Joseph-Louis Lagrange."

"The calculus of variations?" murmured Alison. She made a face. "You might as well be speaking Greek or Hindi."

"I know, I know," said Carrick. "But trust me, it offers a wealth of exciting new possibilities for understanding how our physical world works!"

"We're just beginning to understand how mathematics can be used to create models of natural processes and then applied to science, engineering, mechanics, and the like," explained Cordelia. "These applications include practical problems such as how to design longer, stronger, and safer bridges. For example, the calculus of variations can be used to analyze the distribution of weight loads throughout a bridge and to establish the center of its mass. It can also show how a bridge should be expected to respond to vibrations from wind, traffic, and the stress imposed by its own cables and towers."

"In formulating the calculus of variations, Euler and Lagrange further developed the work of Sir Isaac Newton and the German polymath Gottfried Leibniz, who had invented calculus a century earlier," interjected Carrick. "At the heart of the calculus of variations is something called the Euler–Lagrange equation. A current mathematician—a woman by the name of

Marie-Sophie Germain—has used some of these techniques of the calculus of variations to develop more advanced mathematical models for the issue of vibrations and how they affect structures like bridges—"

"Oliver, let us not overwhelm our friends with such advanced mathematical concepts." Cordelia made a face. "Indeed, I confess that I don't entirely understand the calculus of variations and its ramifications. We need to do more study on it."

"Cordelia is going to borrow some rare mathematical books from a friend of hers at the Royal Institution and bring them back here," said her cousin. "Then we will set to work with Mrs. Guppy and Mademoiselle Benoit to see if we can figure out if I am right in assuming Milton's innovation centers around the calculus of variations."

"Let us hope that is so," murmured Charlotte.

"I am going back to the earl's workroom and will get started," said Carrick, waving off McClellan's offer of breakfast.

Cordelia waited for her cousin to leave the room before turning to a different topic. "While we work on the mathematics, Kit is going to concentrate on discovering the identity of Axe. He has some meetings today with several of the supervisors overseeing the Bristol Road Project, as they are in Town for the transportation conference," she said. "He's also going to make some inquiries regarding the most talented bridge engineers in the area and see if any of them has a connection to Jasper Milton."

"And I will take a careful look through *Debrett's Peerage* for any clue to the identity of Axe," said the dowager. "A mother's maiden name, an image on a coat of arms—there's a wealth of important information within its pages if one knows what to look for."

"I've already done that, having learned from you during previous investigations how much that book can reveal," replied Charlotte. "Alas, no luck."

Raven put down his fork. "What can I do to help?" he said to Cordelia.

"Alas, sweeting, Cordelia may be able to swear her cousin to secrecy, but Mrs. Guppy and Mademoiselle Benoit have seen you as a ragged urchin," said Charlotte. "Were they to learn that you are our ward, it might raise awkward questions—"

"And put our family secrets in danger," finished Raven. Disappointment rippled in his eyes, but he nodded in understanding. "Oiy, I'll be careful to keep out of sight."

"We all will," piped up Hawk.

"Actually, there is something you can do without putting the family at risk," offered Cordelia. "You can gather all the mathematical books in Wrex's library, especially the ones on Leonhard Euler's work, and stack them on one of the worktables for me to fetch when I return from the Royal Institution."

Charlotte gave her friend a grateful smile. "And I had better go and compose my next satirical drawing for Mr. Fores." The previous night's discussion with von Münch had sparked an idea, though it might be a dangerous one. She needed to think it over.

The quiet solitude of her workroom was a welcome respite from the turmoil of the last few days. Charlotte went through the comforting ritual of sharpening her pencils and pens, uncapping her inkwell and selecting a fresh sheet of paper to begin her preliminary sketching.

As always, she closed her eyes for an instant and finished her preparations with a whispered thanks to Hephaestus, the god of art and creativity for both the ancient Greeks and Romans. It was a habit she had formed while living in Rome, a city in which even the smallest sun-bleached stone seemed to thrum with a silent ode to the imagination.

"Perhaps I'm mad," whispered Charlotte. But the moment her pencil point touched the paper and began to move in concert with her thoughts, she felt all her uncertainties unknot and float away.

A. J. Quill was fearless.

Caught up in the rhythm of mind and body at work, she lost track of time. One sketch finished, she moved on to a second idea and then sat back to scrutinize the results.

As her gaze shifted to the first one, Charlotte gave an involuntary gasp. It wasn't often that she could take herself by surprise. The image was powerful—perhaps too powerful.

"A. J. Quill is bold, but not reckless," she told herself. And this particular drawing would stir up a maelstrom within the highest circles of government.

It depicted a massive arched bridge, one thin end planted on the tiny island of Elba and the other widening as it curved and came to rest in the heart of France. Straddling the top of the curve, as if he was riding his war horse, was Napoleon Bonaparte in full battle dress. Charlotte could already envision the title—*A Bridge to the Future?*

She stared at it for a moment longer, then pushed it aside. The second sketch was safer, though it still raised important questions that would no doubt capture the public's attention.

They trust me to tell them about issues that affect their lives.

The drawing was based on the same bridge theme. But this one showed an arched bridge with one end anchored in London and other coming to rest in the industrial city of Manchester. Rather than a single famous figure, it showed a crowd of working-class men and women trudging across its span.

"*A Bridge to Freedom,*" she mused, thinking aloud about a possible title. The captions would discuss the preachings of the French radicals, who claimed that cheap and reliable transportation would give workers a modicum of power by allowing them to seek better wages in other areas of the country if their local employers refused to pay them fairly for their labors.

A part of her yearned to publish the Napoleon print. If war

erupted in Europe again, it would affect millions of lives. But she knew in her heart that she didn't know enough about the situation to make such a risky decision.

"Which one do you intend to submit to Fores?"

Charlotte turned around to face Wrexford, who had entered her workroom without making a sound. "I don't really have a choice. One of them is too reckless, and I know it."

He came to sit on the arm of her chair and brushed a quick caress to her cheek.

A fleeting touch, and yet it lifted her spirits.

"It may feel like we are struggling right now to beat Evil. But we have faced the devil before," he said softly, "and pitched him back into the fires of Hell."

"Amen to that," she murmured as he tucked an errant curl behind her ear.

It was strange how the little everyday gestures were a source of courage to face the unknown threat.

Love, friendship . . . they were far stronger than fear.

"What did Griffin want?" asked Charlotte, after reaching for his hand and twining her fingers with his.

"He took me to a secluded spot across the river to meet with George Pierson, who wanted to have a chat about what happened at Vauxhall Gardens. He's been ordered to find Milton's papers."

"By Lord Grentham, I assume," responded Charlotte. Merely saying the man's name made her skin prickle. They had crossed paths with the minions of Britain's shadowy minister of state security in the past. She didn't relish the idea of getting involved in another encounter.

"But why?" she added.

"I asked Pierson the same question. He did not deign to give me an answer," replied Wrexford. "That's no surprise, of course, but he did offer an explanation of why Wayland and the

Frenchmen were shot dead." A frown. "However, based on the evidence I saw, it can't be true."

His expression turned troubled. "I saw no weapons around the bodies of the three victims. And yet Pierson claimed that his men told him that they did not fire the first shot but responded in self-defense."

"My sense is that Pierson's position as Grentham's top operative requires him to lie without compunction," observed Charlotte.

That's true," agreed the earl. "However, why bother? He had no reason to lie to me. He could simply have said that matters of state security demanded the elimination of the two Frenchmen, and that Wayland was guilty of conspiring with the enemy, so deserved his fate."

Charlotte considered his point and had to agree with him. Pierson was pragmatic. Wrexford had proved helpful to the government in the past, so spinning pointless faradiddles risked alienating a useful ally.

"So, there was one party made up of Wayland and his two French contacts, and a second party made up of the two government operatives," she mused. "Are you thinking that a third party was present and deliberately instigated the mayhem?"

"It seems the only logical explanation," said Wrexford.

"I can't see how that would play to anyone's advantage," she said. "Indeed, if the object was to steal Milton's papers, the strategy was absurdly risky—"

"But what if the third party knew that the papers were false?" interrupted Wrexford, "and used the mayhem to eliminate Wayland?"

An involuntary gasp slipped free as she grasped his meaning. "Axe!" Charlotte steadied her voice. "You think Milton's killer was afraid that Wayland might remember something that would lead him to realize Axe's identity?"

"Perhaps," replied the earl. "Garfield was murdered, and

now Wayland has also been killed. To call it mere coincidence sticks in my craw."

He absently picked up one of her pencils and slowly twirled it between his palms. "I think I should pay a visit to Ezra Wheeler to inform him of what has happened. If I were he, I would come to the conclusion that London is a decidedly unhealthy place for a member of the Revolutions-Per-Minute Society to be until a cunning murderer is caught."

CHAPTER 26

Wrexford had just crossed through the central garden of Berkeley Square and turned down Hay Hill, intent on paying a visit to the Royal Institution, when a figure emerged from the shadows and fell in step beside him.

"I have learned some new information concerning the murder of Jasper Milton, milord," said von Münch. "But I don't think you're going to like it."

'There's a great deal I don't like about this investigation," replied the earl. "But the quest for the truth doesn't allow us to pick and choose." They walked on and turned left onto Dover Street. "Go ahead and say what you have to say."

"Very well." Yet von Münch hesitated a moment longer before going on. "Have you considered that your government might be involved?"

Wrexford gave a mirthless laugh. "Actually, I'm several steps ahead of you on that discovery. I was summoned to meet with Lord Grentham's top operative earlier today." A pause. "I'm surprised you didn't come along and eavesdrop."

"Grentham," mused von Münch, ignoring the earl's sarcasm. "He is not a man with whom to trifle."

"I'm well aware of that," said the earl. "What's your point?"

"I simply wish to reiterate that the movement of raw materials and manufactured goods has huge economic implications, both locally and globally," answered von Münch. "Any country possessing a way to increase its share of the market would naturally be loath to share that method with its competitors."

"Ideas and innovations are not like some exotic djinn that can be kept corked in a bottle," pointed out Wrexford. "Patents are issued, allowing inventors to sell their discoveries to those willing to pay a licensing fee. Technology is shared—"

"Yes, but there are certain innovations that governments try very hard to keep as proprietary information. Military weapons, for example," interjected von Münch. "Things that will alter the balance of economic power are also of grave concern, especially for Britain, as trade is the lifeblood of its global empire."

He looked around before continuing. "His duties to king and country require Grentham to think in terms of black and white, rather than subtle shades of grey. Which is to say, be careful, milord. For whatever reason, it's my sense that the members of your government have decided that it is in their best interests for Milton's innovation to be a secret known only to Britain."

"Assuming that we find the cursed innovation," muttered Wrexford. "But thank you for the warning. I am not so naïve as to think my title or position in Society will protect me if Grentham believes that I am a threat to the greater good of the nation."

"Then I have said enough." After touching the brim of his hat in silent salute, von Münch slipped away through a narrow gap between the buildings without further ado.

Charlotte put the finishing color highlights on her satirical drawing and rolled it in a length of protective oilskin. Raven would deliver it once darkness settled over the city.

Realizing that she hadn't had a bite to eat since breakfast, she quickly cleaned her brushes and made her way down to the kitchen, where the ambrosial scent of baking biscuits perfumed the air with a sugary sweetness.

"I hope those aren't all promised to the Weasels," called Charlotte, knowing the boys would soon be done with their lessons.

McClellan poked her head out from one of the pantries. "I think they can be convinced to share." She emerged carrying a sack of flour, her face ghostly pale from a dusting of its contents. "However, you need more sustenance than ginger biscuits. I'll fix you a collation of fresh bread and roast beef."

Charlotte poured herself a cup of coffee from the pot on the hob and added a splash of cream while the maid prepared a plate of food.

"Ah, here you are." Cordelia entered the kitchen area several minutes later and paused for an appreciative sniff. "Lud, that smells divine. Might I take a plate of those marvelous biscuits back to mademoiselle and Oliver? They refused to interrupt their work to come with me for some refreshments."

"Solving a murder takes precedence over hungry Weasels," replied McClellan with a smile. "You may take these, and I will bake a second batch for the boys." She cut off several extra slices of roast beef and made up a second plate. "Sit and join m'lady in having some proper food. I'll bring a tray of hearty fare up to the others shortly, along with the biscuits."

"Bless you." Cordelia took a seat at the center table after helping herself to a mug of coffee.

"How is the work going?" asked Charlotte after sitting down beside her.

"It's actually fascinating! Mathematics never ceases to amaze and delight me. It explains so much about our world and how it works," replied Cordelia. "I have just been reading about some of the mathematics relevant to bridge design. There is very interesting work being done on how to model the ability of a surface to return to its original form after experiencing vibration or other effects of stress. And that may prove very important in determining the structural stability of a bridge."

"Good heavens, what causes something as large as a bridge to vibrate?" exclaimed McClellan.

"Wind," answered Cordelia. "Or, even more importantly, the type of traffic moving over it. There was an incident on the Continent where a bridge collapsed when an army was crossing it on foot. Some mathematicians think that it was because the soldiers were marching in lockstep to their drummer, which created a destructive level of vibration."

"And you are saying that mathematics can help avoid such calamities?" said Charlotte.

"It may be difficult to comprehend how abstract theory can have such momentous practical applications. But as Oliver indicated earlier, he suspects that Jasper Milton was working with the calculus of variations, and he thinks there is reason to believe that such mathematics would be well suited to predicting which designs would minimize the stresses that seem to cause these disasters."

Cordelia drew in a deep breath. "So to answer your question, yes—Jasper may indeed have discovered the key to revolutionizing bridge building, allowing a structure to be both longer and safer."

After taking a bite of her bread, she frowned in thought as she swallowed. "But let us put abstractions aside for the moment. Mademoiselle Benoit told me something very odd just now."

"Oh?" Charlotte put down her cup.

"I was pressing her and Oliver about Jasper's stay in Paris," continued Cordelia. "I asked them to think hard about any conversations they might have overheard between Jasper and the radicals, and to try to recall whether there was anything unusual or unexpected that might give us a clue as to Jasper's murder."

She swirled the coffee in her cup. "At first, they insisted that there was nothing. But then mademoiselle allowed that she had heard Jasper mention 'Eton' several times during a clandestine conversation with Montaigne."

"Eton?" repeated Charlotte. "You mean the elite school for aristocratic boys?"

"Yes," answered Cordelia.

Charlotte pondered the revelation, trying to make some sense of it. "You mentioned that Jasper Milton was tutored at home before attending Cambridge, so he wasn't a student at Eton."

Which begs the question . . .

"So what's the connection?"

"None that I can see," admitted Cordelia. "But you and Wrex have taught me not to overlook any tiny detail, no matter how irrelevant it might seem. Because sometimes looking at it from a different perspective shows that in fact it's the key to solving the whole mystery."

Charlotte shook her head in puzzlement. "I can't see—"

A small cough interrupted her. She turned to see Peregrine standing in the shadows. "I did not mean to eavesdrop, m'lady. Raven and Hawk sent me down to see if the ginger biscuits were ready, while they helped Mr. Lynsley roll up the maps we used for our geography lesson."

"Fly back in a quarter hour, Falcon," called McClellan as she removed a baking pan from the oven. "The first batch is promised elsewhere."

Peregrine nodded but made no move to leave.

"Is something troubling you, sweeting?" coaxed Charlotte.

"Umm . . . well, since I heard you mention Eton . . . and since Mrs. Sheffield just pointed out that we shouldn't over-look any detail, however unimportant it may appear . . ."

He cleared his throat with another cough. "I think I ought to tell you about something that struck me as very havey-cavey at the school just before I was expelled."

Wrexford paused at the main entrance of St. Paul's Cathedral to look up at the majestic steepled bell towers that framed the columned portico and upper colonnade. Though he had visited Sir Christopher Wren's architectural masterpiece countless times—the nation held many ceremonies for both its triumphs and tragedies here—he never ceased to be awed by the imposing grandeur of the London landmark.

It was not only a work of art but an engineering marvel.

Which was why he was here. One of the porters at the Royal Institution had informed him that Ezra Wheeler was among the half dozen conference attendees invited for a special tour of the magnificent dome, the largest in the world.

Dropping his gaze from the Corinthian columns, Wrexford hurried up the stone steps and passed into the nave, then made his way to the stairwell leading up to the dome—a journey of 528 steps, as he had learned from his father on his first visit to the cathedral.

On reaching the Whispering Gallery, the first of the three viewing areas, he spotted one of the Royal Institution officials who had arranged the tour.

"Hopkins, can you kindly tell me where I might find Ezra Wheeler?" he inquired.

"I believe he's gone all the way up to the Golden Gallery, milord."

"Many thanks."

"Enjoy the view, sir!" called Hopkins as Wrexford hurried away. The cathedral was built on Ludgate Hill, the highest point of London, and the outer walkway at the very top of the dome offered a spectacular panorama of the sprawling city and the River Thames.

A gust of wind ruffled his coat as Wrexford ducked through the opening leading to the narrow ironwork ring that ran around the base of the spire. The walkway was deserted save for a single figure who was standing with his back half-turned as he gazed up at the *tempietto*—a crowning design made of four columned porticos facing the cardinal points of the compass.

"Mr. Wheeler?"

The man turned. "Yes?"

"It seems that designing bridges is a more perilous profession than one might imagine," commented Wrexford, on seeing Wheeler's right arm was in a sling and his hand was heavily bandaged.

"Any designer worth his salt often wields a hammer and chisel during the construction process, sir. It's imperative to understand the materials used, and how they react to stress."

"As someone who is also involved in scientific pursuits, I couldn't agree more about empirical research," responded the earl. "By the by, I'm Wrexford."

"Ah. Your reputation proceeds you, milord," replied Wheeler with a nod of acknowledgment. "Your work on improving the tensile strength of iron has allowed engineers to formulate better designs for bridges."

He waggled his injured arm. "But as for my injury, it was actually *not* related to my work. It seems that being a tourist in Town is even more dangerous than climbing the heights of an unfinished bridge."

Wrexford frowned. "What happened?"

"I was returning to my lodgings last night from an evening soiree given by a member of the Royal Society and chose to take a shortcut through Hyde Park, where I was attacked by footpads." He made a face. "I should have known better, but I confess, I had imbibed more brandy than was wise."

"The members of the Revolutions-Per-Minute Society appear to be attracting a number of deadly attacks of late."

Wheeler's expression turned grim. "Milton's murder and Carrick's unexplained absence are indeed unnerving."

"I am sorry to be the bearer of bad news, but things have taken an even more sinister turn," said Wrexford. "Though it has not yet been made public, both Kendall Garfield and Mercer Wayland have met with violent deaths."

"D-Dear God," intoned Wheeler, his eyes flaring in shock. "Do you mean they were . . . murdered?"

"Yes." Wrexford allowed a moment for his reply to sink in before adding, "As you know, my wife and I are close friends with Lady Cordelia and her husband, and so I have been doing some informal investigation into Milton's murder." Another pause. "Can you think of anyone who knew that Milton was working on a technological breakthrough for bridge design—and would be willing to kill in order to steal it?"

"I . . ." Wheeler looked away to the river, watching a flock of gulls dip and dart above white-capped water. "I can't think of anyone, save for . . ." His voice trailed off into the thrum of the swirling breeze.

"Save for Oliver Carrick?" suggested the earl.

A shrug was the only answer.

Wrexford hesitated, and then asked, "Are you acquainted with any friend of Milton who is called Axe?"

Wheeler pursed his lips as he considered the question. "No," he said slowly. "But there are always a number of carpenters who work at a bridge-building site. Perhaps Milton had formed a friendship with one of them."

"That's an excellent suggestion, and one that hadn't occurred to me." There was, of course, another alternative for the murderer—Wheeler himself. Aside from Milton, the other members of the Revolutions-Per-Minute Society had thought him aloof and a bit of an enigma.

But then again, reflected the earl, *I, too, am considered eccentric and unsociable.*

Glancing down at the lead-covered dome beneath the walkway, Wrexford decided to change the subject. "Are you interested in architecture, Mr. Wheeler? Domes in particular seem a very different type of engineering challenge from that of bridges."

"I'm interested in any construction created by innovative thinking in structural engineering," came the reply. "Sir Christopher Wren had a bold new vision for a dome that appeared airy and light, and yet would be larger than any other one in existence. The technical difficulties he faced—how to deal with stability and the distribution of weight and force—were enormous, and yet he found a way to overcome them."

Wheeler moved to the low railing and leaned forward to observe the lower parts of the dome. "To do so, Wren created an ingenious design of three nested domes. The outer one that you see here is a majestic size and shape that dominates the skyline. Within it is a steeper dome, which is what people see from inside the cathedral. And then there is a hidden middle dome, which helps create strength and stability."

"Interesting," murmured Wrexford.

"As a man of science, you will appreciate the fact that Wren consulted with his good friend the legendary polymath Robert Hooke to use science to solve the structural challenges."

"We are becoming more and more aware of how science is key to solving so many practical challenges."

Wheeler's face lit up with a look of passionate enthusiasm as he continued to expound on the innovative engineering ideas created by Wren. "Come, have a look at what I mean about the outer shape."

As Wrexford approached the rail, Wheeler took hold of the earl's coat sleeve with his good hand. "In my experience, most people get a little giddy when looking down from towering heights. Have a care. I'll steady you."

The earl leaned out, just as the wind changed directions and a gust from the opposite direction swirled around the spire.

Wrexford felt his weight shift, and for an instant he felt himself teetering. Another blast of wind hit . . .

And then suddenly he was pulled back. Wheeler retreated several steps and braced the earl's back against the spire's colonnading.

"One needs good balance and catlike footing when walking in high places," counseled Wheeler.

"As well as nine lives," murmured Wrexford.

That made the engineer chuckle. "Those of us who design bridges count on that old adage being true."

"Speaking of lives," continued the earl. "Given the fate of your fellow society members, and the attack on your own person—"

"A-Are you suggesting that the incident with the footpads in the park wasn't a random attack?" interjected Wheeler.

"Let's just say that I find it an unsettling coincidence," he answered. "So if I were you, I would leave London until the crimes are solved and the culprit is apprehended." The wind gusted again, once again reversing direction. "After all, better safe than sorry."

"Egad." Wheeler blew out his breath. "Well, as it so happens, I have been invited to visit the provost of Eton to discuss taking charge of an important bridge renovation near Windsor Castle, and I'll be spending a week as a guest of the school in order to inspect the nearby site." He paused to blot his brow. "I leave at first light tomorrow."

"A fortuitous happenchance. I am glad to hear it," said the earl. "One never knows when trouble might rear its ugly head."

*   *   *

"My dear Falcon, if you think something is amiss, then it likely is," said Charlotte. "So please don't hesitate to tell us about it, no matter how unconnected it might seem."

"Very well." Peregrine drew in a deep breath. "To begin with, on the first day of classes, it was announced that Eton's long-time drawing master was taking a leave of absence for the coming term, and that his replacement was a Frenchman—"

"A Frenchman," she exclaimed. "You are sure?"

"Yes, m'lady. We were told that we were lucky to have him, for he had lived for the past decade in Rome and so was highly skilled in teaching the elements of classical design and proportion." A pause. "The thing is, Mr. Valencourt knew nothing about art."

He hesitated. "The other boys didn't notice. But because of you and things you've explained to us about the basics of drawing, it struck me as very odd. His lessons consisted of passing out paper and pencils and giving a few muddled platitudes about trusting our eye. He then would tell us to draw a chair, or if the weather was pleasant, he would send us outside to sketch a tree or a detail from one of the buildings, and then went off—I know not where—and left us on our own."

"That does seem to raise some questions," she mused.

"Then one night, I—I climbed out of the window of my quarters in town and returned to Eton," confessed Peregrine, "where I made my way to the main courtyard and crept into the Upper School. I knew the under-master kept a private library of scientific books and a collection of chemicals for his own experiments in his study room,"

A sigh. "You see, scientific subjects are not part of our curriculum, so students aren't permitted access to them."

"Because heaven forfend that such a respected bastion of education should deign to teach the boys any useful subjects for modern life," muttered Cordelia.

"Indeed, it's antediluvian thinking," agreed Charlotte, but then quickly encouraged Peregrine to continue.

"I know it was wrong of me, but I wanted to find a way to make my stink bombs more noxious," he said. "So I took one of the books and the box of chemicals to a nook just below one of the windows, so I could read by the moonlight. But then, I heard the door creak open and saw Mr. Valencourt enter. He had a small shuttered lantern and angled the narrow beam of light so that he could riffle through papers on the under-master's desk and in its drawers."

"Definitely havey-cavey," said Cordelia.

"That's not all, m'lady. The day before, I had hidden in the school chapel after my last class rather than return right away to my lodging house in order to borrow one of the glass bottles used for scented oils for my stink bomb. And I overheard the provost of Eton talking to someone about a collection of very rare and valuable books that he had borrowed from the royal librarian at Windsor Castle, and how they were being kept under lock and key in the under-master's study room to ensure their safety."

"What sort of books?" asked Charlotte.

"They moved on to the passageway leading to the Upper School, so I didn't hear the rest of their conversation, m'lady. But I saw Mr. Valencourt draw a length of thin steel from his boot—just like the type of lockpick that Wrex carries—and open one of the oak storage chests that is used to store valuables."

Peregrine stopped for a moment to steady his voice. "I was frightened out of my wits and didn't dare move a muscle. Punishment for any infraction of the school rules is awfully harsh."

"I'm well aware of the brutal traditions of these prestigious schools," said Charlotte in a taut voice. She knew that boys were often beaten with a cane for even the smallest offense, and while she decided to say no more on the subject for now, she made a mental note for A. J. Quill to compose a commentary on the beastly practice in the near future.

"I trust that he did not spot you," she added.

"No, m'lady. I have a good deal of practice at losing myself in the shadows."

"As Kit is working with the provost of Eton on the Bristol Road Project, perhaps he can make a discreet inquiry about the contents of the specific books," suggested Cordelia. "We can—"

She stopped in midsentence on hearing Mademoiselle Benoit give a tentative hail as she started down the stairs to the kitchen.

"Madame Sheffield? Are you down there?"

Charlotte gestured for Peregrine to exit the kitchens through the passageway leading to the scullery.

"Yes, yes, do come join us," answered Cordelia.

"Would you care for some tea?" called McClellan.

"*Merci.* Tea would be lovely." Lifting her skirts, mademoiselle crossed the kitchen threshold. "Oliver sent me to inquire whether I might bring him a pot of coffee and perhaps some biscuits."

"But of course. Sit and enjoy your tea, while I assemble a more substantial array of refreshment than mere biscuits," replied the maid, as she prepared a teapot and carried it to the table.

"Indeed, you two must be famished," said Charlotte. "Mac will ensure that you don't starve."

"You are too kind," murmured mademoiselle, ducking her head to put a spoonful of sugar into her cup.

As McClellan bustled around the kitchen, Charlotte sought to put the Frenchwoman at ease by asking a question about Paris. Cordelia quickly chimed in with her own query, and the three of them conversed about the highlights of the city until the maid was ready to head to the earl's workroom with the refreshments.

"Oliver, you must sample Mac's famous ginger biscuits," called Cordelia as she flung open the door.

No answer.

"*Oliver?*"

Nothing but a deafening silence.

Oh, surely Carrick hadn't played them all for fools. Charlotte hurried to check the adjoining library.

But it, too, was empty.

"*Merde!*" Cordelia whirled around to confront mademoiselle. "Where did he go?"

The Frenchwoman quickly looked away and lifted her shoulders in a Gallic shrug. "I haven't a clue."

CHAPTER 27

As Wrexford approached his workroom, the sound of raised voices alerted him that something was amiss. He drew his pistol and broke into a run.

"Thank heaven you have returned, Wrex!" exclaimed Cordelia, her voice sparking with hurt and anger. "Oliver and Mademoiselle Benoit have betrayed our trust! I could not bring myself to think it was true, b-but clearly they are guilty as sin!"

The earl quickly tucked his weapon back into his coat pocket. Volatile emotions did not mix well with gunpowder.

She blinked back tears. "Y-You must summon Griffin without delay and have him lock mademoiselle away in Newgate Prison. As for Oliver . . ." A watery sniff. "Justice demands that he answer for his misdeeds."

"Carrick slipped away when Cordelia left him and mademoiselle alone for a short interlude," explained Charlotte in response to Wrexford's raised brows.

"Oliver has committed no misdeeds," insisted mademoiselle.

"You do not know that," retorted Cordelia. "Why would he scarper if he's innocent?"

"I . . ." The Frenchwoman squared her shoulders. "I cannot say."

"Cannot?" asked Wrexford. "Or will not?"

For an instant, a swirl of conflicting emotions clouded her gaze before mademoiselle squeezed her eyes shut and assumed a resolute silence.

"As if there aren't enough variables complicating the equation," muttered the earl, drawing a pinched smile from Charlotte. But for the moment, he decided that Carrick was not their main priority. Something in Charlotte's expression told him that she had other news, and it was best conveyed in private.

"Enough shilly-shallying," he announced to the group. "Mac, kindly escort mademoiselle down to the kitchen and lock her in one of the larders for now." He thought for a moment. "Where is Tyler?"

"Mr. Sheffield sent a note just after you left this morning asking for his help in making some inquiries regarding the Bristol Road Project and its bridge engineers," replied McClellan.

"In that case, when you've finished lodging our guest in her new quarters, please head to Conduit Street and have our footmen bring Mrs. Guppy back here to join her friend," said Wrexford. "Assuming, of course, that she hasn't escaped and steamed off to some hideaway."

Lifting her chin, Mademoiselle Benoit acquiesced without protest when McClellan took her arm and signaled for her to move into the corridor.

"What a conniving little minx. I hope you plan to keep her on bread and water," grumbled Cordelia once the door fell shut. "But I'm even more furious at Oliver for manipulating my love and trust in him for his own ends." She fisted her hands to keep them from shaking. "It seems that he, along with his co-conspirators Mademoiselle Benoit and Mrs. Guppy, saw a way to use us to get their hands on what they thought were Milton's papers."

"Perhaps," responded Wrexford. "Be that as it may, we will soon have two women under confinement, and I will send word to Griffin that Carrick is loose in London. He's had his chance to be forthright with us, and now it's time to let the proper authorities handle the question of whether he is guilty or innocent."

He moved to his desk. "But there is still a missing piece to this damnable puzzle."

A piece that he had been pushing around in his mind, trying to see its contours and where it fit in.

"Carrick could not have been the one who fired the pistol shot that ignited the mayhem in which Mercer Wayland, Monsieur Montaigne, and the French radical were killed," he continued. "And I just had an interesting conversation with Ezra Wheeler. He was attacked by footpads that same evening while returning home from a late-night soiree given for the conference attendees. So it would seem that someone is trying to do away with all of the members of the Revolutions-Per-Minute Society. It could be that Carrick has an accomplice—"

"Wrex," interrupted Charlotte. "In light of that possibility, you need to hear what Peregrine recounted to Cordelia and me. Let me go fetch him. It's best you hear the account in his own words."

She returned shortly, and just as the earl suspected, Raven and Hawk had insisted on accompanying their fellow Weasel.

Catching his eye, Charlotte gave an apologetic shrug. "There seemed little point in telling them they couldn't be part of the meeting."

"Oiy," added Raven. "Falcon would simply tell us everything."

"Sit quietly," commanded Wrexford. "And that goes for you, too," he said as Harper padded in after the boys.

Charlotte flashed an encouraging smile at Peregrine. "Tell Wrex what you witnessed at Eton."

The earl listened without interruption and then asked a few follow-up questions.

"A Frenchman," he mused. "That certainly does raise some unsettling questions."

"I am unclear about something," said Charlotte, once the earl had finished. "Why does a school for elite young gentlemen teach drawing and not mathematics or any scientific subject?"

"Because," answered Wrexford, "the ability to create a credible piece of art is considered the mark of a true connoisseur of civilized culture. The normal rite of passage for an aristocratic young man is to take the Grand Tour through Europe to acquire gentlemanly polish, and the ability to draw the exquisite ancient ruins that he observes in a city like Rome or Florence garners much admiration among his peers."

He made a face. "While the more practical skills of mathematics and science carry a whiff of the working classes."

"Then why did Eton hire someone who knows nothing about the subject?" mused Charlotte.

"A good question," he answered. "We need to track down the former drawing master and inquire as to how a replacement was chosen." A pause. "And we need to learn more about Mr. Valencourt."

But before he could begin to formulate any sort of plan, an out-of-breath Sheffield rushed into the room.

"I've found him!" he exclaimed. "I've found the linchpin of proving Oliver Carrick's innocence!"

For a moment, everyone in the room stared at him in dumbfounded silence. And then Cordelia burst into tears. "I-Impossible! Oliver arranged another clever ruse and slipped away this afternoon. Which is a far more eloquent admission of guilt than any words."

Stunned, Sheffield looked to Wrexford for confirmation.

"It's true, Kit," offered Charlotte. "Mademoiselle Benoit deliberately distracted us long enough for him to leave the house unseen."

"What—or rather, who—did you discover?" pressed Wrexford, curious to know what had Sheffield so certain that he had solved the mystery.

"The identity of O-C—the letters written in blood by Kendall Garfield to identify his killer."

Cordelia's eyes flared wide, hope warring with despair.

"Explain yourself," urged Wrexford.

"I arranged to meet with some of the supervisors in charge of the Bristol Road Project, who are in Town to attend the transportation conference," said Sheffield. "My aim was to learn more about how they hire bridge engineers for the various sections of the route, and who among them are considered the best of the group. It's a massive undertaking, and a number of sites are being worked on at the same time, as the road experts survey the terrain and map out the exact route."

He pulled a piece of paper from his pocket and took a moment to read its content. "Three of the current bridge sites are considered the most challenging. Milton was in charge of the most difficult one. Carrick and a man named Jonathan Edwards were contracted for a design near the town of Bray."

He looked up, a flash of grim satisfaction lighting his face despite Cordelia's earlier assertion. "And the third site was given to Brendan O'Connor, who has garnered acclaim in the scientific world for his work in bridging difficult terrain in the coal country of Wales."

"O-C," observed the earl. "But what makes you think that he's a more likely suspect than Oliver Carrick?"

Sheffield smiled. "The fact that his father was involved in the outlawed Society of United Irishmen, a radical republican group that advocated independence for Ireland."

"Ye gods," whispered Charlotte.

"It gets even more damning," said Sheffield. "The Society of

United Irishmen formed close ties with the revolutionary government in France during its first clashes with our country at the end of the last century. And together they came up with the plan for France to send a large expeditionary force to Ireland to help expel the British."

"The planned landing at Bantry Bay in December 1796," intoned Charlotte.

"Which ended in utter failure," replied Wrexford. "It was one of the stormiest winters on record. A number of the French ships foundered, and a great many lives were lost."

"O'Connor's father was arrested and died in prison, and his mother succumbed to illness a short while later," explained Sheffield. "He went to live with relatives in Scotland—by the by, I know all of this because Tyler happened to know of him and his background—and then attended the university at St. Andrews, which is where he studied mathematics and science."

"So, O'Connor has a good reason to have a grudge against Britain and feel a kinship with the French radicals and their desire to see Napoleon restored to power," observed the earl.

"He's built an admirable career for himself within the world of road and bridge construction, with no hint of any trouble concerning his personal life," said Sheffield. "But of course, we need to dig deeper and see what dark secrets he may be hiding."

"We have already discovered a dark secret relating to Eton, thanks to Peregrine, who just told us about some suspicious activity he witnessed at the school." Wrexford went on to explain about the French drawing master, as well as what the boy had seen and heard.

"Given that O'Connor is working for the Bristol Road Project . . . and given that Lord Fenway, the provost of Eton, is head of the commission that oversees the project," he concluded, "we need to pursue this lead and see if we can uncover any link between O'Connor and the new drawing master at Eton."

The earl glanced at Cordelia. "That would certainly shift suspicion away from Carrick."

"Perhaps the pieces of the puzzle are finally beginning to fit together," suggested Sheffield. "A plausible scenario is that the two villains have Milton's papers and are trying to steal proprietary information concerning construction plans for road building and other techniques that they can also sell to the Russians."

"Let us be careful about jumping to conclusions," cautioned Wrexford.

"Tyler should be returning shortly. Perhaps he can do some asking around among his various contacts in the slums and see if he can sniff out a connection," replied Sheffield.

"We need to do so quickly," mused the earl. "The authorities have been embarrassed by their failure to apprehend a suspect for the murder. Once Griffin gets his hands on Carrick, they will want the wheels of justice to spin swiftly."

"No matter whether they have arrested the right man or not," observed Charlotte.

The sun was settling beneath the horizon, taking with it the last rays of light. The shadows deepened within the workroom.

She hugged her arms to her chest and turned for the door. "Let us head to the dining room and have Mac order up a simple supper. Then I suggest we all get some much-needed rest and reconvene in the morning. In the light of a new day, perhaps the way forward will appear a bit clearer."

By some unspoken agreement, they talked quietly of mundane things over the informal meal—news from friends traveling abroad, the renovations of the manor house on Cordelia and Sheffield's estate, a new art exhibit opening next week at the Royal Academy—rather than the investigation. Sensing the mood, the Weasels were unnaturally subdued and excused themselves from the table as soon as their plates were empty.

"They must be ill," quipped McClellan as a maid cleared the table and then rolled in the tea trolley. "They didn't wait for the platter of ginger biscuits."

Charlotte smiled, appreciating the maid's efforts to add a note of levity to the proceedings.

"I think I shall forgo any sweets as well," announced Cordelia as she stood up.

Sheffield pushed back his chair, but she placed a hand on his shoulder. "Please, you stay and enjoy a postprandial whisky with the others. I—I simply wish to take a short stroll in the back garden for a breath of fresh air."

He hesitated, but after glancing up at her face, he gave a small nod. "Of course."

"She needs some time alone to sort out her emotions," counseled Charlotte after Cordelia had left the room. She thought back to her own fraught past and a shocking discovery about her late husband. "It's difficult to come to grips with the fact that a loved one has been hiding a terrible secret."

"Yes, it does seem likely that Carrick has left a trail of murdered friends." Sheffield's voice held a note of hope that she would contradict him.

But alas, she couldn't make herself lie.

"And yet, why did he run away just now?" mused Wrexford. "We had accepted his word that he was innocent. He must have known that fleeing would force us to think the worst."

"You're right. It makes no sense," agreed Charlotte. "But something must have triggered his actions."

Another mystery.

"That would be a logical surmise. But logic has proven elusive in this investigation." Wrexford rose. "I'll fetch the whisky and four glasses from the parlor."

"Make that five." Tyler removed his hat as he entered the dining room and tossed it on the sideboard before coming to an abrupt halt. "Why the long faces? Has something else happened?"

Charlotte told him about Carrick's disappearance and Peregrine's account of the suspicious activities at Eton.

"Eton," muttered Tyler, once she had finished. He looked to Sheffield. "When you and I parted, I continued to make inquiries about O'Connor. I dug up no dirt on him, but in the process I uncovered some other unsettling information on the Bristol Road Project—"

"Whose commissioner is the provost of Eton," observed Sheffield as Wrexford returned to the room.

"What unsettling information?" asked the earl, as he passed out the libations.

"There appears to be a pattern of corruption within the bidding process for securing a contract to work on one of the many parts of the project," answered Tyler. "Word is, one must pay a hefty bribe if one wishes to be chosen."

"Bloody hell, both Garfield and Carrick mentioned that as a reason why Milton decided to give his innovation to the French radicals. But I thought Milton had been swayed by mere rumors or innuendo," said Sheffield. "Lord Fenway will be appalled to learn of this."

He frowned. "Who is responsible for this nefarious scheme?"

"The people I talked with were too frightened to give me a name," replied the valet. "I will keep trying."

"Fenway is a stickler for propriety," muttered Sheffield. "He needs to know of this right away."

"Give me another day or two," said Tyler. "It would be better to go to him with actual names, not just word of mouth."

"He's right, Kit. You are new to the commission. Making an unfounded accusation that turns out to be false would not make a good impression," counseled Wrexford. "The fact is, it does not reflect well on Fenway that this all happened right under his nose. So even if the information turns out to be accurate, he won't thank you for being the one to bring it to his attention."

Sheffield nodded in understanding. "But the truth is the truth, so once it's confirmed, I can't in good conscience stay silent."

Wrexford chuffed a sardonic laugh. "A conscience is a cursed encumbrance."

"But we all appear to be stuck with one." Charlotte smothered a yawn as she rose. "At the moment, however, mine is demanding a night of rest before we jump back into the fray."

"As is mine," said Sheffield. "I shall bid you good night here and fetch Cordelia from the garden. We shall let ourselves out."

Tyler and McClellan followed him to the stairs. Charlotte lingered, waiting until she and Wrexford were alone before leaning down and feathering a kiss to his cheek. "Are you coming?"

He lifted his glass and swirled the remaining whisky. "I'll be along shortly."

Closing his eyes, he let the silence wrap around him, allowing his thoughts to spin round and round, and then fall into their own order. Logic was all very well, but he had learned from Charlotte that intuition was an equally powerful force.

After savoring the last swallow of Scottish malt, Wrexford extinguished the lamp flames and lit a candle before heading upstairs. But as he stepped into the shadowed corridor, he found the three boys waiting for him.

"Wrex," said Raven. "We have an idea . . ."

CHAPTER 28

"Are you stark raving mad?" Charlotte turned around from the window, the starlight shimmering through the gauzy linen of her night-rail. "It's much too dangerous!"

"Actually, it isn't," responded Wrexford. "That's what makes the plan so ingenious."

"There is a fine line between genius and madness," she shot back. "I think you and the Weasels have crossed to the wrong side."

"Just hear me out," he asked.

"I would rather not," said Charlotte. "But given how many times I have suggested actions that made your hair stand on end, it would be churlish of me to refuse." Her jaw tightened for an instant, "Go on."

He was surprisingly succinct with his reasoning.

"Damnation," she muttered after spending several long moments looking for ways to poke holes in his thinking. "You truly think it's safe to let the boys search Eton's academic offices on their own even though there may be a ruthless killer at large?"

"I do," he answered. "First of all, I will be meeting with the provost in his private lodging in Lupton's Tower, which means I'll be only a stone's throw from where the Weasels are making their covert search."

She averted her gaze.

"Second, the drawing master will have no reason to be in that section of the school late at night," continued the earl. "And third, Peregrine has confessed to making a number of nocturnal forays to the school from his lodgings in town in order to explore all the nooks and crannies of the ancient buildings while he was a student. He knows of ways to bypass the main corridors and where there are secret places in which to take shelter. So even if Valencourt is out and about, he won't spot the boys."

Charlotte frowned. "What about Wheeler? We have agreed that for now he must remain on the list of suspects."

"Yes, but if Wheeler is still at the school as a guest of the provost, good manners will dictate that he be included in our meeting," pointed out Wrexford.

She drew in a breath . . . and then released it in a sigh.

"May I take that as a yes?"

"Only if the Weasels promise not to deviate so much as a hairsbreadth from their allotted roles," answered Charlotte.

A nod indicated his agreement. "I will go inform Tyler and McClellan that they are to leave at first light to begin putting our plan into action."

Twilight was fast giving way to darkness as Wrexford smoothed the folds of his cravat into place and donned his evening coat, patting the hidden inside pocket to settle his snub-nosed pistol into place.

It had taken two days to arrange, but McClellan and Tyler had found a house for rent in the town of Eton to serve as their base of operations, and all was now set for their plan to be put in motion. It was just a short distance from the school, which made the logistics easy.

As for the emotional elements . . .

Charlotte watched his preparations with misgiving, clearly unhappy at her role in the coming evening. "I still say that my presence wouldn't attract any undue attention."

"On the contrary, this isn't the stews of London, where all manner of people prowl through the night. The school as well as the town will be still as a crypt at this hour," reasoned the earl. "Dressed in your urchin garb, you would stand out like a sore thumb."

"But the boys—"

"Even if the boys are spotted, people will assume that some schoolyard mischief is afoot rather than anything nefarious," he pointed out. "I understand your frustration at not being able to participate. But sometimes the simplest strategy is the best choice."

"I know that you are right," she conceded.

"But that doesn't make it any easier to swallow," added Wrexford. As he turned back to the cheval glass to check that he looked every inch the well-tailored, wealthy aristocrat, he mentally reviewed the plan to make sure all the pieces were ready to fit into place.

While Hawk kept watch from the chapel's bell tower—with orders to raise the alarm if he saw anything suspicious by blowing three sharp blasts on the bosun's whistle Wrexford had given him—Peregrine and Raven would sneak into the school under the cover of darkness and make their way into a mysterious locked area near the Ante-Chapel to search for incriminating evidence that would tie the new drawing master to Milton's murder and the theft of his papers.

"It was fortunate that Lord Fenway agreed to meet with you," said Charlotte, drawing him back to the moment.

"There was a note of urgency to my request, along with a few veiled hints that there might be trouble lurking within the Bristol Road Project." Wrexford smoothed a small crease from his trousers. "My friends at the Royal Institution told me that the provost takes his responsibility for this particular project very seriously."

Charlotte raised no further arguments. "I imagine Wheeler will be greatly relieved when the killer of Milton and the other two members of the Revolutions-Per-Minute Society is finally captured," she mused.

"Yes, if I were he, I would certainly breathe a good deal easier." He picked up his curly-brimmed beaver hat. "I must not be late."

She stepped aside and then followed him out to the side entrance of the rented house where his carriage was waiting. The three boys were already hidden under the tarp of the boot. However, a sidelong glance at her taut face showed that all the precautions had done little to assuage her worries.

"We'll be fine," murmured Wrexford, clasping her hand and giving it a squeeze.

"Godspeed," she murmured. "And be careful."

Their soft-soled shoes made no sound as the boys dropped down to the cobblestones from the slow-moving carriage and slithered into the shadows of the brick and stone outer wall of the school.

A moment later, Wrexford's carriage rolled through the main entrance.

"Follow me," whispered Peregrine, rising to a crouch and leading the way along the Long Walk. "There's a wooden gate set into a recessed niche by Corner House that's used for the night-soil cart. It affords some easy handholds for scrambling up and over to a narrow ledge. From there we can crawl to the corner and drop down into Church Yard."

One by one, the three of them scaled the age-dark planking and pulled themselves up to the stone outcropping. "Hawk, once we cross the yard, there's a way to jiggle open the old lock at the base of the left bell tower. Inside is a circular staircase that will take you up to a vantage point overlooking the School-yard."

A silvery mist rose from the nearby river. The crescent moon flickered in and out of the scudding clouds, leaving the school wreathed in darkness. The Weasels hurried across the deserted yard and crept up to the front of the chapel.

"That's the provost's lodge," said Peregrine, indicating the stately brick and Bath stone building to his right. "In the center, rising up from the entrance archway, is Lupton's Tower." He pointed to the glow of golden lamplight illuminating the tower's top two banks of mullioned windows. "That is the private quarters of the provost of Eton. Wrex is meeting with him in there."

He deftly worked open the lock of the door to the bell tower.

"Raven and I will be searching the Lower School, which is straight ahead, and the Upper School, which is to your left," he continued. "You keep an eye on the yard and its surroundings. M'lady has given us strict orders that at the first sign of trouble you are to blow the whistle and then scarper."

"Oiy," acknowledged Hawk.

"Then up you go," said Raven.

As Hawk slipped into the stairwell, he turned to Peregrine. "Where do we start?"

"The Lower School is topped by the Long Chamber, which is where the King's Scholars sleep," answered Peregrine. "So I doubt any important documents are hidden there. Still, let us have a quick look around, and then we'll take a special shortcut from there to the locked section of the Upper School near the Ante-Chapel, where I think Mr. Valencourt has his lair."

The imposing entrance door to Lupton's Tower swung open before Wrexford could give a second rap with the knocker.

"Lord Wrexford." A courtly-looking gentleman with a carefully coiffed mane of salt-and-pepper hair greeted him with a genial smile. "How nice to finally make your acquaintance. I've heard a great deal about you."

"Then it's a wonder that you agreed to meet with me, Lord Fenway" said the earl.

A polite chuckle. "I prefer to form my own judgment regarding both people and the decisions that my position in Society require me to make." The provost gestured for him to enter.

"Excellent, as I am looking to get your thoughts and opinions on several highly important matters."

"Then let us proceed to my study without delay. Serious subjects are best discussed over a glass of fine brandy." Fenway started up the circular stairs, the flames from the branch of candles in his hand casting a skittery light over the ancient stones. "Forgive the informality of the evening. Given the lateness of the hour, I saw no need to keep my servants on duty when I'm perfectly capable of pouring libations."

"That suits me perfectly," answered Wrexford. "What we have to discuss is highly confidential."

"I confess, sir, you have piqued my curiosity." The provost led the way into a tastefully appointed room paneled in dark wood. Carved bookshelves dominated the walls, interspersed with a number of fine landscape paintings—the earl recognized several Constables and a quartet of smaller canvases by Thomas Girtin.

"Do have a seat," continued Fenway, indicating a pair of leather armchairs by the hearth. The glow of the banked coals warmed the dark burgundy hues of the oriental carpet to mellower shades of red. He poured two glasses of amber-colored brandy and passed one to Wrexford. "Mr. Wheeler indicated that you might wish to speak with me, though he did not elaborate."

"Is Wheeler not still here?"

"No." Fenway settled into his seat and clicked open the

cedarwood box on the side table beside his chair. "Would you care for a cigar or cheroot?"

"Thank you, but not at the moment." Wrexford took a sip of brandy, which was indeed superb.

"Wheeler has kindly consented to take over a bridge project for crossing the River Thames at Dorney Reach, and so is spending a few days at the site in order to give me his assessment of when the work can be finished," explained the provost. "He has also agreed to investigate why a smaller bridge just a stone's throw from here is taking so long to complete."

"I imagine a grand undertaking like the Bristol Road Project has a great many complex logistics to oversee."

"That is putting it mildly, milord. But I don't imagine you came here to discuss my problems."

Though we will touch on them shortly, thought Wrexford.

"Please tell me your concerns," went on Fenway, "and what it is that I can do to be of help."

Wrexford had already decided not to dance in circles around his reasons for requesting the meeting. "I am hoping that you might identify the men you feel are the best bridge designers involved in the Bristol Road Project," he replied. "And who among them might be capable of murder."

"Murder? Good heavens, what a question." Fenway set down his glass. "I assume this has something to do with the demise of Jasper Milton?"

"It does. I have reason to believe that Milton was killed by someone who understood the implications of his work in revolutionizing the design of bridges so that they could be built to cross longer distances and support heavier loads. Like many of us in the scientific community, Milton believed that locomotives will soon be the mainstay of moving goods and people around the country," said Wrexford. "Needless to say, his innovation would be worth a great deal—patents, a construction company trained to employ the new methods of building—"

"Not to speak of consulting fees," interjected Fenway. "I can think of a number of foreign powers who would pay dearly for an engineering consortium to oversee the construction of major thoroughfares to connect their cities, ports, and farmlands."

"Yes, I imagine the potential for profit is astounding." Wrexford paused. "Africa, India, the Far East—much of the world is fertile ground for change."

"I agree, milord.' A furrow creased Fenway's brows. "However, as head of the commission in charge of overseeing the building of a network of roads and bridges connecting London with the port of Bristol, I have little personal contact with the individuals hired to create the various components."

"It's my understanding that no more than a half dozen bridge experts have the credentials to work on the major bridges your commission has planned," pressed Wrexford.

"I don't doubt that you are right," responded the provost with an apologetic grimace. "But I can't say for sure."

"Yes, but I imagine that you have had talks with your senior supervisors in which they've discussed the strengths and weaknesses of the men with whom they are working," replied the earl.

Fenway considered the suggestion for several long moments. "Are you interested in anyone in particular?"

"Brendan O'Connor." Wrexford was not about to reveal the secret that Napoleon might be plotting to return to power. "Though I am not at liberty to reveal why."

"I will trust that you have a good reason for that, Lord Wrexford," replied the provost. "I'm afraid that I can't tell you anything about O'Connor at this moment, but I shall make some inquiries and inform you of anything that I learn."

"I am much obliged."

Fenway rose and, after adding a chunk of coal to the fire, refilled the earl's glass. "Now, perhaps we might turn the conversation to more pleasant topics."

"As to that, I'm afraid that I have another unsettling issue to raise before we do so."

"Oh?"

"It, too, concerns the Bristol Road Project," said the earl.

"I'm perplexed by your interest in this monumental undertaking to improve transportation." A note of annoyance had crept into the provost's voice. "Especially as it's an undertaking that has nothing to do with your scientific interests."

"Allow me to explain."

In thinking over all that they had learned over the past few days, Wrexford had decided to take the bull by the horns in order to protect Sheffield from any consequences of being the bearer of bad tidings. He knew how much the position on the commission meant to his friend.

While I don't give a rat's arse as to whether I make an enemy of Lord Fenway, the earl added to himself.

"It concerns the subject of bribes." But before he could go on, the provost suddenly rose.

"Please excuse me for a moment." Fenway moved to the door—rather stiffly, noted Wrexford—and left the room.

The crackling of the coals seemed to take on a sharper edge. Powerful gentlemen were used to people bowing and scraping before them. Their pride was easily offended.

Wrexford watched a tiny flame suddenly flare to life in the hearth.

So be it.

Fenway returned and resumed his seat. He appeared to have mastered his initial ire and regained his composure. "So, kindly tell me about this unsettling issue. If something is amiss, of course I wish to know about it."

"In the course of investigating possible suspects for the murder of Jasper Milton," said the earl, "I have uncovered other information and have reason to believe there is an organized system of corruption regarding the process of awarding contracts for the various components of the project—"

"T-That's preposterous!" exclaimed Fenway.

"I'm afraid that I have evidence to the contrary," replied the earl.

Fenway's face turned ashen. "W-Who?"

"I have not yet discovered that," answered Wrexford.

"I cannot understand..." The provost shook his head in disbelief. "H-How did you come to discover this? Are there others who know of it?"

"As of now, I am the only one who knows about it." Wrexford wasn't about to reveal the fact that others were involved. The less said about his inner circle of family and friends, the better. "I am sure that you will wish to deal with this discreetly."

"Indeed, indeed." Fenway drew in a measured breath, and then reached for his cigar box. "Forgive me, but I must..."

"Of course," murmured the earl.

He looked away to the carved bookshelves and the rows of ornate leatherbound volumes with their gilt-stamped spines, allowing the provost a moment of privacy in which to master his emotions.

A low cough drew his gaze back... only to find himself staring down the barrel of a pistol.

CHAPTER 29

After easing the heavy door open, Peregrine peered through the narrow crack. The glimmer of moonlight outside the diamond-paned arched windows was just enough to show that the Lower School—a long, narrow hall where the younger students were given their lessons—was deserted.

He turned and beckoned for Raven to join him. "We need to stay alert," he whispered. "The night watchman always checks in here right around this hour as part of his last round."

Two rows of rough-cut oak columns created a center walkway that ran the length of the room. The wood was black with age.

"What are all those marks?" asked Raven as they crept up to the first set of columns.

"It's a tradition for boys to carve their names into the walls and columns as a rite of passage when they move to the Upper School," replied Peregrine. After darting a look back the way they had come, he gestured for them to slip in among the rows of narrow trestle tables and benches. "Stay low and move quietly."

"Oiy, did you really have to sit here for hours on end and lis-

ten to a schoolmaster drone on about Latin verbs or some ancient battle between Sparta and Athens?" demanded Raven as
they paused before crossing to another section of the room.

"Yes," muttered his fellow Weasel. "Why do you think I set
off a stink bomb?"

"Ha! I would have been tempted to add gunpowder and
blow a hole in the roof."

Peregrine sniggered—and then sucked in his breath as the
soft shuffle of footsteps came to life in the outer corridor. "The
night watchman's coming! Take cover."

Both boys ducked under one of the tables and flattened
themselves against the floor.

A minute passed, and then another.

The massive iron hinges groaned as the door swung open
and a weak beam of lantern light swept over the room.

A cough broke the silence, followed by a wheezy warning.
"If any of you little devils are in there making mischief, there
will be hell to pay!"

Peregrine held very still.

The beam did another cursory probing through the shadows
before disappearing. "Hmmph. Thank your lucky stars that
you're all fast asleep in your beds."

A weighty thud echoed off the walls before the room settled
back into silence.

Raven started to move, but Peregrine let out a soft hiss and
waited another minute just to be sure.

"We really don't want to get caught," he explained as he rose
to a crouch and began to creep forward. "Punishment is awfully severe for breaking any of the rules."

Raven hadn't pressed for details of life at Eton, as he had
sensed that Peregrine was loath to talk about them. However,
he couldn't help but be curious. "Do they birch your bottom?"

"A birch rod leaves naught but bruises, so that's not so bad.
But some masters use thin, flexible canes, which flay the flesh."

"What sort of perverted monster takes pleasure in beating a boy bloody?" Raven grimaced. "Surely such acts are illegal."

A mirthless laugh. "Who is to stop them? We're told it's all part of turning us into men."

Raven uttered a curse that would have earned him a caning had a schoolmaster caught wind of it.

Peregrine crept over to the raised lectern used by the teachers and checked inside its cubbyholes. He shook his head to indicate that he had found nothing.

"The beatings are bad enough, but all the boys live in fear of being sentenced to the Lockbox," he continued, once he had rejoined Raven.

"What's that?"

"A windowless stone chamber hidden somewhere in Lupton's Tower." Peregrine came to the corner of the room and led the way into a storage alcove. "It's said to be cold and black as Hades." Peregrine repressed a shiver. "Rumor has it that several years ago one of Upper School boys went mad after being confined in there for a week."

"I wager that we would find a way to beat them at their own game," muttered Raven.

"I would prefer not to put that statement to the test." Turning back to the task at hand, Peregrine squeezed between two stacks of wooden crates and felt his way along the wall until he came to a narrow, iron-banded oak door recessed into the bricks.

"Last year, I traded my gold pocket watch to one of the King's Scholars in return for him showing me the ways he and his friends had discovered for exploring the school buildings without getting caught."

"Where does this door lead?"

"It gives access to a hidden passageway through an unused part of the cellar and gives us access to the section of the school adjoining the Ante-Chapel. That has to be where Mr. Valencourt has his secret lair," answered Peregrine. "It's the only place I never had a chance to explore, because the lock was too complicated for me to open. But now that Wrex has taught you how to work the levers . . ."

He fiddled with the rusty latch and finally pried it open. "Let us hope we can find what Wrex and m'lady are looking for."

"If the papers are in the secret chamber," replied Rave, "we'll find them."

Too on edge to sit quietly, Charlotte stripped off her gown and donned her urchin's garb despite the earl's admonition to stay hidden in the rented house. Her fancy silks and satins had felt stifling. The rags made her feel ready for any exigencies.

An illusion, perhaps, she thought as she fetched a sketchbook and pencil from her valise. But it helped steady her spirits.

After heading downstairs, Charlotte entered the parlor. McClellan looked up from her knitting but made no comment on the change of clothing as Charlotte settled into a chair and turned to a fresh page.

She wasn't quite sure of what she hoped to accomplish by sketching—other than distract herself from the painfully slow passage of time. Still she made herself put pencil to paper.

"Shall I go make some tea for us?" asked McClellan a short while later. She, too, appeared fidgety. Tyler had left earlier in the day to make further inquiries about the bridge engineer Brendan O'Connor, leaving her and Charlotte as the only ones without a specific assignment.

"I would ask for whisky, but I'd rather keep my head clear." Charlotte continued her aimless doodling of bridges, hoping her imagination would come up with some brilliant insight on its own.

McClellan rose and came to look at the page. That she said nothing was an eloquent enough statement in itself.

"I know, I know, it's a silly waste of time. I suppose I'm hoping for some sudden spark of inspiration," Charlotte admitted. "Most crimes have a key to unlocking the motivation, and once one sees it, the whole picture snaps into focus."

McClellan gave the squiggles another look and arched her brows in skepticism. "If you say so."

"Milton's murder is connected to bridges," muttered Charlotte under her breath. "And bridges allow people and goods to move from here to there faster and more efficiently."

The maid retreated to her own chair without further comment and resumed her knitting.

Charlotte turned to a fresh page, willing it to speak to her.

It stared back in taunting silence.

Closing her eyes, she exhaled, determined to relax and give her imagination free rein . . . and after a moment, she found herself drawing a gentleman on horseback trotting over a bridge, followed by a pair of farmworkers on foot, carrying sacks of grain.

"What am I missing?"

The coals in the hearth had burned down to ashes, though a sudden flare of firelight showed that a few embers were still burning.

She drew a circle.

"O," whispered Charlotte, hoping to spark some new insight, though she had drawn the letter countless times over the last few days. She stared at the page for a moment before drawing a second half circle beside the first one to form a *C*.

Think!

The exhortation elicited no new inspiration.

Discouraged, she turned her thoughts back to the theme of transportation.

Vehicles were the backbone of commerce. *Carts and carriages, wagons and drays. And they all moved on . . .*

Her breath caught in her throat as she suddenly recalled

Wrexford's description of the marks Garfield had drawn on the floor with his own blood.

What if . . .

What if the line between the two letters wasn't a random twitch of the dying man's finger? *What if it had been intentional?* What if it was meant to be an axle.

Axle . . . *Axe!*

And what if the letters were really meant to be circles . . .

"Ye gods!"

McClellan looked up with a start. "What?"

Charlotte suddenly saw the truth with startling clarity. "I think Wrex and the boys may be in grave danger!" She shot up from her chair and rushed to snatch up her hat from the side table. "I can't explain now—I need to run!"

Wrexford raised his brows. "I am aware that Sophocles said, 'no one loves the bearer of bad tidings.' But might I suggest that perhaps you are overreacting, Fenway."

"Stubble the witticisms, milord."

The earl turned to see Ezra Wheeler standing in the doorway.

"You—and your wife—have been far too inquisitive from the beginning," continued Wheeler as he entered the room. "We had hoped to deflect your interest, but alas, you refused to be distracted." A shrug. "Now you leave us no choice."

The earl shifted his gaze back to Fenway's weapon. "You can't think that you'll get away with shooting me here tonight. A number of people are aware of my visit."

Fenway was no longer looking so genial. "He's right, Ezra. We need to think of something—"

"My dear Hugo, I already have," interrupted Wheeler. He, too, was holding a pistol. "Lord Wrexford is known to have a penchant for sleuthing. God only knows what misguided curiosity about Eton led him to sneak up to the battlements of Lupton's Tower in the dead of night." He turned to Wrexford.

"As I mentioned when we were atop the dome of St. Paul's Cathedral, one needs good balance and catlike footing in high places, especially when some of the ancient stones are loose and crumbling. One slip can prove fatal."

"Ah," murmured Fenway. "That's diabolically clever."

"But just to be sure that the earl has come alone, I'm going to have a look around," added Wheeler. "So in the meantime, let us shut him up in the Lockbox."

That drew an appreciative chuckle from the provost. "A brilliant suggestion." Fenway looked at Wrexford. "Some people consider that a fate worse than death. Several days spent within its walls have been known to turn someone into a blathering idiot."

"The Lockbox?" repeated Wrexford. "Is that a sadistic little game you use to threaten the boys and frighten them half to death?"

"Oh, it's no game," assured Fenway. "The Lockbox is a hidden chamber carved into a special section of the interior stone walls. It's pitch-black inside, the air is foul, and the damp chill quickly seeps into your bones. It's also deep enough in the walls that no one in the tower can hear a cry from someone imprisoned there." A low laugh. "It doesn't take long for a man to lose his reason."

"You have only to ask the younger son of Lord Sudbury," said Wheeler, "who became too curious about the contents of my private workroom."

"Where, no doubt, he found records of systematic graft and fraud regarding the finances of the Bristol Road Project," said the earl.

Another shrug.

"By the by, how did the two of you come to be working together?" added Wrexford.

"I was a King's Scholar here, but Hugo—that is, Lord Fenway—was quick to recognize that my special talents would be wasted if I merely became a well-educated middle-class professional, limited in advancement by my background," replied Wheeler. "And so—"

"Ezra," interrupted Fenway. "There is no reason to reveal all the details about our activities."

"On the contrary," countered Wheeler. "I have read about Lord Wrexford and how he has helped solve crimes that have puzzled the authorities. Clearly, he thinks himself exceedingly clever. And so, he might appreciate—in a cerebral sort of way—that we are, too."

A flash of teeth. "He's no threat. He won't be repeating the information to anyone."

Fenway shrugged and looked away.

"I spent only a term here, and then Hugo arranged for me to apprentice with John McAdam," continued Wheeler. "I'm very good at designing roads and bridges, and I made important connections that allowed me to hear of attractive investment opportunities. And then I met Jasper Milton, who arranged a consulting position for me with Thomas Telford."

"Between my influence in recommending Ezra for lucrative endeavors, and my ability to channel government investment in public works, we have built a very profitable private business for ourselves," interjected Fenway.

Wrexford made a guess, though he was fairly certain that he was right. "So why murder Milton?"

"Because he made a bargain to partner with us to make a fortune with his new bridge innovation and then reneged on the deal," answered Fenway.

"Ah, yes—honor among thieves." Wrexford made no effort to hide his contempt. "How convenient to pretend to such scruples, when in truth your morals are those of a snake."

Wheeler laughed. "Call us whatever names you wish."

"What about Carrick?" asked the earl. That Cordelia's cousin had chosen to slip away demanded the question. "Is he involved in your sordid scheme?"

"Oliver may be brilliant, but he is pitifully naïve," answered Wheeler. "Like Milton, he believes that people are altruistic by nature and are motivated to do the right thing. Though he wasn't happy about Milton's ultimate decision on what to do with his innovation."

Recalling Carrick's description of the murderer as a burly, broad-shouldered man, he made a guess. "So, it was you who murdered Milton. And recalling the quarrel you had overheard, you saw an opportunity to frame Carrick for the crime."

"Milton had only himself to blame. Ezra tried to reason with him," interjected Fenway.

"It had nothing to do with morals. It was all about business," said Wheeler. "Milton wanted to give his innovation to the French—and without receiving a penny." A mournful sigh. "We couldn't allow that. It was key that the innovation remained a secret known only to us. Which is why I also had to eliminate my fellow society members Kendall Garfield and Mercer Wayland. I wasn't sure how much they knew about Milton's work."

He flexed his hand, which Wrexford had noticed was no longer bandaged. "Doing away with Wayland became a little complicated, but it all worked out in the end."

So that explains who fired the shot that killed Wayland and ignited the return gunfire from the British government's operatives that did away with the two Frenchmen, thought the earl. *And one of their bullets nicked Wheeler.*

"After several major bridges are constructed with Milton's innovation, the innovation will no longer be a secret," observed the provost. "And others will begin to use the concepts. But by then, we will have made a bloody fortune."

"You're already very rich men from the bribes," said Wrexford. "Isn't that enough?"

"That is easy for you to say, milord, having been born into wealth and privilege. You've never had to lift a finger to enjoy a life of luxury," replied Wheeler. "I grew up in poverty and worked myself to the bone to hone my skills. And Hugo's father had squandered the family fortune, so he was constantly struggling to maintain a façade befitting his title."

His gaze hardened. "So, no. There can never be such a thing as too much money." He pursed his lips. "Though perhaps we will feel satisfied after the final phase of our plan comes to fruition."

"Indeed, that brings us to the real genius behind our actions." Fenway picked up the narrative. "We have realized that steam-powered locomotives will soon displace traditional horse-drawn vehicles as the main mode of transportation, both in this country and abroad. That will require different bridge designs to carry the weight. Milton was smart enough to realize that too, and he explained to us that his innovation addresses the new requirements."

"Locomotives require flat land for optimum performance, especially at the site of a bridge. So we have quietly been purchasing land along the major rivers that lie between London and the port cities of Bristol and Liverpool," added Wheeler. "Hugo will be in a position to counsel Parliament about the future of transportation and encourage them to pass a bill to make government grants for the public good. And of course, given his experience, he will be appointed to run the undertakings."

"That's quite an impressive plan," said Wrexford. "I have just one question. What, exactly, is this wondrous innovation? Some sort of metal alloy? A special support brace that makes trusses stronger?"

Both Fenway and Wheeler hesitated in answering.

"Good God—you don't know, do you?" Wrexford suddenly recalled something that Carrick, Garfield, and Wayland had all implied about Milton—the fellow put only some of his thoughts down on paper. The rest he kept in his head.

"My guess is, you stole his work papers when you murdered

him, but his innovation revolves around mathematics, and you have not yet figured out exactly what he was thinking." He considered what he had just learned and couldn't resist doing a little needling of his own. "But unlike the other members of Revolutions-Per-Minute, Wheeler, you're not conversant with advanced mathematics."

"Enough talking," snapped Wheeler. He aimed his weapon at the earl's chest. "Place your hands on your head. And be forewarned—one false move and I'll shoot you dead on the spot. It would be an inconvenience, but we'll figure out an alternative way to get rid of your corpse."

To Fenway he added, "Search him for weapons. Then let us put him in the Lockbox while I make sure that no accomplices are lurking in the buildings."

The earl gave no reaction as Fenway relieved him of both his full-sized rifled pistol and the miniature one in the hidden breast pocket of his coat.

"Check his boots as well," cautioned Wheeler. He smiled when Fenway fished out the thin-bladed knife from its sheath. "Boots are handy places in which to hide a blade."

He gave a flick of his pistol, indicating for Wrexford to turn around and face the door to the corridor. "Go ahead of us and unlock the portal of our guest's quarters, Hugo."

"With pleasure."

"Move, Lord Wrexford—but do so slowly," ordered Wheeler. "As I said, I'll shoot you now if I have to, but I'd prefer to take a stroll on the roof with you."

Wrexford responded with a nonchalant shrug and walked into the corridor as directed.

Fenway had the door to the Lockbox open—it was a slab of thick oak with an ingenious faux front of stone tiles that blended into the outer walls. "Enjoy your stay, Lord Wrexford."

"It's not personal, milord. It's merely business." A push from Wheeler propelled him through the narrow opening into the chamber. The door slammed shut with a thud, and the earl heard a locking mechanism click into place.

A hollow silence settled over him. Fenway was right—no sound reached his ears from the outside. The only hint of life was the faint beating of his own heart.

And then Wrexford began to chuckle.

"Fawwgh!" Raven expelled a sharp snort through his nose as he and Peregrine emerged from the passageway. "That was even more disgusting than the sewers of St. Giles."

Peregrine plucked a tangle of silvery strands from a spider-web out of his hair and scraped a smear of ooze from his coat sleeve. "Trust me, there are even more noxious tunnels under the chapel. But never mind that now. We need to get into the locked lair and discover if Mr. Valencourt is working with Milton's killer."

He cracked open the door to the storage room and peered up and down the corridor. The shortcut had brought them to within spitting distance of the door that gave entrance into the mysterious part of the building. "The watchman has finished his rounds, and I don't imagine that we'll encounter anyone at this hour of the night—"

"Still, better to be safe rather than sorry," counseled Raven. "You keep watch at the corner of the corridor while I attack the lock."

He quickly approached the door and pulled a set of three slender steel picks from his boot, each with a different-shaped hook at its tip. From his coat, he took a tiny candle and quickly struck a spark to its wick. After inspecting the keyhole and giving a few experimental pokes, he blew out the flame and set to work.

Snick, snick. A precious minute passed. And then another.

Swearing under his breath, Raven switched hooks, aware that his fingers were growing slippery with sweat.

From his vantage point, Peregrine turned with a nervous look.

Swallowing hard, Raven flexed his hands and tried again.

Snick.

On hearing the latch release, he felt a rush of relief and hissed for his fellow Weasel to join him.

CHAPTER 30

Wrexford dug into the secret pocket hidden in the lining of his coat and extracted a tiny glass vial and packet of thin wooden sticks topped with a chemical compound—an experimental source of illumination that he and Tyler had recently developed.

"Let us hope these work outside the laboratory," he muttered, as he removed the wax seal from the vial and quickly dipped the chemical tip in and out of the vitriolic acid.

A flame whooshed up, the fire-gold light catching the curl of the earl's smile.

Holding up the brightly burning stick, he turned in a slow circle, getting his bearings within the stone chamber. For all their evil genius—Wrexford readily conceded that Fenway and Wheeler were intellectually gifted—the two villains had ignored a basic scientific principle.

"Forming a conclusion without knowing all the facts often leads to an erroneous conclusion," he murmured, after aligning his back with the doorway and moving in a straight line to the opposite wall. Fenway and Wheeler had overlooked a small but key element in the earl's educational background.

It was an understandable mistake. Wrexford never talked about the term—or rather, the three-quarters of a term—that he had spent at Eton.

His father had thought that he and his younger brother, Thomas, might enjoy the camaraderie of other boys after undergoing a rigorous course of study for a number of years with their private tutor. And so he had arranged admission to the elite school for his sons.

The earl's smile stretched a touch wider as he began to tap his fingers over the rough blocks of mortised stone.

He and Thomas—who, alas, had perished in a French ambush during the Peninsular War—had been bored to perdition by the school's uninteresting lectures and the emphasis on memorization rather than any real thinking. However, the company of other boys had been great fun. The two of them had marshaled a small number of them into an adventurous group that proceeded to raise hell with all the rules of the school—without getting caught in the act.

Tap, tap.

That, reflected Wrexford as he continued to examine the wall, was because he and his brother had heard rumors about secret passageways that had been built into the school two centuries ago during the Civil War between the Royalists and the Parliamentarians. They managed to find a couple of them. And then, when he had found an ancient map in the school library's archives, all of Eton's secrets were at his fingertips.

The late-night mischief he and his brother had wrought throughout the school buildings—crowned by playing a movement of Mozart's Requiem in D Minor on the chapel organ at midnight—had driven the headmaster and his under-masters to distraction.

They couldn't prove who were the guilty culprits. But they had their suspicions . . .

And so the headmaster had finally begged Wrexford's father

to withdraw his two miscreant sons before the school's reputation for strict discipline was blown to flinders.

Tap, tap.

Wrexford allowed another smile as he heard a slightly hollow sound from one of the stones. Placing both hands on it, he gave a hard push . . .

And was rewarded a moment later as the hidden door faced with a stone veneer gave a muted groan and swung open several inches.

The earl quickly lit another chemical match and then slipped into the passageway.

Raven pushed the newly unlocked door open, allowing him and Peregrine to enter a narrow foyer. To the left were two archways, each giving access to a small room filled with all manner of old books. Starlight from the narrow diamond-paned windows cast just enough illumination for the boys to see the rest of the layout. To the right was a solid wall of mortared stone.

And straight ahead was another closed door.

Raven carefully relocked the door he had just opened before approaching it. Choosing the smallest of his hooked picks, he gave a tentative touch to the keyhole . . .

Only to have the door swing open on oiled hinges.

He cocked an ear and heard nothing.

Peregrine shifted to a different vantage point and signaled that there was no sign of lamplight inside the chamber.

Without further hesitation Raven darted inside.

Once Peregrine had joined him and closed the door, Raven decided to risk lighting one of the glass-globed lanterns on the entrance table. The room was windowless, and as the flame steadied, it showed that the space was normally used as a storage space. It was crowded with ancient wooden cabinets, crates of textbooks, and other items of schoolboy life.

However, to the right, sitting off on its own in a clearing near the wall, was a large desk stacked with open books and piles of papers. Several pencils and pens—one of them looked as if the point had been snapped off in anger—lay on the ink-stained blotter.

"Poke around and see whether you find anything suspicious among the flotsam and jetsam," he said to his fellow Weasel after handing him the small candle lantern, "while I have a look at the desk."

Peregrine nodded and crept off to explore the numerous nooks and alcoves of the room.

On closer inspection, the nearest pile of papers proved to be covered with scribbled equations. A few of them looked familiar, while others were bewilderingly complicated. And some seemed to trail off and make absolutely no sense.

Cordelia would likely have a better idea of what it all meant, decided Raven, and made himself move on.

After a brief glance at the spines of the books, which all looked to be well-known treatises on mathematics, Raven edged around to the other side of the desk in order to sift through another stack of papers. Frowning, he paged through more scribbles and crossed-out equations—

He looked up with a start on hearing a sudden *thud* but relaxed on seeing Peregrine stick his head out of the far alcove half filled with cricket bats and give an apologetic grimace.

So far, everything appeared to be disjointed scribblings. Surely a momentous innovation would look much more impressive. Raven drew a deep breath and started searching through yet another pile, only to find more random numbers and half-finished equations.

He was beginning to lose heart when finally, beneath a piece of torn oilskin cloth, he found a sheaf of water-stained papers, smaller in size than the rest of sheets that were scattered across the dark wood. And there was a notebook beneath them, its cloth covers frayed from frequent use.

Raven opened it and leaned in to study what was written on the first page. It wasn't the numbers that drew his eye . . .

In the course of working to assess whether the documents that Wayland intended to sell to the French were fakes, Cordelia had taken the time to explain to him what she was doing—and shown him examples of Jasper Milton's handwriting.

"*Eureka*," he whispered.

From all that Charlotte had taught him about the little nuances that a pen or pencil could create on paper, he quickly recognized that he was looking at Milton's missing notebook.

Feeling a surge of excitement, he gave a sharp hiss to draw Peregrine out from one of the nooks.

"I've found Milton's papers—" he began, only to freeze on seeing Peregrine's eyes flare wide in fear.

Raven spun around to see a mustachioed man holding a pistol.

"What the devil are you two imps doing in here?" The man took a step closer.

"M-Mr. V-Valencourt," stammered Peregrine. "We . . ."

"W-We thought maybe we could find some noxious liquids in this storeroom to make stink bombs," interjected Raven, hoping that in the dim light the drawing master wouldn't recognize his former pupil and think them just two mischievous students out on a lark.

The explanation drew a menacing frown. "It's dangerous to be here—" began Valencourt, but the sudden sound of approaching footsteps caused him to cut off with a low curse.

"Hide, lads!" he added. "And don't make a sound."

Raven reacted in a flash. Grabbing Peregrine by the arm, he dove into a side alcove where a jumble of academic robes hung from pegs protruding from the wall. The two of them wiggled beneath the heavy wool and velvet folds and went very still just as the drawing master turned to face the door.

Wrexford crouched down, the horrible smell forcing him to breathe through his mouth. If he remembered correctly, this particular passageway led to a subterranean tunnel that ran under the Schoolyard and would bring him to the section of the Upper School that butted up to the Ante-Chapel. That was where Peregrine had noticed the special lock, and they had all agreed it was the most likely location for any skullduggery going on.

"Damnation." Wrex winced as his shoulders snagged on the rock spurs protruding from the rough-cut tunnel as it slanted deep into the bowels of the earth. The way was narrower than he remembered.

Ignoring the slime of centuries, he dropped down and began to crawl forward on his belly as fast as he could. Time was of the essence . . .

"Valencourt." Wheeler gave a grunt of surprise. He, too, was armed — he had a pistol clenched in each hand. "Might I inquire what you are doing here at this hour of the night?"

"I was returning from the tavern in town and thought I saw a boy dart in the side door to the Upper School," replied the drawing master in a slightly slurred voice. "Knowing our provost's attitude on strict discipline and deportment, I decided to have a look around to make sure no mischief was afoot."

He gave a careless wave of his weapon and let out a belch. "But it seems I was mistaken, and it was naught but a trick of the shadows." A lopsided grin. "Or it's possible that I might have had one too many mugs of ale."

Raven ventured a peek through the folds of fabric. Wheeler did not appear amused by the response.

"How did you open the outer door?" he demanded.

"I . . ." Valencourt swayed slightly as he contemplated the question. "I simply pressed the latch, and it popped open."

"Did it?" Wheeler took several steps into the room and gave a quick glance at the books and papers.

"It must have," answered Valencourt in a puzzled voice. "Because I don't remember having a key."

Wheeler whirled around and took dead aim with both weapons at the schoolmaster's forehead. "Liar. I think you're in league with Lord Wrexford."

Valencourt swayed again. "*Who?*"

A tiny metallic click sounded . . . and then the drawing master dove to his right just as both of Wheeler's weapons erupted in an explosion of sparks and a thunderous *BANG!*

"It's nothing personal, monsieur," intoned Wheeler as he tucked his pistols away and approached the motionless figure sprawled on the floor. "But I couldn't permit you to make off with Milton's notebook. Not when I have gone through so much trouble to obtain it."

He sidestepped a rivulet of blood flowing from beneath Valencourt's head and was about to crouch down beside the body when the clatter of running footsteps caused him to spin around . . .

"You didn't really think I was going to let you get away with your crimes, did you, Wheeler?" said Wrexford as he stepped through the doorway.

A spurt of fear pulsed through Charlotte's veins as the peal of the chapel's bells—sounding loud enough to wake the dead—suddenly shattered the quiet of the night. Heart hammering against her ribs, she broke into a run.

Eton's outer walls were just ahead, looming up from the ghostly mist floating in from the nearby river. She raced along Slough Road and turned into Weston's Yard. The side gate was locked, but the stone coping surrounding the wrought iron allowed just enough of a handhold for her to climb up and over the entrance wall.

Giving silent thanks for the physical training sessions with her fencing master, Charlotte dropped down and made her way through a narrow walkway to the Schoolyard. A gaggle of the King's Scholars had come down from their school lodgings in the ancient college and were milling in confusion by the chapel, staring up at the bell tower.

Recalling the map of the college grounds, she took a moment to orient herself and then slipped into the shadows of the dark brick building and angled her steps for the entryway set in the corner of the yard where the Upper School met the Ante-Chapel. That, she knew, was where Peregrine and Raven were headed.

Dear God, let them be unhurt. Charlotte clenched a fist as she hurried for the stone stairs. No matter that she was un-armed—woe to any villain who tried to harm them.

Wheeler slid a step back from Valencourt's body, the look of shock on his face growing more pronounced as the walls began to shudder with a thunderous clanging coming from the bell-tower.

"Another murder victim?" said the earl, after a glance at the patch of fast-darkening scarlet pooled on the stones.

"And soon there will be another!" Wheeler raised one of his two pistols—

"It's not loaded, Wrex!" cried Raven from the depth of the alcove. "He fired both of his weapons—we saw two muzzle flashes!"

Wrexford kept his eyes on Wheeler, not allowing his relief at knowing the boys were safe to distract him from dealing with his dangerous adversary. "It's over, Wheeler. The townspeople will be here shortly, and you will have to answer for your crimes."

The engineer hesitated, then flung both his weapons at the earl's head and darted for a door set in the center of the far wall.

Wrexford ducked the missiles and was after him in a flash. But the few seconds of delay gave his quarry just enough time to slip through the portal and slam it shut.

"Damnation," he exclaimed after slamming his shoulder against the portal and realizing the bolt was engaged.

He turned back to the room and saw that Peregrine had untangled himself from the academic robes and was kneeling beside the drawing master's prostrate body.

"Mr. Valencourt, Mr. Valencourt." The boy gently shook the man's shoulder. "I—I think he's d-dead," he stammered on getting no response.

Raven crouched down next to him for a closer look. "Naw, it looks like the bullet merely creased his temple, so I think he's just stunned. Head wounds tend to bleed like the devil." His gaze shifted to the bushy moustache—which had come half unglued from the drawing master's upper lip.

"And by the by . . ." Raven shook the man's shoulder a little harder. "His name isn't Valencourt—it's von Münch."

"Bloody hell," muttered Wrexford as he hurried over to join the boys. "You're right."

A wince spasmed over von Münch's face and he managed to pry open one eye. "Before you ring a peal over my head, milord, be advised that I can explain."

"I'm sure you can, but not now," snapped the earl. "Hand over Milton's papers. I don't trust you with them."

"I don't have them—I swear it!"

"That's because we do," said Raven with a grin as he patted his pocket.

"Well done, lads! But now we need—"

"Wrex!" Charlotte flew into the room and let out a gasp of joy at seeing the boys. "But where is Hawk?"

"In the belltower!" answered Peregrine. "He must have heard the pistol shots and was clever enough to sound the alarm."

"Speaking of which, the townspeople are beginning to arrive to see what is causing the commotion," said Charlotte. "In the confusion and crisscrossing lantern light, I just spotted Wheeler fleeing this building. I have reason to believe that he is the killer—"

"He is," interjected Wrexford. "But how did you come to that conclusion?"

"I should have seen it sooner!" she answered. "As I was sketching, I suddenly saw that the marks that Wayland drew on the floor with his own blood could have a whole new meaning. The horizontal line was an axle, and the marks beneath it weren't an *O* and a *C* but were meant to be *wheels*. Axe-Axle-Wheels! So I came to warn you!"

"Alas, I learned of his perfidy myself. But I'll explain that later. Right now we need to ensure Wheeler doesn't escape justice."

"He exited through the gate at Baldwin's Bec," said Charlotte.

Wrexford needed only an instant to decide on their next moves. "Actually, your presence is a blessing in disguise," he said to von Münch. "You can deal with the authorities while Charlotte and the boys slip away with Milton's papers without anyone noticing their presence here tonight."

He paused. "Be advised that Fenway is also the enemy. Tell the town officials that the provost is guilty of several nefarious crimes and must be taken into custody. Let us hope that your head wound will add enough veracity to the claim that they will have no choice but to detain Fenway until the confusion is sorted out."

"Don't worry, milord," replied von Münch as he sat up gingerly. "I shall be very persuasive."

Charlotte gave a reluctant nod, understanding that it was the only way to guard their family secrets. "I take it you are going after Wheeler." It was said as a statement, not a question.

"He must be held accountable for his crimes," said Wrexford simply.

She looked away without arguing, but not before he saw the look of stark fear in her eyes.

"From the bulge in Wheeler's boot, I think he has a knife," piped up Raven.

"I take it you have yours with you?"

"Oiy." Raven pulled out the stag-handled blade that the earl had given him during the first days of their acquaintance and held it out.

Much water has passed under the bridge since that moment, its currents often swirling with perilous eddies, reflected Wrexford as he took the knife and tucked it away.

And yet, he reminded himself, *we have navigated all the dangers.*

"I think I know where Wheeler is headed." He turned for the corridor. "I need to hurry."

"Wrex," uttered Charlotte in a low voice. "He's a cold-blooded killer."

"His victims didn't see him coming. With me, he won't have that advantage." A martial glint gave his gaze a steely gleam. "Don't worry, I won't let him get away."

CHAPTER 31

Mist rose up from the river, fogging the footpath as it narrowed and snaked through the trees. Wrexford could hear the low rush of water against the banks as he quickened his pace.

Clouds scudded across the night sky, darkening the shadows that flitted all around. Still, just a few minutes ago, as the path crested a rise before dropping back down toward the river, Wrexford had caught a glimpse of his quarry silhouetted in a flicker of moonlight.

His guess had been right. Wheeler was heading for Windsor Bridge, where he had been overseeing extensive renovations to the structure, as requested by the Prince Regent, who adored pomp and pageantry and wished to have a more regal look to the main route for traveling from Windsor Castle to the royal palaces in London.

It was a clever choice for making his escape. Crossing over to the vast grounds surrounding the castle would make it easy to move around unseen, and the various stables and outbuildings offered ample opportunity to steal a horse. By dawn, Wheeler could be miles away, with a multitude of choices for reaching the coast and slipping away to the Continent.

The thought spurred Wrexford to greater speed.

Milton's murderer must not be allowed to cross the bridge.

Wheeler was heavyset and not a speedy runner. The earl's long-legged stride gave him the advantage. Spotting a shortcut, he raced across a swath of meadowland, then plunged down a steep embankment, gaining precious ground. As the path flattened and followed the contours of the river, he could see Wheeler up ahead.

His quarry turned for an instant to look behind him and stumbled before regaining his stride.

Wrexford kept up his relentless pursuit. He knew from his military experience that panic would take its toll on Wheeler, both mentally and physically. When the confrontation came, that would give him an advantage.

The gap between them was closing.

"Give yourself up," he called. "I won't let you escape."

Wheeler lowered his head and kept running.

The breeze had freshened, dispelling the silvery vapor, and suddenly the dark skeleton of the bridge renovation loomed up on the hill just ahead. Wheeler raced into a large work area where iron girders and wooden beams sat on trestles covered with canvas tarps. Blocks of stone were stacked in an adjacent section, while another part of the clearing was filled with coils of rope, lengths of chains, and a storage shed for tools.

Zigzagging through the raw materials, Wheeler headed for the half-finished structure spanning the river. He scrambled over the barrier of timbers and chains blocking man and beast from the danger ahead and headed out into the spiderweb of rope handholds strung up as a safety net for the workers.

Wrexford peeled off his coat and flung it aside before jumping on one of the rough-cut logs and hauling himself up and over the obstacle.

Another few steps gained on his quarry.

Wheeler stumbled as the footing turned more treacherous. The paving of the old bridge had been torn away in order to widen it, and temporary planking had been placed for the work being done. Grabbing up a loose rock, he turned and heaved it at Wrexford.

The earl ducked it with ease. "My raggle-taggle urchins can throw better than you do," he called. "Or has fear tied your muscles in knots?"

Wheeler turned and grabbed a handhold on the main guide rope, then picked his way with sure-footed grace to the outer beam. A flash of steel cut through the darkness, followed by a low laugh as the engineer tossed the severed length of rope into the rushing water below.

"You see, you're not quite as clever as you think, milord!" he called. "And by the by, my muscles are functioning perfectly."

Wrexford quickly surveyed the surroundings to gauge his options. A glance up showed that a single thick manila line had been strung from the iron support stanchion next to him to one up ahead where the current work was being done. A pulley rigged with a heavy metal hook for moving buckets back and forth was tethered to a ring just above his head. Wrexford yanked it free and grabbed hold of the hook.

Whoosh!

The wind whistled through his hair as he flew along the length of rope. Wheeler made a grab for him, but Wrexford kicked the engineer's hands away and continued on another twenty feet before dropping down to the widely spaced planks with perfect timing to keep his balance.

"The only way to cross to the other side is to crawl along that one old outer beam left from the original bridge." The earl pointed to a horizontal length of rusty metal to his left that trailed off into the darkness. "And I'm not about to let you try it."

Wheeler shifted his stance and didn't answer right away.

No doubt the gears are turning inside his head, thought Wrexford. His adversary looked to have regained his sangfroid.

It would be a mistake, he reminded himself, *to underestimate the man.*

"Tell me, how is it that you have appeared here when you were locked away in an impregnable cell?" called Wheeler. "I refuse to believe that Fenway would betray me. But the only other explanation is that you're some otherworldly wraith, capable of walking through walls of stone."

"Perhaps I'm an avenging angel," answered Wrexford, feeling no compunction to reveal his secret. "You've committed a great evil, and so you must pay for your sins."

"Do you actually believe that Good always triumphs over Evil?" shot back Wheeler. "Surely you are not that naïve."

"It is an elemental battle—the light and dark sides of human nature are constantly at war," the earl replied. "I've won enough battles to remain optimistic. So I like my chances." A pause. "Do you?"

The question seemed to take Wheeler aback. He hesitated just an instant before dismissing it with a curt laugh. But the telltale pause revealed a hint of doubt.

And in the heat of a clash, Wrexford believed that the engineer's doubt would work against him.

"The fact is, I *do* like my chances." Wheeler brandished his knife. "For I know that you are not armed, while I am. And you're well aware that I'm not afraid to use my blade to take a life, if need be."

"You may try." Wrexford revealed Raven's knife and snapped it open. "Since I believe in fighting fair, be advised that I *am* armed. And I, too, can be lethal with a blade if I so choose."

"Anyone who fights fair is a bloody fool," called Wheeler as he shuffled to his left—and suddenly hurled an open can of turpentine at the earl's head.

Wrexford ducked, but the liquid hit him full in the face. Blinded, he staggered back, his eyes feeling on fire. He heard the creak of the planking. Wheeler was moving . . .

Think! Recalling his surroundings, Wrexford retreated, angling his steps to the right, where one of the stone support pillars rose up from the river. He took cover behind it, blotting his eyes with his shirtsleeve and then blinking furiously to clear his vision.

If the engineer was pragmatic, he would seize the opportunity to escape rather than allow hubris to color his judgment and demand a mano a mano victory.

The light brush of boot leather on wood was suddenly audible as the breeze died for a moment.

A wise move. By the sound of it, Wheeler was creeping toward the opposite side of the bridge where the existing beam offered a path to freedom.

Though his eyes were still blurry, the earl eased away from the pillar, and after another few rapid-fire blinks he spotted the engineer creeping stealthily through the maze of ropes and netting.

"Give it up," called Wrexford. "I'm not going to let you escape."

Wheeler carefully worked his way up a barricade of thin netting, and though it sagged and threatened to snap, which would have resulted in a fatal fall onto the rocks jutting up from the water, he dropped down to safety.

"I don't see how you are going to stop me."

The earl was already moving. Several sections of the bridge expansion's skeleton had been bolted into place, and a narrow strut—barely wider than the palm of a hand—offered a chance to put himself between the engineer and the Windsor Castle grounds.

Without breaking his stride, Wrexford stepped on the thin piece of iron and kept going, trusting his balance . . .

And Clotho, the Spinner of Fate, who seemed to have a soft spot for him.

Ignoring Wheeler's yelp of dismay and the sudden gust of

wind that tugged at his shirt, the earl hurried over the last few
feet of danger and leapt to solid footing on a section of planking.

"As you see, there's nothing wrong with my balance—or my
footing in high places," he called.

"Damn you," cried Wheeler in frustration. "Why the devil
do you care so deeply about vengeance for Milton? His personal flaws were legion."

"I don't care about vengeance, I care about principle." A
smile. "It's nothing personal, Wheeler. It's all about justice."

A look of disbelief spasmed over Wheeler's face. "You are
willing to risk your life over an abstract ideal?"

Wrexford thought about all the light and love he was putting
in jeopardy—*Charlotte . . . the Weasels . . . the family's inner
circle of dear friends*—and felt his heart clench. Would such a
sacrifice be worth it?

"Principles are what challenge us to rise above our own selfish needs and desires and do the right thing. And they matter
most when things are complicated and confusing," he replied.
"The difference between Good and Evil is rarely black and
white. And so for me, drawing a moral line in the sand is what
keeps the Darkness from taking hold of our hearts."

"You are welcome to bask in platitudes," snapped Wheeler.
"I prefer the more tangible pleasures that money can buy."

"You are free to decide what is important to you," said
Wrexford. "But the choices you make have consequences. You
don't have the right to decide who deserves to live and who deserves to die. And so you must answer for your actions."

Wheeler took a step closer and flicked his knife in a menacing gesture. "And so must you."

They stood facing each other, the moon flicking in and out
of the shifting clouds. A gust of wind shuddered through a
nearby copse of trees, rustling the leaves. A squall looked to be
blowing in.

The earl held himself very still. One learned a great deal

about an opponent by allowing him to make the first move. His guess was that Wheeler would use his bulk and muscle to go straight for the jugular.

With a subtle shift of weight, Wrexford balanced on the balls of his feet, ready to react in an instant to whatever attack was coming.

Wheeler dropped his arms to his side and looked away. "Perhaps you're right. Perhaps I must face my faults—"

The blade whipped up without warning, aiming to cut an angled slice between the earl's ribs and thrust upward to pierce the heart.

Wrexford parried the blow with a lightning-fast swing of his forearm, knocking the engineer's knife hand up and away from his body. His own weapon darted in—the engineer's unprotected chest was at his mercy—but merely pricked with the point to draw a tiny bead of blood.

Wheeler recoiled with a grunt. A wink of starlight showed his brow was sheened in sweat.

"Unlike you, I'm not aiming to kill," said the earl as he reset his stance. "I'm taking you back to face justice."

"Never!" cried Wheeler. "I don't intend to be used as a source of entertainment for the masses by being made to dance the hangman's jig at a public execution."

"Then perhaps you shouldn't have murdered three of your friends, all because you lusted for money that you didn't even need," said the earl. "If you're whining for sympathy, look elsewhere. You'll get none from me."

A snort of rage sounded as Wheeler lowered his head and charged.

Wrexford twisted to evade the hit, but a glancing blow from the engineer's shoulder knocked him across the width of the planking. His boots slipped on a patch of grease, and for a perilous moment he teetered on the edge, fighting for balance.

The engineer pivoted.

A rope dangling just out of reach caught the earl's eye, undulating like a snake in the fitful breeze.

He lunged for it just as Wheeler raised his knife and charged again.

For an instant, the bristly hemp slid through his fingers, scraping the skin from his palms. But thoughts of family summoned an extra measure of resolve. His grip held as his momentum carried him over the yawning gap between the center beams and the planking on the other side.

Wrexford released his hold and dropped with a thump just as a scream rent the night.

Hitting up against nothing but air, Wheeler flapped his arms madly to stay upright. But in the next instant he tumbled head over heels into the void.

Expelling a pent-up breath, Wrexford steadied his balance enough to look down over the edge of the plank.

Jutting up from the roiling water fifteen feet below was an outcropping of rocks. Wheeler's broken body lay face down, arms and legs spread-eagled. With a last flicker of life, he managed to roll himself onto his back, revealing the knife impaled in his chest.

A cat may have nine lives, reflected Wrexford, *but we mortals possess just one.*

A rasping cough—or perhaps it was a prayer—and then Wheeler was gone.

"*Corruptio optimi pessimal*," murmured Wrexford, thinking of Charlotte's frequent use of Latin aphorisms. *The corruption of the best is the worst.*

Wheeler's intelligence had given him a great advantage in life, despite his humble birth. That made his decision to use it to commit unspeakable crimes seem even more terrible.

The earl stood for a moment longer, thinking about Good and Evil. This investigation had been particularly distressing. A group of like-minded friends had turned out to be a viper's nest of greed, envy, and self-serving lies.

Has this new age of rapid-fire change and technological wizardry left concepts like loyalty and friendship in the dust?

Wrexford suddenly felt weary to the very depths of his soul.

The wind swirled, and its chill bit through his shirt. Repressing a shiver, he turned and made his way back through the maze of ropes and struts to *terra firma*. At some point during the chase—he knew not when—he had twisted his knee, and it was now aching abominably as he stumbled over the barricade, then paused to catch his breath.

At first, he thought the spectral shape rushing toward him was a figment of his black mood.

But the feel of Charlotte's arms enfolding him in a hug was blessedly real.

Her scent . . . the texture of her hair . . . the softness of her skin.

They stood wrapped together, silently savoring their connection. Words were irrelevant. Their bodies were speaking the only language that mattered.

After feathering a last kiss to his cheek, Charlotte pulled back. "I saw Wheeler fall. Is it over?"

"Yes." He confirmed.

"*Deo gratias,*" she whispered. "The carriage is waiting at the end of High Street. Give me your hand, and let us return to our family."

CHAPTER 32

Afternoon light flooded in through the drawing room windows. Charlotte pressed her palms to the glass panes, welcoming the warmth. It was now the second day after the terrifying night at Eton, and yet a chill still lingered in the depth of her being.

Wrexford came up behind her and placed his hands on her shoulders. "Everyone will be arriving shortly. Are you ready for all the questions and explanations?" The details about the foray to Eton and the subsequent chase after Wheeler had already been recounted to their inner circle. But what lay at the heart of the mystery had not yet been revealed.

A wry sigh. "Knowing our friends, it will likely be a rather rowdy gathering."

Charlotte leaned back, feeling her emotions steady as she fit into the familiar contours of his body. "In truth, I would rather sleep for another day—or another week—but they, too, deserve some closure." She closed her eyes for an instant. "Being part of our extended family is not for the faint of heart."

The earl chuckled. "Think how boring their lives would be without us constantly tripping over Trouble."

McClellan poked her head into the room. "The dowager and Henning are at the door. And I see Sheffield's carriage coming into the square."

"Tell Riche to show them in," said Wrexford. "And have him bring in an extra bottle of whisky."

The maid nodded. "I've baked a triple batch of ginger biscuits, which should be ample sustenance for the crowd—assuming the Weasels haven't turned into locusts!"

"We heard that!" called Raven as he led Hawk and Peregrine into the room, each of them bearing a heaping platter of the sugar-scented pastries. Harper, padding along as the tail end of the procession, added a *woof*. "Don't worry, we left more than enough for everyone."

"Put the biscuits on the tea table and hurry away. Cordelia's cousin, as well as his friends Mademoiselle Benoit and Mrs. Guppy, are accompanying her and Sheffield, and it's best that they don't know your true position in this household," she said. "You may all return once they leave and it's just our inner circle of friends."

"Very well. But since house rules entitle us to attend a council of war, it's not technically eavesdropping if we listen from the adjoining parlor," replied Raven.

"Go!" said Charlotte, punctuating the command with a shooing gesture as the sound of approaching steps in the corridor grew louder.

The room quickly filled, voices raised in greeting echoing off the walls as everyone settled into place.

Alison quickly rapped her cane for silence. "My ancient heart can't stand the suspense a moment longer." She raised her quizzing glass and fixed Charlotte and Wrexford with a basilisk stare. "What the devil has been going on these last few days?" A sniff. "And how dare you leave me out of the fray?"

"First things first," called Henning. He turned to Tyler, who was standing by the sideboard. "Pass out libations before we dive into the details."

More murmurs and shuffling.

"*Sláinte.*" The surgeon raised his glass. "I would propose a toast to peace and quiet, but I'm not an idiot."

"Stubble the sarcasm, Baz. As Alison has suggested, we have a great deal to discuss, so let us begin without further delay." Wrexford turned to Sheffield and Cordelia, who were sitting together facing Cordelia's cousin, Mademoiselle Benoit, and Mrs. Guppy. "Since so much of this mystery and its ultimate resolution revolves around Oliver Carrick and his star-crossed Revolutions-Per-Minute Society, I say we begin with him."

"When he fled from our town house several days ago, we all assumed that he *must* be guilty of Milton's death, despite his assertions of innocence," added Charlotte. "But it seems that, as with so many of the confounding twists and turns in this investigation, we couldn't unravel the truth from all the misleading clues."

"Explain yourself, Oliver," urged Cordelia with a smile. "Thank heaven you were clever enough to spot the thread that led to the ultimate truth."

Carrick rose and cleared his throat. "I regret plunging all of you into such a bubbling cauldron of danger. Had I realized the key to the mystery sooner—"

"Leave off all the shilly-shallying and get to the point," called Henning after a noisy slurp of whisky.

"The point is . . ." Carrick closed his eyes, a look of mingled sorrow and regret shading his face.

"Oliver," encouraged Cordelia.

He expelled a sad sigh. "The point is, we were all chasing papers that didn't exist."

"How can you be so damn certain?" challenged Henning.

"Because Jasper Milton was not only a genius—he also possessed an eidetic memory."

The room went absolutely still.

"An eedee-*what*?" demanded the dowager.

It was Wrexford who jumped in to explain. "Put simply, it is the ability to save an image in the mind's eye and recall it with perfect clarity at a later time."

"But surely that's impossible!" protested Alison.

"For most of us, yes," agreed the earl. "But a few rare individuals are gifted with such powers." He made a face. "I feel like an utter lackwit for not recalling an incident that happened early in 1812. Had I done so, we might have solved this mystery a great deal sooner."

"Don't be so hard on yourself, Wrex," said Charlotte. "It was merely a rumor, and I had heard it, too. But it sounded so far-fetched that I dismissed it out of hand." A sigh. "Even though at the time I had reason to believe that the government was taking it seriously."

"But what—" began McClellan.

"I shall explain," said the earl. He moved to the hearth and turned to face everyone.

"In 1810, an American merchant—or as Kit would call him, an entrepreneur—by the name of Francis Cabot Lowell came to Britain on an extended visit. During that time, he visited a number of our textile mills in Lancashire and Scotland, which used the most advanced technology in the world to manufacture cloth. Lowell knew that America desperately needed such advanced innovations to become an economic power. But Britain had strict laws prohibiting any copy of technical plans for such inventions from being taken out of the country."

"Our government, however, suspected that Lowell meant to try to take a copy of the plans for the steam-powered spinning and weaving machines with him when he returned to America," offered Charlotte. "He was stopped and searched at the docks, but the customs officials found nothing and had to permit him to leave. However, as soon as he was back in Massachusetts, he was able to draw the complex plans of the various machines from memory, as the mill owners had decided there was no harm in letting him have a close look at them."

"Good heavens," muttered Alison. "And here I have trouble

recalling whether I have put two or three teaspoons of sugar in my tea five minutes after I have poured myself a cup."

Charlotte smiled before continuing. "Although the government covered up what happened, they are extremely sensitive about any further technological secrets slipping away from these shores. They had heard rumors from some of Milton's professors at Cambridge that he possessed an extraordinary memory and became worried when their operatives in Paris noticed that he was spending time with several known radicals."

"And that explains why Grentham and his operatives had an interest in our investigation," said Wrexford. "And why they were desperate to know whether Milton's ideas had died with him, or whether someone had convinced him to write everything down."

"Allow me to pick up the thread from here and return to Milton's work." said Carrick. "As mademoiselle and I worked with Cordelia to determine whether the documents that Wayland had intended to sell to the French radicals were actually Milton's work papers, we quickly realized that not only were there too many mathematical errors, but also the handwriting wasn't quite right."

He shook his head. "Wayland tried to imitate Milton's style, but Milton had a very peculiar way of forming the letter *a*. However, Wayland was clever enough to add some scribbled notes in the margins—which was something that Milton often did—in order to make them look authentic. And one of the things he wrote suddenly jarred my memory!"

A note of rising excitement shaded Carrick's voice. "It was simply the name of the professor who served as a mentor to Milton during our university days. They had remained good friends, and when I saw Haverstick's name, it reminded me of a very odd thing he had said to me regarding Milton and his ability to recall information when we had dinner several months ago in Cambridge."

He blew out his breath. "I knew you would think me crazy if I tried to explain, so I arranged to escape and follow my hunch. And sure enough, Professor Haverstick confirmed that Milton had told him about his eidetic memory and said that was why he always burned the work papers containing his best ideas after committing them to memory. That way, he could be absolutely sure that nobody knew about the revolutionary concepts he was exploring."

"Good Lord, what a tale," said McClellan. "But if Milton was such an idealist, why did he agree to work with Wheeler and Fenway on a venture that was funded by the British government, turnpike trusts, and private investors?"

Carrick considered the question for a long moment. "Because he thought the Bristol Road Project would benefit the working man, not just the wealthy. Milton assumed the motives behind the project were all for the higher good, and my guess is that made him even more aghast when he discovered the corruption, and the fact that his friend Wheeler and Fenway had created the bribery scheme and were reaping the profits."

He hesitated and looked to Cordelia, who was blinking back tears, before continuing. "So he reneged on his deal, and when Wheeler couldn't change Milton's mind, he murdered him and stole his work papers and notebook."

A sigh. "But the problem is, Milton's scribbling book was just that—incomplete scribbles of vague ideas. The only complete plans for the momentous innovation were inside his head."

"One thing puzzles me, Carrick," mused Wrexford. "You said that you went to make one last effort to change Milton's mind on the night of the murder because you knew he was going to meet with the French radicals at the Three Crowns Inn to turn over the papers explaining his innovation."

"That's what I thought." Carrick made a wry face. "However, Mademoiselle Benoit subsequently learned that Jasper was going to offer *himself*, rather than any papers. He intended to accompany them back to France."

"Bloody hell," said Henning, then rose to pour himself another glass of whisky. "So you're saying that his momentous idea did indeed die with him."

"His scribbling book offers some tantalizing clues," answered Carrick. "But in truth, we really don't know exactly what he was thinking."

"Mathematics are key in understanding architectural principles regarding things like mass, weight, and structural strength," piped up Madame Benoit. "But as we have all discovered, bridges are far more complicated. There are so many variables, and we really don't understand all the permutations of how they come into play. We think Milton was very interested in vibrations and was studying the work of the German physicist Ernst Chladni, who experimented with vibration patterns in oscillating plates. His work showed practical promise in figuring out ways for stabilizing bridges. In fact, Napoleon took a great interest in the subject."

"Indeed," said Carrick. "In 1809, the French Academy of Sciences offered a prize for the mathematical explanation of what they called the elasticity problem, and Napoleon offered to give a kilogram of gold to the winner."

"My friend Marie-Sophie Germain should have won—indeed, she is recognized as the leader in formulating a mathematical theory of elasticity, which has practical applications for bridge design," said Mademoiselle Benoit. "However, the male judges decided there were small errors in her calculations."

"My brain is now not only oscillating," said the dowager faintly as she looked back and forth between the two bridge experts. "It is spinning in circles."

Cordelia gave a sympathetic smile. "I, too, am having trouble following the technical explanations."

"I am sorry," apologized mademoiselle. "I get very excited

about the subject. But enough of theory. Let's just say I am confident that with Mademoiselle Germain's help, Oliver and I can use Milton's notes and our own creative thinking to pursue new and innovative ways to improve bridge design through mathematics."

But may it happen without any more deaths and deceptions, thought Charlotte.

The sudden rustle of silk drew her back from her brooding. She looked up to see Mrs. Guppy rise from her seat on the sofa and move to the center of the room.

"If I may be permitted to summarize the practical aspects of what we have just heard . . ."

Charlotte signaled for her to go on.

"It seems fair to say that Jasper Milton was working on a number of possibly brilliant theories on how to revolutionize bridge design. But with his death, it will likely be some years before our scientific methods are advanced enough to prove whether any of them are correct."

"Wheeler and Fenway's greed has done much harm to Progress," reflected Sheffield.

"Yes, we have just seen the dark side of scientific thinking and the quest to bring new and wondrous innovations to life," responded Mrs. Guppy. "But allow me to offer a brighter development." She fixed the earl with a smile. "Thanks to you, Lord Wrexford, and your sworn statement to Mr. Griffin and the Bow Street magistrate that Wheeler confessed to you about murdering Jasper Milton, Oliver Carrick has been exonerated and is no longer a fugitive from justice."

Cordelia leaned over to give her cousin a hug.

"And I am delighted to announce to all of you that Mademoiselle Benoit, Carrick, and I have officially formed a company to design bridges. Together we have been working on technological innovations involving traditional methods and materials, and we believe we will improve transportation sooner rather than later. At the same time, Mademoiselle Benoit and Carrick will continue Milton's exploration into using mathematics to develop revolutionary new design concepts."

She smiled at the couple. "My two young colleagues possess just the sort of creative minds to lead our scientific thinking about bridges and bridge building into the future."

So perhaps some real good has come out of tragedy, reflected Charlotte. The thought helped her breathe a little easier, though sadness still weighed on her heart.

"And now," added Mrs. Guppy, "I imagine you have a great deal to discuss among yourselves, so the three of us will take our leave and give you some privacy." A twinkle lit in her eyes. "Assuming we are free to go."

Wrexford acknowledged the question with a polite bow. "I look forward to hearing about your new technologies."

Mrs. Guppy smoothed a hand over her skirts. "If I may be so bold, we may have a few metallurgy questions for you, milord."

"It would be my pleasure to assist."

On that cheerful note, and with a flurry of good wishes all around, the trio took their leave.

"I suppose all's well that ends well. Though it leaves a terrible taste in the mouth to think that four people lost their lives for no good reason." Alison released a mournful sigh. "Will someone kindly pass me a ginger biscuit?"

Raven, his hearing as batlike as ever, appeared in a flash at the sideboard and brought the platter to the dowager. "Have two, Aunt Alison."

A chorus of chuckles lightened the somber mood.

"This has been a particularly difficult investigation," observed the earl.

He knew that Charlotte was troubled by some of the decisions they had made. Their family had been put in grave danger on several occasions, and he sensed that she was asking herself whether they had crossed the line.

He was wondering the same thing, but that was something to be discussed in private. For now there were other matters to resolve.

"Amen to that," responded Henning. "Yes, it was messy. Sometimes Good and Evil aren't clearly defined. Let us just give thanks that this close-knit circle of family and friends came through it unscathed."

Tyler picked up the bottle of whisky from the sideboard and cocked a salute to the surgeon.

"Given that you have the malt in hand, come pour me another wee dram," drawled Henning.

"What will happen to Fenway?" asked Cordelia.

"The government will, of course, cover up the fact that a highly respected member of the ruling class is a corrupt criminal," said Wrexford. "They will announce that Fenway has retired from public life due to health reasons, and he'll be packed off to his estate in Derbyshire, where he will live out his days in poverty, as all his ill-gotten assets will be forfeited to the Crown."

"Assuming Grentham doesn't order a hunting accident in order to be rid of the potential for embarrassment," muttered Henning.

"Hmmm, I wonder . . ." mused Charlotte. "But no," she quickly added, "in this case I think A. J. Quill agrees that some scandals don't deserve the light of day. The Bristol Road Project is important for the country. It shouldn't lose the support of the public or Parliament because of Fenway and Wheeler's machinations."

"As to that . . ." Cordelia mustered her first real smile of the meeting. "Kit has been asked to head up one of the subcommittees."

"I look forward to taking up the challenges," said Sheffield. "But only after my bride and I take our delayed wedding trip to the Continent."

"Bravo!" exclaimed Wrexford. "The government has made a wise choice."

Sheffield drew in a deep breath. "We shall see. But I hope to do some good."

"There is still one thing I am wondering, sir," ventured Peregrine. "You mentioned that Lord Fenway and Mr. Wheeler imprisoned you in the dreaded Lockbox. How did you ever discover the secret passageway?"

"I have a confession to make, lad," replied the earl. "I attended Eton for a term—well, three-quarters of a term—but hated it, so I got myself expelled. However, I didn't want to mention that to you boys, so as not to set a bad example for you."

"What did you do, Wrex?" demanded Raven.

"There were no stink bombs involved," responded Wrexford. "My brother and I formed a small band of like-minded rebels, and we sneaked out of our quarters every night to explore the school. We had heard rumors of the passageways and managed to locate a few of them early on, which allowed us to escape the night watchmen. I then found an ancient map of all the tunnels in the library archives and made a copy, which allowed us to create some outrageous overnight mayhem—a pig in the provost's inner sanctum, itching powder in the headmaster's robes . . ."

The Weasels began to chortle.

"The headmaster couldn't prove that my brother and I were the ringleaders. However, my father was soon requested to find other educational opportunities for us," finished the earl. "But be forewarned. Do *not* consider this revelation to be a license to commit mayhem going forward."

He paused, his expression turning very solemn. "As we have seen in this investigation, actions have consequences—and not always the ones that are intended. I hope we have all learned the lesson of how important it is to consider our decisions very carefully and think through the possible ramifications."

All three boys nodded in unison.

"I, too, have a question," said Sheffield after a moment of reflective silence. "What game is von Münch playing? He claimed to have put his cards on the table, so to speak, and yet he said nothing about his masquerading as Eton's drawing master. What was his motive?"

"He promised to appear here this afternoon and explain," said Charlotte. "But regardless of his motives, I am very thankful that von Münch was there and prevented Wheeler from discovering the boys."

"I have my doubts about whether he will show up," growled Wrexford. "Or whether we will ever get a straight answer out of him. I'm not convinced the explanation he gave us about being an agent for Prince William of Württemberg is true." He looked around, half expecting the fellow to materialize from the woodwork. "Be that as it may, he did play a critical role in making sure Fenway couldn't abscond in the confusion of the night." A grudging smile. "According to the account Griffin heard, von Münch flashed some very ornate and impressive government credentials to the local authorities, which had them obeying his orders without question."

"No doubt forged," grunted Henning.

"No doubt," agreed Charlotte. "But as I couldn't reveal my identity, Fenway would have escaped justice if our friend hadn't improvised."

"You call him a friend despite all his untruths to us," observed Cordelia.

"As I've said before, we all have our reasons to guard certain personal secrets. But I trust that his heart is in the right place." Charlotte turned to Wrexford. "Speaking of friends, has Griffin forgiven you for not revealing everything you knew about the investigation?"

"He was hurt by my lack of trust, but when I explained that I didn't wish to put him in an impossible situation regarding his superiors, he understood and appreciated my reasoning," answered the earl. "I think his feathers may still be a little ruffled, but several hearty meals should quickly assuage any lingering hurt."

"Well then, if there is nothing more to parse through, Cordelia and I are going to return home and begin planning our long-delayed wedding trip." Sheffield stood up. "Rather than a toast I shall offer a resolution—let us all pledge to do everything in our power to assure that the coming months bring nothing but peace and tranquility."

Henning snorted into his glass.

"That is an excellent way to end a fraught few weeks," said Charlotte.

"May the cosmos look kindly on our request," said Wrexford dryly. "I think we've earned it."

Evening had fallen, and the town house was quiet. Their friends had all departed, and the Weasels had happily accepted the dowager's invitation to accompany her home and stay for supper—which, thought Charlotte, would no doubt include copious sweets.

The thought of such normal little pleasures drew a mental vow from her to take Sheffield's exhortation to heart.

"Peace and tranquility," she whispered, as she continued to sketch a few ideas for her next satirical drawing.

"What did you say?" Wrexford looked up from the book he was perusing. The two of them had retreated to the earl's workroom after supper, intent on spending the evening in relaxed contemplation.

"It was just a reminder to the goddess of chaos that we have had enough of Trouble."

He returned to examining the pages.

She saw that a pile of books had been moved from the adjacent library to the back work counter where he stood. "Any further discoveries in your father's books?"

"Nothing of note," came the reply.

"I know you are anxious to pursue the matter of 'A' and the mystery surrounding that individual's identity."

Wrexford appeared lost in thought.

"The search will now have our full attention," said Charlotte in a louder voice.

The sound must have startled him because he turned abruptly . . . and then stared down at his feet in consternation.

"Is something wrong?" she asked.

"The valise. It was here earlier today," he muttered. As he looked around, his puzzled expression turned stormy. "The bloody, bloody rascal! He *was* here, and it appears that he has absconded with money that Sheffield and I recovered from Wayland's rendezvous with the French radicals."

"You think von Münch took it?" she exclaimed.

"Who else?"

He had a point.

"Hell's bells." Clearly agitated, Wrexford closed the book with a snap and stalked to his desk. "I must speak to Riche about having the locks replace—" The rest of the word gave way to a sharp inhale.

Charlotte was out of her chair in a flash. She saw him pick up a plain white square of folded stationery from his blotter.

"Good heavens, what is it?"

He turned it over in his fingers. There didn't appear to be any writing on the outside or any identifying wax seal.

She held her breath, waiting for him to open it.

For a moment, he looked tempted to fling it into the fire. But after unclenching his hands, Wrexford slowly unfolded it.

Her heart was now hammering hard enough to crack a rib. Still, Charlotte heard him mutter a curse.

"W-What does it say?"

"It's from von Münch." He handed it to her without further words.

Forgive me, she read, *but pressing circumstances require my presence elsewhere. You have my word that I shall communicate with you again soon.*

Charlotte felt an odd sound well up in her throat.

And when I do, I will have some important information for you about the mysterious person mentioned in your father's letter.

"Have you any idea what this could mean?" she whispered.

Wrexford shook his head. "Like every situation concerning von Münch, it seems like we have no choice but to wait and see."

AUTHOR'S NOTE

As readers familiar with this series may have noted, I've taken a little twist in this book's plot on the theory that it's fun for both you and me to keep things evolving. The mystery here doesn't revolve around a tangible physical object/innovation, such as a computing engine, a voltaic battery, or a multi-shot pistol. Instead, the "MacGuffin" is based on abstract mathematical ideas. In this day and age, we are all familiar with the innovative importance of mathematics—algorithms, software codings, AI—and yet, so were engineers of the Regency era, inspired by the thinking of mathematicians in the past. So I wanted to play with the fact that mathematical insight can represent every bit as much of a practical innovation as any physical invention.

But more detail on mathematics a little later (I don't want to scare you away!). First let's explore some of the other back stories to the plot.

The idea of easy, inexpensive travel allowing freedom of movement to all segments of society may not seem very revolutionary to all of us, but in the Regency era the improvements in basic infrastructure, like roads and bridges, coupled with the advent of railroad and steamship travel, changed the world. At the grand Peace Conference, which convened in Vienna in the fall of 1814 in order for the leading powers to discuss how to rebuild and reorder Europe now that Napoleon had been exiled to the isle of Elba, a major topic was transportation and the movement of populations. According to noted historian Paul Johnson, author of *The Birth of the Modern*, improved roads and bridges were one of the basic keys to modernity. (I highly recommend his fascinating book for anyone interested in how the western world underwent radical changes in all aspects of society during the early part of the nineteenth century)

I think it's worth noting that the Federal-Aid Highway Act of 1956, which aimed to construct an interstate highway system of 41,000 miles connecting forty-two state capitals and 90% of American cities with a population over 50,000, is widely considered to have changed (for better and perhaps worse) the face and community of the United States. So quantum change brought about by transportation infrastructure is something that continues to affect our lives in modern times.

As always, I like to weave cameo appearances of real-life scientific luminaries into my books—especially when my research turns up unsung heroines! In this case, I found two fascinating women who rarely receive full credit for their accomplishments in traditional narratives of history. Sarah Guppy, who plays a role in this story, was an engineering expert, inventor, and entrepreneur who helped run her husband's businesses. As noted in this story, she and her spouse created a system of copper sheathing to protect the bottom of ships from destructive worms—one of ten patents the family received—which won a very lucrative contract from the British Admiralty. Guppy went on to become the first woman to receive a patent in Britain by creating an engineering innovation for building suspension bridges, then a new type of design that suggested further possibilities for quicker travel routes because they could span wider crossings.

Mathematician Marie-Sophie Germain, who is mentioned in these pages, is also a real-life person. Her contributions to the mathematical theory of vibration of a rigid surface, spurred by German physicist Ernst Chladni's famous experiments with vibrating metal plates, eventually played a big role in understanding how to deal with the stresses that affect bridges. (I will not bore you with the scientific principles, figuring that those of you who have a deep interest in the science of bridge building can satisfy your curiosity with further research on your own.)

Another real-life person making a cameo appearance is Marc Isambard Brunel, a leading engineer and inventor of the era.

His creation of machinery able to mass-produce pulley blocks— a key component of naval rigging—for the British Navy in 1805 was a milestone in the Industrial Revolution. It so happens that Brunel's son, Isambard Kingdom Brunel, also a famous engineer, was a key player in building the Great Western Railroad in Britain—and Sarah Guppy was one of his early investors! Isambard Brunel also designed the famous Maidenhead railway bridge, which J. M. W. Turner featured in one of his later paintings.

Also mentioned throughout the story is Thomas Telford, a legendary Scottish road, bridge, and canal engineer who paved the way for modernizing travel throughout Britain. He also consulted on major transportation projects in Europe and Russia.

Now, switching from fact to fiction, the other inventors and mathematicians who play a part in the main plot are fictional. I also want to stress that the villains in this story are purely imaginary! I mean no disrespect to Eton in making its fictional provost an unsavory character, as well as for setting some of the serious skullduggery within its hallowed walls. (The Lockbox and secret tunnels are also my own creation.) However, Eton was such an iconic place during the Regency—and remains so today—that I couldn't resist using it for the final action scenes, especially as my fictional Peregrine was a student there for a short while. As for the description of corporal punishments meted out on the students, that's a dark part of the school's past that was, alas, true back in the early nineteenth century.

As I said earlier, for me research is a very fun part of starting a book because I always make unexpected discoveries that spark plot twists. For this book, one of the fascinating stories I stumbled upon turned into a key element of the story. Jasper Milton, my murdered inventor who lies at the heart of the mystery is fictional, but his character is inspired by the real-life Francis Cabot Lowell.

Lowell was a successful American businessman who is credited with helping to spark the Industrial Revolution in America by creating the first modern textile mill in the country. How he did this is definitely the stuff of novels!

During the early 1800s, America was dependent on Britain and Europe for manufactured goods, but war between the Europeans and America's resulting Embargo Act of 1807 disrupted trade. Francis Lowell came to Britain with his family in 1810 for a two-year visit—supposedly because of ill health. However, while he was there, he toured extensively throughout the steam-powered textile mills in Britain, which were the most advanced in the world. The British government, aware that the new technology gave their nation a great economic advantage, had very strict rules in place which forbade taking any technical plans of the machinery out of the country. Although the British mill owners were in full support of this ban, they saw no harm in allowing Lowell to inspect their operations. After all, what harm could a tour do?

Well, little did they know that Lowell possessed an eidetic memory—what we today call a photographic memory—which allowed him to file away perfect mental pictures of all the complicated machinery.

The British government knew of Lowell's business acumen and his involvement in international trade, so they were careful to search him and all his luggage at the time of his return to America to make sure he wasn't trying to sneak any proprietary technical information out of the country. (I imagine Lowell was smiling as the custom officers did their duty.) On arriving home, Lowell set to work—and in 1814, the Boston Manufacturing Company in Waltham, Massachusetts, began cranking out textiles with machines created from Lowell's memory.

Lowell's story got me to thinking . . .

Bridge engineers of the era were exploring new designs involving innovative ways to use traditional materials (such as the advent of suspension bridges). But they were also becoming aware that mathematics was key in creating revolutionary improvements. (Yes, yes, we'll get to the math in a moment.) So it occurred to me that a plot revolving around an eidetic memory and mathematics would be a fun twist. It also struck me as plausible that the British government would be keen to keep any revolutionary breakthroughs in bridge design from leaving the country, as improvement in transportation had great economic implications. So I created Jasper Milton. He would, of course, have known of the Lowell story, and clever fellow that he was, his plan was to give *himself* to the French, rather than turn over any technical papers.

And now, as promised, here comes a brief explanation of the basic concepts that were likely spinning around in Milton's head.

Mathematics can play a number of important roles in the design of bridges—a range of mathematical tools are employed to optimize the shape, design, and dimensions of bridges to ensure their strength and stability. Mathematical models can also be used to analyze the effects of various forces, such as the loads exerted by the weight of the bridge itself, traffic, and external forces such as wind or shifting terrain.

Calculus and the calculus of variations, as described in this story, are distinct but related areas of mathematics. These tools can be used to analyze the distributions of weight loads throughout a bridge, the center of mass of the structure (important for ensuring structural stability), and the efficient use of materials. Mathematical methods also permit various analyses to understand safety and cost trade-offs in the use of materials and design alternatives. Specific examples of the early use of mathematics in bridge design include determining the most efficient curvature for the arches supporting a bridge and the best dimensions of beams supporting the bridge roadways to determine the optimal distribution of stress throughout the structure.

These methods proved particularly important when it first became desirable to design bridges capable of supporting moving trains. Even earlier, however, there were a considerable number of bridge collapses due to pedestrian traffic (including marching troops). At the time, these incidents were difficult to explain in that forces or stresses on bridge structures appeared to be tolerated well until sudden structural deformation or dangerous oscillation would occur, in many cases resulting in the collapse of the bridge. Mathematics and other scientific investigations provided a basis by which to begin to understand these phenomena.

It is hard to pinpoint the exact start of the use of mathematics in the engineering of bridge projects, but the most relevant mathematical concepts were developed beginning in the eighteenth century and were gradually introduced into practical engineering practices in the nineteenth century (though their use did not become prevalent until later in the century).

In the 1750s, the legendary Swiss mathematician and physicist Leonhard Euler began developing a specific set of mathematical tools applicable to various optimization problems—and even noted their possible ramifications for bridge design. Euler built upon the branch of mathematics known as calculus, which as Cordelia points out in the story was developed by Newton and Leibniz in the previous century. Working independently, Italian mathematician Joseph-Louis Lagrange made important advances in Euler's developing theory, causing Euler to abandon his own largely geometric approach and adopt Lagrange's more analytic one. In 1756, Euler named this emerging mathematical methodology the "calculus of variations."

Rather than try to explain this very complicated—at least to all of us non-mathematicians—methodology, which might very well run longer than the actual story, I shall merely say it became very important in the development of bridge design.

During the Regency, there was an emerging awareness in

some quarters that vibrations from various stresses imposed upon the elements of a bridge design might play a big role in determining structural stability. As knowledge of the mathematics of vibration developed gradually (very gradually), it became clear that an understanding of vibration patterns, as well as ways to model the ability of a surface to return to its original form after experiencing vibration (the "elasticity" of the surface), were important to bridge construction.

As noted above, the German physicist Ernst Chladni had performed a series of experiments concerning vibration line patterns in oscillating plates, and it therefore became of great scientific interest to better understand the complex patterns revealed by the Chladni Experiments. The mathematics of this and the relevant implications for bridge design took decades to achieve some level of practical usefulness, but in 1809 an early attempt was made when the French Academy of Sciences set up a competition to provide an explanation of these experimental results (the "elasticity problem"). Napoleon himself was apparently very interested and offered a one-kilogram gold medal as a prize for the winning entry. After several tries, Marie-Sophie Germain was awarded the prize in 1815—though unfortunately for her, Napoleon's gold was no longer a part of it.

Following upon Germain's great initial work, the formulation of a general mathematical theory of elasticity capable of use in actual construction work was set out by Claude-Louis Navier in 1821. However, for the purposes of this story I'm assuming Jasper Milton, my fictional mathematical genius, was brilliant enough to have come up with the advanced concept six years before Navier.

We now know, however, that the mathematics of bridges is even more complicated than Jasper Milton could have realized. In fact, to my surprise, my research led me to discover that even today, bridge design is not an exact science. Mathematicians and engineers still debate which structural issues caused the famous collapse of the Tacoma Narrows Bridge ("Galloping Gertie") in the 1940s. (You can watch the available online videos of this catastrophic structural failure.)

More recently, just a fifteen-minute bicycle ride from Charlotte and Wrexford's fictional Berkeley Square town house, there is the carefully planned and widely celebrated London Millennium Bridge. After opening to much fanfare in 2000, the bridge had to be closed after barely one day of operation for two years of redesign due to unexpected lateral swaying which, when amplified by the adjustments in stride made by pedestrians to maintain their balance, threatened to collapse this icon of the new—and supposedly wiser—millennium.

Without going into excessive detail, the difficulty of mathematically modeling bridges is due, first, to the large number of independent factors (variables) which must be accounted for. Engineers call this the number of "degrees of freedom" required in these models. A second, and highly important, reason is that the systems which need to be modeled mathematically for bridge design turn out to be nonlinear, meaning that changes in the output (results) of the models are not proportional to changes in the inputs (the factors being modeled in bridge design). As a result, very small changes in these initial factors can produce huge differences in structural soundness. This phenomenon was widely observed by Regency-era designers of these structures but remained highly perplexing given the mathematical knowledge of the day. It was not until the twentieth century that the mathematics was developed for modelling—at least approximately—such non- linear systems.

And here I shall (almost) cease all talk of mathematics. But I don't want to leave you feeling worried about crossing your next bridge! Because of the mathematical modeling we can now do, as well as the knowledge base we have developed as to what has proved structurally sound in the past and the margin of safety built into today's bridges, there is no reason for alarm. The Golden Gate Bridge, for example, sways about twenty-seven feet and exhibits vertical waves of almost ten feet but still has proved to be entirely safe.

I hope you've enjoyed these glimpses into the back stories of the book. —*Andrea Penrose*